The Game

Mary was shocked. Since when had Lynne done smack? But she obviously had, judging by the way she was doing it now – sucking the bitter-sweet-smelling smoke up like an old hand.

'Mary?' Lynne held out the black-streaked foil. Her pupils had shrunk to two tiny dots of black in a sea of blue – so pale it seemed almost transparent.

Mary shook her head. She'd heard that smack made you do crazy things, and there was no way she was making a fool of herself in front of the men.

'Try it,' Ali urged her huskily. 'You'll like it.'

By the same author

The Front
Forget Me Not
Tainted Lives
The Charmer
The Club

About the author

Mandasue Heller was born in Cheshire and moved to Manchester in 1982. There, she has found the inspiration for her novels: she spent ten years living in the infamous Hulme Crescents and has sung in cabaret and rock groups, seventies soul cover bands and blues jam bands. She still lives in Manchester with her musician partner, three children and a tarty squirrel-tailed cat.

Copyright © 2005 by Mandasue Heller

First published in Great Britain in 2005 by Hodder & Stoughton
A division of Hodder Headline

This paperback edition published in 2005

The right of Mandasue Heller to be identified as the Author
of the Work has been asserted by her in accordance with the
Copyright, Designs and Patents Act 1988.

A Hodder paperback

16

All rights reserved. No part of this publication may be
reproduced, stored in a retrieval system, or transmitted, in any
form or by any means without the prior written permission of the
publisher, nor be otherwise circulated in any form of binding or
cover other than that in which it is published and without a similar
condition being imposed on the subsequent purchaser.

All characters in this publication are fictitious and any resemblance
to real persons, living or dead, is purely coincidental.

A CIP catalogue record for this title is
available from the British Library

ISBN 978 0 340 73507 7

Typeset in Plantin Light by Palimpsest Book Production Limited,
Grangemouth, Stirlingshire

Printed and bound by Mackays of Chatham plc, Chatham, Kent

Hodder Headline's policy is to use papers that are natural,
renewable and recyclable products and made from wood
grown in sustainable forests. The logging and manufacturing
processes are expected to conform to the environmental
regulations of the country of origin.

Hodder & Stoughton Ltd
A division of Hodder Headline
338 Euston Road
London NW1 3BH

To the many branches of my tree,
for all that was and is yet to be . . .

Acknowledgements

Special thanks as always to my family:

Jean Heller, my mum. Wingrove Ward, my partner. Michael, Andrew and Azzura, my children. Ava, my sister. Amber, Martin, Jade, Reece and Kyro, my nieces and nephews. Auntie Doreen. Pete and Ann. Lorna, Cliff, Chris and Glenn. Daniel and Natalie. You're all fantastic.

As are the rest of my family and friends who have supported me along the way, not least, Norman Kaine Fairweather Brown. Heartfelt gratitude to you all.

The more I see of the publishing world, the more I realise how vital a role each person within the industry plays. As I can't hope to name them all individually, I extend an allencompassing thank you to everyone at Hodder – particularly Carolyn Caughey, Emma Longhurst, Lucy Hale, and Phil Pelham.

Many thanks as ever to my agents, Cat Ledger and Faye Webber.

Nick Austin.

Lovely Betty and Ronnie Schwartz.

Martina Cole.

And, last but not least, Wayne Brookes – your help was invaluable.

PROLOGUE

The clock was driving Jane crazy – tick-tick-ticking a relentless tattoo into her pounding head, mocking her: *It's only twelve o'clock . . . It's only twelve o'clock . . . It's only—*

Struggling to her feet, she winced as a knife-slash of pain sliced across her eyes. She had a terrible headache, and the unbearable tension wasn't helping.

Looking at the drawn faces of her friends as they stared at the floor, contemplating their own versions of the hell they'd found themselves in tonight, Jane was swamped by guilt. She should never have involved them in this. It was nothing to do with them – not really. It was all her stupid fault. Why could she never leave things be?

'Anyone want a brew?' she asked, her voice too loud in the clock-ticking silence.

No one answered and for a moment she wondered if she'd actually spoken the words or only thought them. Given how messed up everything was right now, she couldn't be sure. She wasn't sure about *anything*.

Hobbling into the kitchen, she filled the kettle and set about finding cups amongst the mountain of dirty dishes heaped in the sink. Sensing movement at the window, she froze, the fine hairs rising on the back of her neck. Heart in mouth, she turned her head and stared at the thin curtains. There was definitely somebody out there: she could see the shadow shifting slowly along.

When the knock came, Mike crept up to the kitchen doorway and pressed a finger to his lips before moving on to the front door.

'Yeah?'

'It's me,' the shadow whispered. 'Let us in.'

'It's a bit late for a visit,' Mike said, breathing an audible sigh of relief that it was only speed-freak Roy. 'What's up, mate?'

'Aw, come on,' Roy wheedled. 'I've been here later than this before. Open up, man. I've got something to tell you.'

'No way!' Pete hissed from where he was perched on the edge of the couch. 'Don't let him in.'

'Er, not now, Roy,' Mike said. 'It's a bit . . . inconvenient.'

'Jane there?' Roy asked.

As she stood in the kitchen doorway, Jane's heart gave another painful lurch. Bringing her hand to her mouth, she bit down hard on her knuckles to stop herself crying out.

Half-turning, Mike raised a reassuring hand. 'No, she's not,' he lied. 'Why?'

'Oh, something and nothing.' Roy lowered his voice to a sly whisper. 'It's just that we had a little chat about *evil* the other night, and I wanted to tell her I was right.'

'What d'y' mean, mate?

'Aw, look, just open the door,' Roy persisted. 'This is dead important.'

'Sorry, man, no can do. I'm, er, not dressed.'

'Entertaining?'

'Yeah, that's right. So, hurry up and tell us what you want, eh?'

'All right, I'm going. But do us a favour, yeah?'

'Sure.'

'When you *do* see Jane –' Roy sounded muffled now, as if he had his lips pressed close to the wood '– just tell her I saw the Devil today. Tell her he was looking for her, but she's not to worry 'cos I didn't tell him where to find her. Later, yeah?'

Going back to the others when Roy's footsteps had died away, Mike slumped down on the couch beside Pete.

'Oh, fuck,' he muttered, sounding as freaked as they all felt. 'That's all we need. What we gonna do now?'

'We know what we've got to do.' Pete sighed wearily. 'Only now we'll have to do it sooner rather than later, 'cos if Butler's gripped shit-for-brains, there's no telling what he's let slip.'

'You don't think Roy would say anything, do you?' Jane asked, nervously wringing her hands.

Looking up at her as she wandered fully into the room, Pete nodded grimly. 'Probably, yeah. You know what he's like.'

'This is doing my head in,' Tina snarled, bringing her fist down hard on the arm of her chair.

'Yeah, well, it's not exactly fun for any of us,' Pete snapped, flicking her an impatient glance. It was the first time she'd opened her mouth in an hour, but the sound of her complaining voice was enough to raise a dead dog's hackles. He wanted this over with – *now*. Pulling his sleeve back, he checked his watch and frowned. 'Shit. We've got hours yet.'

'God, this is awful,' Jane moaned, swiping at a tear as it trickled slowly down her cheek. 'I don't think I can take much more.'

'Don't you dare start snivelling,' Tina warned her unsympathetically. 'You're not the only one who's suffering, you know. My back's *killing* me, and I've got a—'

'Why don't you do everyone a favour and piss off to Mimi's if you're not up to this?' Pete cut in coldly.

'What for?' she demanded.

'To give us all a bit of fucking *peace*.' He was openly

glaring at Tina now, his dislike of the overweight, over-bearing bitch intensifying by the second. 'And don't start kicking off, 'cos we're in enough shit as it is without you making things worse.'

Bristling, Tina said, 'Don't tell *me* what to do! I'm sick to death of you and your orders. You think you're a right hard knock, but you're not. You're just a—'

'Pack it in!' Mike interrupted sharply. 'Pete's right. You *should* go – both of you.'

'No way,' Jane protested. 'I'm not leaving you to take the flak if it comes on top.'

'We'll be fine,' Mike assured her, his pale face belying his words. 'It's you they're looking for, don't forget. They don't know me and Pete. If they come and you're not here, they'll probably just leave it.'

'Yeah, *course* they will,' Jane snorted sarcastically. They all knew that Butler would stop at nothing to get what he wanted. Folding her arms, she shook her head determinedly. 'No, I'm staying, and that's that.'

'Me too.' Tina shot Pete a defiant glare.

'Suit yourself.' Holding his hands up in a gesture of resignation, Mike got up and went to the bathroom, his slumped shoulders clearly displaying his unhappiness.

The room fell quiet when he'd gone, and Jane felt the sound of the clock worming its way into her frazzled mind again.

Tick . . . tick . . . tick . . .

'Aw, this is fuckin' crazy!' Pete barked suddenly, slapping a hand down on his thigh like a whip-crack. 'Are you *sure* you didn't find out where that gear's stashed, Jane? This would all be over if we could just get it back to Butler.'

Jane's mouth flapped open with disbelief. 'Are you *mad*? How's it going to be over? Someone's *dead*, in case you've forgotten.'

'Yeah, and I don't want to be next!' Leaping angrily to his feet, Pete paced to the window and eased the edge of the curtain back to peer out at the road down below. 'Shit, man, I can't see a thing. They could be watching us right now for all we know.'

'Losing your bottle?' Tina gave a scornful sneer.

'Fuck off!'

'Hate to say it,' Mike said, coming back with a worried frown creasing his brow. 'But there's an awful smell coming from the bedroom.'

Glancing at the wall-mounted thermostat, Pete tutted when he saw that it was pushed up to its highest mark.

'Great. We forgot to turn the heating off. There'll be maggots and all sorts by now.'

'*Don't*,' Jane groaned.

'No point turning it off now,' Tina grunted, giving an exaggerated shiver. 'I'm already freezing.'

'Stop thinking about yourself for just *one* flaming minute, will you!' Pete bellowed at her. Then, turning to the others, his face completely drained of colour, he said, 'Right, I've had enough of this. Let's get moving.'

'What, *now*?' Jane gasped.

'Yes, *now*. And seeing as you two are so dead set on staying, you can get your arses in there with us. *MOVE IT!*'

Gulping down the grapefruit-sized lump that was forming in her throat at the thought of the gruesome task that lay ahead, Jane helped Tina up and clutched at her arm as they followed Pete and Mike to the bedroom.

PART ONE

I

Hiding behind the stinking metal bins lining the wall beneath the grimy kitchen windows, Mary James buried her nose in her skirt to block out the stench of boiling cabbages wafting out through the clattery old air vents. Shifting a couple of inches to the left when a stream of hot grey water spewed out of the drainpipe and gurgled down the grid, she scowled at a burst of raucous dinner-lady laughter. She didn't know what they had to laugh about. It was a shit school, and they had to be thick as shit to want to work here.

The morning bell began to clang out its warning. Staying where she was, Mary listened to the thunderous roar of footsteps as her fellow pupils ran through the scarred black doors. *More thick shits*, she thought with a sneer. Running along to boring assembly like their lives depended on it. God, she couldn't wait to be free of this dump.

Reaching into her pocket for the fag that she'd dimped on her way in that morning, she was just about to light it when she heard hushed voices at the far end of the bins. Thinking it was the wag squad, she shuffled deeper into the shadows and held her breath.

But it wasn't the nuns on the prowl, it was the so-called cock-of-the-first-year Jeanette Craig, and her sidekicks, Susan Murray and Sally-Ann Corbett.

Dipping her head, Mary peered through the gap between the bin's wheels. She could only see the group's feet as they gathered in the corner at the far end, but it was enough to wind her up. If they thought they were going to skip assembly out here, they had another think coming. The last thing she needed was for those dozy bitches to draw attention to her. Anyway, she was in second year and that gave her seniority. They could just piss off and find themselves another hiding place.

Pushing herself to her feet, Mary was just about to go and send them packing when she caught the nasty tone in Jeanette's voice and realised that they were up to no good. Hesitating, she cocked her head and listened.

'Where d'y' think *you*'re going?' Jeanette hissed.

'The bell's gone,' another girl mumbled. 'I'm g-going to assembly.'

Mary gritted her teeth. So, that was their game, was it? They were ganging up on someone.

There was a dull thud as Jeanette slammed the girl back against the wall.

'No, you're not,' she snarled. 'We ain't said you can go nowhere.'

'Yeah,' Susan sneered nastily. 'We ain't give you *permission*.'

'We'll get in trouble.' The girl almost crying now. 'We'll get the cane.'

Jeanette and the others laughed. They could see that she was crapping herself and it gave them a kick. They'd been planning this all weekend, and they weren't going to let a little thing like being late for assembly stop them. Anyway, it was only Sister Ferdinand on duty on a Monday morning, and she was a wimp compared to the other nuns. If they didn't do it now, they mightn't get another chance for ages.

Whimpering as they closed in some more, the girl said, 'Why are you picking on me? What have I done?'

Jeanette gave a nasty bark of a laugh. 'It wants to know what it's done, girls. Shall we tell it?'

'Yeah,' Susan hissed, her mean little down-turned mouth forming a perfect arch around her pointy chin. 'Tell it we hate it 'cos it's a filthy doggy bitch.'

'I'll tell you what you've done.' Jeanette poked the girl's skinny chest with a rigid finger. 'Your mam's a scrubber, that's what.'

'A proper slag,' Susan chipped in. 'And your dad's a pervy old wanker.'

'And *you* stink.'

'Of piss and shit.'

'And mouldy old bread. Haven't you got no better clothes, you tramp?'

'State of you. You look like you've been rooting in the bins. Can't your mammy get no decent punters now she's such an old scrubber?'

'Get lost!' The girl was crying now, tears of fear and humiliation streaming freely down her cheeks. 'She's not a scrubber!'

'That's not what *my* mam says.' Jeanette shoulder-barged her into the bins. 'You calling her a liar, or something?'

'No! I've never even met her. How am I gonna—'

Slapping the sobbing girl hard across the face, leaving a stinging red palm print, Jeanette said, 'Shut your bleedin' mouth, you. No one calls my mam a liar and gets away with it.'

'You've had it now,' Susan crowed. 'She's gonna kick your face in for that.'

'Nits!' Sally-Ann squawked suddenly. 'She's got nits!'

'You what?' Jeanette jerked back.

'There!' Sally-Ann pointed. 'I seen something move.'

'*Oooer*, yeah,' Susan yelped. 'I seen it an' all! Look, they've got a nest.'

'You manky little cow.' Lunging forward, Jeanette grabbed at the girl's hair with both hands. Crying out when a bloated louse scuttled across her finger, she jerked back and wiped her fingers on her skirt. 'Right, that's it,' she declared. 'We'll have to cut it off.'

'I've got them scissors I nicked from art,' Susan volunteered gleefully.

'Giz 'em 'ere, then,' Jeanette demanded, seizing the girl by the neck of her jumper – careful not to let the stringy hair fall onto her hand again. 'And hurry up before someone comes.'

As Susan fished about in her satchel, Jeanette and Sally-Ann flicked furtive glances around the yard for approaching nuns. Finally, Susan pulled the scissors out and handed them over.

'Grab her,' Jeanette ordered. 'Keep her still.'

'Don't!' the girl cried as Jeanette snapped the scissor blades together just inches from her nose. 'I'll tell.'

'And I'll cut your bleedin' throat,' Jeanette warned.

Incensed by what she was hearing, Mary burst out of her hiding place and marched around to where the gang had the girl up against the wall.

'What the *fuck* is going on here?' she demanded, putting her fists on her hips.

Jumping, the girls turned around and blanched when they saw who it was. Mary James catching them at it was worse than all of the nuns put together. She would kick the shit out of the lot of them if she felt like it.

'Nothing,' Jeanette said, all trace of cockiness gone now.

'Don't look like nothing to me,' Mary snapped. 'It looks like you lot are causing trouble.'

'We wasn't doing no harm,' Susan ventured nervously. 'We was only gonna cut the nits' nest out.'

'Nest?' Mary repeated scornfully. 'They don't have nests, you thick bitch. Anyhow, didn't I see Nitty Nora dragging *you* out of assembly last week?'

Blushing furiously, Susan looked down at her feet.

'We wasn't gonna do nothing,' Jeanette murmured. 'We was only messing.'

Fixing her with a fierce stare, Mary said, 'That right, is it? Well, you'd best not let me catch you messing with *her* again or you'll have *me* to deal with. Got it?'

'Yeah.'

'Good. Now, give me them and piss off.' Snatching the scissors, Mary used them to motion the bullies away. 'Go on – get moving before I change me mind and give *you* lot a haircut.'

Turning to their victim when they had fled across the yard, Mary looked her over and immediately knew why they had targeted her. She was a newcomer, for one thing, and she was skinny and scruffy, and smelled musty – like stale biscuits dunked in hot wee. The poor cow was asking for it.

'Who are you, then?' she asked.

'J-Jane Bates,' the girl stammered, peering up at her fearfully.

'So, you've got nits then, have you, Jane?'

'N-no. I don't think so.' It was a lie, but Jane wasn't about to admit it to this tough girl and get her head kicked in.

'What d'y' mean, you don't *think* so?' Mary tutted. 'You must know if you've got them or not. Let's have a look.'

'Don't!' Jane covered her head with her hands as Mary came towards her. 'Please don't.'

'Stop whining,' Mary scolded. 'It's no big deal. Shit, I've had 'em enough times myself. Even had to have me head shaved once.'

'Yeah?' Lowering her hands, Jane looked up at her cautiously.

'Straight up.' Mary grinned, showing surprisingly even white teeth. 'I looked like I was on day release from Borstal.'

'Did it grow back?'

'You taking the piss?' Frowning now, Mary waggled the end of her thick auburn plait. 'This look like a wig, or something?'

'No.' Jane's chin began to wobble. 'I – I just . . .'

'God, I'm only messing. Can't you take a joke?'

'S-sorry. I just thought . . .'

'Aw, forget it. And quit snivelling or you're really gonna piss me off.'

Sniffing loudly, Jane wiped her nose on the back of her sleeve. Pulling a used tissue from her pocket, Mary handed it to her.

'I'm Mary James. You live round here?'

'Yeah.' Jane blew her nose. 'We've just moved to Charles Barry Crescent.'

'Eh, that's where I live,' Mary said. 'What number?'

'One-twelve.'

'No shit? That's just down the landing from me. I used to go in yours all the time when old Eileen had it.' Pausing, Mary gave a sly grin. 'Here, I hope you decorated when you moved in. She kept it a right pigsty, her.'

'Not yet,' Jane admitted, blushing deeply. 'My mum's waiting for the grant.'

'She'll be lucky.' Mary snorted. 'My mam's *still* waiting, and we've been here donkey's. Where'd you come from?'

'Rusholme,' Jane told her, sighing at the memory of the lovely house they had left behind: the big old Victorian terrace, with its whitewashed walls and ornate bay windows.

'Rusholme?' Mary raised an impressed eyebrow. 'It's dead nice round there. How come you ended up in this dump?'

'We, er, sort of lost our house,' Jane admitted shamefacedly. 'The council said we had to come here or Wythenshawe.'

'Ah well, owt's better than Wythy, eh?'

'Suppose so. But I still wish we hadn't had to move.'

'Missing your mates, eh?' Mary nodded sagely. 'Well, never mind, you'll soon make more. So long as you stay away from bitches like Jeanette Craig and her lot. They're nowt but trouble, them.'

'I was *trying* to stay away from them,' Jane muttered. 'They've been picking on me all week.'

'Yeah, well, you've just got to learn how to stand up to them. Anyhow, what was all that shit they were going on with about your mam?'

Blushing again, Jane looked down at her feet. 'They called her a scrubber, and when I said she's not Jeanette got mad and said I was calling *her* mum a liar.'

'Typical.' Mary rolled her eyes. 'Can't just have a decent scrap without making up some poxy excuse. So, is she one, or what?'

'Who?'

'Your mam.'

'*No!*' Jane's head shot up in protest, but she immediately lowered her gaze when Mary stared back at her. God, why couldn't she ever keep her big mouth shut? She'd land herself in worse trouble than she'd just been saved from at this rate.

Mary felt a bubble of amusement rise into her throat. Jane might be a scrawny little cow, but at least she had a bit of bottle – which was more than could be said for Jeanette's lot. Those yellow bitches were happy enough picking on the helpless kids, but they shit themselves when someone harder had a go at *them*. You could call *their* mams and dads all the names under the sun and they wouldn't say a word.

'You don't want to be letting them get to you,' she advised now. 'They're all mouth, that lot.'

'Easy for you to say,' Jane murmured miserably. 'I bet they wouldn't dare try and cut *your* hair off.'

'Too right they wouldn't. They know better than to mess

with me. Anyhow, I've warned them now, so they should stay clear. If they hassle you again, just let me know and I'll sort it.'

'Thanks.'

''S all right.' Shrugging, Mary squatted down in the shadows and pulled the dimped cigarette from her pocket. Striking a match on the wall, she lit it and inhaled deeply before offering it to Jane.

Casting a nervous glance around the yard, Jane said, 'No, ta. I don't smoke.'

'You what?' Mary squinted up at her. 'How old are you?'

'Eleven.'

'And you don't smoke?' Mary shook her head in mock despair. 'No wonder you get picked on. You wanna try it, it'll make you look hard – 'specially if you can do rings. Look.'

Jane watched in awe as Mary jutted out her pretty chin and released a stream of perfect smoke Os. She did look hard, but then she *was* hard. Jane doubted that it'd have the same effect if *she* did it.

She was saved the embarrassment of having to try when the bell began to clang again, heralding the end of assembly.

Pushing herself to her feet, Mary dusted her skirt off and ground the cigarette out with her heel.

'Best make a move before the penguins send out a search party. I've got maths first. What've you got?'

'Games.'

'Oh dear, Sister Let's-be-friends.' Mary chuckled. 'Just don't go in the showers, whatever you do. Say you're on the rag or something.' Laughing at Jane's puzzled expression, she said, 'You'll learn.' Then, linking her arm through Jane's, she walked her across the yard.

Reaching the door, she pulled it open and poked her head inside to check for nuns. Seeing nothing but a mass of pupils spilling down the corridor, she slipped inside, pulling Jane with her.

'I'm going this way,' she yelled above the noise. 'Meet me in the yard after school. You can come to mine and I'll help you get rid of the crawlies.'

'Really?' Jane blushed again.

'Said so, didn't I?' Waving, Mary rushed away.

Jane was late out at home time and Mary was irritated at having to wait around. She hated school, and if it hadn't been for the fact that hanging about at home with her family was *worse*, she wouldn't come at all. Still, if things worked out with her new friend, at least she'd have someone to wag it with now. There was nothing more boring than wandering about on your own all day.

Sitting on the wall separating the yard from the car park, she aimed rhythmic kicks at the Sisters' convent-owned Citroen 2CV, smiling slyly when a dent appeared in the smooth paintwork. It served the bitches right; always preaching against the sin of pride when everyone knew that they'd kill for this shitty heap of metal.

Hurtling out of the doors a few minutes later, Jane glanced all around the yard. Spotting Mary, she ran across to her, gasping, 'Sorry I'm late. Sister Henry made me stay behind to empty the bins.'

'Sounds about right,' Mary grunted, jumping down. 'She's a right lazy cow, her. Anyhow, let's get out of here. I've had enough of this place for one day.'

Leading Jane to a gap in the dense bushes alongside the high school wall, she clambered through into the field beyond and held the branches back for the other girl to follow.

'It's dead quick this way,' she said. 'But don't ever come without me or some pervert will get you.'

'You're joking?' Jane gasped.

'I'm bloody not,' Mary intoned grimly. 'A girl in my class got raped in here last month, and she never come back to school after. They reckon she's gone a bit loony, but I suppose you would if a bloke did shit like *that* to you.'

Stepping into the field, Jane cast a nervous glance around, half expecting to see a rapist hiding in the tall grass. There was no one there – no one she could see, anyway – but she was spooked enough to stick close to Mary's side as they made their way to the other side.

Emerging onto the main road a short while later, they crossed over and turned the corner. A feeling of dread washed over Jane as the four huge concrete Crescents with their network of connecting steel-railing walkways came into view. They were so big and dark: house upon house, each hemmed in above, below and beside by an exact replica of itself.

Her heart sank further still when they reached their block and climbed the pissy-smelling stairs to the first-floor landing. She'd have to tell her mum where she was going or there'd be hell to pay, but she didn't want Mary to see the disgusting state of the house. Reaching her door, she hesitated.

'Er, you'd best wait here a minute.'

'Don't be soft,' Mary scoffed. 'I know this place like the back of my hand – probably better than *you*. Anyhow, it's rude to make your mates stand outside like a dog.' Reaching past Jane, she pulled the handle down and shoved her inside.

Following her into the familiar front room, Mary felt a tug of nostalgia. She hadn't been in here since Eileen had died, but before that she'd called in at least once a week – running errands in order to gain access to the sideboard where the silly old cow had kept her pension money stashed.

She'd helped herself to a small fortune over the years, but she figured she'd earned it – not least for the trauma of finding the body. That had been horrible: Eileen scrunched up on the floor behind the door, her face all grey and blotchy, with flies crawling over her open see-nothing-no-more eyes. And the stink had made Mary sick to her stomach – almost as sick as the sight of Eileen's mad cats fighting over the bits of her that they'd managed to chew off in the week they'd been trapped with her corpse.

Yeah, she'd earned every penny of that stolen money.

The sideboard was gone now, as was the rest of Eileen's dusty old furniture and cat-shit-encrusted carpet, but the wallpaper was the same tobacco-stained flowery crap. There were heaps of bulging bin-bags stacked in the corners now, and boxes littered the floor, their contents spilling out every which way.

Blushing scarlet as the stench of overflowing bin wafted out through the kitchen door, Jane scuttled into the dark hallway. She was just about to call up the stairs when the back-room door was suddenly wrenched open and her mother stepped out. Gazing up at the woman in horror, Jane wished the ground would open up and swallow her into its murkiest depths. Why, when her mum was *always* in bed when Jane got home from school, had she chosen *today* to get up? And why wasn't she dressed yet? She looked awful.

Spotting the girl hovering about in the background, Alice Bates pulled her dressing-gown belt tighter and gave her daughter a furious look.

'Who the hell is *that*?'

'M-Mary,' Jane stuttered, praying that Mary was too busy snooping to notice.

No such luck.

'Hiya, Mrs Bates.' Smiling, Mary stepped forward. 'I'm Mary James from down the landing. Me and your Jane are mates from school.' Stopping in the doorway, she raised an eyebrow. In her nightclothes, with her unbrushed frizz of hair standing on end, Jane's mother was the spit of old Eileen. It gave Mary quite a turn.

'I – I was just coming to ask if I could go to Mary's for a bit,' Jane said. 'Is that all right?'

Alice's nostrils flared. Ordinarily, she'd have refused, but right now she just wanted this scruffy, far-too-forward child out of her house. Telling Jane that she had an hour, she gave her a last warning glare and stalked up the stairs with her nose in the air.

'Jeezus,' Mary whispered when a door slammed up above. 'What's up with *her*?'

Shrugging, Jane dipped her gaze and rushed to the door, desperate to escape.

'She always like that?' Mary persisted, following her out.

'No!' Jane folded her arms defensively. It was one thing *her* seeing her mother in that state, but someone else seeing Alice Bates at her worst was utterly humiliating.

Grinning mischievously, Mary nudged her as they made their way around the landing.

'Here, has Jeanette's mam met her then, or what?'

'No, why?'

'Nowt. Only, if she had, you could see why she said that about her, can't you? No offence, but she's a right state.'

'She's still not a scrubber.'

'I'm not saying she is, but you can't blame no one for saying it if she goes about looking like that, can you? Christ, I thought mine was bad, but yours takes the biscuit.'

Jane's eyes were brimming with tears. Mary was only voicing what anyone would think if they'd seen her mother like that, but she wasn't always such a mess, she still got dressed up when she went outside. It was only at home she'd stopped making the effort – and that wasn't her fault. Not all of it, anyway. Alice couldn't help it if she was ill.

Seeing the turmoil on Jane's pale face, Mary felt a rush of pity. It must be terrible to be so ashamed of the woman who'd brought you into the world. Mary's own mother was a proper little battleaxe, but at least she kept herself clean. As Catholic as they came, Agnes James would rather flog herself in public than give anyone cause to question if her knickers were fresh.

'Look, don't get upset,' Mary said, forcing Jane to unfold her rigid arms and linking her own through hers again. 'Everyone thinks they're better than everyone else round here, but they're all the same behind the nets. See them, there.' Lowering her voice, she pointed at the door they were passing. 'They thought they was well posh when they moved in, just 'cos they were the first to get out of the old terraces. But when the rest of us moved over, they'd already stunk the place out. You have to hold your nose when you walk past in summer 'cos you can smell the piss all down the landing. So, like I said, there's no point getting mardy about your mam. She'll fit in a treat.'

'Mmm,' Jane murmured unhappily, not believing it for a minute. Her mother would rather die than 'fit in' in a place like this.

Reaching her own door, Mary eased it open and peeped inside before shooing Jane quickly up the stairs.

'Sorry about that,' she said when they were safely in her room. 'But my lot can be a right load of funny bleeders when they want. You never know if they're gonna say hello or tell you to piss off. Hope you're Catholic, by the way?'

'Yeah, why?'

''Cos me mam would kick my arse from here to Rome if she caught me bringing a Proddy home.' Grinning, Mary shrugged her jacket off and tossed it onto the floor. 'Sit down, then.'

Perching on the edge of the bed, Jane peered around the

room as Mary set about rooting through a small set of drawers. There were clothes, shoes, magazines and comics everywhere, and the dressing table was barely visible beneath a mess of make-up, nail-varnish bottles, tissues and lotions. Jane could take every single thing she owned out of *her* drawers and throw it around, and it wouldn't cover the *bed* – never mind the bed *and* the floor.

'How come you've got so much stuff?' she asked enviously. 'Is your family rich, or something?'

'Do me a favour,' Mary grunted, slamming the drawer shut when she found the fine-tooth comb she was looking for. 'Even if they were, they wouldn't buy *me* nothing. Everything I've got, I've nicked for myself.'

'Nicked?' Jane repeated incredulously.

'Yeah. What's up with that? Don't tell me you've never done it?'

'No.'

'God, you really are a baby, aren't you? Don't smoke, don't nick. Bet you've never been pissed, either?'

Jane shook her head.

'Christ!' Mary gave her a mocking grin. 'I can see I'm gonna have to teach you loads. But let's get this sorted first. Sit on the floor so I can get at you.'

Doing as she was told, Jane winced when Mary set about wrenching the comb through her hair.

'Don't you get scared?' she asked. 'Nicking stuff, and that.'

'Nah, it's easy. I hardly ever get caught.'

'What happens when you do?'

'I leg it. But if I can't, I either give 'em a good kick, or bawl me head off. Either way, they have to let me go 'cos I'm too young to go to court. Anyhow, never mind all that. Tell me what's going on with your mam.'

When Jane didn't answer, Mary gave her a sharp prod in the shoulder.

'Oi, I'm talking to you. Don't you trust me, or something?'

'Yeah, course. It's just . . .'

'Just nothing. You either do, or you don't.'

Noting the hint of belligerence, Jane said, 'All right, I'll tell you. But you've got to promise you won't hate me.'

'Don't be stupid,' Mary chided. 'I've seen her, don't forget. There's nowt you can say that'll shock me.'

'Suppose not,' Jane muttered. Then, taking a deep breath, she said, 'It's just that . . . well, she's not been too well, lately, and she's always in a bad mood.'

'About what?'

'I don't know.' Jane gave a miserable little shrug. 'I think she's still mad at my dad for walking out.'

'Is that all?' Mary cut in. 'Bloody hell, I thought you was gonna say something really terrible. It's no big deal if they've split up, you know. My mam and dad are about the only ones still together round here – and that's only 'cos he's too lazy to go.'

'They haven't split up,' Jane insisted. 'Well, not really. They *kind* of did, but he came back.' Pausing, she bit down hard on her lip. Why was she running off at the mouth like this? Her parents would *kill* her if they knew she was telling a stranger their private business.

'And?' Mary prompted impatiently. 'He's back, so what's her problem?'

'Nothing, really,' Jane said. Then, trying to change the subject: 'So, have you got loads of friends round here, then?'

'More than you'll ever have if you treat everyone like your enemy,' Mary told her huffily. 'I'm talking about your mam and you're trying to fob me off. You said you trust me, so why don't you just tell me what her problem is?'

Squeezing her eyes shut, Jane said, 'Honest, it's nothing. Just . . . well, my dad reckons she drinks too much.'

'No *kidding*?' Mary murmured dryly.

'He doesn't like it,' Jane went on guiltily. 'He says it's not good for her so soon after the baby.'

'What baby?'

'The one she lost.'

'Where?'

'What?' Confused, Jane looked up at her.

Gripping her head firmly, Mary turned it back around.

'I meant where did she lose it, stupid. At the shops, or something? It was a *joke*.'

'Oh.' Jane frowned, wondering how anyone could find something so bad amusing. 'No, it wasn't like that. She fell down the stairs.'

'Pissed?'

'How d'y' mean?'

Tutting irritably, Mary said, 'I mean was she off her head, like she was at yours just now? Are you thick, you, or what?'

'No, I just didn't get you.' Jane was getting upset again. Grimacing at yet another hard tug on her hair, she said, 'Ow! That really hurts. Do you have to be so rough?'

'If you weren't acting so dumb I wouldn't be getting mad,' Mary retorted, digging the comb in even harder.

'I'm not acting dumb,' Jane protested, struggling to her feet. 'You wanted me to tell you about my mum and I was, but you're just being horrible. I'm going home.'

Rolling her eyes when Jane made for the door, Mary said, 'Get back here, you narky mare. I'm only trying to make you feel better.'

'Yeah, well, you're not.'

'*Sorry*, I'm sure.'

It sounded sarcastic, but Mary actually meant it. It was ages since she'd had a real friend and she didn't want to fall out with Jane at this early stage. Most of the girls round here either thought they were too good for Mary or they were just too scared to disagree with her – and that was mega boring. Anyway, she quite liked this moody little cow. There was something about her that brought out Mary's protective instincts. Christ knew Jane needed *some*one to look out for her. Her parents were obviously doing bollocks all.

'Look, I'm sorry,' she said again, less aggressively. 'Just let me get on with this before the eggs hatch and I've got to do it all again, eh?'

Inhaling deeply, Jane did as she was told and sat back down. She didn't want to fall out either. Not only because Mary was the first friendly person she'd met since moving here, but also because she sensed that Mary would make a fearsome enemy.

'Go on, then.' Mary resumed her combing. 'Tell me about the baby.'

Hugging her knees to her chest, Jane sighed heavily. She'd never told anyone about this before – didn't know if she should be telling Mary now. But Mary would only get mad again if she didn't.

'I don't think she wanted it,' Jane admitted after a while. 'She got dead angry when she found out she was pregnant and they used to argue about it at night when they thought I was asleep. My dad wanted it, but she reckoned it'd ruin everything.' Pausing, she gave another deep sigh. 'I think that's when she started drinking.'

'And he took off?'

'Yeah, but he came back a few weeks after.'

'That's stupid,' Mary scoffed. 'Why did he bother going in the first place?'

'I don't know.' Jane shrugged. 'We were supposed to go and see her when she went to hospital, but when he got home from work he said I'd have to go by myself 'cos he was going away for a bit. He gave me a fiver to get the bus and that, then he just went.'

'Wow, I'd have had a great time on me tod with a fiver!' Mary grinned. 'Fags, booze, chips. I'd have stuffed myself stupid. So, did he go off with another woman, or what?'

Jane fell silent again. This was getting too close to the bone now, and she was regretting ever starting it.

'I knew it!' Mary declared gleefully. 'I'm right, aren't I? I can tell. So, who is she? Have you seen her? Does your mam know?'

'It's not like that. Anyway, I don't want to talk about it.'

'Just tell us who she was and I'll never mention it again. *Please.*'

'I don't know anything.' Jane gritted her teeth. 'And I don't want to, neither.'

'Did your mam kick her head in?' Mary persisted. 'Mine would have. She'd have battered the pair of 'em. Is that how come you had to move?'

Blushing deeply, Jane shook her head. This was getting worse and worse. Mary would know every terrible thing about her family in a minute. It was so embarrassing.

'My dad got sacked,' she muttered. 'And we lost the house 'cos we couldn't afford it no more.'

'Bloody hell!' Mary exclaimed, laughing. 'Talk about bad luck. He sounds like a right useless bastard.'

'No, he's not!' Jane protested, jumping to her father's defence. She loved him dearly, and would have given anything to be with him during those awful weeks when her mother came home from hospital. 'He just gets fed up of my mum shouting all the time.'

'Yeah, well, you would shout about something like that, wouldn't you?' Mary reasoned. 'It's no wonder she's an alkie with all that shit to deal with.'

'She's *not* an alkie.'

'Whatever!' Shaking her head, Mary plucked the last wriggling louse from the comb and cracked it between her nails.

Wiping it onto the tissue she'd been using, she shoved it proudly under Jane's nose. 'Look! There were *loads*, but I think I got them all. Is it still itching?'

'No.' Jane recoiled from the bloody little graveyard. 'It feels tons better.'

'Good.' Balling the tissue, Mary threw it out of the window. 'You can pay me later.'

'Oh . . .' Jane's face fell. 'I didn't know you wanted . . .'

'*Joke*.' Mary rolled her eyes. 'God, you're hard work, you.' Reaching under her mattress, she pulled out a crumpled pack of Number 6 cigarettes. Lighting two, she handed one to Jane. 'Get sucking, dopey,' she chuckled when Jane just stared at it. 'It won't kill you. Anyhow, we've got to do everything the same now we're best mates, haven't we?'

Gazing up at Mary's pretty face, Jane felt a flush of warmth course through her body. She'd told her all of her family's dirty secrets and she *still* wanted to be mates. Bringing the cigarette to her lips, she sucked on it like she'd seen Mary doing. She choked herself half to death, but she didn't care. They were best mates, and that was all that mattered in the world.

2

Four years on, they were as close as ever. So close, in fact, that when Mary reached sixteen and left school, Jane stopped going too.

It was a risky thing to do, given the severity of the consequences should she be caught: her parents would kill her, the *nuns* would kill her, and then they'd send her to a home for bad kids where she'd get her head kicked in every day just for breathing too loud. Jane knew all that, but still she did it. She just couldn't face spending day after day in that God-obsessed zoo without her friend to keep her sane. And the longer it went on, the harder it was even to contemplate going back.

It was easy enough to hide the truth from her dad now that he'd finally managed to land himself another job after all those years on the scrap heap. And her mum was drinking as much as ever, so it was a breeze putting one over on her. But she had to be careful, all the same. It was all very well leaving the house in her school uniform each morning and arriving back at the normal home-time in the afternoon, but several letters bearing the school frank had arrived in the last few months, and she'd worried herself sick over each one. Fortunately, she was always first to get her hands on the post because her dad left for work before it came and her mum was rarely out of bed before noon. But, sooner or later, she was sure to miss one.

As she almost had that morning.

Her dad had forgotten his wallet. Coming back to get it,

he'd missed the postman by less than two minutes. It was way too close for comfort and Jane was shaking like a leaf when she snatched the all-too-familiar letter off the mat and shoved it into her pocket. Her legs still felt like jelly when she went to knock for Mary.

'What's up with you?' Mary asked when she came out. 'You look like you've seen a ghost.'

'This.' Jane showed her the unopened envelope as they set off down the stairs. 'My dad nearly got it.'

'You're really pushing it,' Mary warned her. 'You know what they're like. They'll have you straight down to Mother Superior if they find out.'

'Don't!' Jane moaned, blanching at the thought of the terrifying old witch who presided over the school with her see-all, know-all, hate-all eyes. 'There's no way she's getting her hands on me. I'd rather die.'

Mary shrugged. There wasn't much she could say. It wasn't *her* who was going to land in the shit, but Jane wouldn't be told.

'So, what they saying this time?' she asked, reaching for the letter and ripping it open. 'Dear Mrs Bates,' she read out loud, 'despite several letters asking you to contact us regarding Jane's continued absence, we still don't seem to have had a response from you. As it has been ongoing for almost three months now, we feel it necessary to warn you that we will soon be forced to take official action. To avoid this, we advise you to contact us with an explanation forthwith . . . blah, blah, blah.'

'They won't do anything.' Jane was far less confident than she sounded. 'They said that last time, but they haven't done nothing yet.'

'You'd best watch it, all the same.' Mary handed the letter back. 'They'll have the welfare round before too long.'

'They'll have a job getting an answer. She never opens the door when she's in on her own.'

'Well, it's up to you, but I know what *I*'d do. I'd go in for a couple of weeks to throw them off the scent. Forge a letter saying you've had some mad disease, or something.'

'Fuck off!'

'Well, don't say I didn't warn you when it comes on top.'

Taking a pack of cigarettes from her pocket, Mary lit two and passed one to Jane.

'What's this?' Jane stared at it in disgust. 'Where's the filter?'

'They're me dad's Capstans. Don't have it if you don't want it, but it's all I've got now me mam's hiding her purse – tight bitch.'

'Still nagging you about getting a job?' Jane took a tentative drag on the foul-smelling cigarette.

'Never stops.'

'What you gonna do?'

'God knows.' Mary shrugged. 'I'll have to start looking, sooner or later, I suppose. I can't live on fresh air, and *she* won't give me nothing. She does me head in.'

'Stupid cow,' Jane murmured.

'Oi!' Mary scolded. 'That's my mother you're slagging off. Only I'm allowed to talk about the stupid cow like that.'

Laughing, Jane linked her arm through Mary's.

'Leave off, you dozy cow.' Shrugging her off, Mary walked quickly ahead. 'I can't be seen with you in your uniform. You'll have the pigs after me for encouraging you to wag it.'

'You *are*!' Still laughing, Jane ran to catch up.

'Am I, bollocks,' Mary snapped. 'I'm not a kid, like you, you know. And stop letting that fag burn down. I've only got five. Dimp it if you don't want it.'

'I'm smoking it,' Jane protested, taking a puff to demonstrate – and coughing till her eyes watered. Handing it back, she said, 'Here, I can't be doing with that. I'll look for my mum's bag later – try and get some of hers.'

'You'll be lucky if you find anything but gin in *her* bag.'

'Oi! That's *my* mother you're slagging off.'

'And only *you*'re allowed to do that?' Mary retorted. 'Yeah, *right*!'

Jane grinned. She didn't mind Mary taking the piss out of her mother; the bitch deserved it for all the trouble she caused. Her poor dad couldn't do right for doing wrong, these days, and Jane wondered why he put up with it – but she was glad he did if him taking the flak let her off the hook.

Reaching the park gates, Jane was surprised when Mary didn't go through them as usual. This was where they spent most of their wag-time, playing on the deserted swings and roundabout, and cadging cigs and cups of tea off the workmen on the building site on the other side of the fence.

'Where we going?' she called as Mary continued on up the road.

Turning, Mary gave a secretive smile and tapped her nose, saying, 'Somewhere special.'

'Where?'

'Wait and see.'

Following Mary across the dual carriageway and on through a maze of back streets, Jane began to get irritated. Especially so when Mary suddenly started to run.

'Aw, hang about,' she yelled, running to catch up again. 'Bleedin' hell, Mary, I'm sick of *walking*, never mind running. We'll be in Stockport in a minute, the rate you're going.'

'Stop moaning and look!' Grinning, Mary pointed to a park up ahead.

Glancing through the fence, Jane felt her pulse quicken. 'It's the fair!' Mary yelped, as if Jane hadn't already sussed it out for herself. 'I saw it in the paper last night. I knew you'd love it. Come on.'

Panting as she struggled to keep up when Mary pulled her through the gate and across the grass, Jane stared around in wonder. She'd never even *seen* a real live fair before, much less been to one. Her mother had always refused to let her go, proclaiming them to be dirty, dangerous places, run by unscrupulous shysters who just wanted to fleece decent people like the Bateses out of their hard-earned money. Looking now at the gangs of shirtless, long-haired men and boys who were busy erecting the various colourful rides, she felt a thrill of excitement. It didn't look dirty or dangerous, it just looked glamorous and romantic.

'Oh, my *God*!' Stopping dead in her tracks, Mary yanked Jane to a standstill and dragged her behind the stout trunk of a tree.

'What's up?' Jane glanced around to see what had caused Mary's eyes to widen like that. 'What you staring at?'

'Him!' Mary pointed to a group of lads who were working on the half-built speedway some yards ahead.

'Who?' Jane frowned, peering at them. 'I can't see anyone that nice.'

'*Him!*' Mary insisted, pointing frantically. 'The one with the black hair. Oh, my God, just *look* at him. He's totally *fit*!'

Amused, Jane shook her head. In all the time she'd known Mary, she'd never seen her going gaga over a lad. Not a real one, anyway. Only Donny, and Davids Essex and Cassidy, whose faces adorned her bedroom walls – and Michael Jackson, whose lovely mug resided safely under her mattress to stop her family from having a complete shit fit.

'Right, come on,' Jane said. 'We're going to talk to them.'

'No!' Mary squealed, grabbing at Jane's arm to stop her marching away. 'I can't. I'm bright red. He'll know what I'm thinking.'

'Which is what?' Jane was chuckling now. 'That you can't wait to tear his scrods off and play doctors and nurses?'

'Don't be disgusting.'

'Oh, get a grip. We're only gonna *talk* to them.'

'No!'

'*Yes!*' Grabbing Mary's sleeve, Jane wrenched her out from the cover of the tree and dragged her towards the lads. 'Stop struggling,' she hissed. 'You're making a fool of yourself.'

'You're the one who's doing that,' Mary hissed back. 'Get off! They're looking.'

And they were.

As a group, the lads had downed tools and settled back against the unfinished construction to ogle the girls. As they got closer, a few of them blew wolf whistles at Mary, who was extremely pretty, with long, glossy hair, a slim waist and large, bouncy breasts. They barely glanced at Jane, who was nowhere near as well developed, but she didn't care. She'd just spotted her own hunk, and her heart was hammering in her chest.

Del Murphy folded his arms to better display his muscles as the girls approached. As boss of the speedway crew, he got first dibs with any skirt they met. And, with his thick, dirty-blond curls, his cheeky, lopsided grin, his ice-blue eyes, and the gold gypsy hoop he wore in his ear, he rarely fared too badly.

'Well, hello there, ladies,' he drawled in a soft Dublin brogue. 'And what can we be doing for youse?' This he addressed to Mary's tits.

Barely glancing at the smooth-talker, Mary folded her arms to obscure his view and smiled shyly up at the dark-haired lad standing beside him.

Nodding, Mick Murphy picked up an oily rag and wiped at the sweat trickling down his chest. The girl was stunning, but he knew better than to make a move until his cousin had declared his intentions. Del might only be five feet six but he was the best bare-knuckle fighter in the family and Mick didn't fancy copping for one of his punches.

'You working on the fair, then?' Mary asked, indicating the assorted pieces of metal stacked up all around them with a nod.

'No, we're building a ginormous doll's house,' Del quipped huskily. 'Feel free to step inside and whip us up a nice cup of tea.'

'Yeah, like I look like some sort of maid,' she retorted, snorting softly. 'When are you open?'

'I'm always open when it's a beautiful lass like yourself knocking.'

'Grow up, you mong.' Mary shook her head in mock despair. 'I just want to know when you're open so we can go and get some money.'

'Ah, you won't need money, angel,' Del told her, laying it on thick as he noticed her gaze drifting towards his cousin. 'You won't have to pay for nothing.'

'What about her?' Mary thumbed towards Jane, whose cheeks immediately flared to a brand new shade of crimson.

'And who's she, when she's at home?' Del asked, frowning when he noticed Jane's uniform.

'My best mate.'

'Don't tell me *you*'re a schoolie?' Stepping back, he looked Mary over with open disappointment.

'Do I *look* like a kid?' she challenged, jutting her hip forward to affect a more woman-like stance.

'So, you're babysitting, then?'

'No, she's my mate, like I said. And I don't do nothing without her.'

'In that case, she's free an' all.' Del tossed Jane a wink now – almost causing her to stop breathing altogether. 'So, what're your names?'

'I'm Mary.' Mary touched a hand to her chest. 'And she's Jane.'

'Del Murphy.' He reached out to shake their hands. Then, pointing to the others in turn, he said, 'Mick Murphy, Joe Murphy, Kelly Murphy, Charlie Murph—'

'Bloody hell!' Mary cut in incredulously. 'You all brothers, or something?'

'Cousins,' he said, the soft teasing lilt of his voice mesmerising Jane. 'If you ever need a helping hand, just yell "Murph" at the top of your lungs and one of us'll come running.'

'Yeah, *right*. Like we'd ever need *your* help.' Turning to Jane, Mary rolled her eyes scornfully. 'So, you gonna tell us what time you open, or what? 'Cos we can't just hang about here all day.'

'You could if you want to watch us get all dirty and sweaty,' Del drawled, grinning lewdly. 'But if you'd rather come back later, we'll be kicking off at five.'

'See you later, then.' Linking her arm through Jane's, Mary flounced away with her nose in the air. Glancing back after a few seconds, she smiled when she saw that the lads were still watching. 'Don't forget what you said about us not paying,' she called. 'I'll be holding you to it.'

'You can *tie* me to it hand and foot, if you like,' Del called back. 'I've some nice silk scarves in the van.'

Dismissing this with a wave, Mary marched Jane across the grass and out of the gates.

'Why've we got to go?' Jane protested, reluctant to leave. 'We've got all day. Can't we just hang about for a bit?'

Flagging down an approaching bus, Mary said, 'No way. I need to get some new clothes.'

'What for?'

'To knock lover boy's eyes out.' Mary shoved Jane up the step.

'I think you've already done that,' Jane muttered, unable to mask the envy in her voice. 'They couldn't stop staring at you.'

'Rubbish.' Mary grinned, pushing her towards the back seat. 'Anyway, it's only that Mick one I'm after, so you can have your pick of the rest. Which one do you fancy, anyhow?'

Blushing, Jane said, 'Del.'

'You have *got* to be joking?' Mary drew her head back, a cynical smile on her lips. 'That shortarse?'

'He's not *that* small,' Jane protested. 'He's bigger than me.'

'Everyone's bigger than you,' Mary retorted playfully. 'But even if he wasn't such a dwarf, I can't see how you could fancy him. He's not a patch on Mick. God, he's *gorgeous*, him. Do you think he fancies me?'

'Probably,' Jane said, glancing back through the window. The lads were back at work now. Watching Del until the bus turned the corner, she sat back and sighed. 'Do you think Del noticed me?'

'Yeah, course,' Mary assured her airily. 'He winked at you, didn't he? Anyway, never mind him. Did you see the way Mick was looking at me when we were going? Like his eyes were burning into me . . .'

Later that evening, dressed to the nines in the new outfits they'd shoplifted that afternoon, Mary and Jane went back to the park in high spirits.

Thrilled by the unfamiliar sights, sounds and smells, Jane pointed out all the rides she wanted to go on as they made their way across the grass to the speedway. But the minute she saw Del, all those plans flew out of the window and she knew that she wouldn't move from his side until she was forced to.

True to his word, Del didn't let them pay a single penny to go on his ride – and he made sure they got the best carriage all to themselves. Stopping to chat to them each time he collected fares, he asked how they were doing, could he get them anything, did they want to go faster, slower, upside down . . . ?

Waving them to come off after an hour, he reached for Mary's hand to help her down the steps.

'Me and Mick are taking a break and we thought you might fancy a go on something else?'

'Like what?' Mary asked, yanking her hand free and wiping it on her skirt.

'Oi,' Del protested with a twinkle in his eye. 'I haven't got a disease, you know.'

'And I don't need any help,' she retorted. 'Help *her* if you want to play the hero. She can hardly stand up.'

'I'm all right,' Jane lied, dipping her head to hide her flaming cheeks.

'*She*'s all right.' Del smirked, nudging Mick. 'Think we ought to take her on the waltzers?'

'The waltzers?' Eyes widening, Mary gave a squeal of excitement. 'God, yeah! I haven't been on them for *years*! I love them.'

Jane hated them. From the moment the ride started to the moment it stopped, she closed her eyes tight and clamped her mouth shut to stop herself from screaming as she clung to the restraining bar for dear life. The speedway had been scary enough, but this was terrifying. And Del urging his waltzer-cousin to spin the little scoop of a carriage ever faster didn't help. Jane's stomach was heaving by the time it stopped, and her legs felt as if she were trying to balance on water.

'Let's stay on for another go,' Mary laughed, her glowing cheeks making her look even more beautiful than usual.

'No way!' Jane yelped, struggling to get out of the carriage and as far away from the platform as possible. 'You can stay on if you want, but I'm never going near it again.'

'Would you look at the state of her?' Del scoffed – loudly enough for everyone around to hear. 'I've never seen such a green face in all me life. It's like puked-up peas.' Lowering his voice to a grotesque rasp now, he snarled, 'Your mother cooks socks—'

'Pack it in!' Mary snapped, loyally following Jane off the ride. 'She can't help it if she's never been to the fair before. Isn't there something a bit slower she can go on?'

'What, like the babby rides, you mean?'

'Don't be so tight.'

'Now, see, that's the trouble with babysitting,' Del teased, leading them to the Hook-a-Duck stall. 'You can't do any of the big grown-up things without the bairn tossing its dummy out of the pram.'

'We can do anything we want, mate,' Mary told him frostily. 'Probably done twice as much as *you* already.'

'Doubt that.' He gave her a lewd grin. 'We'll have to swap stories sometime. You'd be shocked what me and him have got up to with the ladies – eh, Mick?'

'Yeah, whatever,' Mary drawled, feigning boredom because the last thing she wanted was a rundown of what Mick had got up to with other girls. Snatching the hooked stick that the stallholder offered her, she thrust it at the tiny plastic ducks bobbing about in the water.

'Here now, there's a knack to this,' Del said. 'Let me show you.' Getting right up close behind Mary, he guided her arm, whispering, 'Anyone ever tell you you're gorgeous when you're angry?' Laughing softly when she squirmed, he tightened his grip. 'Don't jerk or you'll never catch anything. That's it . . . just keep it steady and wait for papa duck to come to you.'

Watching from the corner of her eye, Jane pursed her lips and jabbed her stick savagely at the ducks. Del's digs about babysitting were getting to her, but it was the way he kept touching Mary that was really pissing her off. Still, at least Mary wasn't encouraging him, which was something, she supposed.

'I got one!' Mary yelped suddenly. 'Look!' Dodging Del, she clutched at Mick's arm and waved her captured duck in the air.

'Great,' he muttered, shrugging her off.

Seconds later, Jane got lucky, too. Yanking her catch from the water, she grinned widely, too excited to remember that she was annoyed. 'I've got one, an' all. Have I won something?'

'Here you go, darlin'.' The stallholder handed her a tiny, palm-size teddy bear.

Wrinkling her nose when she saw Jane's prize, Mary said, 'I don't want one of *them*. What else have you got?'

The man handed her a goldfish in a water-filled plastic bag.

'Gee, *thanks*,' she muttered, peering at it with disgust. 'Just what I've always wanted – *not!*'

'It's got a black dot over its eye,' Mick remarked shyly, pointing it out. 'That's supposed to be lucky – like the third eye, or something.'

'Really?' Mary simpered, thrilled that he was actually talking to her. 'Is that an Irish thing?'

'Best get back,' Del interrupted, glancing at his watch. 'The takings go right down when we're not there to supervise. Them randy cousins of ours let all the birds go free if you don't watch them.' Winking at Mary, he motioned everyone forward with a nod.

Trailing behind as the others headed back to the speedway, Jane slipped the teddy she'd already secretly named Del into her pocket and squeezed it softly between her fingers.

Mary had no such romantic notions about the goldfish.

Plonking it down beside the DJ's booth back at the ride, she promptly forgot all about it.

Nine o'clock came around all too soon.

'We've got to go,' Mary announced, reluctantly going down the steps. Stopping, she smiled back up at Mick who was resting his elbows on the handrail alongside Del. 'Thanks for tonight. It was really great.'

'No problem,' Mick murmured.

'Coming back tomorrow?' Del asked, standing on tiptoe to peer down her top.

'Might.' Shrugging, Mary tilted her head to one side and gave him a coy smile. 'Depends if we can go free again.'

'Course.'

'We'll be here, then.'

'Great.' Del winked. 'I'll be looking out for you.'

'Bye,' Jane said, giving him a shy smile.

'Yeah, see you,' he said, already turning back to the ride.

Skipping out through the park gates, Mary linked her arm through Jane's and squeezed it excitedly.

'Wasn't that great? Didn't I tell you you'd love it?'

'Yeah,' Jane muttered sulkily, sticking her hands deep into her pockets.

'What's up with you?' Mary frowned. 'I thought you'd be dead happy spending all that time with lover boy.'

'I would if he hadn't spent so much time drooling over you,' Jane complained. 'He didn't even *look* at me.'

'Don't be daft,' Mary protested. 'He's probably just shy – like Mick is with me. Anyhow, it'll be different when he gets to know you. You watch, he'll be all over you tomorrow.'

3

Del wasn't all over Jane the next night. Or the next. In fact, he barely noticed her at all during the rest of that week. Sick to death of listening to her moaning on about him – and frustrated that shy Mick still wouldn't look *her* in the eye – Mary finally took matters in hand.

Jumping off the speedway just as it started up, leaving Jane strapped into the carriage and unable to follow, she grabbed Del and dragged him down the steps into the shadowy alley between the rides.

'Look, I know you know my mate fancies you,' she blurted out, surprising even herself with her bluntness. 'And I'm pretty sure you know I fancy the arse off your Mick. So, what we gonna do about it?'

Del narrowed his eyes thoughtfully. He was no fool. After a week of knock-backs and evasions, he'd pretty much sussed that he stood next to no chance with Mary because, left to choice, she'd pick their Mick every time. But he'd also worked out that Jane was into him in a big way and, knowing how fond Mary was of her, he reckoned he could use that to his advantage.

But this was one ride that Mary wouldn't be getting for free.

'You what?' Mary gasped when he'd told her his conditions for setting her up with his cousin. 'You have *got* to be joking!'

'Nope.' Folding his arms, Del gave her a sly smile. 'I never joke about a thing like this. So, what's it to be?'

Glancing back at the speedway, Mary caught a glimpse of Jane's face as it flashed by. Jane looked so lost stuck on the speeding ride by herself. So . . . *helpless.*

Sighing heavily, Mary bit her lip. Del's suggestion was ludicrous, but would it really hurt to agree to it? She could always change her mind when it came to it. He certainly couldn't *force* her. Anyway, Jane wouldn't stand a chance if she didn't. And, as he'd just pointed out, neither would Mary – not without his say-so, anyway.

'Just once?' she asked, folding her arms and looking him in the eye.

'Just the once,' Del confirmed, holding her gaze as he added, 'But I won't say no if you come back for more.'

'Don't flatter yourself,' Mary huffed. Then, after more lip-chewing, she said, 'All right. But you've got to be nice to her. And you've got to swear you won't mess it up with me and Mick.'

Del smiled. He wasn't worried. Mick might be the looker of the family, but Del was the champion *fucker.* All he needed was a chance to prove it to Mary – and if blackmailing that chance out of her was what it took, so be it.

'I won't be messing nothing up, darlin',' he drawled. 'Just stick to the deal and we'll be sweet.'

Mary didn't mention the date to Jane that night. Knowing that the silly cow would go home and work herself into a state over it, she waited until the following evening – ensuring, she hoped, that Jane wouldn't have enough time to back out of it and screw everything up.

'No *way*!' Jane yelped when Mary finally told her what they would be doing when they got to the fair that night. 'I won't know what to say. And what will I *wear*? I can't go like this!'

'You can wear this.' Pulling a denim minidress from the

mess of clothes littering the floor, Mary tossed it to her.
'And you won't have to say *anything*, 'cos you'll be too busy
necking to talk.'

'No, I can't.' Jane was truly terrified now. 'You know I've
never – *you* know.'

'Oh, so what.' Mary flapped her hand dismissively. 'That's
nowt to worry about.'

'It's all right for you. You've done it loads of times.'

'Yeah, but I didn't know what I was doing the first time,
did I? Look, it's easy. You just shut your eyes and open your
mouth; he'll do the rest. Now, stop panicking or I'll go and
tell him it's off.'

'No, don't.' Exhaling nervously, Jane closed her eyes and
flapped her hands in front of her face to calm herself down.
'All right, I'll do it,' she said after a moment. 'It wouldn't
be fair on Mick if I bottled out. He's really into you.'

'You reckon?' Grinning, Mary turned to fluff her hair in
the dressing-table mirror. She suspected that Jane was right,
but she wasn't *sure* yet. Mick still wouldn't look her in the
eye for more than a second, much less *talk* to her. Still, that
should all change tonight.

Frowning as Del's smirking face popped into her mind's
eye, reminding her of the deal they'd struck, she said, 'You'd
best not mess this up after all the trouble I went to, you
know. I'm counting on you to make sure your Del never
looks at another girl again.'

'Shut *up*!' Jane squawked, blushing and grinning at the
mere prospect of Del falling so hard for her that he wouldn't
look at anyone else. 'Tell me again . . . What did he say?'

'If you ask me one more time, I'll knock you out,' Mary
warned, reapplying her lipstick for the third time in an hour
and smacking her lips together. 'He said he's liked you since
he first saw you . . . Oh, and he hopes you give a good blow
job.'

'He *didn't*? Oh, my God, Mary! You didn't tell me *that* before.'

Grinning, Mary shook her head. 'You're too easy to wind up, you. I'm only messing. But, then again . . .' Tilting her head, she pursed her lips. 'You never know what might happen, do you? What'll you say if he asks you to give it a lick?'

'Piss off!' Jane spluttered. 'He wouldn't – *would* he?'

'If he's owt like the lads at the youthy, yeah,' Mary told her blithely. 'Still, he can't make you, can he?'

Frowning worriedly, Jane said, 'What if he packs me in for saying no? I don't want him to finish with me straight off, but I don't think I could do something like *that*.'

Mary was getting bored now. Shrugging, she pulled a jacket from the drawer and gave it a good shake.

'Look, I don't know *what* he'll do, and I don't really care. Anyway, it probably won't even get that far, so stop freaking out.'

'I can't help it. He's gorgeous.'

'Is he bollocks,' Mary snorted. Then, 'Here, let me put some slap on you. You look like a ghost, all white like that.'

'All right,' Jane agreed, giggling now. 'But make sure I can wash it off before I get home. You know what my mum's like.'

'Even if she noticed, which I *doubt*, I don't think she'd be too worried about a bit of mascara and lippy,' Mary said, squeezing a blob of foundation onto her palm. 'It's what you're putting it on *for* she'd freak about.'

'Don't remind me.' Jane grimaced as Mary rubbed the liquid onto her cheeks. 'Here, you don't reckon he'll think I look stupid, do you? He hasn't seen me in make-up before.'

'Probably won't even see it,' Mary said, frowning as she applied black liner to Jane's eyelids. 'It's dark in there at night, don't forget.' Finishing off with a coat of glossy red lipstick, she stood back. 'There you go.'

Glancing at herself in the mirror, Jane gasped. She looked ridiculous – like a cheap, crudely painted doll.

'I can't go out like that,' she complained, rubbing at her lips. 'He'll kill himself laughing.'

'Cheeky bitch.' Snatching up her cigarettes, Mary lit one and pointed it at Jane. 'It took me ages to get you looking that nice, but I won't be doing it again if that's all the thanks I get. I only nicked that lippy last week. It's a right waste, that.'

'I'm sorry.' Jane stopped rubbing and gave a guilty smile. 'But you always look brilliant. I only wanted to look as good as you. You can do it again, if you want? I promise I'll leave it on this time.'

'Get lost!'

'*Please* . . . ?' Jane pulled a pitiful face. 'Pretty please with knobs on?'

'All right, but if you touch it again, I'll knock you to next week and back.' Relenting, Mary picked up the lipstick and reapplied it, squinting as the smoke from the cigarette dangling out of her mouth swirled up her nose. 'You're not used to it, that's all. You'll love it when you get the hang of it. And Del will flip out – you watch.'

'You reckon?' Jane gave a doubtful frown. 'I still think it's you he's after.'

'Is he hell,' Mary lied. 'It's you he's having the date with, don't forget.'

'Yeah, but only 'cos you asked him to. They'd do anything for you, that lot.'

'Well, they're stupid then, aren't they? Honest, Jane, you look great.' Drawing her head back, Mary peered at her. 'You trust me, don't you?'

'Course.'

'Right. Well, get off your arse and let's get moving before they think we've stood them up.'

★　　★　　★

By the time they reached the small play area at the rear of the park where Mary had arranged to meet the lads, Jane was more nervous than she'd ever been in her life. For most of the walk there she'd silently prayed that they wouldn't turn up, convinced that it would be a total disaster, that Del would change his mind as soon as he saw her – or, worse, tell her that it had all been a horrible joke; that it was Mary he really wanted, after all.

Glancing at Mary now as they walked through the narrow gate, Jane wished for the umpteenth time that she had half of her friend's looks. Even a *tenth* would be great. And a bagful of her self-confidence wouldn't go amiss either. Still, even if she wasn't a patch on Mary, she had to admit that once she'd put the dress on and let Mary tie up her hair, she did look nice. And the make-up wasn't half as bad as she'd initially thought – not once she'd scrutinised her face in the mirror a few thousand times and got used to it.

Lying lazily back on the roundabout as Mick pushed it around, Del sucked on a cigarette and released a trail of smoke rings into the air, trying to make a continuous circle as he turned.

Unlike the girls, he'd made no effort with his appearance whatsoever. There was no point. He'd only wangled a couple of hours off, and he'd be straight back to work once he was done. Anyway, he didn't want to be giving Plain Jane the wrong idea. She might think he'd got himself togged up for *her*, or something.

Like *that* was ever going to happen!

Propping himself up on his elbow when Mick told him that the girls were here, Del watched Mary sashaying across the grass, her hips swaying seductively in her tight black skirt, her breasts jiggling promisingly beneath her equally tight white T-shirt. It was too dark to see details, but he knew she looked horny as hell. She always did.

Pity he had to have it off with her mate to get a look in, but if that was the price he had to pay . . .

'Evening, ladies,' Del called out. 'See you're looking gorgeous, as usual.'

Hopping onto the still-revolving roundabout, Mick twisted his head round to look them over. Mary did look amazing. And, surprisingly, Jane didn't look half bad, either. Her legs were quite nice when she wore heels, and her face was a lot prettier when her stringy hair wasn't lying flat on either side of it. Maybe Del would quit griping when he took a proper look at her and leave Mick and Mary to get on with it. Fat chance, but he could hope.

Del didn't care how pretty Jane looked. There was only one girl for him in this town – and only one way of getting to her. Unscrewing the cap off the bottle of cider he'd brought along, he held it out to the girls.

'You first.' Mary nudged Jane.

Reaching for the bottle, Jane took a quick sip of the vinegary liquid.

'Thanks,' she whispered shyly, handing it back. 'It's nice.'

'It's all right,' Del drawled, passing the bottle to Mary who had already jumped up beside Mick. 'You'd best hurry up if you want to catch up, 'cos we've already had a bottle,' he went on, lying now, because the Murphys wouldn't be caught dead supping the commercial gut-rot they pushed onto the punters.

'Cheers, my dears.' Taking a long drink, Mary passed the bottle back to Jane, egging her on to drink as much as she could take in one go. 'More . . . more . . . more . . .'

Jane soon began to feel tipsy. Too shy to join in, she just smiled as the others chatted and laughed. Leaning her head back when Mick started the roundabout moving again, she gazed happily up at the stars flickering overhead. She could hear the thumping music from the assorted rides beyond the dark canopy of trees, and she could see the multi-coloured lights of the rides strobing the dark night sky. It was all so beautiful . . .

Jane gave a little squeal of surprise when Del's grinning face appeared above her. She hadn't realised that she'd slid so far down on the pitted wood, but she was flat on her back now, and Del was clambering over the metal dividing rail to join her in her segment.

His lips felt harder than she'd expected when he kissed her, but she didn't resist when his tongue darted between her lips.

Nor did she stop him when his fingers crept down the neck of her dress and groped at her barely existent breasts.

And she followed without a murmur when he unceremoniously pulled her by the hand into the bushes.

Before Jane knew it, it was all over. But she didn't mind the haste. It was the best night of her entire life, and she would cherish the memory for ever.

A few feet away, Mary struggled to contain her disappointment as Mick, too, came to a speedy conclusion. For such a stunning boy, he was a crap kisser, and nothing to write home about in the shagging stakes, either. Not that she was overly experienced in that department, but she'd expected a bit more than she'd got. She could still feel the wetness of his slobbery kisses on her lips, and it was all she could do not to push him away when he zipped himself up and came in for a cuddle.

'We'd best be off,' she said, getting to her feet and heading out into the open of the park.

'Not coming on the rides tonight?' Del followed her out, leaving Jane in the bushes.

Peering after Mick who was making his way into the far

corner to have a piss, Mary shook her head. He really was gorgeous, but she couldn't go through that again.

Smiling slyly as he saw the disappointment in her eyes and realised that Mick had failed to impress, Del stepped closer and pressed his lips softly against hers.

Jerking back as a small thrill of pleasure tingled between her legs, Mary glanced quickly around.

'They didn't see anything,' Del assured her quietly. 'The deal still on?'

Confused, Mary nodded and pulled her jacket tighter around herself. She was shivering, but she wasn't sure if it was the cool night air or the kiss that was causing it.

Stumbling out of the bushes just then, Jane was smiling, oblivious to the sparks shooting between her friend and her boyfriend.

Boyfriend . . . The word danced in her mind. *I've got a boyfriend.*

'See you tomorrow?' Mick asked, coming across and taking Mary's hand in his.

Slipping it free and shoving it into the safety of her pocket, Mary nodded. 'Yeah, sure.' Then, 'Come on, Jane. Let's make a move.'

Glancing back as Mary hurried her towards the gate, Jane waved – a little disappointed when only Mick waved back.

4

Jane groaned when the all too familiar nausea gripped her stomach. This was the third week running that she'd woken up feeling as sick as a dog, and she didn't know how much more she could take. Everything she ate or drank came straight back up, and the smell of anything, from cigarette smoke to perfume, sent her rushing for the loo.

This morning, it was her own breath that propelled her out of bed.

Yanking her dressing gown on, she dashed to the bathroom, reaching it just in time.

Splashing her face with water when she'd stopped throwing up, Jane sloped miserably back to her bedroom. It was four months since that night with Del – that one glorious moment that had never been repeated because Del had never spoken to her again, not even to say goodbye when the fair packed up and left town. She'd been due a period a week later, but it hadn't come. Still hadn't. When the morning-noon-and-night sickness came, she'd finally had to accept the awful truth.

In a mixture of terror of her parents finding out and crazy delusions of Del somehow hearing the news and rushing back to declare undying love and devotion, she had hidden the truth beneath baggy jumpers and unzipped skirts. But her days were definitely numbered. The only thing that still fitted was an elastic-waisted skirt and an oversized old shirt of her dad's. It wouldn't be long before people started questioning why she never wore anything else. She just thanked God that it was the six-week summer holidays so she didn't have to try and squeeze into her uniform.

She didn't even want to *think* about what she'd do when it was time to go back to school.

Dropping her dressing gown to the floor, Jane peered down at her swollen belly. Touching the lump tentatively, she tried to imagine what lay beneath the thickened flesh. It would have arms and legs by now, and a face – a real face, with a nose, eyes, and a mouth. Would it look like her, she wondered, or . . .

The door opened.

'Jane, I just need you to go and—' The words died in Alice's mouth. Recovering after several eternity-long moments, she pointed at Jane's stomach. 'What the bloody hell is *that*?'

Snatching the skirt up, Jane covered herself and turned her back. 'Get out, Mum! I'm getting dressed.'

'Don't you tell me what to do in my own house,' Alice screeched. 'Turn round – let me get a proper look at you.'

Rushing across the room, she seized Jane's arm and pulled her roughly around. Seeing the lump in profile, she threw a hand up to her mouth.

'Oh, my God, look at the bloody size of you. What have you *done*, you stupid girl?'

'Get off!' Jane cried, tearing her arm free. 'You've got no right to—*Aagghhhh!*'

The slap crashed against her cheek, knocking her down onto the bed. Looking up at her mother's livid face, she felt a rush of genuine fear. She'd gone too far this time and no amount of cheek or bravado was going to get her out of a beating. Covering her head with her arms when her mother snatched up a hairbrush from the dressing table, she curled into a defensive ball as the blows rained down on her naked buttocks.

'No right?' Alice roared. 'I'll give you no right, you little *whore!*'

Rushing in to see what all the noise was about, Frank was horrified to find his wife laying into his daughter.

'Alice,' he yelled, snatching at her arm as she raised it above her head. 'Stop it. You'll kill her!'

'Too right I'll bloody kill her,' Alice snarled. 'Look at her, Frank . . . Go on – take a good hard look at your precious daughter, then tell me I shouldn't beat the living daylights out of her!'

Glancing down at Jane, Frank blinked rapidly when he saw the cause of his wife's fury. For a moment it didn't register, then the blood drained from his face.

'No . . .'

'Oh, yes,' Alice hissed, breathing heavily now as her exertions caught up with her. 'Now do you see what I've been putting up with? This is all *your* fault.'

'*My* fault?' he spluttered. 'Now, hold on a minute . . . This has got nothing to do with me.'

Turning on him, Alice narrowed her eyes spitefully.

'Oh, *really*? Well, I think it has. If you hadn't messed everything up in the first place we wouldn't be in this dump, would we? And *now* look. She's as bad as that lot of scum out there!' Alice gestured angrily out of the window. 'Well, she's not having it,' she went on, her nostrils flaring with rage. 'I'll rip it out of her with my bare hands if I have to, but she's not having it. I told you once there'd be no more unwanted children in my house, and I'm telling you the same now.'

Frank's mouth flapped open but nothing came out. He didn't know what to say. Alice was right. It *was* his fault.

Jane would never have got away with running wild if they had stayed in Rusholme. If only he hadn't . . .

But, no. There was no point raking over old coals. This had to be dealt with – now.

Averting his gaze from Jane's nakedness, Frank picked up the gown she'd dropped and tossed it over her.

'When did this happen, Jane?'

The calmness of his tone brought a snort of disdain from Alice.

'Listen to him, talking to her like she's done nothing wrong. Well, she *has*. She's a dirty little slut, and she needs to know how disgusting she is.'

'Stop bloody *shouting*,' Frank hissed. 'Do you want the whole world to know what's going on? Go and make an appointment with the doctor if you want to do something useful.'

'Do it your bloody self,' Alice snarled, stalking from the room. 'I'm washing my flaming hands of her – the good-for-nothing, dirty little . . .'

Closing the door quietly on his wife's retreating form, Frank told Jane to get dressed. Turning his back to give her privacy, he wandered across to the window and peered out at the wall of concrete facing him.

Lord, how he hated this place. It was little wonder that things had turned out like this if this was all that Jane had in her life: a God-awful view of the outside world, a useless fuck-up of a father, and a drink-addled mother. What kind of life was that for a young girl?

'I'm very sorry, Mr Bates.' Wiping his hands, the doctor sat down behind his desk and shook his head slowly. 'If you'd brought her in a couple of weeks ago there might have been a possibility, but now . . . ?' He shrugged help-lessly. 'I'm sorry.'

Frank pursed his lips and folded his arms and concentrated

on his jiggling foot for what seemed like an eternity. Then, nodding, he stood up.

'Thanks, doctor. Come on, Jane.'

Jane glanced nervously at her father's profile as they walked home from the surgery. He'd barely spoken a word since they'd left the house, but she could feel the disappointment coming off him in waves – and that frightened her even more than her mother's anger. Without him, she had no one.

No one but Mary – and what was *she* going to say when she found out?

Wrapping her arms protectively around her stomach as she struggled to keep up with her father's rigid-legged stride, Jane felt a tiny glimmer of hope. At least Mary would understand how she was feeling.

Reaching the phone box at the foot of the sloping entrance to their block, Frank yanked the door open and went inside to make a call.

Hopping from foot to foot outside, Jane strained to hear what he was saying, but she couldn't make out a word. When he came out some minutes later, his face was whiter than she ever remembered seeing it as he set off up the slope without so much as glancing at her. Running to catch up with him, her blood ran cold when he calmly told her to pack her clothes as soon as they got home.

'Why, Dad?' she asked, sounding like the terrified young girl she was right then. 'Where are we going?'

'*We*'re not,' he replied stiffly. '*You* are. You're going to stay with my sister.'

'Aunt Margaret?' Jane murmured, her tongue beginning to feel numb and invasive in her mouth. 'But I don't even *know* her. I haven't seen her since I was a baby – and I don't remember that. I don't want to stay with her, Dad. Please, don't make me.'

'You're going,' Frank muttered through gritted teeth, steeling himself against her tears. This wasn't what he wanted either, but it was the best solution he could think of. At least if his daughter wasn't here, Alice couldn't make her life a complete misery – *or* his.

5

Unaware of the drama, Mary didn't know what had hit her when she called for Jane later that morning.

'You've got a bloody nerve, coming round here,' Alice spat, wrenching the door open with a furious scowl on her face. 'How *dare* you come knocking like you haven't a care in the world!'

'What have *I* done?' Mary protested, stepping back from the stronger than usual alcohol fumes.

'Don't come the innocent with me,' Alice sneered, narrowing her glazed eyes spitefully. 'I *know* you, lady. I got your measure the first time I laid eyes on you. And you can wipe that smirk off your face, because you've nothing to be proud of.'

'I don't know what the *hell* you're talking about,' Mary retorted, jutting her chin out as anger loosened her tongue, 'but if you want to get into a slanging match, fine, 'cos there's nothing for *you* to be proud of either. Your Jane doesn't deserve half the shit you give her – pissed out of your head day and night.'

'You *what*?' Alice's face was a picture of righteous indignation. 'How *dare* you talk to me like that, you cheeky little bitch! I'll rip your bloody head off!'

'Like to see you try,' Mary challenged, spreading her arms wide and stepping back to let the neighbours get a proper eyeful. There was no way she was taking the blame for this unprovoked attack. If Alice Bates wanted to play dirty, she could damn well do it in front of witnesses. 'Come on, then . . . Let's have it, you rotten old cow.'

'Enough!' Frank barked, coming up behind his wife and yanking her away from the door. Pushing her firmly inside, he said, 'Go home, Mary. This has got nothing to do with you.'

'What's going on, Mr Bates?' Forcing herself to stop shouting, Mary stepped forward. She liked Jane's dad. At least he always had the decency to say hello when he saw her – unlike his stuck-up bitch of a wife.

Frank had already begun to close the door. Hesitating, he ran a weary hand through his hair. As disappointed and angry as he was about the situation, it wasn't fair to take it out on Mary. This wasn't her doing. It was Jane who'd opened her legs.

'You might as well know,' he told her quietly. 'Jane's gone away for a while.'

'Away?' Mary repeated despondently. 'But *why?*'

'Don't you know?' Frank peered at her disbelievingly.

'No.' Gazing innocently back at him, she shook her head. 'Honest, Mr Bates, I don't know anything. What's happened? She's not . . . *ill*, is she?'

'In a way,' Frank admitted glumly. 'She's, um, pregnant.'

'*Pregnant?*' Mary couldn't have been more shocked if he'd physically slapped her. '*How?*'

'I'm sure I don't need to explain that to you.' Frank flicked her a knowing glance. If this girl with her well-developed body and far too adult tongue hadn't already tasted the forbidden fruit, he was a monkey's uncle.

Mary shook her head slowly, incredulity ringing through her words as she said, 'I just thought she was getting fat.'

'Mmmm,' Frank murmured, frowning guiltily because he himself hadn't actually noticed the change in his daughter. 'Please don't come round again,' he said then, closing the door.

Mary walked back to her own house in a daze. Jane pregnant. How? When?

But then, she knew the answer to that already. It was that time with Del in the park. It had to be – there was no way Jane had been within sniffing distance of any other lad after that. And Del certainly hadn't entertained her again – Mary knew that for a fact.

He'd been far too wrapped up in entertaining Mary.

Contrary to what she'd vowed at the time, she hadn't done it just the once with him, she'd done it several times – right up until the night the fair had packed up, in fact.

If Mick hadn't been such a sloppy kisser she might not have gone off him so fast. But he had been. And then Del had put him to shame, and . . . well, she hadn't seen any harm in it.

Oh, she'd thought she was so damn clever at the time, doing it right under Jane's nose without her knowing a thing about it. Now she just felt stupid. Really, really stupid.

Jane . . . *Pregnant* . . .

Agnes James was drying dishes in the kitchen when Mary came back just ten minutes after going out. Already in a temper after having received the telephone and electricity bills that morning – both of which were much higher than she'd budgeted for – Agnes slammed down the plate she was holding and stomped into the hall to confront her daughter.

'I thought I told you to go and look for a job?'

'Leave off, Mam,' Mary said miserably, heading for the stairs.

'Never mind leave off,' Agnes squawked. 'You left school near on a year ago, and I'm up to bloody *here* with it.' She flapped a hand beneath her chin to demonstrate. 'I've got bills coming out of me ears, and not a sod lifting a finger to help. So get yourself down to that flaming careers office before I *drag* you there.'

Tutting, Mary continued on her way.

'I'm not joking,' Agnes yelled after her. 'I've had it with wiping your flaming backside while you waste time with your little mate. Swanking about like Lady bloody Muck when you should be out grafting.'

'Like them, you mean?' Leaning over the banister when she reached the top of the stairs, Mary thumbed down towards the living room where her father and brother were sleeping off the excesses of the night before. 'Gonna tell them the same, are you? 'Cos neither of them's kept a job for more than a week.'

'They *have* worked, for your information,' Agnes contradicted her primly. 'And our Joey still does.'

'Once a year when they need a Santa at the precinct? Don't make me laugh.'

'Right, you – out of it!' Furious, Agnes stomped to the front door and yanked it open. 'Go on, bugger off. And don't come back till you've got a job.'

'You don't get them just like that,' Mary argued. 'I don't see why you don't just let me sign on.'

'In your dreams.' Agnes pulled in her chins at the very idea. 'That's for honest God-fearing men what can't get steady work, that. Not for the likes of you – a lazy mare who's got nowt better to do than sponge off her mother.'

Thundering back down the stairs at this last insult, Mary marched outside and pulled the door to with a resounding slam. It was so unfair. Her brother was *years* older than her and he was a right lazy-arse, but it was all right for *him* to sign on. And her dad hadn't worked in yonks, but no one was allowed to *mention* that. Christ, the hardest thing the pair of them ever did was prop up the bar down the pub!

Lighting her last cigarette she screwed the empty pack up and dropped it to the floor. Kicking it ahead of her, she wandered aimlessly around the landing. What was she supposed to do now? She had nowhere to go, nothing to do.

Passing Jane's door, Mary hesitated, wondering if she should knock and ask Mr Bates where they'd sent Jane. She doubted he'd tell her, but even if he did, she didn't have enough money to take the bus from one stop to the next, never mind to wherever Jane was.

Continuing on to the end stairwell, she finished the cigarette and flicked the butt over the balcony. Without Jane to hang about with, there really was nothing stopping her from getting a job, she mused. It would beat the hell out of staying in the house with her nagging mother, and she could certainly use the money.

Decided, she set off down the stairs and headed to the careers office.

Walking to a small industrial estate beside the flyover a short while later, Mary was nervous as she entered the doors of the factory.

The careers adviser hadn't rated her chances too highly, given that she had no qualifications or experience, but Mary had insisted that she wanted the chance of an interview, at least, and she'd made the woman ring the factory to set one up.

Taking a deep breath now, she composed her face into an eager smile and knocked on the office door.

Miss Jennings, the supervisor, called her in and waved her to take a seat. Still smiling, Mary perched nervously on the edge of the chair facing the desk. She knew that they were desperate for staff because the careers adviser had told her that they'd been advertising for ages without success – poor wages being the cause, she'd intimated. Mary hadn't cared about that. Any wage was better than the nothing she had now.

'I'd have preferred someone with experience,' Miss Jennings said with more than a hint of disappointment when Mary admitted that this was her first ever interview. 'But beggars can't be choosers, I suppose. What qualifications do you have?'

'Well, none really,' Mary told her sheepishly. 'But the careers woman said it wouldn't matter as long as I'm willing to work hard – and I *am*. She said you'd train me up, as well.'

'Did she now?'

'Yeah.' Mary smiled. 'So, what will I have to do?'

'*If –*' Miss Jennings stressed the word '– I decide to give you a try, you'd be involved in the production of high-quality lingerie. Have you *any* experience with sewing machines at all? Maybe your mother has shown you how to use one?'

'No.' Mary shook her head. 'We sew everything by hand at our house. But I'm a dead fast learner. You'd only have to show me once, and I'd pick it up.'

'Oh, dear,' Miss Jennings murmured wearily. 'I suppose we *could* train you . . . But you'd be expected to reach a high standard in a very short space of time. Some of our ladies are nearing retirement, and their work will have to be picked up by those remaining.'

'No problem,' Mary replied confidently. 'When can I start?'

Resting her elbows on the desk, Miss Jennings steepled her fingers beneath her chin and peered at Mary. The girl was a good deal younger than desired, but she seemed eager enough – and there wasn't exactly a queue of applicants looming on the horizon.

Standing decisively, the supervisor walked to the door, saying, 'Okay, I'll give you a one-day trial. You won't be paid, of course, but if you show promise you can come back tomorrow and make an official start.'

'Great!' Mary squawked, leaping to her feet. 'I won't let you down – you'll see.'

Pleased with herself for proving her mother so wrong – so quickly – she followed Miss Jennings onto the factory floor.

The noise hit her in the face like a sledgehammer. It was horrendous – like nothing she'd ever heard before. An endless cacophony of machinery in motion: the whirring and clankety-clank of the industrial sewing machines; the thumpety-thump of the steam presses; the swish and grind of the cloth-cutting machines. And, above all that, the raucous chatter of twenty-plus workers hard at it.

Grinning at the welcoming smiles she received from the women she passed on her way to the kettle – where, she soon discovered, most of her first week's work would take place – Mary knew she was going to like it here.

Mary was aching from bone to muscle and back when she climbed into bed that night, but she felt great.

So, she'd lost her best friend, and her mother was making her life hell.

So what?

She'd soon make new friends. And now that she had a job, she'd have money coming out of her ears before too long. Life was going to be one long party from here on in.

Closing her eyes, Mary was smiling as she drifted off to sleep.

Miles away, in a tiny attic bedroom in her aunt's dismal old house in Wigan, Jane was crying her heart out.

She'd never felt so alone in her entire life and she didn't know how she was going to survive the next five months in this horrible place with her horrible aunt.

Meeting Jane off the train that afternoon must have been the first time her aunt had set foot outside the house in years, judging by the greyness of her skin – which, Jane thought, was a perfect match for the plait snaking down her back like a disgusting string of steel worms. She probably hadn't spoken to another human being in all that time, either. She certainly hadn't spoken to Jane throughout the fifteen-minute bus ride from the station to the house. But, once there, she'd more than made up for the silence, telling Jane exactly how things were going to be from now on.

In accordance with her parents' orders, Jane would not be allowed out until it was time for her to go to the nursing home – where a place had already been arranged for her, apparently. She was to stay inside at all times, except to take the bins out or do odd jobs in the yard. And she would earn her keep by getting on with household chores – a seemingly endless list of which her aunt had already prepared. When the chores were finished, she would eat. Then she would be allowed to select a book from the dusty old collection on the shelves dominating the parlour wall, which she could read in her room for precisely one hour before switching out the light.

That last bit had depressed Jane beyond belief. She didn't want to *read* – and certainly not the rubbish her aunt seemed to favour: Shakespeare, Dickens, and Thomas stupid Hardy. If she'd known that this was all the entertainment she would have to fill the long, lonely hours, she'd have packed her *Jackie* and *Bunty* comics. But how could she possibly have known that it would be like this?

Falling into bed that night, having spent the entire afternoon on her knees scrubbing the kitchen floor, she'd been too tired to do more than climb beneath the rough old army blanket and try to find a spot in the pillow that didn't have a cheek-piercing lump in it.

Closing her eyes, Jane had prayed for sleep. *Any* dream that cared to darken her mind would have been a welcome release from her new reality, but it wasn't to be. Her mind's eye replayed every terrible moment of the day over and over again – from her mother intruding into her privacy, to her father coldly packing her off on the train to hell, to her aunt collecting her and bringing her back here.

And *as* for her aunt . . .

How one woman could be so dirty, Jane did not know. The house looked like it hadn't been cleaned in a hundred years. But then, it probably hadn't, seeing as the only time her aunt had actually got off her backside all day was when her ratty little dog needed feeding. The rest of the time, she'd stayed put in her chair, ordering Jane to fetch and carry. Jane had no doubt that every filthy inch of this house would be spotless by the time she finally escaped.

Escape.

Just thinking the word brought a fresh flood of tears to her eyes.

Covering her head with the blanket to deprive her miserable aunt of the satisfaction of hearing her cry, Jane contemplated holding her breath until she died. No one would miss her. No one would even care. And when they found her skeleton years from now they'd wonder who it was, because by then everybody would have forgotten that she'd ever existed.

Jane's last thought as she finally succumbed to sleep was that, when – *if* – she ever got away from here, she was never going home again. Her mother had betrayed her in the worst possible way, and Jane would never, *ever* forgive her for that.

6

Mary's first month at 'Henshall's Smalls' was the toughest of her entire life. She'd never had to work so hard at anything before, and she was almost dead on her feet at the end of each day. She was the go-get-me girl, running up and down the huge factory like a blue-arsed fly, carrying uncut cloth here, sewn-up knickers and bras there. She made numerous cups of tea for the other women, and she was sent to the shop at least fifty times a day for newspapers, butties, ciggies, Tampax . . .

It was exhausting, but she enjoyed every minute of it, and wondered why she hadn't done it sooner.

When the Thursday pay day came around at the end of the month and she finally got her very first wage packet, she was so proud she thought she'd burst. She knew it wouldn't be much after tax and her week-in-hand were deducted, but it felt like the crown jewels to her, and she bounced home full of the joys of adulthood.

Greeting her on the doorstep with an outstretched hand, her mother soon pricked that bubble.

Gazing down at the envelope she was still clutching, Mary's heart sank at the prospect of handing it over. She hadn't even opened it yet – hadn't had the joy of counting, touching, sniffing the money.

She couldn't do it.

Folding her hand around the envelope, she pushed it

deep into her pocket and shook her head. 'Sorry, Mam, but I've worked my arse off for this. I'll give you your share when I've worked it out, but you're not having it all.'

Agnes's face was a picture of disbelief. Her lot were as rough as they came, but none of them had ever dared disobey a direct order.

Recovering quickly, she placed her hands on her ample hips.

'Oh, no, we're having none of that. Not after everything I've done for you over the years. I've worked every day God sends to keep you lot, and by *Christ* it's time one of you started paying me back.'

'I'm not saying I won't give you *nothing*,' Mary reasoned, making a vain attempt to calm the situation down. 'Just not everything. That's fair, isn't it?'

'There's no bargaining going on here,' Agnes told her flatly. 'I've given you leeway so far – subbing you for dinners, and what have you. Now you've earned your bit, you can do what I had to do when I was your age and hand it over.' Folding her arms now, she shrugged. 'Take it or leave it.'

'Right, well, I'll leave it,' Mary snapped, stepping right up to her – and noticing for the first time how small Agnes had become.

They stood like that for a while, Mary towering over her mother, the air thick with challenge. Then, all fear of the woman who had ruled their family for as long as she could remember momentarily gone, Mary shook her head and pushed her way through the door.

'Where the hell d'y' think you're going?' Agnes squawked, whirling around and following her in. 'This is *my* house, and don't you forget it.'

'I'm getting my things,' Mary yelled back over her

shoulder. 'You want me out, so I'm going. All *right*?'

'Fine. Then you can bugger off.'

'Fine.'

Muttering curses under her breath, Mary stomped angrily up to her bedroom. They were such hypocritical wankers, this family – one rule for the lazy bastard men, another for Mary. It made her sick.

Dragging some clothes from the dresser drawer, she stuffed them into a carrier bag, knowing that she had to be quick to avoid her dad or thuggish brother getting wind of what was going on. There was no doubt about whose side *they*'d take, and she didn't want to be on the receiving end if one of them decided to give her a clip around the ear for cheeking Agnes Almighty James.

Taking a last look around when she'd finished, Mary galloped back down the stairs and out of the front door with her mother's cry of 'Good riddance!' ringing in her ears.

Heading instinctively for Jane's house, she was almost there before she remembered that Jane was gone. Standing like a lost lamb at the head of the stairwell, she shivered when a cold draught curled around her legs. Peering up at the dark clouds hanging ominously low overhead, she muttered, 'Go on, then, God – you might as well piss on me, an' all. Every other bugger has.'

Almost as soon as the words left her mouth, the clouds burst and the rain began to lash down. Trotting down the stairs, Mary dashed for cover in the so-called garages that ran beneath the flats.

No cars were ever parked in these doorless concrete boxes because it was too easy for the joyriders to get at them, so the residents just dumped all their old furniture and unwanted household crap there instead. And the local prostitutes and junkies made good use of them, too – as was testified by the number of used condoms and blood-stained syringes littering every floor.

Trudging slowly past each archway, Mary almost smiled when she saw an abandoned mattress propped against the wall in one. At least she'd have somewhere to sit and brood for a couple of hours – until her stubborn old bitch of a mother saw sense.

Stepping carefully over the rotten, stinking debris, Mary kicked the mattress flat. A cold dampness immediately seeped through her jeans when she eased herself down onto it. Gritting her teeth, she drew her carrier bag up close to her chin and wrapped her arms around it.

It was growing darker outside by the second and, one by one, the street lamps were flickering to life; a faint glow of red before the final eerie orange, casting only the barest hint of illumination through the doorway – not nearly enough to see anything but sinister shapes in the rapidly increasing gloom of the garage.

Mary was so cold and hungry that she felt like crying, but she was too tired after work – and the exhausting confrontation with her mother.

Yawning wearily, she nestled her cheek into the comforting softness of the clothes in the bag and closed her eyes. She'd just get a bit of rest – prepare herself for continuing the argument if her mother still wasn't willing to be reasonable.

Roused by the rattle and shake of a milk float trundling past, it took Mary several minutes to get her bearings. Groaning when she realised where she was, she heaved her aching body off the mattress and stumbled out into the dawn light.

Shivering violently in her damp clothes, she looked at her watch and was dismayed to see that it was only six a.m.

There was no way she'd get into the house at this time of the morning. The bolts would be across, and her mother would kick off good-style if Mary disturbed her sleep.

Hopping from foot to foot as her breath swirled around her face in a cold, wet cloud, she decided to risk sneaking into work early. It was strictly against the rules because of all the thieving that went on between shifts, but she'd freeze to death if she stayed outside for much longer. And it was a safer bet than risking her mother's wrath.

Treating herself to a twenty-pack of Regal King-Sizes from the shop on the corner – no more piddling Number 6s for *her* now she was earning – Mary slipped in through the material-delivery hatch at the rear of the factory and dashed into the toilets.

Locking herself into a cubicle, she sat on the cistern and waited until the women from her shift began straggling in. Strolling casually out then, as if she had just arrived, she had a quick wash, then went to the canteen and downed three hot cups of tea in quick succession.

Warmer and less stressed, Mary started up her machine and got to work, vowing that she would never *ever* go through a night like that again. She would put things right with her mother if it killed her.

Slotting her key into the lock that evening, Mary was looking forward to sleeping in her nice warm bed – and she was more than ready for dinner. It was always fish on a Friday, and Agnes James made the best Finny-Addy and mash in the world. She couldn't wait.

The door didn't open.

Pulling the key out, Mary frowned down at it, wondering if she'd inadvertently picked somebody else's up by mistake at work. But, no . . . that wasn't possible. No one left anything lying around at Henshall's.

Bending down, she raised the letter-box flap.

'Mam . . . let me in. The lock's bust.'

Getting no answer, she knocked a few times and shouted some more, but still nobody came. Then Hilda the next-door neighbour came out and delivered her a crushing blow.

'They're not in, Mary, love. They took off this affy on the coach.'

'Coach?' Mary repeated blankly. 'What coach?'

'For Bucklin's,' Hilda said, sucking wetly on a match-thin roll-up. 'Forget you was going, did you?'

'Oh, shit!' Mary hissed. She *had* forgotten. Her mother had booked the holiday the previous year, using the special coupons from *The Sun*. She'd collected them religiously as if they were blessings from the Pope himself, stashing them away in her enormous handbag, along with her never-ending pile of money-off coupons. Mary had been so wrapped up in her job that it had completely slipped her mind.

'Can't you get in?' Hilda was asking now, squinting at Mary with streaming eyes as the smoke from the noxious-smelling roll-up swirled up her nose.

Sighing, Mary said, 'No. The lock's bust.'

'Oh . . . that'll be your dad fiddling with it, I suppose.'

'Fiddling with what?'

'The lock.' Hilda pointed her roll-up at the door. 'He was messing with it before they set off.'

Glancing at the lock as realisation kicked in, Mary gasped when she saw the shiny new brass face.

''Spect they thought you'd be meeting 'em at the coach, eh?' Shrugging, Hilda turned and went back into her own – *accessible, warm, inviting* – house, slamming the door firmly in Mary's bewildered face.

Mary stared at her own door for several minutes, unable

to believe what was happening. It couldn't be true. They wouldn't have gone and left her locked out for two whole weeks. They just wouldn't . . .

7

Mary set up home in the garage. She didn't want to, but she had no choice. There was nowhere else *to* go. Her best friend had abandoned her, and now her family had disowned her. And the neighbours wouldn't help – she knew them well enough to know that without making a fool of herself by asking. She'd caused them too many problems over the years.

Work was her only salvation. There, she soaked up the warmth, luxuriated in the hot water, and drank all the hot tea she could pour down her throat throughout the day in preparation for yet another night outside.

Slipping into Henshall's on the Wednesday of the second week, she was confident that no one had sussed her out. She was just praying that her luck held out for another few days, until her family came back.

It didn't even last for the next few seconds.

At the very moment she dashed into the toilets, Miss Jennings stepped out of one of the cubicles.

Stopping in her tracks, Mary's mouth flapped open.

'Miss Jennings . . .' she bleated lamely. 'I, er, just—'

Holding up a hand, Miss Jennings closed her eyes and said, 'Office. I think it's time you and I had a little chat.'

Mary's heart sank as she followed the supervisor to the office. She was going to get the sack, she just knew it. Perching on the edge of the chair, she waited for the hammer to fall.

Taking her own seat, Miss Jennings peered across the desk, wondering how best to broach the unpleasant subject she knew she had to tackle. Struggling to find a balance between the sympathy she knew she ought to be feeling and the distaste she actually was, her voice was low when she finally spoke.

'Mary, I've noticed that something is a little *amiss* of late. Would you care to enlighten me?'

'I don't know what you mean,' Mary lied, shrugging innocently.

Sighing disappointedly, having given Mary a fair chance to come clean, Miss Jennings said, 'Well, dear, I didn't want to have to be as blunt as this, but I'm afraid you've left me no choice. You're dirty, your clothes are creased, and, quite frankly, dear, you smell. I know you've been coming in early for some time now, and I'd like you to tell me what's going on.' Smiling softly as she watched her words strike home, she added, 'I only want to help. That's what I'm here for, after all.'

Blushing furiously, Mary poured it all out, half rising from the chair as she spoke, sure that she would be told to leave once the truth was known. She was surprised when Miss Jennings waved her back down.

'It must be very difficult, but I'm afraid I can't get involved in private affairs like these. I must, however, insist that you buy some deodorant. You see there have been a number of complaints about your . . . *odour*.' Pausing, Miss Jennings gave a small sympathetic smile before continuing: 'Now, there's plenty of hot water, and I shan't keep a tab on how much you use in the mornings. But you absolutely *cannot* continue to come in so early. I'd hate to have to let you go now that you've shown how capable you are, but if Mr Henshall were to get wind of this . . . Well, I'm sure you understand?'

Nodding, Mary stared down at her feet, her cheeks ablaze with shame.

'Right, then.' Satisfied that she had sorted the problem out, Miss Jennings pushed her chair back with a scrape and stood up. 'Run along and get cleaned up. And why don't you go and get yourself a newspaper while you're at it? I'm sure you'll find a cheap room if you look hard enough.'

'Oh, no, I'll be all right,' Mary insisted. 'Me mam'll be back at the weekend.'

'And if she hasn't changed her stance?' Peering down at Mary, Miss Jennings raised an eyebrow and frowned pessimistically. 'From what you've told me, she doesn't sound the sort to forgive and forget. Having left you on the streets for so long while enjoying a *holiday*, I think it highly unlikely that she'll welcome you back with open arms, don't you?'

'I don't know,' Mary muttered unhappily. In fact, it hadn't even occurred to her that her mother wouldn't let her back in. But now that it had been said she realised that it was a distinct possibility. They *had* gone away and locked her out – and she'd *never* have believed they'd do something like that.

'I wouldn't take the chance, if I were you,' Miss Jennings intoned grimly. 'If this situation were to continue, then your personal condition would only deteriorate further, and I couldn't allow you to subject the others to that – now could I?'

'No, Miss.'

'Mmm. Well, run along. And do make an effort to sort this out as quickly as possible. It's for your own good.'

Mary couldn't get out of the office fast enough.

Seconds later, Miss Jennings smoothed her skirt down and went to have a good old gossip.

At lunchtime, Mary sat alone at the back of the canteen. Mortified that she apparently smelled bad – and that the women had been complaining – she stared studiously down at the *To Let* ads in the local paper, looking for anywhere, no matter how small, that wouldn't eat up every penny of her wages.

When Lynne Raymond, the woman who worked on the huge steam press at the far end of the factory, came and sat down at her table, she leaped to her feet.

'Stay put, you silly cow,' Lynne said, waving her back down. 'I don't bite – not straight off, anyhow.' Smiling, she took a pack of cigarettes from her overall pocket and offered one to Mary. Lighting one for herself, she inhaled noisily and leaned back in her seat. 'Look, love, I hope you don't mind me saying, but I've heard about your problem and I think I might be able to help.'

'Oh?'

Avoiding Lynne's gaze, Mary self-consciously pinned her arms to her sides to stop the reported B.O. from escaping. Her hands were shaking and her cheeks were burning. She'd seen Lynne around but they'd never actually spoken, and Mary found her a little intimidating. She was older, for one thing, and really sophisticated with her dyed blonde hair, bold blue eyeliner and glossy red lipstick.

But it wasn't just this that was causing Mary's embarrassment. It was the fact that Lynne had heard about her problem, which could only mean one thing: that Miss Jennings had been blabbing. And if she'd told Lynne, who else had she told? Flicking a surreptitious glance around the canteen, Mary was dismayed to see several of the women pretending not to look at her.

'Don't mind, do you?' Reaching across the table, Lynne picked up the jam tart Mary had bought but hadn't yet touched. Stuffing it into her mouth, she said, 'Sorry, but I can't resist the strawberry ones.'

'It's all right.' Mary smiled nervously. 'I wasn't really hungry, anyway.'

'You're like me,' Lynne chuckled, spraying pastry onto the table. 'Eyes bigger than your belly.' Wiping her mouth on her sleeve when she'd finished, she said, 'Right, about your problem. If you're interested, you're welcome to come and kip at mine for a bit.'

'Really?' Mary spluttered, looking her fully in the eye for the first time. 'How come? You hardly know me.'

'I know you're in the shit,' Lynne replied quietly. 'And I think everyone deserves a helping hand sometime – especially when they're as young as you. You can always say no, but I'd think about it if I was you. Where've you been kipping this last few weeks – some garage or other?'

'Yeah.'

'Well, don't you think it'd be better to have a proper bed? Even if it's just for a night or two.'

'You're not winding me up?'

'Dead straight,' Lynne assured her, smiling. 'What d'y' say?'

'God, yeah! I'd love to.' Mary grinned. 'It won't be for long 'cos I'm really gonna try and get a place of my own. And I promise I won't get in your way. I'll be dead quiet, and—'

'Steady on!' Lynne laughed. 'If I wanted to live with a corpse I'd just move me bed in here. You could get your menopause early just *sitting* near this lot. Anyhow, tonight's good for me if you're up for it.' Pushing her chair back, she stood up. 'See you later, yeah?'

'Yeah, see you.'

Smiling as she made her way out, Lynne aimed challenging eye-daggers at the women who looked up as she passed. Just let one of the bitches *dare* say anything and she'd tear their heads off! It was because of them she'd done it in the first place – a spit in the eye for gossiping behind the poor kid's back like a pack of bloody hyenas.

As soon as Lynne was out of the room, two women who'd been eavesdropping from a neighbouring table rushed over to Mary.

'Did we hear that right?' one of them said, plonking herself down on the chair Lynne had vacated. 'You're gonna stop with *her*?' She thumbed over her shoulder in the direction of the door.

'Yeah, why?' Mary said warily.

'You know what she is, don't you?' the other said in a quiet, disapproving tone.

'No.' Mary narrowed her eyes, her hackles beginning to rise.

'A whore,' they both hissed at once.

'Disgusting,' the first woman added, wrinkling her nose. 'Who knows what kind of filth she gets up to? You want to watch yourself, love, or she'll have you at it, too.'

'She's only giving me a bed for a couple of nights,' Mary told them indignantly. 'And I haven't exactly got a lot of choice, have I? I mean, no one else is rushing to offer a helping hand, are they?' Staring coolly at them now, she shook her head when neither could meet her eye. 'Didn't think so.'

'I can't,' the first muttered. 'My hubby wouldn't . . .' Trailing off, she stood up. 'Best get back to work, eh?'

'Yeah, best had,' Mary sniped. 'Before you get infected, or something.'

'We was only trying to warn you,' the second informed her huffily. 'If you don't want our advice, that's your look out. Just don't blame us if you end up as bad as her.'

Smiling sweetly, Mary said, 'Piss off.'

It was pouring with rain when they came out of the factory that evening. 'Sack the bus,' Lynne said, dragging her hood up over her hair. 'I think this calls for a taxi.'

Mary's face fell. 'I, er, don't think I can afford it.'

'My treat,' Lynne said. 'I had a little win on the bingo last night.' Stepping to the edge of the pavement, she glanced up and down the road. Seeing a taxi after a couple of minutes, she put her fingers to her lips and whistled shrilly.

Dashing out from the shelter of the doorway, Mary climbed into the cab just seconds after Lynne had told the driver where to take them. Settling back in her seat as they swished their way through the darkening streets, she wondered if she hadn't better mention what the women had said before it was too late. She doubted it was true, but if it was, there was no way she wanted to get involved.

Gazing out of the window as she contemplated how best to broach the subject without offending Lynne, her brow began to crease with concern when the cab turned off the Mancunian Way and headed towards the Crescents.

Slinking down in her seat as they turned onto the road fronting her mother's block, Mary prayed that none of the neighbours would see her. That would be all she needed – *not!* If any of the nosy sods round here had heard the same rumours as the women at work, her mother would know everything before she'd even had a chance to put her new key into the new lock.

They might have disowned her, but there was no way her family would tolerate her staying with a *prostitute*. Her mother would be convinced that Mary was up to all sorts, and she'd have their Joey keeping tabs on her left right and centre. It would be a living hell.

She was relieved when they bypassed her mother's block and continued on to John Nash – the one furthest away. Her family never came down this end, it being too far from the pub, the shops, and the bus stop. Unless someone told them, they might never even find out that Mary was here. If she kept her head down – and got on with looking for her own place as soon as possible – she might just get away with it.

But there was still the other problem . . .

'Lynne,' she said, when they'd climbed out of the cab and paid the driver. 'Can I ask you something?'

'Fire away,' Lynne said, dashing head-down for the shelter of the stairwell.

'It's just something the women at work were saying,' Mary panted, following at a run.

'Oh, yeah?' Stopping in the narrow entrance hall, Lynne shook the rain from her coat. 'And what's that?'

'I didn't believe it,' Mary assured her. 'But, well, they sort of said you're a . . .' Pausing, she swallowed hard, too embarrassed to say it.

'They sort of said I'm a *what*?' Lynne prompted, a strange smile on her lips as she led Mary up the stairs to her floor. 'Prostitute, by any chance?'

Blushing, Mary nodded, sure that Lynne would deny it – and be mad at Mary for even entertaining the idea.

Instead, laughing out loud, Lynne said, 'What if I was? Would it bother you?'

'No, course not,' Mary said quickly, still sure that the denial was about to come.

'Well, I am,' Lynne said, her voice suddenly serious. 'And, what's more, I'm *proud* of it.' Coming to a stop at her front door, she unlocked it but didn't go inside. Looking at Mary, she said, 'Way I see it, I'm just using the cunts before they use me. But if you've got a problem with that, you'd best toddle off back to your garage, 'cos I ain't apologising to no one for nothing.'

'I haven't got a problem with it,' Mary murmured shamefacedly. Awed by the passion behind Lynne's logic, she thought that Lynne was just the most glamorous, amazing woman she'd ever met.

Smiling when she saw the sincerity in Mary's eyes, Lynne said, 'We'll get along just fine, then, won't we? Come on . . . Let's get that kettle on before my tits drop off.'

Grinning, Mary followed her new friend inside.

If anyone had told her that, in the space of just one short month, she would lose her best friend, land her first job, get kicked out of her home and have to sleep in a garage, then move in with a *prostitute*, she'd never have believed them in a million years. But Mary had a feeling that life was about to become very interesting indeed.

8

Sister Hadley ran The Pines nursing home with compassion and efficiency, priding herself on having the new-breed mentality – despite being of the old-breed age. She didn't hold with the outdated 'have it in secret, get rid of it in haste' principle, believing instead that every woman, whatever her age, had the divine right to choose her own destiny – *and* that of the child she alone had borne for nine long months. She conceded that there were circumstances where it was advisable for a child to be given up, but it was her firmly held belief that each case had to be viewed on its individual merits.

And that belief would never be swayed by the likes of Alice Bates.

That woman, as Sister Hadley thought of Jane's mother, was a mean-minded tyrant whose only concern was that *she* should not be tainted by the stigma of her daughter's illegitimate child. She hadn't an ounce of grandmotherly feeling – and even less motherly love, judging by the coldness with which she had made her demands regarding her daughter's confinement.

There was to be no mollycoddling. No familiarity, which could potentially lead Jane to believe that her behaviour was acceptable. The baby was to be removed immediately it was born, and the adoption papers signed at the first possible moment. And she was to be informed the very instant that Jane went into labour, because she absolutely *had* to be there to ensure that her directions were carried out to the letter.

The first thing that Sister Hadley did when Jane arrived was talk to her – both to assess her condition, and to ascertain what she expected and wanted from the situation.

The second thing she did was to encourage Jane to mingle with the other girls, knowing that it would do her no end of good to learn that she was not as alone as she so obviously felt. Helping the girls whose babies had already arrived would also reassure her that she was perfectly capable of holding, feeding, and changing a newborn. There was no great mystery to it, but Sister Hadley knew that childbirth was one of the most daunting prospects for these young, inexperienced girls.

Watching Jane throw herself right into everything from the off, Sister Hadley had no doubt that she would be just fine. Pity she was going to have such a battle with her mother, but Jane seemed determined, and Sister Hadley had to admit to a sneaking respect. A very difficult road lay ahead but, God willing, Jane would get through it.

Jane's labour took her completely by surprise. She was helping out in the kitchen at the time and thought she'd wet herself when she saw the pool of water around her feet. When the first cramp took hold seconds later, she knew exactly what was happening – and she was petrified.

'Oh, God!' she cried. 'Help! It's coming! *Aaagghh!*'

Alerted by her panicked screams, Sister Hadley came rushing in. Taking instant control she pushed Jane down into a chair. 'Stop that noise at once. You'll frighten the poor mite to death before it's had a chance to snatch a breath. Now, remember what I told you and breathe – quick, quick, slow . . . That's right.'

All the time she was talking to Jane, she was also issuing orders to the other girls: 'Lesley, go and tell Nurse Sullivan to prepare the birthing suite . . . Julia, away and fetch a wheelchair . . . Alexis, mop up that mess before someone slips and breaks something . . . Carole-Anne, stop staring like a blasted fool . . .'

Jane screamed and grunted and panted and pushed her way through the next fourteen sweat-soaked, pain-filled hours. Then, finally, just when it felt as if her entire lower half was being turned inside out and hacked to pieces with a blunt machete, she felt a rush of heat between her legs and a huge, smooth, wet blob came slithering out.

'You've a baby boy!' Sister Hadley announced, scooping the bloody bundle up. 'A beautiful, perfect, baby boy.'

Jane laughed and cried all at once. 'Can I see him?' she begged, terrified that her son would be whisked away before she'd had so much as a glimpse of him.

'You can do better than that,' Sister Hadley reassured her. 'You can have a hold of him. Just give me a minute to clear his wee lungs and he's all yours.'

Swiping at her tears, Jane craned her neck to watch what the sister was doing to her baby. She was alarmed when she heard his first cry. It was so thin and weak, like a tiny, distant wail of distress.

'Is he all right?' she gasped, struggling to sit up. 'What's wrong with him?'

'He's fine,' Sister Hadley beamed, bringing the swaddled child back to his mother and laying him gently in her arms. 'He's just doing what all men do when they realise they're awake – looking for a titty. Now, are you going to let him have a suckle, or are you wanting me to fetch a bottle?'

Jane gazed down at the baby in her arms. He was snuffling at her covered breast, his mouth open as he sought to fulfil his primitive needs. It was the most instinctive thing in the world, and Jane recognised it on a purely spiritual level.

'I want to do it,' she said.

'You're sure?' Sister Hadley asked; all too aware that Jane would be embarking upon a difficult path if she went ahead and bonded with her son in this way. It would be twice as difficult for her to contemplate adoption once he had drawn from her well.

Nodding decisively, Jane said, 'Yeah.'

'Right, then. Let's help the little fella out, shall we? Show him how to get what he wants – not that he wouldn't learn fast enough all by himself, mind. What are you calling him, by the way?'

'I don't know. I hadn't really thought about it.'

Picking the baby up, Sister Hadley peered at his face for a few seconds, then said, 'He looks like a David to me. Baby David.'

'David?' Jane repeated the name. Then, smiling, she nodded. 'Yeah . . . that's nice.'

'Ah, good. That's settled then.'

Handing David back to his mother, Sister Hadley guided them through the first tricky feed then left them to it, retiring to her own bed for a well-earned rest.

Early the next morning, she called Jane's father to let him know that he had a beautiful grandson – smug in the know-ledge that there was nothing his wife could do to sour the event.

The next three weeks passed all too quickly. Before she knew it, Jane was saying her tearful goodbyes to Sister Hadley, the staff, and the girls at The Pines.

Carrying David in the second-hand Moses basket that Sister Hadley had given her, she boarded the train to Manchester with a feeling of impending doom. Her parents hadn't visited during her confinement, and she was dreading the reception she'd receive when she arrived home. She was quite prepared to take whatever her mother threw at her if there was even a chance that clearing the air would make way for reconciliation, but she very much doubted it would turn out like that. Still, she had to try for David's sake.

Getting off the train at Piccadilly, Jane made her way to the bus station, feeling a little sicker with each step. The scenery was familiar, but it seemed alien – like a place she'd seen in pictures but had never actually visited. It was as if she didn't belong there, and she hoped it wasn't an omen of what she would find at home.

Stepping off the bus when it reached the Crescents, she gazed up at the curved bank of windows with a sinking heart. It felt like she was being watched – as if all the neighbours had their noses pressed up against the nets to see the outcast and her illegitimate child.

Scolding herself for being so paranoid, Jane forced herself to calm down. No one was watching; no one even knew – her mother would have made damn sure of that.

Peering down at David, she gave him a shaky smile.

'Well, this is it. Wish me luck.'

Getting a tiny gurgle in reply, she took a deep breath and set off up the stairs.

She'd just emerged onto the landing at her floor when her father popped his head out of the front door.

'*There* you are!' he called, unable to mask his relief as he rushed out to help her. 'I've been worried sick. I thought you weren't coming.'

'Sorry.' Reaching up, Jane kissed his cheek. 'The train was a bit late, then I had to wait ages for the bus.'

'Never mind. Better late than never, eh? So, this is him, is it?'

'Yeah, that's him.' Jane watched her dad's face closely for signs of disappointment. 'His name's David.'

'David?' Frank raised an eyebrow. 'Where did that come from? Is it . . . ?'

Understanding the unspoken question, Jane shook her head. She'd never told them about Del, and had no intention of doing so now. There was no point. He was long gone.

'It was Sister Hadley's idea,' she said. 'But I kind of like it.'

Peering down at his grandson for a moment, Frank said, 'Me too. Sorry I didn't meet you, by the way. I was a bit tied up.'

'It's all right,' Jane assured him, knowing full well who had tied him up. 'Is she okay?'

'Not really, no.' Frank gave a sheepish shrug. 'But give her time, eh? She'll come round.'

Jane gave him a small, tight smile. Who was he trying to kid?

Following her father into the house, she sat awkwardly on the couch and peered around the living room. It looked exactly the same as it always had, but it felt much worse than she'd anticipated. Despite her father's attempts at jollity, there was a distinctly unwelcoming atmosphere.

David began to whinge. Scooping him quickly out of his basket, Jane rocked him gently and shushed him as she felt his nappy, praying that he didn't start bawling and give a bad impression of himself. With the odds already stacked against them, that was the last thing they needed.

'He's not wet,' she said, looking up at her father who was hovering above her. 'He must be hungry.'

Frank's face fell. 'You're not going to . . . ?'

'Bottle.' Smiling shyly, Jane reached into her bag for one of the prepared ones that Sister Hadley had packed for her. 'I did try the other way, but it hurt too much.'

'Ah, right.' Frank was visibly relieved. Breastfeeding was a strictly private mother-child event, in his opinion – one he absolutely did *not* want to witness his own child doing. 'Um, how about a cuppa?'

Biting her lip when her father rushed from the room, Jane blinked rapidly to stop the tears from escaping. He was trying so hard to be nice, but it was obviously as difficult for him as it was for her. Whatever came of this home-coming, *he* was the one who'd have to deal with the fallout, and that wouldn't be easy.

If only he'd stayed away that time he left, she mused as she gazed into her baby's trusting eyes, she and David would be safe with him in a real home now – not sitting here, waiting for Her Ladyship to make an appearance.

In the bedroom above, Alice was pacing back and forth, a glass of gin clutched in her hand. She'd heard Frank welcoming Jane home as if she were the most wonderful sight he'd ever seen, and his indiscretion had infuriated her. He should have waited until they were inside. The whole neighbourhood would know the shameful truth by now.

Downing the drink, she poured herself another and cursed Jane under her breath. The girl was so selfish; she had no idea of the hell she was putting her mother through. No thought for anyone but herself – herself, and the unwanted child she'd dared bring home with her.

Well, she needn't think it was staying; or that Alice was having anything to do with it. Or with *her*, for that matter. If her mother meant so little to Jane that she would delib-erately disobey her, then she'd just have to live with the consequences.

Changing her decision about not seeing her daughter, Alice slammed the empty glass down on the dressing table and stormed downstairs to give Jane a well-deserved piece of her mind. Her eyes narrowed to slits when she burst into the room to find Jane feeding the baby, a fresh cup of tea sitting beside her on the floor.

'Well, well,' Alice sniped, shoving her sleeves roughly

up her arms as if preparing for a fight. 'Isn't this *cosy*?'

'Alice,' Frank warned, getting up from his seat. 'Just leave them be, eh? They've only just—'

'Shut up.' Alice cut him dead, her gaze never leaving Jane's face. 'I'm talking to *her*, not you. Well, what've you got to say for yourself?'

'Hello, Mum,' Jane murmured, giving her mother an uncertain smile.

As incensed by the quiet greeting as she'd have been had Jane been insolent, Alice bared her gritted teeth. 'Don't you *dare*,' she snarled, spittle flying from her lips, her hands balled into fists. 'Don't you bloody *dare* try to worm your way around me!'

'I wasn't.' Jane struggled to appear calm despite her wildly hammering heart. 'I was only saying hello.'

'Well, *don't*,' Alice retorted furiously. 'I don't want your hellos – not when you couldn't stick to your end of the bargain.'

'What bargain?' Jane blurted out before she could stop herself. 'There was no bargain. It was just *you* telling me what to do.'

'You're a *child*,' Alice spat. 'It's not listening that got you into this mess in the first place.'

'I'm not *in* a mess.' Jane stared fixedly at the floor as the anger began to rise into her throat. 'I've had a baby, that's all.'

'That's *all*?' Alice gave a contemptuous snort. 'That's all, she says.'

'Yeah, that *is* all.' Snapping her gaze up, Jane eyed her mother coldly. 'And if you can't accept it, you can get stuffed, 'cos he's mine and I'm keeping him. Oh, and his name's David, by the way.'

'Not to me, it's not.' Alice refused to even look at the baby in her daughter's arms. 'To me it's just that bastard that should have been scraped out of you when we had the chance.'

'That's enough!' Frank barked, stepping forward and seizing his wife's arm. 'You're drunk.'

'So what?' Alice screeched, wrenching herself free and glaring at him, her face contorted with disgust. 'It beats the *hell* out of being sober and having to look at you two playing happy families. You make me *sick*.'

'I'm warning you, Alice—'

'It's all right, Dad,' Jane interrupted sharply. 'I'm going.'

Standing, as calmly as her quivering legs would allow, she laid David gently in his basket and tucked the little blanket around him. She could take whatever abuse her mother levelled at *her*, but she couldn't bear to see her father suffer. And he *was* suffering – it was all too obvious. He looked so much older than she remembered, and his skin seemed to be as grey as his hair was becoming. But it was the dullness of his eyes that upset her the most – as if the light of his very soul had been extinguished.

Hoisting the basket onto her hip, she bent to retrieve her bags then turned to her mother.

'Right, I'm off. And don't worry – you won't see us again. I don't want my baby to know what a sad old alkie bitch his gran is.'

'Get *out*!' Alice hissed, her back hunched as she struggled to restrain herself from attacking the stranger standing in front of her – the stranger who, she realised despite the drink, would most probably beat her senseless if the fight became physical. For Jane had obviously grown in more ways than one during her time away.

Sensing that she had won this round of the battle, Jane gave a contemptuous shake of her head, then walked calmly over to her father. Kissing him, she said, 'Bye, Dad. I'll ring you at work sometime – let you know where I am so you can visit us.'

Walking out then, she set off down the landing with her head held high.

There was one last person she had to see before she threw herself on the mercy of the Social Services.

'I haven't seen her for months,' Agnes James said, pursing her lips primly as she peered into the Moses basket. 'I take it that's why *you* disappeared so fast?'

Blushing guiltily at the disapproving tone, Jane nodded.

'Fine kettle.' Shaking her head, Agnes slipped a cigarette out of the pack in her apron pocket. Lighting it, she folded her arms. 'So, how's Her Ladyship taking it? I can't imagine she's best pleased?'

'Er, not exactly, no,' Jane admitted. 'She didn't want me to keep him.'

'But you're going to anyhow?' Agnes rolled her eyes. 'Ah, well, the Devil makes his choices the same as His Good Self, I suppose.'

Frowning as she tried to make sense of what Mary's mother had just said, Jane hoisted the basket up a little higher.

'I'd best get going, Mrs James. I only wanted to see your Mary, but if you don't know where she is . . . ?'

'No, I don't.' Agnes sighed her disappointment. 'But that's kids for you. You give them everything you've got and they walk away without so much as a backward glance. But you'll find that out soon enough if you keep him.'

'I *am* keeping him,' Jane said, meaning it more than she'd ever meant anything in her life before.

Peering closely at her for a moment, Agnes nodded slowly.

'Good luck to you, then, love. You'll need it. He's a bonny 'un, I'll give you that.'

Thanking her, Jane went on her way with fresh tears brimming at her eyes. Why couldn't her own mother have been as understanding? Why couldn't she find it in her heart to accept the blood of her blood?

Boarding the bus back to town, Jane stared straight ahead until the Crescents were far behind. If she never saw the place again, it would be a lifetime and a day too soon.

PART TWO

9

Ali and Raiz tugged their collars up around their ears and tried to be as inconspicuous as possible as they made their way through the dark streets. They had spent the last few hours hiding out in the ice-covered park and they were numb-bollock cold, but it was more the fear of bumping into their dealer before they made it home that was making them shiver.

Terry Hardman would be spitting blood by now. He'd laid half an ounce of smack on them over a week earlier and they were supposed to have his cash by ten tonight – or else. It was two a.m. now, and they still didn't have it. But what could they do? They couldn't magic it out of thin air. And they couldn't give the smack back because, apart from the little they'd actually sold, they had polished the lot off.

It disgusted them that they had sunk so low, but they blamed the decadence of this Western society. All they had wanted was the chance to make a fresh start in a country whose government didn't punish its people for living and breathing. But they hadn't anticipated the effect such freedom would have upon them. They had seized it and embraced it and loved it – and, ultimately, abused it, landing themselves with a heroin habit that had rapidly taken over their lives and trampled the shit out of their high hopes.

Dealing was the worst mistake they could have made, but they had thought themselves too intelligent to fall into the user/dealer trap. How wrong they had been. The moment they'd had that gear in their grasp, they had partied like there was no tomorrow.

Well, tomorrow was here with a vengeance. And if they didn't manage to avoid Terry until they'd figured out a way of getting their hands on some easy money, it would be the last tomorrow they would ever see.

Rounding the corner to their block, they stopped in their tracks when they saw Terry himself walking towards them. They wanted to turn and run, but it was too late – he'd already spotted them.

'What fuckin' time d'y' call this?' he demanded, marching towards them with murder in his eyes. 'I said ten, you pair of piss-takers. I've got better things to do than chase your fuckin' arses all over town. Give us me money, and fuckin' hurry up about it.'

Peering at him fearfully, Raiz stuck his hands into his pockets and shuffled his feet. Terry was furious now, but when he found out that they didn't have his money, he'd lose it for real.

'Where is it?' Terry's narrowed eyes flashed from one to the other of them.

'It's . . . well, we . . .' Faltering, Ali swiped at the sweat that was breaking out all over his brow. 'It's just that, well, we haven't got it right now.'

'You what?' Terry stared back at him. 'You fuckin' me about?'

'We thought we'd have it,' Raiz chipped in, fear making his voice as shaky as his legs. 'Believe me, Terry, we wouldn't mess you about on purpose. We've just had a bit of trouble getting the punters to pay up.'

'I should have known a pair of Paki cunts like youse couldn't hack it,' Terry snarled. 'If you ain't got a counter to hide behind, you ain't got a clue, you lot. But that's your problem, not mine. Cough up, *now*, or I'm gonna do you.'

Ali felt the anger spark in his gut. He hated being mislabelled, but it happened all the time here. The people were so ignorant. And Terry Hardman was the most ignorant of them all.

'Could you give us a few more hours?' he asked, struggling to keep his hatred of the man standing in front of him from his voice. 'We've just been putting the frighteners on, and there's three who'll be here first thing in the morning to pay up. We'll bring it straight round.'

'On Christmas fuckin' Day?' Terry sneered, cracking his knuckles menacingly. 'You think I want *you* round my gaff when I've got me kids opening their presents? Do me a favour!'

'All right.' Ali held up his hands in a gesture of compliance. 'Look, we have got *some* of the money, but not all of it. If we give you what we've got, will you wait till tomorrow for the rest?'

'Ali!' Raiz hissed. 'What are you—'

Silencing his friend with a sharp elbow in the ribs, Ali said, 'What do you say, Terry?'

'Depends how much we're talking.' Terry flicked an impatient glance at his watch. 'I'm supposed to be somewhere, and if you cunts have made me miss out, I'll be double pissed off.'

'There's about two hundred,' Ali lied, bringing a groan of despair from Raiz who knew full well that they'd be lucky to rustle up *two* pounds, never mind two *hundred*. 'Only thing is, it's stashed round the back,' Ali went on, gesturing down the pitch-dark alleyway that ran between the flats and a row of derelict shops.

'Fuck's it doing down there?' Terry demanded.

'You know what thieving bastards they are round here,' Ali explained. 'If you carry cash you get mugged, but if you leave it in the flat they kick the door in, so we just hide it out back. Come on, we'll show you.'

'This best not be a wind-up.' Giving them a warning glare, Terry set off up the alley. 'If I find out you're lying, I'll break every fuckin' bone in your body.'

'What the hell are you doing?' Raiz hissed as they followed Terry. 'There's no stash back here.'

'*We* know that, but *he* doesn't,' Ali hissed back. 'Look, he's on his own. We won't get a better chance than this.'

'For what?' A prickle of apprehension disturbed the thick curls on Raiz's scalp. 'What are you planning, man?'

Sliding his knife from its sheaf in his inside pocket, Ali showed it to him.

'Oh, shit,' Raiz muttered fearfully. 'No way, man. You can't. He'll kill us.'

'He will anyway when we don't give him the money,' Ali reasoned. 'Come on, man, what else can we do? It's him or us.'

'It's not just him, though, is it?' Raiz argued in an urgent whisper. 'His men will suss it. We'll never get away with it.'

'They won't know it was us.'

'It's right behind our *flat*. It's fucking crazy, man.'

'Yeah?' Ali challenged, his coal-black eyes glittering madly in the faint moonlight filtering through the gaps in the roof-less shop's wall. 'So, what do *you* suggest?'

'I don't know,' Raiz admitted miserably.

'Exactly. So just shut up and leave the thinking to me.'

'What are you muppets up to?' Terry demanded in a harsh whisper. Waiting at the corner up ahead, he waved impatiently for them to get a move on. 'It fuckin' stinks down here. Shift yourselves before I change me mind and kick the fuck out of you.'

'We're coming,' Ali whispered back, grabbing Raiz's arm and forcing him on. 'He's scared of the dark, that's all.'

'Wuss,' Terry sneered. 'That's the problem with you lot. You've got no balls.'

Flicking a hate-filled glance at Raiz, Ali gripped the handle of the knife in his pocket. Hardman was scum. If anyone deserved this, he did. Surely Raiz could see that?

'Right, where is it?' Terry demanded when they reached him. Glancing up and down the deserted alley, he couldn't see anywhere that would make a suitable hiding place – just towering walls and locked gates. 'Come on, you greasy twats . . . I haven't got all night.'

'Oh, don't worry, it's here,' Ali snarled.

'Aw, shit,' Raiz groaned. 'Don't, man. It isn't worth it.'

'Fuck's he whingeing about?' Terry grunted.

Stepping right up to him, Ali's whole body was shaking with rage and fear as he stared into the white man's contemptuous eyes.

'Don't *ever* disrespect my friend,' he warned him quietly. 'He's a good man. But *you* . . . you're *nothing*.'

'You *what*?' Terry's eyes narrowed to slits as his face contorted with disbelief. 'What did you fuckin' sa—'

The word died in his mouth as Ali whipped the knife out and rammed it into Terry's chest. The man's eyes widened for a moment, then sank slowly back into their sockets as, slumping to his knees, he fell sideways, his head hitting the icy cobbles with a dull crack.

'Oh, Christ!' Raiz gasped, leaping back and flailing his arms. 'What've you done, man? What've you done?'

'Shut up!' Ali hissed, squatting beside Terry and rummaging through his pockets.

'Is he dead?'

'I hope so. Don't just fucking stand there, man. Come and help me.'

'What – what are you looking for?' Wringing his hands, Raiz stepped hesitantly forward.

'Money. We've got to make it look like a mugging.'

Raiz glanced nervously up at the flats beyond the wall.

Despite the late hour, several lights were still on, but there were no faces at the windows. Thanking God for that small mercy, he squatted down to help.

'Christ,' Ali exclaimed. 'Look at *this*.'

Pulling a clear-plastic package from where it had been stuffed down the back of Terry's jeans, he held it up for Raiz to see. Raiz's eyes widened when he saw that it was heroin. Even compressed by its mode of travel, it still looked a fair amount – an ounce, give or take.

'There's money, too.' Ali extracted Terry's bulging wallet and glanced into it.

'How much?' Raiz was still staring at the heroin, a wild craving twisting at his gut.

'Enough for now.' Glancing furtively around, Ali pushed himself to his feet. 'Come on. Let's get out of here before someone sees us. And don't run. Just stay cool.'

Following him shakily out of the alley, Raiz tugged his collar high again. The road was deserted, but he knew from experience that there could be numerous hooded thugs lurking in the shadows, waiting to pounce on vulnerable passers-by and relieve them of their belongings. He pitied any that tried it on with Ali right now, though. His friend was wired to the max – armed and more than a little dangerous.

'Where are we going?' Raiz asked when they had been walking for what seemed like hours but was in fact only fifteen minutes.

'Town,' Ali said, walking on with purposeful strides. 'We'll book ourselves into a hotel – get ourselves an alibi.'

'There's a taxi.' Raiz pointed across the road to where a black cab was pulling in to the kerb.

'Get it,' Ali said, setting off. 'Come on, man . . . *run!*'

Lynne had had a terrible night. It was icy as hell, and the sub-zero temperature had obviously put the punters off leaving their cosy homes because she'd been walking up and down for hours without so much as a *sniff* of a kerb-crawler. All she'd done all night was a couple of hand jobs on a pair of piss-heads making their way home from the pub – and the bastards had ripped her off.

'Two for the price of one,' one of the cunts had joked, shoving a fiver down her top. 'Come on, darlin' . . . It's Christmas. We're skint.'

Furious with herself for not checking that they had the cash before servicing them, she'd had to let it go. But she'd remember their faces – and God help them if she ever saw one of them on his own.

Knowing that the fiver wouldn't cover the cab she'd just flagged down, never mind buy the weed she so desperately needed to chill herself out, she decided to do a jump when the cab slowed down as it neared the Crescents. It was a risk if the driver fancied giving chase, but if worse came to worst and he caught her, she'd just have to offer him a free blowie.

Climbing into the cab, Lynne flopped down on the seat and was just about to tell the driver where to take her when the door was wrenched open and two men clambered in, bringing a blast of chill air with them.

'Oi!' she protested. 'This is mine. Piss off and get your own.'

'It's ours,' Ali argued, holding the front of his jacket together with one hand. 'We saw it first.'

'Did you bollocks!' She clung to the seat as he tried to shove her out. 'I flagged it – ain't that right, mate?' This she directed at the driver.

'I don't give a toss who takes it,' he replied gruffly. 'Sort it out between you, or get out. I've got a Santa suit waiting at home. I can't be doing with time-wasters.'

'Don't tell me, tell *them*.'

'Maybe we could share?' Raiz suggested, desperate to

avoid a scene. They needed an alibi, but this was the wrong place to be getting one. 'We'll pay,' he added, pleading with his eyes now.

'Oh yeah?' Lynne peered back at him with suspicion. 'Why would you do that?'

'Gratitude.' He gave a sheepish shrug. 'It's your cab. You'd be doing us a favour.'

Amused by his over-politeness, Lynne relaxed her stance. He wasn't as good-looking as his mate but he was a bit of a sweetie, whereas his mate was rude and arrogant. Not that she was looking for anything with *either* of them after the night she'd just had. She'd rather sew her pussy lips together than spread her legs. But they *were* offering to pay.

'Sure you've got the money?' She cocked an eyebrow at him.

Nodding vigorously, Raiz nudged Ali. 'Show her.'

Rolling his eyes with irritation, Ali eased Terry's wallet out and flapped it open for a second before stuffing it back into his pocket – time enough for her to see the thick wad of notes it contained.

Smiling broadly, she settled back and patted the seat.

'Go on then. You've twisted my arm.'

'Where to?' The driver was tapping his nails on the steering wheel. 'But I'm warning you now, I'm going home in exactly ten minutes and anyone who's still with me is out – wherever we are.'

'Crescents, you moody old sod,' Lynne said. 'And I pity your kids if you're the only fucking Santa they've got. They'll be getting nowt but lemons if your sour mush is anything to go by.'

'Don't push it,' he threatened, throwing her a dirty look through his rear-view mirror.

'Please, can we just go?' Raiz implored. 'We've got to be somewhere.'

'Oh yeah?' Lynne turned to look at him. 'Off to a party, are you? I'll come, if you're asking. I could do with a good old knees up after the night I've had.'

'There's no party,' Ali told her curtly.

'Shame,' she teased, grasping at the hanging strap as the driver swung out onto the road. 'You'd be a bit of all right if you loosened up.' Thinking about the money in his wallet then, she pursed her lips. 'You know, if you were a bit more friendly I'd invite you back to mine for a Christmas drink. We'd have to stop off for a bottle on the way, though.'

'No, thank you.'

'Suit yourself.' Shaking her head, Lynne gave Raiz a *What's up with him?* smile.

Smiling sheepishly back at her, Raiz glanced out of the window. They were heading off the Princess Parkway into Hulme and the darkness was descending like a blanket, but there was no safety in the gloom. The gangsters who ruled these streets were so used to conducting their dealings in the dark, they had cat vision. If anyone was looking for him and Ali right now, they were dead.

Held up for several minutes by a red light on a deserted stretch of road, the driver checked the time on his dashboard clock and tutted loudly.

'Know what,' he told the men when he finally set off again, 'I'd accept her offer if I was you, 'cos there's no way I'm going into town once I've dropped her off.'

'Aw, no, man,' Ali protested. 'You've got to. You promised.'

'I didn't promise nothing, mate. I'll drop youse at the Crescents with her. Or I can stop right here if you wanna argue about it. Your choice.'

'Ah, well, looks like Shitty Santa's made your mind up for you,' Lynne chuckled. 'So, you on for that drink, or what?'

Slipping into their own language, Raiz asked Ali what he thought.

'I don't know,' Ali replied tetchily.

'We'd still get an alibi.'

'Yeah, but what then? We can't go back to the flat, and we'll never get another cab now. We'd have to walk to town, and we can't risk it – not while we're carrying this gear. And I've got blood on my shirt. If the police pull us, we've had it.'

'Maybe we won't have to walk anywhere.' Raiz flicked a surreptitious glance at Lynne. 'Why don't you chat her up? See if we can't get a drink *and* a bed.'

'Why don't *you*?'

'You're better at it.' Raiz gave a weary grin. It was true – Ali had a far better pick-up rate. In the time they'd been here, it was Ali the girls chased, leaving Raiz to cop off with their less attractive mates by default. 'Come on, man. It's the perfect solution.'

'Don't you know it's rude to talk foreign when there's a lady present?' Lynne cut in peevishly. 'Heard that saying, haven't you – when in Rome . . . ?'

'Excuse me?' Raiz frowned with confusion.

'You're in England, speak *English*,' she scolded. Then, tapping the driver's shoulder as he turned a corner, she said, 'You can stop here, mate. We'll walk the rest of the way.'

Pulling over, the driver adjusted his meter and said, 'Seventeen quid.'

'You what?' Lynne was outraged. 'That's daylight fuckin' robbery. It's only a fiver from the Parkway.'

'Not at Christmas,' the driver growled, activating the automatic door-locks and snatching up his radio. 'Pay up *now*, or I'm calling the cops.'

'Pay him,' Raiz urged, his eyes showing panic again.

'All *right*.' Extracting a twenty from the wallet, Ali thrust it through the grille. 'Keep the change.'

'Ta very much.' Grinning victoriously, the driver released the doors. 'Merry Christmas.'

'Up yours,' Lynne hissed, climbing out onto the pavement in a clatter of stiletto heels. 'And I hope your reindeer's dead when you get home, you miserable cunt!'

'Here, I hope you've got enough left to pay for *her*,' the driver said to Ali. 'She might look like a cheap slag, but you can bet your life she's gonna fleece the arse off of you. Her type always does.' Flipping Lynne the finger, he took off with a squeal of burning rubber.

'Wanker!' she yelled after him. 'I do *not* look cheap! This dress probably cost more than your fuckin' *cab*!'

'Ignore him,' Ali said, spurred on by a desperate look from Raiz. 'You look very nice. In fact, that's what we were discussing in the cab – how . . . *attractive* you are.'

Squinting up at him, Lynne pulled a face. Not only rude and arrogant – but a bullshitter, too.

'Oh, per-*leease*,' she drawled, completely unimpressed. 'Do I look like I fell out of the stupid tree?'

'Sorry?'

'Look, I asked you back for a drink, that's all. If I wanted a bit of the other, I wouldn't be taking you home.'

'You have a husband?' Ali frowned with disappointment as his plans went up in smoke.

'Like hell!' Lynne laughed. 'Christ, d'y' think I'd be bringing fellas back if I had a bloke? I don't know how you lot do it, but our lads don't take kindly to that kind of shit. Nah, there's no bloke . . . Just me mate. She's only a kid, but she's nice enough.'

'A kid?'

'Yeah.' Nodding, Lynne set off up the road. 'Well, I say kid, but she's not really. She's eighteen. Anyhow, you'll meet her in a minute. The name's Lynne, by the way.'

'Ali and Raiz,' Ali told her, ignoring a warning stare from his friend. It was better that she knew their names if the police ever questioned her – unlikely, but you had to cover every eventuality.

'Rai-*eece*,' she repeated, smiling when he nodded. 'So, you're Rai-eece, and he's Ali?'

'No, *I*'m Ali. He's Raiz.'

'Right.' Rolling her eyes, Lynne stopped at the corner. 'Well, whatever your names are, do us a favour and wait here a minute.'

'Where are you going?' Ali glanced nervously around.

'What's up?' she teased. 'Not scared of getting mugged or something, are you?'

'It's cold,' he snapped. 'Why don't you just tell us if you've changed your mind about that drink?'

'Did I say that?' Amused, she held out her hand. 'Give us some money, then.'

'Excuse me?' Ali glowered at her. 'Why would I give you money?'

'You can't expect *me* to pay for the booze. I'm doing you a favour here, don't forget.'

Sighing irritably at another nudge from Raiz, Ali slapped a twenty into her hand.

'You'd better not be ripping us off,' he warned. 'We know where you live.'

Laughing, Lynne cocked her head at Raiz. 'Thinks he's a bit hard, him, doesn't he?' Then, to Ali, she said, 'For your information, sunshine, you haven't got a *clue* where I live. Look around . . . There's tons of dark little side streets to disappear up.'

'So, that's your game?'

'No, it ain't.' Reaching up, she gave his cheek a rough tweak. 'I don't play games, me. I'm just going to get that

drink, like I said, then we're going up to my place to celebrate. It's Christmas, don't you know.' Winking at Raiz, she
put her head down and dashed around the corner to the
all-night blues.

Mary was curled up on the couch watching TV. She was
knackered, but there was no way she was going to bed. She
never did when Lynne was working the streets – hadn't done
since Lynne came back battered and bruised after a brush
with a psycho punter. Lynne had said it was rare, but Mary
lived in dread of it happening again, and waited up until Lynne
was home now – however late – for fear of waking up to the
news that her friend had been found dead in some ditch.

Already scared half to death by the horror film she was
watching tonight, she jumped when she heard hushed male
voices in the hall. Almost screaming out loud when Lynne
burst in and flipped the light on, she said, '*Christ*, Lynne!
You scared the crap out of me! I thought it was burglars,
or Dracula, or something!'

Laughing, Lynne plonked the bottle she was carrying
down onto the table and switched the TV off.

'Shouldn't watch shit like that on your own,' she scolded.
'You know it gives you nightmares. Anyhow, cover yourself
up. We've got company.'

Pulling her dressing gown together, Mary twisted her head
to see who was there. Her eyes widened when she saw the
men standing in the doorway. One was a little short, with
a mop of raven curls and a baby-plump face that made him
look a bit feminine. But the other was absolutely gorgeous
– tall and slim, with sleek, glossy black hair, glittery coal-
dark eyes, and smooth olive skin.

'This is Raiz, and this is Ali.' Lynne motioned to the men
in turn. 'That's right, isn't it?'

'Yes, you got it right this time,' Ali drawled, his heavily

accented voice sounding as rich and as smooth as velvet to Mary's ears.

'Thank Christ for that.' Laughing, Lynne slumped down on a chair and pulled her patent-leather shagging boots off. 'This is Mary – the mate I was telling you about.'

Smiling shyly when the men said hello, Mary drew her knees up and tightened her grip on the front of her gown. She couldn't believe how good-looking they were compared to Lynne's usual punters. Especially the tall one. Surely he didn't need to pay for sex?

'Can I use the toilet?' Ali asked as Raiz entered the room.

'Upstairs, second right,' Lynne said, rubbing at her feet. 'I don't think there's any bog roll, but there's a couple of newspapers under the sink.'

Sitting down cross-legged on the floor, Raiz gazed around the room with a twinge of something he couldn't quite define in his heart. Compared to the cold starkness of his and Ali's flat, this was a palace. The walls were a warm peach, blending nicely with the by no means new blue velour suite and navy patterned carpet. There was a small, glass-topped coffee table in the middle of the floor, a colour TV and an all-in-one hi-fi unit on one side of the window, and an artificial Christmas tree on the other – its spiky arms a riot of multicoloured tinsel and twinkly fairy lights. The gas fire was giving off a warm, orange glow, completing the picture of womanly homeliness, and Raiz felt a lump forming in his throat as a sudden vision of his mother and sisters invaded his thoughts.

'You all right?' Lynne was peering at him with concern. 'You've gone a bit pale.'

Blinking rapidly, Raiz forced the heart-rending vision out of his mind. 'I'm fine, thank you,' he murmured, reaching into his pocket for his cigarettes. 'Do you mind if I smoke?'

'Only if you're sharing,' Lynne said, adding with a

chuckle, 'And *please* stop being so polite. You're in *my* house now – no airs and graces allowed.'

'Sorry.' Smiling shyly, Raiz leaned forward to offer her a cigarette from the packet.

'You could have chucked it,' she grumbled, edging forward in her seat and snatching one. Reaching into her bra, she pulled out the small bag of skunk she'd scored at the blues with the change from the twenty. Rolling a spliff, she lit it and sat back, taking a couple of deep, relaxing drags before offering it to Raiz.

'Warmer now?' she asked as he reached for it.

'Yes, thanks.'

'Good. You looked freezing before. So, where was it you said you were going? Town?'

'Yes.' Raiz nodded, dropping his gaze. 'We were, erm, just going to see if there were any clubs open.'

'At that time of a Christmas Eve?' Lynne pursed her lips disbelievingly. 'Come on . . . You were going to a party, like I said, weren't you?'

Blushing, Raiz agitatedly flicked his cigarette ash. He hated lying. He was terrible at it.

'You two brothers, or something?' Lynne asked then.

'Kind of.' His blush deepened.

'Kind of, like you are but you've got different dads?' Lynne probed. 'Or, kind of, like all our mum's mates are our aunties when we're growing up?'

Not understanding, Raiz just smiled tightly.

'Just mates, then?' Lynne concluded.

'Yes, but I think of him as my brother.'

'Oh, so it's a black thang?' she teased. 'Like, "Yo, Bro!"'

Embarrassed for him when he began to squirm, Mary tried to change the subject.

'Your friend's been a long time, hasn't he? Do you think he's all right?'

'Yeah, he *is* taking his time, isn't he?' Lynne agreed, frowning as it suddenly occurred to her that Ali could be robbing them blind upstairs while his mate was distracting them down here. 'Think I'd best go and see what he's up to.'

Blanching as she got up and headed for the door, Raiz said, 'No! He'll be fine – really. He always takes a long time.'

'No harm checking,' Lynne insisted, even more certain from his reaction that something funny was going on.

Running lightly up the stairs, she popped her head into her own and Mary's bedrooms. Finding them in darkness, she went to the bathroom and listened at the door for a moment. Hearing muffled scraping and banging noises coming from within, her eyebrows puckered together with suspicion. Whatever he was up to in there it certainly wasn't bog-related.

Thanking God she'd never got around to fixing the broken lock, she pushed the handle down and burst in, her eyes flicking every which way for signs of wrongdoing as she said, 'Oops! Sorry. Forgot you were in here.'

Ali was kneeling on the lino between the bath and the sink. He was bare-chested, his jacket laid neatly on the closed toilet seat, his wet shirt hanging over the side of the bath.

'I was, er, just fixing the panel,' he explained, leaping to his feet. 'It had come away from the wall.'

'Oh?' Lynne walked forward, her frown deepening. 'I never noticed.'

'It's fine now.' Stepping in her way, he snatched up his shirt. 'I hope you don't mind, but I washed this. I spilt sauce down it earlier. Is there somewhere I could hang it to dry?'

'Stick it on the radiator,' Lynne muttered. Ali was acting awfully jumpy all of a sudden; he was definitely up to something. Narrowing her eyes when she spotted a small wrap on the cistern, she reached across and picked it up.

'What's this?'

'Nothing,' Ali lied, snatching it from her.

'Bollocks!' She put her hands on her hips. 'You can't fool me. I know a wrap when I see one. So what is it? Coke? Speed?'

'Smack,' he admitted, picking up his jacket and slipping it on. 'Look, I'm sorry. It was disrespectful to bring it into your home. We'll leave.'

Drawing her head back, Lynne narrowed her eyes and nodded knowingly.

'Oh, I see. First you don't want to take me to your party, now you don't want to share your drugs with me. Well, that's nice, I must say.'

'You *want* some?'

'I don't bother as a rule, but I don't mind a dabble every now and then – specially if it's going free. Got enough for everyone, have you?'

'Well, yes,' Ali replied, relief that he wasn't about to be turfed out written clearly on his face.

'Come on, then.' Rubbing her hands together, Lynne headed back out onto the landing. 'Let's get this party started.'

Mary almost choked on the smoke she'd just inhaled when Ali followed Lynne back into the room with his chest bare beneath his jacket, his exposed flesh taut and smooth with just a faint smattering of silky black hair running down to his navel.

'Don't have a heart attack,' Lynne teased, seeing her expression and guessing that she'd flipped out over him. 'He's just washed his shirt, that's all. Don't be thinking anything funny was going on.'

Blushing furiously, Mary muttered, 'I wasn't thinking anything.'

Raiz's face was a soggy mask of concern when Ali sat

beside him. Speaking in Arábic, he said, 'I couldn't stop her. Did she see anything?'

Smiling and talking out of the side of his mouth, Ali said, 'Yes, but she's okay about it. She wants to share it.'

'*All* of it?' Raiz was aghast.

'No, she didn't see it all,' Ali reassured him. 'I'd taken a bit out. The rest is under the bath – don't let me forget it when we go.'

'What about the money? How much was there?'

'Nearly two grand.'

'Oi!' Lynne scolded, frowning at them both. 'What've I told you about talking foreign?'

'Sorry,' Ali apologised. 'I was just telling my friend how lucky we are to have met two such lovely ladies.'

'Not that crap again,' she snorted, rolling her eyes at Mary. 'You've got to watch this one. He thinks he's a right smoothie.'

Still smiling, Ali took the wrap, a pack of cigarettes and a lighter from his pocket.

'Do you have any foil?'

'Should have a roll in the kitchen.' Lynne snapped her fingers at Mary. 'Go get it, babe.'

Leaping up, Mary ran and fetched the foil. Handing it to Ali, she felt her stomach turn to hot liquid and melt into her legs when his thumb brushed against her fingers.

Sitting down before she fell, she watched in fascination as Ali carefully unfolded the wrap. As soon as she saw the square of brown powder she guessed that it was heroin. It was the first time she'd actually seen it, but she'd heard all about it, and it excited and frightened her all at once.

Preparing the foil, Ali heated the powder and chased the resulting oil, sucking in the smoke through a rolled-up twenty-pound note. Mary's stomach did another little flip when he held his breath. He looked so sexy with his eyes half closed, his face frozen in an expression of ecstasy.

Raiz did his chase, then offered the foil to Lynne. Sure that she would refuse, Mary was shocked when she accepted it. Since when had Lynne done smack? But she obviously *had*, judging by the way she was doing it now – sucking the bitter-sweet-smelling smoke up like an old hand.

'Mary?' Lynne held out the black-streaked foil. Her pupils had shrunk to two tiny dots of black in a sea of blue – so pale it seemed almost transparent.

Mary shook her head. She'd heard that smack made you do crazy things, and there was no way she was making a fool of herself in front of the men.

'Try it,' Ali urged her huskily. 'You'll like it.'

Dipping her face to hide another blush, Mary said, 'No, thanks. I don't really feel like it just now. I was, er, just going to make a brew, actually. Anyone want one?'

'You're an angel.' Smiling silkily, Ali rested his head back against the couch and closed his eyes. Lynne might not be interested, but this girl most definitely was. He doubted he'd have a problem getting *her* into bed – which would almost certainly guarantee Raiz the same privilege with her friend. They were all the same, these Western women – where one went, the other followed. So predictable . . . So *easy*.

Scurrying into the kitchen, Mary leaned her back against the door and cursed herself for being such a baby. Why couldn't she just be cool, like Lynne? Ali must think she was a right idiot. Damn! Damn! *Damn!*

Forcing herself to get a grip, she filled the kettle and switched it on, dipping down to check her reflection in its shiny side. Smoothing down her hair, she ran a fingertip under her eyes to tidy up her smudged eyeliner.

Reassured that she looked fine, Mary made the teas and carried them into the living room with a carefully arranged smile on her face. It quickly slipped when she saw that they had all fallen asleep.

Deflated, she quietly placed the cups on the table and tiptoed back to her seat. Sitting close enough to see Ali clearly, but far enough away not to wake him with her thudding heart, she stared at him in wonder. She'd never seen anyone quite like him before. Even that gypsy lad Mick hadn't been this nice, and she'd *really* fancied him – before she'd found out how crap he was in bed, anyway. Ali was stunning, with his long black eyelashes curling onto his cheeks and a hint of perfect white teeth showing between his slightly parted, beautifully shaped lips.

She was just fantasising how it would feel to kiss him when Lynne said, 'He's nice, isn't he?' in a slow, dreamy voice. 'He likes you, too. He said so when you were in the kitchen. Said you were really . . . pretty . . .'

Then she was asleep again, leaving Mary to savour her few words. Was it true? Had Ali really said it, or had Lynne made it up to make her feel better? Closing her eyes, she hugged herself, thrilled by the possibility that such a gorgeous man could actually be interested in her.

Lynne woke up half an hour later.

'Christ, that's nice gear,' she said, rubbing lazily at her nose as she sat up and rolled another spliff. 'You should have had some, Mare. You'd love it.'

'Maybe next time,' Mary lied, blinking herself out of a light doze. She had no intention of getting into smack. If the rumours were anything to go by, you had to be super-strong not to get addicted.

Waking just then, Ali stretched languidly. Turning his head, he smiled up at Mary. 'Was I snoring?'

'Course not,' she murmured, wondering how he could imagine himself to have such a human defect.

'Good.' He winked at her, melting her heart all over again.

'I wouldn't want you to think I was a pig.'

Glowing from his attention, Mary rolled the word over in her mind. It was such a silly word, but his accent had made it sound so exotic. Peeg . . . *Peeeg.*

Leaning forward with the spliff dangling from her lips, Lynne took one of the cups off the tray. 'Aw, it's cold.'

'Want me to make another?' Mary offered.

'Nah, we might as well have a proper drink.' Getting up, Lynne turned the hi-fi on and slotted a Marley tape in. Pressing *Play*, she padded into the kitchen, coming back with four glasses and a bottle of coke. Twisting the cap off the rum, she poured the drinks and handed them out. Raising her own into the air, she said, 'Happy Christmas, everyone.'

Settling back in her seat, Mary smiled. This was more like it. She knew where she was with booze and draw; she didn't feel quite so young and inexperienced now.

Humming along when her favourite track came on, she began to feel ludicrously, deliriously happy as she listened to the others chatting. It felt so adult and sophisticated – as if they were in a bubble floating far above the rest of the world.

Mary was so chilled out when Ali came and sat beside her and offered her the foil he'd just prepared, she took it without question. Blushing at the nearness of him when he held the lighter flame beneath it, she sucked the smoke up through the twenty-pound note and held it in like she'd seen him doing.

Seconds later, she clamped a hand across her mouth and leapt to her feet.

Following her as she dashed to the bathroom, Ali stroked her back as she vomited, crooning, 'You'll be all right . . . It's always like this at first, but it's nice when you get used to it – you'll see.'

When the awful heaving finally stopped, Mary began to

feel the full exquisite force of the heroin high. A warmth spread through her entire body like an orgasm, lifting her out of her skin and enclosing her in satin.

Closing her eyes, she felt as light as a feather floating on a breeze when Ali lifted her up and carried her to bed, slipping quietly in beside her.

10

Waking, Ali groaned and pushed himself into a sitting position. Rubbing his eyes, he gazed confusedly around the strange room. It was morning; winter sunlight leaked weakly in through the flimsy curtains.

Looking down at Mary asleep beside him, he frowned as the memories came flooding back. She was attractive enough, he supposed, but he really resented the circumstances. It was one thing fucking women when he *wanted* to; quite another when he *had* to. Still, it hadn't been too bad. At least she'd been practically unconscious.

Stirring just then, Mary opened her eyes and blushed to see Ali gazing down at her. 'Morning,' she said, giving him a tentative smile.

Returning it, he said, 'How do you feel?'

'Fine,' she lied, forcing the thumping headache to the back of her mind. 'You?'

'I'm good.' Pushing the quilt aside, he stood up and stretched. 'Do you mind?' he asked, taking her dressing gown from the back of the door.

'No, go ahead.' Watching as he slipped it on, Mary smiled shyly. It was a pink satin number which reached her calves, but on him it barely scraped his knees.

Going to the bathroom, Ali ran hot water into the sink and washed himself – thoroughly. He'd been stupid not to use a condom, but he hadn't anticipated needing one when he'd left his flat the night before. He just hoped Raiz hadn't made the same mistake. Lynne looked a lot more *used* than Mary.

Tapping on Lynne's door on his way back to Mary's room, he said, 'Raiz . . . you awake?' Hearing the muffled affirmation, he said, 'Well, hurry up and get dressed. We've got things to do.'

'Are you going?' Mary asked when he came back and immediately began to pull his clothes on.

'Business,' he told her cagily.

'On Christmas Day?'

'Yes.' His tone was clipped now.

'Oh, right.' Reaching for the gown he'd slung onto the end of the bed, Mary struggled to mask her disappointment as she slipped it on. She should have known it was too good to be true. She couldn't remember how they'd ended up in bed together, didn't even know if they'd had sex, but it didn't matter – she'd just been so happy to see him there. And now he was going, and she'd probably never see him again.

Trotting downstairs when Raiz was ready, Ali thanked Lynne for letting them stay, then shook Mary's hand – ignoring the look of despair on her pretty face. She'd served her purpose; there was no point dragging it out. Wrenching the front door open, he hustled Raiz out and rushed him away.

'Thank fuck for that,' Lynne said, locking the door behind them. 'I thought they were never gonna go.' Going into the kitchen, she switched the kettle on.

'I wouldn't have minded if they stayed,' Mary moaned, hugging herself. 'Ali, anyway.'

Turning, Lynne gave her a disapproving frown. 'Get a grip, you dozy bitch. You don't even know him.'

'I know, but he's gorgeous. God, Lynne, did you see his eyes? They're, like, so *sexy*.' Sighing heavily, Mary gazed off into the distance.

Shaking her head, Lynne stirred sugar into the teas, then carried hers into the living room.

Trailing miserably in behind her, Mary flopped down on the couch and nursed her own cup. Wincing when Lynne threw the curtains open, she said, 'How come you ended up with Raiz, anyway? I thought you said you weren't in the mood.'

'I wasn't.' Lynne shrugged. 'But it seemed rude not to after you and the other one buggered off like that. How come *you* did, anyway?' She smirked at Mary over the lip of her cup. 'You haven't had a shag in over a year. I thought you was planning on being a nun, or something.'

Blushing, Mary pursed her lips. 'I didn't mean to, it just sort of happened . . . I think.'

'Don't you know?'

'Not really. I just woke up this morning and he was there.'

Chuckling, Lynne shook her head. 'Must have been pretty shit if you can't remember it. You'd best lay off the smack in future if that's what it does to you.'

'I forgot about that.' Mary frowned. 'God! You don't think I'll get hooked, do you?'

'Will you hell, you muppet!' Lynne snorted, looking at her as if she was stupid. 'You have to do it loads before you get addicted. Did you like it, though?'

'I think so,' Mary admitted shyly. 'After getting sick, anyway. I thought I was going to die when I couldn't stop puking, but it was quite nice after. But what about *you* . . . You never said you'd done it before.'

Shrugging, Lynne reached behind her chair and switched the fairy lights off.

'I haven't for ages, but it's a buzz now and then. Anyway, it's Christmas, so we had a good excuse.'

'Suppose so.' Mary sipped her tea. 'Wonder what they're doing today?' she said after a moment. 'Ali said they had business, but no one works at Christmas.'

'Asians do,' Lynne reminded her. 'Which is just as well,

seeing as we've got nowt in the freezer. I'll nip down to Pasha's when I'm dressed – see if they've got any turkey crowns going cheap.'

'Do you think Ali and Raiz eat proper Christmas dinners?'

'Don't know, and I don't care.' Finishing her drink, Lynne put her cup on the table where the cold brews were still sitting on the tray. 'They've been – they've gone. Forget 'em.'

Mary nodded her agreement, but she doubted she'd ever be able to do that. How could anyone forget the most perfect, most handsome, most fantastic man in the world?

Pushing herself to her feet, Lynne frowned.

'Actually, come to think of it, I've just remembered something I forgot to check last night.'

'Eh?' Mary gazed up at her confusedly.

'Your fella.' Lynne headed for the door. 'When I went to see what was taking him so long in the bog last night, he was acting dead cagey – like I'd caught him up to something.'

Jumping up, Mary followed her up to the bathroom.

Squatting beside the bath with a thoughtful look on her face, Lynne said, 'He was kneeling here when I came in. Said he'd been fixing the panel.'

'What was wrong with it?'

'Nothing, as far as I knew, but he reckoned it'd come away from the wall.' Squinting, Lynne scrutinised the panel. Seeing a series of tiny marks, she ran her fingertip down it. It felt rough, as if it had been recently gouged. Noticing some tiny paint-chips on the lino under the sink, she said, 'The lying shit! I *knew* there was nothing wrong with it. He must have pulled it out.'

'What for?' Mary frowned. 'It doesn't make sense.'

'Oh, doesn't it?' Reaching for a metal nail-file that was lying on the bath ledge, Lynne wedged it down the side of the panel and pried it away from the wall. 'Bingo!' she said when she saw the package.

'What is it?' Mary was craning to see over her shoulder. Bringing it out, Lynne showed it to her.

'Wow!' Mary murmured.

'Wow, indeed.' Lynne gave a sly smirk. 'No *wonder* they were in such a hurry to nick that cab. They were probably bricking it in case they got pulled by the pigs.'

'Do you think they'll come back for it?' Mary's heart had quickened at the prospect of seeing Ali again.

'Too right they will.' Lynne assured her confidently. 'But if they think they're just waltzing in and picking it up, then waltzing out again, they've got another think coming.'

11

Kenny Butler parked up at the kerb beside the payphone. Glancing in the side mirror, he watched the police officers milling about at the taped-off mouth of the alley on the opposite side of the road. Climbing out after a moment, he took his cigarettes from his pocket and scanned the road with narrowed eyes as he lit one.

The residents from the new-builds on this side were out in nosy force. Old yellow-eyed Jamaican men leaning on their garden gates with their homies, while the wives gossiped loudly on the chairs they'd dragged onto the doorsteps. Young sassy white girls pushing their expensively dressed mixed-race babies' prams with one hand, defiantly displaying their spliffs in the other. And in every corner, hordes of hooded, shifty-eyed youths were lurking, trying to suss who'd been offed without being seen by the five-o.

Nodding his respect to the older guys, Kenny strolled into the phone box and made a call.

'It's me,' he said when he got an answer. 'There's too much dibble about, so I can't get to the Paki's flat. Do us a favour and go to Terry's while I'm here. I don't know if he had that ounce on him, but they're gonna be all over Nerys when they suss who he is, and she needs to do a proper clean-up in case he left it at home. I'll give it half an hour here. Make sure she don't miss anything.'

Hanging up, Kenny pushed the door open and went back to his car. Leaning back against it, he folded his arms and scanned the street, checking his watch every now and then as if he were waiting for someone.

Spotting two familiar figures turning the corner at the far end of the street ten minutes later, he narrowed his eyes.

Well, well . . . If the mountain won't come to Mohammed . . .

Glancing across to the alley as they passed by on the opposite side, Ali saw the white-suits at the far end and knew that Terry was dead. Good. That was one problem less for him to deal with.

'Shit! There's Kenny,' Raiz hissed, nudging him sharply. 'What are we going to do?'

Exhaling nervously when he saw Terry's right-hand man looking straight back at them up ahead, Ali said, 'Leave it to me. And don't panic, for God's sake. Just stay cool and act naturally.'

'Are you mad?' Raiz hissed when Ali continued strolling casually forward. 'We can't *talk* to him.'

'We've got to,' Ali said from the corner of his smiling mouth. 'It would look suspicious if we didn't. We don't know anything – remember.'

Keeping pace with his friend, Raiz wasn't at all happy. He knew that Ali was right, but it didn't make him feel any better. Kenny mightn't be too pleased to be approached by two of Terry's punters in broad daylight with police all over the place.

Reaching Kenny, Ali held out his hand.

'All right, Kenny. What's going on back there? Someone been mugged, or something?'

Ignoring the hand, Kenny glared at him.

'Where the fuck have you two been? I've been trying to get hold of you all morning.'

'We stayed with our women last night.' Ali gave him a

conspiratorial grin. 'You know how it is . . . Once they've got you in bed, they don't want to let you go.' Pausing when Kenny carried on glaring, he frowned. 'What's up, man? Aw, don't tell me Terry's changed his mind about giving us extra time?'

'You what?'

'To pay what we still owe.' Ali's eyebrows puckered as if he was confused. 'We sorted it out with him last night.'

'What time was that?' Kenny demanded, wondering how come Terry hadn't mentioned it to him.

'About ten, wasn't it?' Ali looked to Raiz for confirmation. Unable to speak or look Kenny in the eye, Raiz just nodded and gazed back at the police across the road.

'Where?' Kenny was scowling now.

'Up at the flat.' Ali's voice was smooth, despite the fear that was making his heart thud painfully in his chest. 'He called round to do the pick-up.'

'Oh, yeah? And what did he say?'

'Just that he'd give us another week.' Ali gave an innocent shrug. 'He was a bit pissed off at first that we didn't have it all, but we weren't far off, so he said he'd let us off this time – it being Christmas, and that. He hasn't changed his mind, has he?'

'I don't know nothing about it,' Kenny admitted. 'You sure that was at ten?'

'Yeah. Why? What's up?'

'I saw him at twelve,' Kenny murmured, almost as if thinking aloud. 'He never mentioned nothing about seeing you then. You sure it wasn't after that?'

'Definitely not.' Ali shook his head and held Kenny's accusing gaze with a steadiness born of terror. If he slipped up now, the big man would be all over him in a flash. 'We were getting ready to go out when he came because we'd arranged to meet our girls at half-past. We gave him what we had, then we all left together.'

'What happened then? Where did he go?'

'No idea.' Ali shrugged. 'He was standing on the corner over there when we left him, talking to someone on his phone.'

'Who?' Kenny was still staring at them with open suspicion. Ali sounded sincere, but you could never be too sure with these shifty black-eyed bastards.

'It wasn't our business to ask,' Ali replied indignantly. Then, 'Look, I'm not being funny, Kenny, but why are you questioning us like this? We made our deal with Terry. Shouldn't you check with him?'

'I would if I could,' Kenny muttered, lighting another cigarette. 'Believe me, I would.'

'Is something wrong?' Ali forced concern into his voice now. 'Terry's not been busted or something, has he?'

Blowing his smoke out noisily, Kenny ran a hand through his hair. If Ali was lying, he was doing a fucking good job of it. But Kenny doubted the skinny shit would dare try and front it out like that. More likely, he was innocent.

'You obviously haven't heard, then?'

'Heard what?' Ali asked innocently.

'That.' Kenny nodded towards the alley. 'It's Terry. They found him this morning. Some cunt's only gone and knifed him.'

'No!' Ali gasped, feigning shocked disbelief. '*Terry?* Who'd do a thing like that?'

'Probably one of these skanky bastards,' Kenny growled, casting murderous glances at the hooded youths. 'And when I find out which one, he's a walking fuckin' dead man.'

'We'll keep our ears open,' Ali assured him solemnly. 'If we hear *any*thing, you'll be the first to know. They won't get away with this.'

'Thanks.' Pulling himself together, Kenny headed for his car. Opening the door, he turned back. 'How much do you still owe, by the way?'

'Only thirty,' Ali lied. 'I think that's why he wasn't bothered about giving us extra time. We'll honour it – don't worry about that. Terry was a good man.'

Nodding, Kenny said, 'Yeah, he was.' Then, 'Look, pass it to me when you get it, but don't call his gaff. His missus has got enough shit to deal with. Just wait till you see me, yeah?'

'Absolutely,' Ali agreed. 'Take it easy, man. They'll catch whoever did it.'

'Not if I catch them first,' Kenny snarled. Taking one last look back at the alley, he climbed into his car and drove away.

'Shit, that was bad,' Raiz moaned, lighting a cigarette with wildly shaking hands. 'He knew it was us. He *knew*.'

'No, he didn't,' Ali told him sharply, gripping his arm and walking him away from any ears that might be listening. 'Not that *you* helped – standing there, looking guilty as hell.'

'I couldn't help it. I thought he was going to kill us.'

'Yeah, well, he would have if he'd thought we'd done it.'

'In front of the police? I don't think so.'

'Don't underestimate him. If he'd wanted us dead, he'd have forced us into the car and taken us somewhere deserted. No, we're definitely in the clear.'

Gazing at his friend's grinning face, Raiz wished that he shared Ali's confidence, but he wasn't so convinced that they were out of the woods.

'I don't think we should celebrate just yet. You could be wrong about Kenny, and I don't want to be sitting in the flat if he comes back after the police have gone.'

'So, what do *you* suggest we do?' Ali asked him irritably. 'Hide – and make ourselves look *really* guilty?'

'No, but I'm not going back until I'm sure it's safe. And we'll have to find somewhere safe to stash the gear, as well. If anyone finds it on us . . .'

'Shit!' Ali slapped a hand to his forehead. 'I left it under that woman's bath. I told you to remind me, man!'

'Don't blame me,' Raiz protested. 'It was your idea to hide it there.'

'I didn't hear you coming up with any better ideas.'

'I don't remember being asked!' Frowning, Raiz dropped his half-smoked cigarette to the floor and ground it out with his heel. 'Anyway, shut up. We're in enough shit without arguing.'

Sighing, Ali nodded. 'Yeah, you're right. We'll just have to go back for it. Anyway, that might be for the best.'

'How so?'

'Well, we're going to need proof if Kenny starts hassling us, aren't we? He said he saw Terry at twelve, so if we get them to say we were with them *before* that and stayed all night, he'll know we couldn't have done it.'

'But we *weren't* with them before that,' Raiz reminded him. 'It was hours later.'

'I'm sure they'd bend the truth if we asked them to.'

'What makes you think they're going to lie for someone they hardly know?'

'They're women, aren't they?' Ali gave him a sly grin. 'Anyway, it mightn't come to that. I think Kenny believed me. This is just a precaution.'

12

Mary did as Lynne had told her to when the men arrived back at the house. Sitting calmly on the couch, she smiled as if she was really surprised to see them.

'Well, well . . . Fancy seeing you again.'

'We, er, bought you these.' Ali handed her the box of chocolates they'd bought on the way over. 'It's just a little thank-you for last night. We had a really good time – didn't we, Raiz?'

'Yeah.' Blushing, Raiz thrust a bottle of white rum into Lynne's hand. 'Happy Christmas.'

'Well, isn't this nice,' Lynne drawled, smiling widely. 'You didn't have to, but I won't refuse. Sit down. I was just about to make a brew if you want one?'

'That would be nice.' Ali smiled, rubbing his hands together. 'Do you mind if I just use the toilet?'

'Weak bladder?'

'Excuse me?' His smile faltered, but he forced it to stay in place.

'Nothing,' Lynne said lightly. 'Just that you dashed straight off to the loo when you first came in last night. I thought you might have a *medical* problem, or something.'

'No, no, nothing like that. It's just the weather. The cold gets to me.'

'I know *just* what you mean,' she said, waving him towards the stairs. 'Help yourself. You know where it is.'

Humming softly, Lynne followed Ali out into the hall and

gave him a little wave as she went into the kitchen. Filling the kettle, she switched it on, then wandered back to the living-room doorway. Folding her arms, she leaned against the frame.

'So, you couldn't stay away, eh?'

Smiling nervously, Raiz fiddled with the toggle on his jacket.

'We just thought it would be rude not to thank you properly.'

'*Really?* So, you didn't forget something?'

'Sorry?'

'Well, that's the *usual* excuse for coming back after a one-night stand. They say they've come to see you, but really they've just come to pick up something they left in your bedroom. Ah, there's the kettle . . . Won't be a minute.'

Back in the kitchen, Lynne peered up at the ceiling and smiled with amusement at the scraping noises coming from the bathroom above. The bastard was having a good old root around. He'd be shitting bricks in a minute.

Making the teas, she carried them out on a tray, just as Ali thundered down the stairs.

'You look flushed,' she commented, walking calmly ahead of him into the living room. 'I hope you haven't been bothering yourself with any more repairs. It's very kind, but there's really no need. That's what the council's for. In fact, they sent someone over just this morning to fix a leak under the kitchen sink, didn't they, Mare?'

'Yeah,' Mary agreed, playing along. 'We were amazed that they came out on Christmas Day, but they said it was no problem – with it being an emergency, and that.'

'Oh, they were fantastic,' Lynne went on, sitting down and casually lighting a cigarette. 'Fixed that leak in no time, then had a look at that bath panel for me. To be honest, I thought they'd say there was nothing wrong with it, but you must have been right, Ali, 'cos it took them absolutely *ages*. I said they needn't bother, but they insisted. Don't you think that's *really* good of them?'

Dropping down onto the couch beside Raiz, Ali flapped his hands, muttering sickly, 'Yeah, great.'

'Ahh,' Lynne crooned sympathetically. 'You don't look at all well. Upset stomach, is it? Do you think you'd feel better with a drink inside you? I'll open that bottle, if you want.'

'No, thank you. I think we'd better just go.'

'So soon?' Lynne raised her eyebrows. 'Aw, not yet . . . Just stay for a drink. It might be just what you need – the old hair of the dog.' Still smiling, she slipped her hand down the side of her cushion. 'Or maybe you need something a bit *stronger* to get you back on your feet? *This*, for example.'

Giggling at Ali's shocked expression when Lynne pulled the package out, Mary said, 'Had you going there, didn't we? You *well* thought the council blokes had nicked it.'

'Oh, God, you don't know how glad I am to see that,' Ali said, standing up and reaching for it.

'Not so fast!' Scowling, Lynne yanked it out of reach. 'I think you've got a bit of explaining to do first. I don't remember giving you permission to use my house to stash your fuckin' gear. Do you know what could have happened if I'd been busted?'

'I'm sorry.' Dipping his gaze, Ali affected shame. 'It was wrong, but I didn't know what else to do when you invited us here. If I'd told you I was carrying it, you might have turned us away.' Pausing, he glanced up and gave her a sheepish smile. 'And we didn't want that, because we . . . well, we liked you.'

'Bull!' Lynne scoffed, not believing a word of it.

'It's true,' he insisted. 'But it was wrong, and I can see I've offended you. We'll just take it and go.' He held his hand out again. 'I promise we'll never bother you again – if that's what you want?'

'As opposed to what?' Holding tightly onto the gear, Lynne peered up at him, narrow-eyed.

'Well, we were hoping you'd agree to see us again. Maybe go out for a drink, or something?'

'A *date*? Do me a favour. I'm a bit old for all that.'

'You're *not* old,' Mary said, desperate to stop Lynne from chasing them away. If Ali wanted to carry on seeing her, she was more than willing. 'Anyway, I think it's nice that they wanted to see us again.'

'You would,' Lynne chuckled, amused by her friend's obvious infatuation. Sighing then, she tossed the gear to Ali. 'Here . . . But don't think you're just pissing off without giving us a bit. I think you owe us that, at least.'

'Absolutely,' Ali agreed. 'You can have some now, if you like?'

'Don't mind if I do.' Grinning, Lynne rubbed her hands together. 'Take your coats off, then,' she said when Ali sat back down and opened the bag. 'You could be here for quite a while with all this to get through.'

'You want us to *stay*?' Ali glanced up at her as he prepared a chase. He hadn't expected it to be quite as easy as this. He'd thought they would have to do a fair bit of creeping to get round her.

'I'm not asking you to move in, if that's what you mean,' Lynne snorted, taking the foil and the straw from him. 'But I'm sure madam wouldn't object if you wanted to stop for a few nights.'

'Would that be all right?' Ali turned to peer into Mary's adoring eyes.

She nodded quickly, ecstatic that he wanted to stay – amazed that he'd thought he needed to ask.

'Thank you.' Leaning forward, he placed a gentle kiss on

her cheek. Then, acting on impulse, he said, 'Do you think you could do me a favour?'

'Yeah, course. Anything.'

'It probably won't happen,' he told her, smiling sheepishly, 'but if anyone should happen to ask, do you think you could say you're my girlfriend?'

'Oh, Christ!' Lynne chuckled, struggling to hold the smoke in. 'Don't say that, she'll think you're asking her to get engaged, or something.'

'Of course I'll say it,' Mary told him, casting a warning glare in Lynne's direction. 'Is that all?'

'Well, you could say that we got here at around half-ten last night.'

'Shady bastard,' Lynne drawled, her pupils already shrinking. 'What you running from?'

'Jealous women,' Ali lied. 'They live in the flat above ours and they've been pestering us to go out with them. We tried to turn them down nicely, but last night they got nasty and told their brothers we'd been harassing them. That's why we needed your taxi,' he went on, almost convincing *himself* with the sincerity in his voice. 'The brothers were on their way over to sort us out.'

'Big bastards, eh?' Lynne smirked.

'*Huge*,' he confirmed, widening his eyes for effect. 'We went back this morning to see if the coast was clear, but they were still there.'

'So you did another runner.' Lynne shook her head. 'They're bound to catch up with you sooner or later.'

'There's not a lot we can do except talk to them.' Ali flapped his hands in a gesture of hopelessness. 'Try to convince them that we were somewhere else when their sisters claim we were hassling them.'

'Like here, you mean?'

'Well, yes . . . That would be perfect.' Smiling shyly, he

looked up at her through his lashes. 'They'd have to know we wouldn't look twice at their sisters if they knew we had such beautiful girlfriends.'

'There you go again with the bullshit,' Lynne chuckled.

'No, really,' Ali insisted. 'What man would be crazy enough to go after other women if they had one of you waiting for him at home?'

'I'll do it,' Mary said, indignant on his behalf. How dare the little slags try to set him up like that! Just let her get her hands on them – she'd make them regret ever even *looking* at him.

Squeezing Mary's hand, Ali turned back to Lynne. 'And you, Lynne? Will you help us?'

'Yeah, whatever,' she purred, closing her eyes. 'Ain't no bitch ever done *me* no favours.'

The rest of the day passed in a lovely blur of drink, smoke, and easy chat. Falling deeper under Ali's spell with every word he spoke, every glance he flicked her way, Mary knew that she had finally found the man of her dreams.

Climbing into bed with him that night, she gazed at his face as he fell into an immediate sleep, and vowed that she would never let him go. Nothing and no one would ever get between them. She would be the best girlfriend any man had ever had, and he would never even *think* about leaving her.

Snuggling up to him, Mary closed her eyes and laid her cheek against his back, drifting away on the heady scent of his smooth olive skin.

Opening his eyes when he knew that Mary was at last asleep, Ali slid out from beneath the quilt and padded quietly across the room. Picking up his jacket, he eased the door open and crept along the landing to the bathroom.

Wedging a towel beneath the door to prevent anyone from bursting in on him again, he took his spoon and his syringe out of his pocket and prepared himself a fix. Chasing was all right when you didn't want people to think you were a junkie, but there was no replacing the rush of the needle.

Drawing the liquid up into the barrel, Ali clamped the belt he'd wrapped around his arm between his teeth and eased the sharp spike into his vein.

No, there was no substitute for this. And, if he ended up staying beyond the few days Lynne had promised, he'd make sure that she and Mary started doing it this way, too.

For people who professed not to do it often – or, in Mary's case, never – these greedy women sure had taken a liking to the gear. It would be gone in no time at the rate they were smoking it, and there was no way he was financing that.

Oh, no . . . They had walked into this with their eyes wide open, and if they intended to carry on, they would just have to pay their own way – and his, too, if all went according to plan.

13

Mary and Lynne got the sack.

It was six months since Ali had weaned them onto the needle, and they had slid into the murky depths of this new scene with such ease, they had no idea how much they had changed as a result.

Miss Jennings, on the other hand, had seen the change almost immediately – although it took her a little longer to figure out the cause.

Lynne had always been stand-offish, but she'd become distinctly spiky of late – never letting the sly comments she'd previously ignored slip her by; challenging every assumed slight to the point that no one dared approach her for fear of having their heads bitten off. And then there were days when she seemed to be present in body only – a spooky kind of 'lights on, no one home' scenario that Miss Jennings found quite disturbing.

As for Mary . . . She'd been quite naive and friendly when she'd first joined them, but that had soon changed after she'd moved in with Lynne. Under the wing of her older, not-so-respectable friend, she had soon lost her innocence. She was edgy and rude now, and the other women disliked her as intensely as they'd always disliked Lynne.

Nobody's fool, Miss Jennings knew that the two were taking drugs. Just as she knew, if the rumours were correct, that they were prostitutes – the lowest of the low. Unfortunately, until she actually caught them doing something untoward on the premises, there was nothing she could do about it. So she waited and watched, biding her time, praying for an excuse to haul them over the coals – and kick them into the gutter where they belonged.

For a while there was nothing, which frustrated her beyond belief. Then, finally, they slipped up.

Finding Mary and Lynne asleep at their machines one morning, Miss Jennings slammed the heavy folder she was holding down onto the counter between them.

'You're sacked!' she declared, a little too gleefully. 'Get your things and leave. And think yourselves lucky I haven't called the police.'

Flipping into surly mode at the rude awakening and the mention of police, Lynne was on her feet in a flash.

'For what? It ain't illegal to have a kip when you're on a break, you know.'

'Break-time finished ten minutes ago,' Miss Jennings informed her primly. 'But, that aside, you're in direct contravention of the health and safety regulations. Falling asleep at a machine is a hazard. You've put yourselves and everybody else in danger.'

'Don't be stupid!' Lynne sneered. 'How's anyone else in danger? It's *my* head that'll get squashed, not theirs.'

'Yes, but they could get hurt if they had to help you,' Miss Jennings countered smugly. 'And I can't allow you to put them in that position. Now, if you don't mind . . .' She waved towards the door.

'You stuck-up *tart*,' Lynne spat, fixing her with an evil glare. 'You need a good fucking slap, you.'

'It isn't very wise to threaten me in front of witnesses.' Miss Jennings cast a gloating glance at the women who were watching avidly from around the room. 'I'm sure you'd rather just leave without a fuss. That's what you people do, isn't it – make a quick getaway before the authorities become involved.'

'*You people?*' Infuriated by the supervisor's supercilious tone, Mary jumped to her feet and came around the machine to stand beside Lynne. 'Who the fuck do you think you're talking to? Just 'cos we work for you, don't mean you can treat us like shit!'

'As your superior,' Miss Jennings informed her frostily, taking a step back towards the safety of the crowd, 'it's my job to make sure that *you* do *yours*. As you haven't, it's my duty to fire you – with immediate effect.' With that, she stalked away, praying that nobody noticed how badly her legs were shaking.

'Leave it,' Lynne said when Mary made to go after her. 'She'll have the pigs round before you can say "Boo!"'

'Let her,' Mary snarled. 'We haven't done anything wrong.'

'I've got gear in my pocket,' Lynne reminded her sharply. 'D'y' want me to get busted, or something? And *you* ain't exactly clean, neither. Just get your stuff and let's get out of here.'

'I can't! Ali will go mad if I tell him I've lost my job. You know how bad he feels about not being able to pay for anything.'

'That's his problem,' Lynne hissed. 'Anyway, we'll stop off at the social on the way back and sign on. That'll keep him quiet. Come *on*.'

'What are you lot gawping at?' Mary yelled at the other women as she followed Lynne out. 'You wanna watch it, or we might just come back and blow the fuckin' lot of you up!'

'Will you shut your bleedin' neck before you land us right in it,' Lynne snapped, hauling her from the room.

Ali was furious when Mary got home and told him the news. Sitting at the small dining table in the corner of the living room, he glared up at her as she hovered in front of him, nervously wringing her hands.

'Oh, that was very clever, wasn't it?' he spat. 'How are we going to survive without your wages? We're only just scraping by as it is. How could you be so *stupid*?'

'It's not my fault,' Mary whined, upset by his lack of concern for the unfair way in which she'd been treated. 'Anyway, we'll be all right. I've still got my in-hand money to pick up at the end of the week, and we've already been to sign on.'

'Did they give you a giro?'

'Not yet, no. But it doesn't work like that. You have to wait till they've processed the forms.'

'Stupid!' He brought his fist down on the table. 'How many times have I warned you about gouching out at work?'

'Lynne *needed* some,' she protested. 'She was starting to get sick.'

'That's *her* business. You should have waited till you got home.'

'It's not fair.' Mary folded her arms sulkily. 'I work my tits off to pay for the gear, but I can't do it any time *I* want. *I* can't stay in bed till all hours, then sit on my arse all day getting mashed.'

Peering up at her, Ali's face twisted into a bitter sneer.

'Oh, so you think I'm a layabout, do you? Think you deserve better? Well, fine. If that's the way you want it, I'll leave.'

'No!' Mary gasped when he scraped his chair back and stood up. 'Don't go, Ali. I didn't mean it. I don't care about the money. I was only shooting my mouth off.'

'Nothing new there, then,' he sniped, pulling his jacket on.

'Don't go,' she begged, grasping at his arm. 'Please, Ali. I'm really, *really* sorry. I'm just wound up about getting sacked. I'll never say it again, I swear.'

'I've got things to do.' Shaking off her grip, Ali made for

the door. Pausing there, he turned and gave her a cold look. 'I suggest you take a good long look at yourself, Mary. I've stuck by you when most men would have walked away, but I won't stay where I'm not wanted.'

'You *are* wanted,' Mary insisted. 'I love—' The rest died in her mouth as the door slammed shut behind him.

Bursting into tears of self-pity and dread, Mary threw herself down onto the couch and buried her face in the cushion. She'd lost her job, and now she'd lost Ali, too. How could she have been so stupid?

'Oh, put a sock in it, for fuck's sake,' Lynne grunted when she walked in. 'I've already got a headache. I don't need you making it worse.'

'He's l-left me,' Mary sobbed. 'I said some terrible things and he walked out. What am I going to do? I can't live without him.'

'*Grow* up,' Lynne sneered, shoving Mary's legs aside and flopping down beside her. 'You'll survive. It ain't like you've lost an arm, or something.'

'That's what it feels like.'

'Aw, belt up, you pillock. He'll be back.'

'He won't.'

'Yes, he *will*. Trust me, I know these bastards. He ain't gonna lose his meal ticket over a stupid row. Now, button it before I knock you out.'

Sniffing loudly, Mary gulped back the tears and rubbed at her eyes.

'D'y' really think he'll come back?'

'Yeah, I really do. Shit, girl, he ain't given us a minute's peace since he first turned up. What makes you think we'd be lucky enough to shake him off now?'

'I don't *want* to shake him off.'

'Whatever.' Lynne sighed. 'Tell him you've signed on, did you?'

'Yeah.'

'And that you've still got your week-in-hand to come?'

'Yeah.'

'Well, there you go, then.' Lynne gave a knowing nod. 'He'll be back in plenty of time to spend it – you watch. Now, if you've done with soaking the cushion, get the kettle on. And give us a smoke while you're at it.'

Taking her cigarettes from her pocket, Mary tossed one to Lynne, then went to make a brew. Splashing her face with cold water while she waited for the kettle to boil, she scolded herself for being such a drama queen. She wished she could be calm and carefree, but it seemed like she was forever bobbing up and down these days – one minute ridiculously happy, the next low and weepy. It was no wonder Ali had walked out. *She* wouldn't put up with a moody bitch like her, either.

Making the teas, her self-pity turned to shame. She'd been well out of order for having a dig at him about money. It wasn't his fault that he wasn't allowed to get a job because he didn't have a British passport. Anyway, he'd paid *her* way when she'd first started on the gear, so she owed him. It had been nasty to throw it in his face like that. No wonder he'd been so mad at her. But he'd understand, she was sure. Once he'd calmed down, he'd know she hadn't meant it.

'I reckon you're right,' Mary said when she gave Lynne her tea. 'I think he will come back. I mean, he must love me, mustn't he? He's always here.'

'So's Raiz, but it don't mean nothing.' Lynne swung her feet up onto the table. 'Still, least *he* isn't bleeding me dry, 'cos I'll tell you something for nothing, he wouldn't get through that door if he tried playing me like Ali plays you.'

'He doesn't play me. He's my boyfriend.'

'If you say so.'

Lynne drank her tea in silence, then stood up and reached

for her coat, saying curtly, 'I'm off to find a punter. *Some*one's got to pay the lecky.'

Alone, Mary brooded over Lynne's words. She was a bitch for implying that Ali was using her – just because Raiz wasn't serious about *her*. Or maybe it was just that *she* didn't really fancy Raiz and was jealous of Mary for getting the gorgeous one? Either way, Mary wished she'd keep her snide comments to herself.

Lynne had changed a lot since they'd started on the gear, and Mary wasn't sure she liked her very much any more. Everything she said had a nasty edge to it, and she always had to get the first hit and the first toke on the spliff – because it was *her* house and she was doing them all such a favour letting them stay there.

Mary would have told her to stick her house up her arse if she had anywhere else to go, but she didn't, so she couldn't. Not yet, anyway.

Ali came back at two a.m.

Mary had gone to bed hours earlier, convinced that he'd decided to spend the night at the flat he and Raiz only ever visited now to collect mail – and to shag any women they'd picked up, but she didn't know about that.

Still wide awake when he lumbered into the room and got undressed, she held her breath, waiting for him to make the first move. But he hadn't come bearing flowers or declaring undying love, as other men might have after the row they'd had. He didn't even say he was sorry for walking out. He just climbed into bed and fell into a deep, snoring sleep.

Mary felt a range of conflicting emotions wash over her as she lay beside him listening to his snores. She was ecstatic that he was back, of course, but pissed off that it had taken him so long – and that he hadn't even kissed her goodnight.

Sometimes, she wondered if he felt the same way about her as she felt about him.

But no . . . She wasn't going to think like that. She was going to find the positive and hang on to it for dear life. He *must* love her, because he'd come back.

Now, if she could only get him away from Lynne and Raiz, everything would be just perfect.

Sliding an arm around Ali, Mary closed her eyes and drifted into a dream world of attentive husbands, beautiful babies, and smart new houses far away from the Crescents.

14

Lynne's eyes popped open at the usual time – force of habit after years of getting up for work. Even now, after months of injecting, her body clock was still more reliable than any alarm clock – proof, as if she needed it, that she *wasn't* a junkie, whatever the moralistic straights like Jennings chose to believe.

So, she'd fallen asleep at the machine for two measly minutes . . . Big deal! What difference did it really make in a nine-hour day? *None!* Jennings was just being a spiteful bitch.

Getting annoyed all over again, Lynne threw the quilt back and got up. She'd spent the whole of the previous day going over and over this, and it was a complete waste of energy. There was no way Jennings was going to reconsider and give her back her job. She just had to accept it and get on with her life. But there would be a few changes around here in the meantime.

'What are you doing?' Raiz croaked, rubbing at his eyes as she stomped around the room.

'Getting dressed,' she snapped. 'And you can get up, an' all, 'cos I want a word with you and Ali. Go give him a shake and fetch him downstairs. But don't wake Mary. I don't want her to hear this till I've told you two.'

Groaning when Lynne flounced from the room, Raiz sat up with a sick feeling of dread in the pit of his stomach. This sounded ominous. He just hoped she wasn't going to kick them out. He'd grown too used to the luxury of this nicely furnished house. And the area felt safer, too. They hadn't seen Kenny once since they'd been here – and, with any luck, never would again.

Pulling his jeans and jumper on, he shuffled along the landing to Mary's room. Shaking Ali until he opened his eyes, he whispered, 'Get up, man. Lynne wants to talk to us. But don't wake Mary.'

'What does she want?' Ali grunted, pissed off at being summoned like some sort of dog.

'No idea,' Raiz said, handing his clothes to him. 'Hurry up, man. She sounds mad about something. I'll go and see if I can suss her out.'

Reluctantly getting dressed, Ali grumbled all the way down the stairs. Seeing Lynne and a very pale Raiz sitting at the table, he jerked his chin up.

'What's up?'

Pushing the pot of tea she'd brewed across the table towards him, Lynne said, 'Sit down. We need to talk.'

'About what?' Dragging a chair out, he sat down and poured himself a cup.

'Work,' she said.

Ali frowned as he stirred three heaped sugars into the tea. He hoped she wasn't about to suggest that he and Raiz started working. She knew full well that they weren't allowed. And if she expected them to start running around dealing, or any other shit like that, she could piss off. He'd tried that. It didn't suit him.

Lighting a cigarette, Lynne squinted at him through the smoke.

'I don't know about you, but I reckon it's a piss-take me being the only one who's still earning. I had to do three punters yesterday just so I could pay that fucking electric bill, and it made me really mad 'cos I'm not the only one who uses the bleedin' stuff. So, I got to thinking, and I decided it's about time someone else chipped in.'

'You know our situation,' Ali told her curtly.

'I'm not talking about *you*,' she snapped, flicking her ash with irritation. 'I'm talking about *her*.' She indicated upstairs with a jerk of her thumb. 'She's got a pussy, and I don't see why she ain't using it.'

'Mary?' Ali's frown deepened.

'Yeah, *Mary*.' Lynne scowled at him, defying him to tell her that his girlfriend was too good to sell herself. Just let him *dare* . . .

'That's not a bad idea,' he murmured thoughtfully.

'So, you agree?' She narrowed her eyes.

'Absolutely.' Nodding, he looked up and gave her a sly grin. 'I don't know why I never thought of it.'

'Good. Well, you can tell her when she gets up, then.' Lynne smiled, relieved that she wouldn't have to force the issue. 'Now that's sorted, who's got the gear?'

'Raiz.' Ali nudged his friend.

Frowning worriedly, Raiz took his wrap out of his pocket and opened it up on the table. Using a knife to split it three ways, he took his and heaped it into his spoon.

'I don't think Mary's going to be too happy,' he commented, staring intently at the powder as he heated it.

'No one's asking you,' Lynne snapped, pulling her belt tight around her arm. 'Anyhow, I'm not too happy that you think it's all right for *me* to do it, but not precious Mary.'

'I never said that,' Raiz muttered. 'I'm just saying she might get angry.'

'You big wuss,' Lynne sneered, jabbing the tip of the spike at her vein. 'Anyhow, don't you worry your little self about her. I'll kick her bloody head in if she dares say no.'

'She won't,' Ali cut in confidently. 'I'll make sure of that.'

Turning to Raiz then he saw that his hands were shaking and said, 'Do you want me to do that?'

'Yeah, thanks.' Raiz handed him the syringe. 'I don't know what's wrong with me, these days . . . I can't seem to get it in.'

'No kidding,' Lynne sniped.

Waking up, Mary was dismayed to find Ali's side of the bed empty. Had she only imagined that he'd come back? she wondered. Or had he changed his mind about sharing her bed and gone to sleep on the couch? Throwing her dressing gown on, she ran downstairs to check.

Hearing the slow, drawling voices coming from the living room, she felt the knot in her stomach tighten. If they were doing what she thought they were doing . . .

Pushing the door open, she was just in time to see the others shooting up. Marching across to the table, she snatched up the empty wrap.

'Oh, thanks a lot,' she complained, flinging it back down. 'You could have said you were getting up.'

'You were asleep,' Ali drawled. 'I didn't want to disturb you.'

'Yeah . . .' Lynne dragged her gaze up for just a second before her eyes rolled shut. 'That's what . . . he said . . .'

Snatching a cigarette from Lynne's pack, Mary went to the couch and flopped down on it. Taking deep, angry drags, she watched narrow-eyed as, one by one, they nodded out.

Getting up after a minute, she tiptoed across to check the syringe still hanging out of Ali's arm. Reaching for it when she saw that it was half-filled with blood, she began to ease it from his flesh.

Coming to, he gripped her wrist hard.

'What do you think you're doing?'

'Getting *my* bit,' Mary cried. 'There's still gear in that, and *you* don't need it.'

Tossing her hand aside, Ali depressed the plunger and scowled darkly up at her.

'Don't *ever* do that again,' he warned. 'My blood is not for you.'

'I don't want your fuckin' *blood*,' she yelled. 'I just want my share of the gear! God, I hate you lot sometimes! You don't give a stuff about me!' Close to tears now, Mary ran from the room.

'We've upset her,' Raiz murmured guiltily.

'She'll be fine,' Ali assured him, closing his eyes again. 'I'll sort her out.'

Mary had cried herself to sleep by the time Ali got it together to go and check on her. Sitting beside her on the bed, he shook her shoulder.

'Don't be mad at me,' he crooned when she opened her eyes. 'We *were* going to save you some, but we figured you'd still have a bit left over from yesterday.'

'You knew damn well I'd finished that,' she muttered, giving him an accusing glare as she sat up. 'You just didn't care.'

'Don't whine,' Ali snapped, irritated by her petulance.

'It's all right for you,' Mary protested. 'You've already had *yours*. I'm the one who's all wound up, but what am I supposed to do? I've got no money till the end of the week.'

'Actually, we were just talking about that.' Ali passed her the cigarette he was smoking. 'And we think you should start working with Lynne.'

'You *what*?' Coughing as she swallowed the smoke, Mary squinted up at him.

'It's good money.' He shrugged. 'You said so yourself.'

'Sack that!' she snorted. 'I don't know how you can even *ask* me. You're supposed to be my boyfriend.'

'Grow up!' he spat, his increasingly gaunt but still

handsome face darkening. 'I thought you were more mature than this.'

'What's *that* got to do with it?' she challenged. 'I thought you loved me.'

'Love?' Ali sneered. 'Love doesn't come into it when you need money. And let's not forget whose fault *that* is. When we started out, you said you didn't need the gear, and I believed you. Now look . . . I'm doing more than I've ever done in my life, and it's *your* fault. You've *got* to do it – for me.'

'Can't you just wait till my giro comes? And I'll find another job, no trouble. I'll go round all the pubs tonight.'

'It's not *enough*!' He slapped his hand down on the bed. 'Your wages from Henshall's weren't enough, and you wouldn't even make *that* at a pub – not even with your giro on top.

'Anyway,' Ali went on in a low, mean voice, 'if you're so selfish that you'd place a ridiculous word like *love* above my health, I might just as well leave and get myself clean. I'd be off it in no time without you holding me back.'

'No!' Mary yelped. 'You can't! I won't let you.'

'Well, what's it to be?' He gazed coolly back at her. 'Are you going to be a silly child for the rest of your life, or will you grow up and do the right thing?'

Swiping at the tears that were rolling down her cheeks, Mary nodded. 'All right, I'll do it. Just don't go.'

'I knew you'd see sense.' Smiling, Ali forced himself not to push her away when she leaned against him.

'Whose idea was it?' she sniffled, miffed that he and Lynne had discussed her when she wasn't there to defend herself. 'Yours or hers?'

'We all agreed it was for the best,' Ali told her, raising her chin with a finger and peering deep into her eyes. 'But you'll be doing it for *us*, not them. Okay?'

Nodding, Mary gave him a trembling smile.

'Good girl,' he said. 'Now, go and have a wash and sort things out with Lynne.'

Lynne was brewing up when Mary came down to the kitchen. Stirring sugar into a cup, she handed it to her – pretending not to notice the red-rimmed eyes and shiny nose.

'He's told you, then? Great idea, isn't it?'

'I'd rather work in the pub,' Mary muttered, sipping the tea with her gaze downcast. 'It makes me sick thinking about dirty old men *touching* me.'

Lynne's smile dropped from her face in a flash. 'Oh, get off your fuckin' pedestal and get real, will you! You seem to think this is all some sort of game, but it's *not*, and you'd better just grow up. You've lived off my fanny for long enough – it's time yours had a workout.'

'All *right*,' Mary protested sulkily. 'There's no need to shout. I've already had the lecture off Ali, I don't need it off you an' all.'

'Yeah, well, I'm glad he had a go at you, 'cos someone had to.'

'Back off. I've said I'll do it, and I will.'

Making a small huffing noise, Lynne folded her arms. 'When?'

'Don't know.' Mary gave a miserable shrug. 'I don't even know *what* to do. Do I just stand on the corner and wait for a car to stop, or what?'

Narrowing her eyes, Lynne sipped her tea and pondered this. If Mary went straight out on the beat, she'd keep all of the money she earned for herself and Ali. But if she did it at the house, she'd have to give Lynne a cut. And Lynne could start her up by offloading some of her own more unsavoury regulars onto her, giving Lynne an even bigger cut – sort of an *introduction* fee. Like George, with his terrible breath and his slobbery lips, who liked to take his teeth out and . . . Ugh! Mary could have him, for a start. And then there was pervy Nigel. She was welcome to him as well.

Mary began to feel a glimmer of enthusiasm when Lynne outlined what she was thinking. She'd feel safer doing it here in her own room, and it would be a lot easier if it was with a punter she'd already met.

'You can start tonight. Nigel's coming over,' Lynne said, smirking at Mary's horrified expression. 'Don't worry, I'll tell him the score when he gets here. You can take it from there.'

'Just like that?' Mary squawked. 'But I won't know what to say, or anything.'

'Whatever comes into your head.' Lynne shrugged. 'The nastier the better.'

'Like what?'

'Jeezus, d'y' want me to write you a fuckin' script, or what? Look, he's a bit kinky, yeah? I just say stuff like . . .'

Mary's eyes widened with alarm as Lynne reeled off an example of what Nigel liked to hear. It was the first time she'd heard the details of Lynne's work – and she didn't like the sound of it one little bit.

'He loves it,' Lynne assured her. 'And if I get nasty enough, he does all the dirty work for me. Then I make him lick it up like the dog he likes to think he is. It's a doddle.'

'No way. I can't say stuff like that.'

'Bollocks!' Losing her patience, Lynne slammed her cup down on the ledge. 'I've heard you say worse to the neighbours so don't come the innocent. Anyway, if you're thinking of backing out, you can piss off upstairs and start packing, 'cos I'm not keeping you – not when you think you're better than me.'

'I've *never* said that. And I'm not backing out, neither. Just don't blame me if I cock it up, that's all.' Taking a deep breath, Mary shook her head to clear the obscene images from her mind.

Looking at Mary's unhappy face, Lynne remembered how hard her own first time had been and felt a twinge of remorse for coming down so hard on her. Lighting two cigarettes, she handed one to Mary and dipped down to peer up into her face.

'You won't cock it up, kid,' she said, giving her a sly grin. 'That's Nigel's job. Anyway, he's a right soft cunt. And I'm here if you really can't handle it.'

'Thanks,' Mary muttered, not at all reassured.

15

Mary had seen Nigel many times before, but now that she knew about his little 'peculiarity' she didn't know where to look when he arrived that night.

Hurrying ahead of him up the stairs, she grimaced when she saw the fluorescent-pink padded bra and matching knickers laid out on her bed. They were absolutely hideous, but Lynne had assured her that Nigel loved them.

Closing the door when he followed her in, she took a deep breath and pointed at the outfit, saying, 'Get them on!' in the domineering tone that Lynne had coached her to use.

When Nigel just gazed stupidly back at her with his piggy little eyes, Mary almost turned and ran. This was a joke – one big, pathetic joke. She'd never be able to do it.

Reminding herself that they were broke – and that she stood a very good chance of losing Ali if she didn't sort it out – she gritted her teeth and tried again.

'I said get them on – *NOW*! And don't take all night about it, you shit-sniffing little mongrel!'

Nigel responded immediately. Dropping to all fours, he waggled his backside in the air and tried to lick Mary's foot.

'Get the fuck off me, you disgusting pervert!' she yelped, leaping out of the way. 'Go on – get over there before I put you on a lead and take you for a walk round *your* road. Want your wife to see what you've been getting up to, do you?'

Panting, with his tongue hanging out, Nigel scampered

obediently across to the bed. Tearing his clothes off, he pulled the ridiculous outfit on.

Kneeling up when he was ready, he whimpered softly, his paws dangling in front of his grotesquely fat belly as he waited for her next command.

Mary didn't know whether to laugh her head off, or kick *his* head *in*. But she had to admit that Lynne was right. If this was all it took to earn more money than she'd made in a week at Henshall's, she'd gladly do it three times a night.

Smiling nastily, she said, 'Right, you – get your disgusting little worm out of my nice silk knickers . . .'

Lynne was lying on the couch when Mary kicked Nigel out forty minutes later. Seeing her drooping eyes and slack mouth, Mary glanced at the table where she'd left her purse containing the gear she'd had to beg the dealer to lay on her that afternoon. It had been moved. Lynne had obviously been in it.

'Bloody hell, Lynne,' she snapped when she checked the wrap and saw how little was left. 'What am I supposed to do with *this*?'

'Sorry,' Lynne drawled insincerely. 'I'll pay you back when I get mine later.'

'Yeah, you'd better.' Pursing her lips, Mary shoved what was left into her pocket. 'You should've asked.'

'Oh, belt up,' Lynne groaned. 'You've done it enough times with mine. There wasn't even that much there.'

'Fuck off! It was a tenner wrap, that.'

'Well, you got ripped off, then, didn't you?' Pushing herself upright, Lynne rubbed lazily at her nose. 'Anyhow, shut up moaning and tell me what happened with Nigel.'

Mary wanted to carry the argument on, but hearing Nigel's name reminded her of what she'd just been through. It had been hilarious – *gross*, but funny all the same.

Grinning, she said, 'Piece of piss.'

'How much did he give you?'

'Don't know – I haven't checked it yet.'

'What you waiting for? Let's have a look.'

Pulling the money Nigel had stuffed into her hand out of her waistband, Mary flapped it sheepishly. Snatching it, Lynne counted it out on the coffee table.

'A hundred and twenty quid!' she exclaimed. 'He's never given *me* that much. I'm lucky if I get fifty. What did you get up to, you dirty bitch? You must have done something *I* won't to get that out of him!'

Lynne was smiling, but it was brittle and Mary knew that she was peeved.

'I didn't do anything,' she insisted. 'Only what you told me – calling him names, and that. He did the rest himself. I never even touched him.'

'Yeah, I bet.' Giving a disbelieving snort, Lynne split the money and handed a rough half back to Mary. 'You earned it, I suppose. Just don't forget whose punter he is.'

Mary's cheek muscles jumped as she gritted her teeth and forced herself not to argue. Nigel *had* been Lynne's punter, but he'd obviously enjoyed himself more with Mary. And if Lynne thought she could take him back just like that, she had another think coming.

As for Lynne waltzing off with half the money, Mary would let it go this time, but it wouldn't happen again. She wouldn't be stupid enough to reveal how much she'd made next time.

Right now, it was time to pay her debts and get another wrap before Ali got home. He'd be pissed off if there was no gear waiting – and that was the only reason he'd agreed to let her do this, after all.

Ali was pleased when he learned that Mary had gone through with it. Telling her that he was proud of her for proving her commitment to him, he did something he hadn't done in months and kissed her.

It wasn't deep and meaningful by any means, but it was more than enough to convince Mary that she was doing the right thing, and she threw herself into her new career with an enthusiasm that surprised them all.

She didn't exactly like it – not once she'd had a taste of the punters who *did* want sex, sometimes much rougher or weirder than she was entirely comfortable with. But she definitely enjoyed the rewards.

Within a month, she had six regulars of her own – excluding Nigel, whom Lynne had jealously reclaimed after his second high-paying visit. She also had more passing trade than she could handle when they went out on the beat.

Having such a pretty face was a definite advantage, but it was Mary's age that was the real draw. It appalled her that there were so many perverts roaming the streets looking for under-age girls. She was regularly paid twice as much as Lynne for the exact same service – and she'd have got *three* times more if she'd been thirteen or fourteen because, unlike everything else in this fucked-up world, the money came down as the years went up for players of this game.

Still, Mary wasn't complaining. If dirty old bastards wanted to shell out all their hard-earned cash for a meaningless shag, she was more than willing to take it.

16

Ali and Raiz had a problem – a big problem, which required a quick solution.

Sitting in their cold, uninhabited flat, they stared at each other in silence, too dismayed to voice what they were both feeling. After everything they had been through to get this far, after everything they had sacrificed . . . To have it all snatched away now was just too unbearable for words.

After two years of waiting, their asylum applications had been refused. They could appeal, the letters they were holding informed them, but if that failed they would be deported in exactly one month's time.

It was the worst possible news. Not only because they seriously hadn't expected it but also because they knew that they now had to do something they'd never intended to do. It was the last thing either of them wanted, but it was the price they had to pay for drifting along in their dark little smack-bubble for so long. Time had run out. There were no options left, and no room for manoeuvre.

After a while, Ali broke the unbearable silence.

'We've got to do it, man. It's either that, or go back.'

'I know,' Raiz agreed miserably. 'But I don't know which is worse. Couldn't we just . . .' Lost for words, he brought his fist down hard on his leg. 'Shit!'

'Don't torture yourself,' Ali told him firmly. 'We've got no choice.'

'It's easy for you,' Raiz moaned. 'Mary will do anything you say. But, Lynne . . . I'm not so sure.'

'Don't worry about her,' Ali assured him grimly. 'She'll do it. And if she doesn't, well . . .' He shrugged with his hands. 'We're in this together, man. If one runs, we both run. But it won't get to that. She'll do it. I know she will.'

Raiz was grateful for Ali's reassurances. His friend was the closest thing he had to family, and he didn't think he'd survive if they were forced to separate.

Sighing wearily, Ali pushed himself to his feet and slipped his jacket on. Handing Raiz's to him, he said, 'Come on, man. Let's get it over with.'

Locking the door behind them, Raiz leaned his forehead against the wood and said a silent prayer before following Ali down the stairs.

Mary was stunned when Ali proposed, but it took her all of two seconds to accept. Never mind that he'd never said that he loved her. And so what if they hardly ever had sex because he was always too busy shooting up or nodding out to get it up. He'd asked her to be his *wife*.

'Yes!' she yelped, flinging herself at him and wrapping her arms around his neck. 'Yes, yes, yes!'

Raiz looked at Lynne, his eyes asking the question that his proud mouth refused to voice. It wasn't that he disliked her, as such, he'd just rather have waited until he'd found a bride his mother would approve of.

Lynne frowned for a while. Then shrugged. Then said, 'Ah, sod it. Why not?'

As Ali and Raiz gave each other congratulatory slaps on the back and shook hands, Mary giggled.

'Married, Lynne! God, it's so brilliant. Can you believe it? I can't. It's just so . . . Wow!'

Lynne smiled, but she had no such romantic notions about

the union. She knew exactly what the men's game was – and more, thanks to Raiz's amusing habit of talking in his sleep. The daft sod had revealed quite a few of his and Ali's dirty little secrets in the year Lynne and he had been together. Not that she gave a toss about any of it – it just gave her a buzz to know that he couldn't hide anything from her. And the only reason she'd agreed to marry him was because it would be a kick in the bollocks for everyone who had ever labelled her unlovable – her own family, for example.

'Let's go to town and book it,' Mary said, jumping up and dragging her coat on.

'What, now?' Lynne frowned. 'Don't be soft. You can't just walk in and do it. You've got to have all your documents.'

'What documents?' Mary was already at the door.

'*Birth* certificates.' Shaking her head, Lynne lit a cigarette as if she had all the time in the world. 'Oh, and passports.' This she aimed at Ali and Raiz.

'They won't need them.' Mary flapped her hand, impatient to get things moving. 'So long as their visas haven't run out. They haven't, have they?' She turned to Ali.

'Not yet.'

'And you've got everything else – birth certificates, and that?'

Snatching the documents when he conveniently produced them, Mary flapped them at Lynne. 'There you go! Happy now?'

Giving in, Lynne stubbed the cigarette out. 'Right, fine. I'll just go and see if I can find mine, shall I? I take it you've got yours?'

Mary's smile slipped. In her excitement, she'd completely forgotten that she didn't have her own birth certificate – had never even seen it, come to that. It was one of those things that her mother kept stashed away in the bowels of her bedroom.

'It's at me mam's,' she said, coming back into the room and slumping down on the couch. 'What am I going to do?'

'Go and ask her for it.'

'Oh, yeah, right. Like she's really gonna give it to me.'

'Well, buy another one when we get there,' Lynne said irritably. 'Bloody hell, girl, why d'y' have to make a song and dance about everything?'

After queuing for an hour for a copy of Mary's birth certificate, they then had to wait another two hours while the registrar checked that Ali and Raiz's documents were valid. Finally, it was done.

Skipping outside with the magical receipt gripped firmly in her hand, Mary hugged an ashen-faced Ali and blew him a kiss as he and Raiz headed for the nearest pub to drown their sorrows.

'I can't believe it,' she cried, grabbing Lynne and dancing her along the pavement. 'Three weeks from now I'll be Mrs Elbani. *God*, Lynne! I can't wait.'

'Dozy bitch,' Lynne teased, disentangling herself as people began to give them funny looks. 'Anyone would think this was for real.'

'It *is*,' Mary assured her quite seriously. 'Once I've got that ring on my finger, it's never coming off.'

'We'll see,' Lynne snorted. Then, to cheer Mary up because her face had fallen, she said, 'I'm only messing. I'm sure you'll last for ever and ever.'

'We will,' Mary insisted. 'You watch.'

Dream on, Lynne thought but didn't bother saying. Mary was setting herself up for a huge fall, in her opinion. But some people just had to learn the hard way.

The next two weeks passed in a crazy blur of activity; planning and replanning, ordering food and drink – and more drink. Everything had to be perfect, and Mary and Lynne literally worked their backsides off to earn the money to fund it all.

As her excitement grew, a cloud managed to creep in to darken Mary's rose-tinted sky. Her family. The more she thought about them, the more she knew that she wanted them at her wedding. But after two years of not contacting them, she didn't know how to approach them. With just days to go, she asked Lynne's advice.

'I don't know why the hell you want them there,' Lynne said. 'But if it means so much to you, just go and see them.'

'You sure you don't mind?' Mary asked. 'I know it won't be much fun for you with none of *your* family there, but I just want mine to see me doing all right for myself.'

'I won't miss my lot,' Lynne assured her. 'I haven't seen them for years, and I ain't about to start looking them up now. If you want yours there, it's down to you.'

'I think I do.' Mary chewed agitatedly on her bottom lip. 'But I'm dreading seeing my mam after all this time. She'll probably have a right go at me.'

'Only one way to find out,' Lynne said, pushing her firmly aside to get at the syringe on the table. 'Bite the bullet and go.'

After more lip-chewing, Mary said, 'Right, I will . . . when I've had a hit.'

'Great idea,' Lynne remarked sarcastically, pulling her skirt up to her knicker line and opening her legs. 'Gouch out while you're talking to her. She's *bound* to come then, isn't she?'

Mary knew that Lynne was right, but she didn't know if she could face her mother straight. She needed a fix just to get moving in the morning. How was she supposed to walk all the way there and back without so much as a sniff?

'Just go and get it over with,' Lynne muttered, peering down at her crotch as she tried to get the point of the needle into the vein at the top of her inner thigh. 'The faster you get it done, the faster you'll get back.'

Agnes James was surprised when she opened her door and saw the daughter she had all but forgotten existed standing there. Looking her up and down, taking in the drawn cheeks, the sallow skin, the lank hair, she pursed her lips.

'Well, well. Look what the dog's sicked up.'

'I didn't come for a fight, Mam,' Mary murmured shamefacedly. 'Can I come in?'

'Suppose so.' Agnes stepped back. 'But if it's money you're after, forget it. I'm skint.'

'I'm not after *anything*,' Mary protested, following her inside. As soon as she was over the threshold, the familiar smell of home struck her to the heart. Sweat, furniture polish, cabbage, cheesy feet . . .

'Our Joey still here?' she asked, knowing full well that he would be. Men like him never left home – not when they had a mother to do everything for them.

'Yeah.' Waddling into the kitchen, Agnes put the kettle on. Folding her arms, she leaned back against the counter. 'So, where have you been hiding yourself?'

Blinking back the tears that she *so* didn't want to cry, Mary shrugged. 'Oh, you know . . . Here and there. So, how are you, Mam?'

'Apart from the crippling rheumatics?' Agnes lit a cigarette – offering one to Mary as an afterthought. 'All right, I suppose. Your dad's been a bit rough with his chest, but I've told him it's his own fault for smoking them Capstans.'

'Still on them, is he?'

'Some things never change,' Agnes remarked wearily. Then, narrowing her eyes, she peered at Mary hard. 'Anyhow, never mind him. What you after, our Mary? And don't say "Nowt", 'cos I know you.'

'I'm not after anything. Honest. I'm . . . well, I just wanted to ask you something.'

'Oh, yeah?'

'Yeah . . . I'm, er, getting married, and I want you to come.' There, she'd said it.

'Oh, aye?' Agnes raised a cynical eyebrow. 'When's it due?'

'I'm not pregnant,' Mary retorted primly. 'I'm getting married because I love him and he loves me, not 'cos I've got to.'

Giving a grunt of disbelief, Agnes turned to make the tea. Handing a cup to Mary a minute later, she said, 'So, what colour is he?'

'You what?' Mary frowned. 'What kind of question is that?'

'An honest one, so let's have an honest answer. Is he foreign?'

'He's Libyan, actually.'

'A *Paki*?' Agnes spat, her face contorting with disgust. 'Oh, for Christ's sake, Mary, what am I supposed to tell your dad? He'll go mental if I tell him you've taken up with a bleedin' Paki. And our Joey'll hit the roof. You know what he's been like since that one pulled a knife on him that time.'

Staring at her, Mary gave a tiny laugh of incredulity. 'He was trying to kick the poor bastard's head in for fuck all, Mam! Shit, you were right when you said nothing changes – not in this family, it don't.'

'Don't take that tone with me,' Agnes warned, slamming her cup down on the ledge. 'There's nowt wrong with *us*. It's *you* who seems to think you're a step up these days. Well, let me tell you something, lady, any fool can see you're not. You look like one of them bloody junkies, if you ask me.'

'Good job I'm not asking you, then, isn't it?' Mary was fighting the tears now. 'Jeezus, Mam—'

'Don't you dare blaspheme in my house!'

'Or what?'

'Or I'll punch your fuckin' lights out, that's what!'

Jumping at the sound of her brother's voice, Mary turned around and saw Joey glaring at her from the doorway, his beer gut hanging much further over his unbuckled belt than she remembered, his arms a meaty mess of cheap tattoos.

'Hello, Joey.' She folded her arms defensively. 'You all right?'

'I'm just great,' he grunted, looking her up and down with a sneer. 'What the fuck have *you* been doing?'

'Nothing.'

'Yeah, *right*, and I'm a monkey's uncle.' Turning to his mother, Joey nodded at the kettle. 'Brew us a cup, Mam.'

'I'm – I'm getting married, Joey,' Mary said, smiling to lighten the atmosphere.

'To a Paki,' Agnes spat, immediately regretting it when her son's whole body seemed to swell with rage.

Whipping his head around, Joey roared, 'You what? You fuckin' *what?*'

'Now, Joey . . .' Rushing across to him, Agnes used every ounce of her strength to force him back out into the hall. 'I'm only saying . . . It's not set yet, or nothing.'

'Get out, you dirty whore!' Joey yelled at Mary over his mother's shoulder. 'Go on . . . Get out of my fuckin' sight before I slap the bleedin' face right off you!'

'Don't worry, I'm going,' she yelled back, dodging past them and yanking the front door open. 'I don't know why I bothered coming in the first place. I should have known you wouldn't've changed. You're just a bunch of fuckin' retards!'

Legging it before Joey could shake their mother off, Mary ran all the way home.

She was dismayed to find the house empty, but glad to

see that Lynne had left her a tiny bit of gear – not enough
to completely wipe out the pain, but it would have to do
for now.

Going up to her room when she was done, Mary climbed
into bed and cried herself to sleep.

Lynne was writing out a guest list when Mary woke up and
dragged herself down to the living room some hours later.
Glancing up, Lynne frowned when she noticed the girl's
red-rimmed eyes.

'Didn't go too well with your mam, I take it?'

'Not exactly, no.' Flopping onto the couch, Mary told her
all about the awful confrontation.

Listening patiently until she'd finished, Lynne calmly
crossed Mary's family off the list, saying, 'Thank Christ
for that. I was terrified they'd said yes, 'cos I know what
you Catholic Paddies are like for the booze. We'd have
needed ten punters a minute for the next three years to
pay for it all.'

Mary had to laugh. It didn't matter how bad things looked,
Lynne had a real knack of cutting through the crap and
making light of it. She was also more than capable of making
a bad situation seem even worse, but Mary loved her when
she was like this. There was no better feeling in the world
than to know that, no matter who turned their backs on
you, your mates were with you all the way.

When the big day finally arrived, Mary spent the entire time
looking over her shoulder in the vain hope that her mother
would change her mind at the last minute and come. She
didn't.

By the time the wedding party traipsed out of the pub
and headed back to the Crescents for the party, Mary was
so drunk that she no longer cared. If she meant so little

to her family that they would snub her on her wedding day, she was done with the lot of them. She was Ali's wife now. She had him, Lynne and Raiz. She didn't need anybody else.

17

Mary had a miserable pregnancy. Despite the GP's warning that her habit would probably bring on a premature labour, the process lasted the full, sickly, bloated nine months.

Going a week over her due date, she was alone when her labour started because the others had given up waiting. Not that they *had* been waiting. Ali had been so wrapped up in himself since the wedding that she was lucky if he gave her a glass of water, never mind asked how she was doing. And Lynne was bitchier than ever, complaining to anyone who'd listen that the more weight Mary piled on around her belly, the less weight she pulled at work. Even Raiz, soft-hearted as he was, hadn't paid her that much attention. To all intents and purposes, she had suffered the pregnancy alone – and now she was going to suffer the birth alone, too.

Scribbling a quick note telling Ali what had happened, hoping – but sincerely doubting – that he might just rush to her side when he saw it, Mary propped it against a cup on the table and waddled out, case in hand, to the bus stop.

Flat on her back on the roughly sheeted bed some hours later, worn out from the agonising contractions and the constant probing examinations, Mary began to suspect that something was wrong when she saw conspiratorial looks passing between the nurses and the midwife.

'What's going on?' she demanded, swiping at the sweat pouring from her brow. 'Tell me . . . I've got a right to know.'

'Nothing for you to worry about,' the midwife told her, worrying Mary even more with her refusal to look her in the eye. 'You just get on with your part and leave us to do ours, eh?'

Panic began to well in Mary's breast like a living, breathing thing. Sure that she was dying, her Catholic upbringing sprang to the fore.

'I want the priest!' she cried. 'Get me the priest!'

Nodding for one of the nurses to go and fetch him, the midwife forced Mary to lie down.

'You just calm yourself down and stop all that shouting, young lady,' she scolded. 'The baby's coming and you're going to need all your energy for that. Now, push when I tell you to, then stop when I say. Do you hear me, Mary? This is really important.'

'What's wrong?' Mary screamed, tears running down her cheeks. 'Just tell me what's—*Aaaggghhh!*'

Minutes after Mary had finally pushed her son into the world, the hospital priest delivered the last rites and christened him Patrick Ali Elbani.

Almost immediately, as if he'd only hung on for the blessing, the sickly baby died.

Beside herself with grief for having survived at his cost, Mary cried when the nurses wrenched him from her. And she carried on crying until they finally sedated her.

Waking the following morning, Mary was shocked to find her mother sitting beside the bed.

'Mam,' she croaked, coughing as she tried to sit up, her throat sore from the medication. 'How did you know I was here?'

'Heard it on the grapevine,' Agnes said. 'How you feeling?'

'Like shit,' Mary muttered, wincing at the cramping pains in her stomach. 'Where's Ali?'

'No idea.' Sniffing loudly, Agnes fussily rearranged her handbag on her lap.

'Aw, you haven't said anything nasty to him, have you?' Mary peered at her worriedly. 'Please, Mam, tell me you haven't sent him away?'

'If he'd been here, I would have,' Agnes admitted. 'But he wasn't, so I didn't need to.'

'Oh.' Mary was deflated. 'Maybe he was here before you came, eh? When I was asleep.'

Giving a disappointed sigh, Agnes shook her head.

'I thought you had more gumption than this, our Mary, I really did. If you must know, the nurse said no one's been near but me since they brought you in.'

'They'll come.' Mary sank further down in the bed. 'Ali will, anyway. You'll see.'

'Oh, why don't you just stop kidding yourself and come home where you belong,' Agnes hissed. 'Don't think I haven't heard what you've been getting up to, 'cos I have. And it's not right.'

Gazing up at the ceiling, Mary felt a tear trickle slowly down her cheek.

'Is that all you've got to say, Mam? Aren't you even gonna *ask* about the baby?'

Agnes sniffed again. Then, glancing quickly around, she said, 'It's God's way to rescue innocent bairns from bad mothers, Mary. What did you expect? If it wasn't the drugs what killed it, it probably would have died of some nasty disease you'd picked up.'

Listening as her mother went on about how ashamed she'd been to hear from a neighbour that her daughter had been seen walking the streets and picking up strange men, Mary turned her head and gave her an accusing glare.

'You don't care that he's dead, do you? It doesn't even mean as much to you as what the fucking neighbours think, or how you're going to hold your head up in the fucking church!'

'Don't you *dare* talk about God's house like that.' Agnes pursed her lips, her eyes ablaze with indignation. 'This is none of His doing.'

'Maybe not,' Mary retorted. 'But it's *His* doing that He's landed me with a mother who doesn't even care about her grandson dying.'

'That's not true.'

'Yes, it is!'

'I came didn't I? More than can be said for its father.'

'See!' Mary gasped. 'That's how much *you* care. You called him *it*. Well, he's not an *it*, Mam, he's my little boy.'

Sighing wearily, Agnes said, 'I know . . . But he's dead, Mary.'

'You don't have to tell *me* that,' Mary sobbed, balling her hands into fists and bringing them down onto the bed with a thud. 'I was *holding* him.'

'Stop shouting.' Agnes reached out a hand to quieten her. 'People are listening.'

'Get *off* me!' Mary snatched her arm out of reach. 'I don't care about them – *or* you. Why should I? You don't care. You're just glad you're not saddled with a *Paki* grandson.'

'That's not fair,' Agnes protested quietly.

'Oh, just go, for God's sake,' Mary groaned, closing her eyes. 'Just go . . . Just go . . . Just—'

'All right, I'll go, if that's what you want.' Agnes stood up. 'But, mark my words, you'll regret turning me away. One day, you'll realise you've only got one true friend in this world.'

Snapping her head round, Mary said, 'If that's true, Mam, it certainly ain't you.'

Two days later, having received no more visitors, Mary discharged herself from the hospital.

Finding nobody in when she got home, she made herself a cup of tea and wearily took herself off to bed, too numb even to feel sorry for herself.

'I wasn't expecting you,' Ali said when he got home some time later and found her there. 'Nobody rang.'

'You're supposed to ring them,' Mary reminded him – not bothering to add that he was supposed to have visited her, too; brought flowers, held her hand, mopped her brow. 'Anyway, it's done now,' she went on, gritting her teeth to say what had to be said next. 'The, er, hospital needs to know when to release his body.'

'*What?*' Ali gazed down at her as if she'd gone stark staring mad.

'The funeral,' she explained. 'We have to arrange for the undertakers to pick him up.'

'What for?'

'To *bury* him.' Squinting up at him, Mary wondered if it were the shock that was causing him to act this way. 'Anyway, we can't leave it too long. I don't know how you do it back home, but we have time limits. We really need to get on to someone soon.'

'And who's going to pay for this?' he demanded curtly

'Us, of course.'

'Oh, no.' Ali shook his head. 'No way! I'm not paying anything.'

'Don't be stupid,' she snapped. 'We've got to. He's our *son*.'

'I never even saw him,' Ali retorted angrily. 'Why would I want to waste money on a fancy box for a . . . a *stranger*?

It's ridiculous! Anyway, they can't make me. I'll deny having anything to do with it.'

'How *could* you?' Mary gasped, staring at him in disbelief. 'That's a terrible thing to say.'

'No, what's terrible is expecting me to pay for something I don't want.' Ali lit a cigarette and sucked deeply on it.

Trying desperately to excuse him, sure that he was lashing out because he was as shocked and as heartbroken as she was, Mary said, 'You're only saying this because you didn't give yourself a chance to get to know him. If you'd only seen him, Ali . . . His skin was the exact same shade as yours, and his tiny mouth had the same curve. And his hair was straight and silky and really, really black. You'd have fallen in love with him if you'd seen him, just like I did.' Pausing, she swiped at the tears cascading down her cheeks. 'When I held him in my arms after he'd . . . after he'd *gone* . . . I just couldn't stop looking at him. He was so beautiful, they had to tear him out of my arms.'

'Shut up,' Ali hissed, balling his hands into fists and baring his teeth. 'Just shut up, for God's sake! You're making me feel *sick*.'

Reaching out, Mary touched his hand.

'I understand what you're going through, Ali. I don't want to think about it either, but we've got to. And if it's the money you're worried about, don't. I'll work extra hard. I could probably manage about ten a day, no problem, until everything's sorted. I know it'll be tiring, but—'

'You what?' Ali interrupted sharply. 'You mean to tell me you could do ten punters in your condition?'

'I know it's a lot,' Mary said, believing that he was displaying concern for her. 'But I'll do whatever it takes to—'

'Whoa, whoa . . .' Holding up a hand to silence her, he narrowed his eyes accusingly. 'How come you can manage that many, all of a sudden? For the past few months you've only been doing about six – and you've been complaining about *that*. What was it you said?' Pulling a face, he mimicked her: '"I'm *pregnant* . . . I'm too *tired*."'

'I *was*,' she protested. 'I still am. You don't know what I've been through.'

'Oh, but I do,' Ali sniped. 'You've been flat on your back in bed, leaving me to fend for myself. Well, the holiday's over, Mary. You've been shirking your responsibilities for long enough. It's time you got off your backside and got back to work.'

'What about Patrick?'

'There *is* no Patrick. And the sooner you accept that, the better.' Pausing, Ali took a deep breath and exhaled noisily. 'I need a hit,' he muttered then, walking towards the door. 'There's enough for you, if you want some.'

Too numb to carry on fighting, Mary pushed the quilt aside and followed him slowly down the stairs.

So, he wouldn't let her have a funeral for their son, but at least he was willing to share his gear to ease her pain. That showed he cared – no matter what he said.

18

Mary had been back at work for two months, and felt much better for it. It was so refreshing to be out in the open again, and she found she'd missed the banter of the other girls much more than she'd realised. At least they showed concern for her – which was more than could be said for Ali or Lynne – always asking how she was feeling, did she need a rest, was there anything they could do for her?

Growing stronger by the day, she felt sure that she could cope with anything after everything she had suffered and survived. So she was totally unprepared when she came home one night to see that the front door was wide open, light spilling out onto the landing.

It was two in the morning and the men would usually be sleeping by now. But even if they'd been awake, they were far too paranoid to leave the door open. It didn't feel right.

Looking at Lynne wide-eyed, she said, 'What do you think's going on?'

'I don't know,' Lynne muttered. 'But I hope it's not a bust. All my gear's in there.'

Suddenly, Ali's fearful voice drifted out to them.

'I'm telling the truth,' he squawked. 'She's not here.'

'Look, man,' Raiz said then, sounding equally scared. 'We swear we don't know where she is. Why don't you come back tomorrow?'

'Don't fuck with me, you Paki bastards,' a third voice

bellowed, aggression tearing through the words. 'Tell me where she is before I drop the fuckin' pair of you off the fuckin' *balcony*!'

The blood drained from Mary's face. It was her brother, Joey, and he was more than capable of carrying out his threat. But what was he doing here? Was he drunk? Had he come to cause trouble?

Running the rest of the way down the landing, Mary skidded to a halt at the door, just in time to see her brother grab Ali around the throat and shove him up against the wall.

'Stop it, Joey!' she screamed, stumbling over the step. 'You'll kill him!'

Dropping Ali to the floor like a limp rag doll at the sound of his sister's voice, Joey turned to face her, his shoulders hunched, his nostrils flaring with anger. Pushing him aside, Mary helped Ali to his feet.

Sneering scornfully when Ali rubbed his throat and hid behind her, Joey said, 'Don't think *she* can protect you, you pussy cunt. If I want you, I'll have you.'

'What's going on?' Lynne demanded, walking in and glaring at the intruder. 'Who the fuck are *you*, and what are you playing at, trashing my house?'

'Don't talk to me, you slag,' Joey growled, grabbing Mary by the arm and hauling her towards the door. 'This is family business.'

'Get your hands off me!' Mary yelled, clutching at the door frame. 'I'm warning you, Joey . . .'

'I need to talk to you,' he hissed. 'Alone!'

Yanking her arm free, she gritted her teeth and said, 'Whatever you've got to say, just say it and piss off, 'cos I don't want you here.'

Joey gave her such a fierce look that she thought he was going to hit her. But after a foot-tappingly slow minute, his eyes filled up and his chin began to wobble.

Concern immediately overrode Mary's anger. In all the years she'd known him, she had never *once* seen their Joey cry. Whatever he'd come for, it had to be bad.

'What's happened?' she murmured, her mouth suddenly dry. '*Tell* me, Joey. It's not Mam, is it?'

Gulping noisily, Joey nodded. 'She's in the Royal, Mare. She's been there all week an' I've been here loads of times trying to get hold of you, but these knob-heads keep fobbing me off.' He flicked an accusing glare back at Ali.

Despite the fear gripping her heart, Mary gave a defiant jerk of her head.

'You shouldn't have bothered, Joey. Mam disowned me, remember? I'm the last person she'd want to see.'

Peering down at her with pain-filled eyes, he said, 'She's *dying*, Mary.'

Mary's mouth flapped open but nothing came out. She couldn't speak. She didn't know what to say.

'Your mother didn't care when our baby died,' Ali muttered behind her. 'Why should we care if *she* dies now?'

Quickly blocking Joey's way before he could go for Ali again, Mary whipped around and glared at her husband with real hatred in her eyes.

'If anyone didn't care about that baby, it was *you*,' she spat. 'And since when has he been *ours*, eh? He wasn't *ours* when I wanted a decent burial, was he? Wasn't *ours* when I was crying my heart out and you were telling me to pull myself together – *was* he?' Rigid with fury now, Mary pointed a warning finger at Ali. 'And another thing, you heartless bastard . . . If you ever speak about my mother like that again, I'll personally rip your bollocks off!' Turning to Joey then, she motioned him out with a jerk of her head.

As soon as she saw her mother, Mary knew that she'd never see her again after this night. She could smell it, and she could see it in the grey sunken mask that her face had become.

Her dad was sitting beside the bed, his head bowed onto his chest as if he was sleeping. He looked so old and frail that Mary wanted to hug him, but she couldn't bring herself to do it. She was too afraid of being rejected again.

Looking up after a moment, Billy James saw his daughter and smiled.

'He found you, then?' His voice sounded as old and worn as he looked. Holding out a shaky hand, he gripped Mary's tight. 'You okay, love?'

'I'm fine, Dad.' Squeezing his hand, she looked at her mother again. She'd never seen her lying so still before – never heard her breathing so painfully shallow.

'Talk to her,' Billy said. 'I know she don't look it, but she's awake. She'll be made up that you come.'

Leaning forward, Mary said, 'Hiya, Mam. It's me – Mary. You all right?' The words sounded absurd, but she didn't know what else to say.

A flicker of a smile shone faintly from the skeletal face on the pillow, momentarily illuminating the parchment-like skin.

'I – I've been meaning to come round for ages,' Mary went on. 'But you know how it is . . . Something always comes up, doesn't it? You've . . . well, what can I say?' Lost for words, she sniffed back the tears that were stinging her eyes. 'Dozy sod,' she blurted out then. 'Fancy landing your-self in here, eh? Who's gonna keep this pair in line without you to kick their arses?'

Agnes made a strange gurgling sound in the back of her throat, almost as if she were laughing. Then, with a heavy sigh, she was gone.

Biting down hard on her lip as the tears streamed from her eyes, Mary leaned down and kissed her mother's cheek.

'Bye, Mam. I do love you, you know . . . Always did.'

Straightening herself up then, she went to fetch the nurse.

After the doctor had been to certify Agnes James's death, the family were left alone with their grief. Sitting in a row beside the bed with the curtains drawn around them for privacy, they stared at the woman they had all loved so deeply in their individual ways.

'You must have known she was this ill,' Mary said quietly. 'Cancer doesn't come on just like that. How come you didn't tell me sooner?'

'We only found out a few weeks back ourselves,' Billy murmured sadly. 'And it was too late by then 'cos she was too far gone. Anyhow, you know what she's like,' he went on, talking as though his wife were still alive – not dead and rapidly cooling in front of his eyes. 'Whatever happens, whatever life chucks at her, she just gets on with it. She doesn't like to bother no one.'

'But you must have known how bad she was,' Mary persisted. 'She must have been sick, or *some*thing. That doctor said she was riddled with it.'

'She does get tired,' Billy admitted. 'But she ignores me when I tell her to take a break. That's her all over, though, isn't it? You can't tell her nowt. Even when the pain's real bad, she just says I'm fussing over nothing.'

'She wouldn't even stop working,' Joey interjected quietly. 'Three bleedin' jobs she had. Kept at it right to the end.'

'*Three*?' Mary repeated numbly. 'Why didn't you stop her?'

'It ain't our fault,' Joey muttered defensively. 'It's like me dad said, you couldn't tell her nowt. She reckoned she loved it.'

'He's right,' Billy confirmed. 'Loves her work, she does.'

'Cancer.' Joey shook his head sadly. 'You wouldn't believe it, would you? Not our mam.'

'She's been talking about you a lot,' Billy went on. 'Going on all the while about how you'd come home soon, and how it was all going to get back to normal. Talks about the babby, an' all. Says he was proper bonny – like the big 'un here when he was little.'

'She *saw* him?' Mary gasped. 'She never said.'

'She wouldn't, would she?' Joey gave a tiny, sad smile. 'Too proud for her own good, her. Just like you, our Mary.'

'Aye, you're her spit, all right,' Billy agreed, leaning forward to pat his wife's cold hand. 'Mary this, Mary that. That's all we ever got from her these last few weeks. That's why our Joey come looking for you.'

Picking up the story, Joey said, 'It wasn't easy tracking you down, I can tell you. But I bumped into Paddy McKay down the pub last week and he said he'd seen you going to that house. I thought you must've been visiting a mate, or something, but when them idiots answered, I remembered what you'd said about marrying one of that lot and put two and two together.'

Mary was stunned to realise that her mother had never let on that she knew Mary was still in the Crescents – or, apparently, what she'd been doing for a living. It was a good job she *had* kept it secret, too. Joey would've kicked off good style if he'd known, and Mary would probably be sitting beside *Ali*'s deathbed right now. Wise old Mam.

'Thanks for looking for me, Joey. Sorry I put you to so much trouble.'

'It's all right,' he murmured, nodding towards the bed. 'I did it for her.'

Hearing the rattle and swish of a tea trolley behind them, Mary eased back the curtain and saw that the ward was beginning to come to life. Looking at her watch, she saw that it was almost seven a.m.

'I'd best get going,' she said, standing up. Patting Joey's

shoulder when he began to rise from his chair, she said, 'No, you stay with Dad. I'll get a taxi.' Leaning down to kiss her father's cheek then, she said, 'Bye, Dad. I'll come and see you soon, I promise.'

They both knew she wouldn't – not once the funeral was out of the way, anyway. With Agnes gone, there was nothing left to hold them together.

19

Ali's passport arrived on the morning of the funeral –
which he wouldn't have attended even if he'd been
invited.

Pouncing on it when he saw the distinctive Home Office
stamp, he tore the envelope open and gave a jubilant yell.

'Raiz! . . . *RAIZ!* Get down here!'

'What is it?' Raiz ran down the stairs with a concerned
look in his eyes. 'What's wrong?'

Thrusting the second envelope at him, Ali took his friend's
face in his hands and planted several kisses on his cheeks,
saying, 'We've done it, man! We've done it! We're free!'
Kissing the precious passport then, he slipped it into his
pocket and raced upstairs to pack.

Pulling his dust-covered suitcase down from the top of
the wardrobe, he tossed it onto the bed and unzipped it,
ignoring Mary who was sitting at the dressing table
attempting to make herself look presentable by plastering
her drawn face with make-up.

Ali's contempt for her had festered and grown in these
last few days, having to endure her moping about the place
as if *she*'d died, refusing to speak to anyone, and giving
them all dirty, accusing looks. There were times when he'd
had to fight himself not to tell her exactly what he thought
of her, and only the anticipation of this moment had
stopped him from walking out.

Mary would have reported him to the Home Office in a

heartbeat if she'd known that he'd been planning to leave her and move in with Caroline, the new woman in his life. But it was too late now. She'd well and truly missed her chance. He'd served his two years, and there was nothing that she or the authorities could do to stop him.

Tossing his clothes haphazardly into the case, Ali couldn't help but smile as he imagined Caroline's face when he gave her the good news. She would be so happy. And if she was happy, so was he.

Caroline was different from all the other women he'd fucked throughout his so-called marriage. Mary was prettier, despite the ravages of the needle which had shrivelled her once-curvaceous body to the disgusting, skinny mess it was today. But Caroline was more vibrant, more *alive*. Where Mary nagged for sex, Caroline *begged* – and that was a huge turn-on. And as for her *mouth* . . . Just thinking about her snakelike tongue gave him a hard-on.

'What are you doing?' Mary asked after watching him for a while in the mirror.

'Don't question me,' Ali told her icily. 'I'm going. That's all you need to know.'

'Where?' She turned to face him. 'And why now? Don't you think I've got enough to cope with today?'

'You don't seriously think I *care*, do you?' Shaking his head incredulously, Ali took his underwear from the drawer and dropped it in the case. 'Actually, no, I take that back,' he said then, turning to face her with a malicious smile twisting his lips. 'I *do* care – about *this*.' Pulling the passport from his pocket, he flapped it beneath her nose. 'It's all I've *ever* cared about. And now I've got it, I'm free to get the hell away from *you*!'

'You bastard,' Mary croaked.

'That's right,' he agreed, smirking nastily. 'I'm a bastard. But what are *you*? Shall I tell you?' Leaning over her, he brought his face down close to hers. 'You're a cheap, stupid, disgusting *whore*. Your mother must have been *so* proud of you.'

'Don't!' Mary cried, covering her face with her hands. 'Not today, Ali . . . *Please*.'

Yanking her hands aside, Ali gritted his teeth and snarled, 'Why? Don't you want to hear the truth? That I can't stand the sight of you. Can't bear to touch you?'

Wrenching her hands free, Mary tore at his hair and scratched his cheeks with her nails, crying, 'I hate you, you bastard! I *hate* you!'

'Oh, yeah?' Struggling to restrain her, Ali slapped her repeatedly across the face. 'Well, not half as much as I hate *you*, you disgusting slag!'

'What the hell's going on?' Lynne demanded, running in. 'Pack it in before someone calls the pigs. Me and Raiz have got gear out all over the fuckin' shop down there.'

'Don't blame me,' Ali snarled, using the interruption to toss Mary aside. 'It's her – she's a fucking crazy bitch. And she wonders why I'm leaving!' Zipping up his case, he snatched it up from the bed. Turning to Mary, he spat in her face and stalked from the room.

Blocking Mary's path when she tried to follow him, Lynne said, 'Let him go. You can't force him to stay if he doesn't want to.'

'You didn't hear what he said,' Mary yelled. 'He *spat* on me, for fuck's sake!'

'So wipe it off,' Lynne barked unsympathetically. 'Fuckin' hell, man, get a grip. I told you from the start he didn't give a toss about you, but you wouldn't listen, would you? It was shite, Mary – all of it.'

'He's my *husband*.'

'Bollocks! He's just a cheating cunt, and you know it.'

'Fuck off!' Bringing her hands up, Mary shoved Lynne

roughly away. 'You're just jealous 'cos Raiz doesn't give a toss about *you*.'

'Like I give a toss about *him*. He's hardly a fuckin' sex god, is he?'

'Like *Ali*, you mean?'

'Behave yourself! I've had hotter bleedin' curries.'

'What's that supposed to mean?'

'Figure it out, you thick bitch. We wasn't exactly *hiding* it.'

Mary felt the blood drain from her face. 'No way! You're lying.'

'Am I?' Folding her arms, Lynne raised a mocking eyebrow. 'Think back to when you were pregnant. *How* many times did you catch him coming out of my room?'

'He was in there talking to Raiz.' Mary gritted her teeth, her breath sounding ragged in her ears.

'If you say so.' Lynne gave a casual shrug. 'He was after me for ages before that an' all, but I kept saying no 'cos I didn't want to *hurt* you.' Shaking her head, she laughed nastily. 'Imagine that.'

'So what changed?' Mary's voice was icy now as she struggled to keep herself from attacking Lynne. She had to hear the full story first – gauge whether it was true, or if Lynne was just being spiteful.

'*You* did,' Lynne spat, her face contorting with contempt. 'Christ, have you *seen* yourself lately? Slopping about all over the place – moaning and whining if there's a bit of fucking mess on the floor.'

'We're not all as filthy as you.'

'Piss off, you cheeky bitch!' Lynne glared at her with genuine hatred in her eyes. 'That's half your problem, that – you think you're better than me. Well, you're *not*! You're exactly the fucking same.'

'I'm nothing like you,' Mary snarled. 'You're just a

disgusting *whore*, selling yourself to every Tom, Dick and Harry that'll have you.'

'And you *don't*?' Lynne retorted incredulously. 'Fuckin' hell, sweetheart . . . talk about deluding yourself!'

'Shut your mouth!'

'Why? Truth hurts, does it?'

'You wouldn't know the truth if it bit you in the arse, you skanky slag!'

Narrowing her eyes, Lynne said, 'Oh, you'd be surprised what I know, *bitch*. You've always thought you were better than me, but you don't know the half of it. All them times you moaned about him not giving you none? Well, he was getting it up for *me* no problem. And I wasn't the only one, neither.'

'Like he'd ever touch *you*,' Mary hissed, nostrils flaring as she struggled to contain herself. 'Know what he calls you behind your back? The scabby *minge*.'

'Maybe so,' Lynne retorted angrily. 'But at least he can't call me a *mug*. You wouldn't catch *me* working *my* arse off for a low-life murdering cunt who's never given a shit about me.' Pausing when she saw the confusion cross Mary's eyes, she smirked. 'Oh, yeah, you didn't know that one, did you? Remember that first night, when he convinced you to say you were his girlfriend 'cos those girls were hitting on him? Well, it was all *crap*. He'd *knifed* someone, and you were his alibi. So, *now* how do you feel, Lady Muck? Still think he ever gave a toss about you?'

'Liar!' Mary roared, lunging at Lynne, punching and biting and tearing at her hair. 'Dirty fuckin' *liar*!'

Running in when Lynne started screaming, Raiz saw what was happening and dragged Mary off her. Wrapping his arms around the younger woman, he lifted her feet off the floor and carried her out of the room.

'Get off me,' Mary yelled, struggling to get free herself as Raiz hauled her down the stairs. 'I'm gonna kill her!'

'No, you're not.' Raiz held on to her tightly. 'There's no point fighting over him. He's not worth it. Now, just calm down and I'll let you go. Okay?'

Slumping in his arms after a moment, Mary nodded. He was right. There *was* no point fighting. This wasn't really happening – it was just a nightmare. She'd wake up in a minute and everything would be back the way it used to be.

Letting her go when he trusted that she'd behave, Raiz opened the front door and ushered her outside. Pulling the door to behind him, he lit a couple of cigarettes and passed one to her. Thanking him, Mary walked to the balcony ledge and leaned her elbows on it.

'Is it true?' she asked when he came and stood beside her. 'About her and Ali.'

Sighing, Raiz nodded. 'And before you ask, yes, I did know.'

Frowning, she turned to face him. 'So why didn't you do anything about it?'

'Like what?'

'Like kick their fucking *heads* in. Christ, Raiz, she's your *wife*. And he's supposed to be your best mate. Doesn't it bother you that he went behind your back?'

'No. He's welcome to her, if that's what he wants.'

'And is it?' Mary gritted her teeth as the simmering anger began to resurface. 'Is that what this is all about? Is he going off with her?'

'I doubt it.' Raiz snorted softly. 'He's got more sense than that.'

'So, where *has* he gone?'

Torn between putting her out of her misery and loyalty to Ali, Raiz didn't answer for a while. Despite everything, he liked Mary and didn't want to contribute to her heartache. But Ali would be his friend long after all of the women were gone.

'I'm not his keeper,' he said at last. 'I'm his brother. The only family we have is each other.'

'What about me and *her*?' Mary peered at him with real pain in her eyes. 'We're your family, too.'

'No offence, but you're not,' Raiz said, frowning apologetically. 'We all knew these marriages weren't real.'

A tear trickled a slow path down Mary's cheek. 'Mine was.'

'But Ali's wasn't,' Raiz reminded her gently. 'You must have known that deep down.'

'No, I didn't,' she murmured, turning her face from him when her chin began to tremble uncontrollably.

Sucking hard on the cigarette until she'd got herself under control, Mary blew a thick plume of smoke into the air and watched it disperse in the breeze.

'What about that other thing?' she said then. 'About him knifing someone?'

'Oh, Christ,' Raiz muttered, dropping his face into his hands and pressing his thumbs into his temples, which were beginning to throb.

Mary's stomach gave an unpleasant lurch at his reaction. Surely it wasn't true? Surely Lynne had just been spouting her usual brand of nasty, spiteful shit? Despite everything, Mary didn't want to believe that the husband she had adored was capable of *that*.

Steeling herself for the worst, she said, 'Tell me, Raiz. Please . . . I need to know.'

Taking a deep breath, he forced himself to meet and hold her gaze, knowing that she *knew* he found it impossible to look anyone in the eye when he was lying.

'There's nothing to tell,' Raiz lied, injecting as much sincerity into his voice as he could manage. 'Whatever Lynne said, she was just trying to hurt you because she's jealous of you. You're better than her, and she can't stand it.'

Only half-believing him, but willing it to be true, Mary nodded and said, 'Thanks.'

'You don't have to thank me,' he replied guiltily. 'You're

too good for her – *and* Ali. I've always known it, even if you haven't.'

'So, why did he betray me if I'm so good?'

'Because he's a fool.'

Frowning, Raiz finished his cigarette and tossed the butt over the ledge. He felt as if he was betraying his best friend, but *some*body owed this girl an explanation. She hadn't done anything to deserve this pain. And he had a feeling that she wouldn't give up on Ali unless she knew exactly what he'd done.

'Look, I'm not going into detail,' he said after a moment, 'but I *will* tell you that he's gone to live with another woman. Her name's Caroline, and he's been seeing her for months.'

'Go on,' Mary prompted when he hesitated.

Glancing at her colour-drained face, Raiz felt as guilty as if he'd slit her throat.

'I shouldn't have said anything,' he murmured, dropping his face into his hands again. 'I'm so sorry, Mary.'

'I need to know,' she insisted, clutching at his arm and forcing him to look at her. '*Please*, Raiz . . . Tell me.'

'There's not much more to tell.' He sighed wearily. '*I* don't like her, but he obviously does. She's lasted longer than all of the others, anyway.'

'What does she look like?' Mary's cheek muscles were jerking as she struggled to keep herself from screaming.

'Fat.' Raiz shrugged. 'Red hair, big mouth.' Shaking his head with disgust, he added, 'Not a patch on you.'

Checking his watch then, he saw that it was almost time for her to meet her family for the funeral. Taking her hand in his, he squeezed it.

'Look, take my advice and go and say goodbye to your mother, because that's more important than *any* of this. Then do yourself a favour and get the hell away from here while you've still got a chance to start again.' Peering deep into her eyes for a long moment, he gave her hand a final squeeze and went back into the house.

Seeing the hearse turning onto the road up ahead, Mary pulled herself together. Raiz was right about this being more important than everything else right now, and she refused to allow Ali to take precedence over it.

There was time enough to deal with him when today was over and done.

20

Lynne and Raiz had gone by the time Mary got home from the funeral. Lynne had left a note propped on the table, threatening to have Mary arrested for assault if she hadn't moved out by the end of the week. That was all. No 'Sorry' . . . No nothing to make up for the pain she'd caused.

Screwing the message up, Mary threw it at the wall. Bending down when she noticed a second piece of paper sticking out from under the table, she smirked when she saw that it was a note to Lynne from Raiz: an address in Salford where he wanted her to forward his and Ali's mail.

Well, well . . . So, Ali thought he'd got away scot-free, did he?

Clutching the address, Mary went upstairs to get changed.

Standing naked in front of the mirror, she really looked at herself for the first time in a long while. Saying goodbye to her mother had lifted the last of the veils from her eyes, and she was horrified by what she saw.

Not yet twenty-two, she looked like an ugly old hag, with grey, sunken cheeks, and hollow, black-ringed eyes. Purple track-marks laddered both arms, her once-full breasts resembled the empty sacs of a seventy-year-old, and the skin of her stomach looked as if it had been shrink-wrapped onto her ribs.

No wonder Ali had been desperate to leave if this was what he saw across the pillow each night . . .

Cutting the thought dead as soon as it crossed her mind, Mary turned her back on the disturbing reflection. No *way* was she excusing him again. From the start, he'd blamed her and manipulated her, using her – if Lynne was to be believed – as a cover for the worst possible of crimes. And now, possibly worse than everything else, he'd abandoned her for a bitch called *Caroline*. Well, no more. She'd been a fool for long enough. It was payback time.

Sitting at the computer in the library a short while later, Mary tapped in the date that she wanted to look up. It was easy enough to remember: Christmas Day – and hadn't she thought they'd all come at once, stupid bitch!

A few seconds passed before the front page from the December 27th edition of the *Evening News* appeared. Staring at it, she was sickened by the stark confirmation of the headline.

MOSS SIDE MAN STABBED TO DEATH.

Reading the article, she learned that the body of 33-year-old Terry Hardman had been discovered in an alley behind a block of flats housing refugees on Claremont Road in the early hours of Christmas Day morning. He'd suffered a single, fatal stab wound to the heart, and the police said they were following a number of leads.

Forwarding to the following day, under the headline MURDERED MAN KNOWN TO POLICE, she read that Terry Hardman was a well-known criminal with a string of convictions for possessing and supplying heroin and cocaine; GBH; witness intimidation; and an arrest on suspicion of manslaughter – charge dropped before it reached court. The police now said that they believed Hardman had been targeted by rival dealers, and they were still following leads.

Pressing on, Mary saw that the 'leads' hadn't come to

anything. Nobody was ever charged with the murder, and the story was quickly relegated to the inside pages. Soon, it was just a couple of lines, stating that the police had, to all intents and purposes, given up on ever solving the case due to a 'disappointing lack of public cooperation'.

The only other mention of Terry Hardman when she entered his name into the search box was in an article more than a year later, concerning a man called Kenny Butler who had, apparently, been Hardman's right-hand man. Having taken over when Hardman died, he'd been arrested at Manchester Airport collecting a large consignment of heroin that the authorities had been tracking.

That was the last mention of Terry Hardman.

Numbed by the realisation that Lynne had been telling the truth after all, Mary stared off into the distance. How long had Lynne known, she wondered, and why hadn't she mentioned it before?

Lynne must have been in on it from the start, she concluded when she'd gone over and over it all in her mind. Ali was way too tight-fisted to give away for nothing all the gear he'd given them when he'd first moved in on them. It was obviously part of the plan – payment to Lynne for setting him up with a willing victim, and a sure-fire way of keeping Mary under control.

'Excuse me, love . . . We're closing. You'll have to go now.'

Looking up, Mary saw that the librarian was waiting to switch off the computer. Apologising, she got up and wandered out into the darkening afternoon. Lighting a cigarette as the door was locked behind her, she gazed around the quiet street with narrowed eyes, wondering how best to use the knowledge that she now possessed.

If she reported Ali, she was in danger of being labelled an accomplice. He *had* come straight to her after he'd done it, after all – stayed the night, and then moved in.

Why would anyone believe that she had been absolutely innocent?

But what if she didn't report him? He'd be free to set up his cosy little love nest with this new bitch he was screwing – and Mary was determined not to slink away and allow *that* to happen.

She wanted to destroy him for that – destroy them *both*.

Taking the address Raiz had left from her pocket, she marched to the nearest phone box with the rage of betrayal burning fiercely in her heart.

Going home when she had done what she had to do, she spent the rest of the night packing everything she owned into bin bags.

Mary took the first flat she viewed the following morning.

Described in the ad as a 'pleasant, compact apartment in a sought-after area, close to amenities', it turned out to be a poky little dive in a scruffy block overlooking Moss Side's indoor market. But it was cheap, and furnished, and far enough from the Crescents that there was little danger of bumping into anyone she knew.

Taking a cab back to Lynne's, she told the driver to wait, then ran up to the house and gathered her bags together. Walking out again, she left the door wide open behind her – knowing full well that the local scallies would strip the place bare before she'd reached the foot of the stairs.

Dropping her bags off at the new flat, Mary went out and spent the last of her money stocking up on the basics to see her through the next few hellish weeks.

She'd deliberately missed her last fix and withdrawal was already starting to kick in. Her entire body was shaking, her teeth chattering madly as the shivers tore a painful path through her muscles. It would have been so easy to anaesthetise herself just one last time, but she'd made up her mind and there was no way she was giving in now.

Leaving everything else where it lay, Mary threw a sheet on the bed and dragged her quilt around herself – all set for the hardest fight of her life.

21

Cold turkey was the worst experience of Mary's entire life. There were times when she truly believed that she was dying; when the pain was hammering at her bones and drilling into her soul, and sweat was gushing from every pore as the toxins poisoning her body burst out from both ends at once. Her internal thermostat had a complete breakdown – one minute freezing, the next boiling hot. And her mind played tricks, creating terrifying hallucinations in the dark.

Slowly but surely, these symptoms receded.

Waking up one morning after her first real sleep in what seemed like months, Mary felt weaker than she'd ever felt in her life before – but stronger, too. She had fought the devil and won. Life could only get better from here on in.

Dragging herself out of bed, she forced herself to eat a round of stale toast, washing it down with a cup of sweet tea. Nauseous after reacquainting her stomach with food, she got dressed and ventured outside to escape the stifling stench of illness in her flat.

Walking aimlessly, Mary was surprised to find herself at the gates of the park where she and Jane had spent so much of their time when they were wagging school. Smiling nostalgically, she went inside and headed for their old bench beside the murky lake.

Sitting down, she felt the tears pricking at her eyes as she traced a finger over the names they had carved into the wood: 'Jane luvs Del' . . . 'Mary 4 Mick 4 eva'.

It had been so childish, but they'd had so much fun doing it. So much fun doing *every*thing, back then. Where had all that innocence gone?

Gazing at the swans floating serenely among the discarded chip wrappers and beer cans littering the water, Mary felt a sense of peace wash over her. She hadn't thought she'd get through those awful times when she'd lost Jane and been kicked out, but she had. Just like she'd get through this now.

Closing her eyes, she stuffed her hands into her pockets and leaned her head back, enjoying the feel of the weak sun on her face, the cool breeze brushing across her cheeks. This was life as it should be lived – not that awful dark existence she'd been enduring since she had met Ali.

Several hours passed before she finally got up and went home. Refreshed from being out in the fresh air, she slept like a log that night.

Sitting at her window opposite the gate at the rear of the park, Tina Barrett narrowed her eyes when she saw the skinny woman making her way to the bench by the lake for the fifth day on the trot.

Innate nosiness getting the better of her, she slipped her coat on and wandered across the road.

After strolling twice around the lake, she casually sat down at the far end of the bench and lit a cigarette, wondering how to start a conversation with the woman who was gazing into the water as if she were in a trance.

'Cold, isn't it?' Tina said after a minute.

'Uh?' Confused, Mary blinked and looked around. Surprised to see that she had company, she said, 'Sorry, I was miles away.'

'Wish *I* was.' Tina smiled. 'A nice hot beach would be heaven on Earth right now. Want a smoke?' She offered the pack to Mary.

'Er, yeah . . . Thanks.' Taking a cigarette, Mary lit it and sat back, glancing at the woman out of the corner of her eye. She was hugely fat, with a too-short, too-tight curly perm, and red, broken-veined cheeks.

Eyeing her in like manner, Tina sussed that Mary wasn't as old as she had initially thought. And she guessed from her pallor that she'd been ill. Probably drugs, she surmised – either that, or cancer.

Shit! She hoped she wasn't chatting to a terminal case . . . She'd end up having to listen to all the miserable details – and she couldn't be doing with that.

'Do you live round here?' Mary asked just then, feeling obliged to make conversation since the woman had been kind enough to share her smokes.

Now it was Tina's turn to say 'Uh?' and look confused.

'I said, do you live round here?' Mary's eyebrows puckered. She hoped this woman wasn't one of those care-in-the-community freaks. That was the last thing she needed.

'Sorry . . . Yeah.' Tina gave a backward jerk of her head. 'Over there. What about you?'

'By the market.'

'Oh, right.'

Lapsing into silence again, they finished their cigarettes. Then, flicking her butt into the lake, Tina said, 'It's bloody freezing out here. Fancy a brew?'

Looking at her, Mary thought, *What the hell.* If she *was* mad, at least it would give her something to laugh about when she got back to her own boring flat.

'Yeah, all right,' she said.

Slapping her hands down on her knees, the woman pushed herself up with a grunt. 'My name's Tina, by the way,' she said, heading for the gate.

'Mary.' Standing up, Mary followed her out of the park and across the road.

She was surprised when Tina went up the path of a small house on the end of a row of three new-builds. She'd assumed that the woman lived in one of the flats in the ramshackle shared houses that lined the rest of the street. This looked like a proper family-type house.

'Are you married?' she asked when Tina slotted the key into the lock and went inside.

'Am I buggery!' Tina grunted, tossing her keys onto the small hall table and hanging her coat over the stair banister. 'I'm on me own since my mum passed on. It's small, but it suits me. Tea or coffee?'

'Tea, please.'

Following Tina into the tiny, spotlessly clean kitchen, Mary felt a twinge of envy as she gazed around and saw that it contained everything you could possibly need: microwave, fridge-freezer, deep-fat fryer, matching blue kettle and toaster. There was even a free-standing electric can-opener.

And she'd thought she was doing well because she'd bought herself a portable TV off the flea market. It was pathetic.

'Coming?' Picking up the tray onto which she'd loaded the cups and a plate of biscuits, Tina carried it through to the equally nice lounge. Putting it down on the table, she flopped into a well-worn, comfy-looking armchair with a satisfied sigh.

Perching on the edge of the couch, Mary clasped her hands together between her knees. This was all so respectable, she almost felt too dirty to be here.

'Make yourself comfortable,' Tina said, picking up the half-smoked spliff she'd left in the ashtray. 'Fancy a toke? You look like you need it.'

Mary's eyes widened. 'You do draw?'

'Doesn't everyone?' Tina gave her a questioning smile.

'Bloody hell, girl, I wouldn't have had you down as a *straight*.'

'I'm not,' Mary replied, frowning worriedly. 'But please tell me that's all you do?'

'Yeah.' Tina gave her a funny look. 'Apart from a drink, anyhow. Why, what's up?'

'Long story,' Mary said, sighing wearily.

Intrigued, Tina lit the spliff and settled back in her chair. 'I'm listening.'

The quick brew turned into several as Mary unburdened herself over the next few hours. Listening, as promised, Tina shook her head, tut-tutted and sympathised.

'You *have* been through it, haven't you?' she said when Mary was all talked out. 'But it sounds like you've got it sorted. You *are* going to stay off the gear, right?'

'Too right,' Mary stated emphatically. 'I can't believe I ever let myself sink so low in the first place. My mam must have seen right through me – and there was me thinking I was doing an ace job of fooling her.'

'Well, I must say I did wonder when I first saw you,' Tina admitted. Then, giving a throaty chuckle, she added, 'I'm just glad it wasn't cancer.'

Laughing when Tina had explained this, Mary said, 'That's all right, I thought *you* were mad.'

'I might be, for all you know,' Tina deadpanned. 'You'll just have to wait and see.'

Smiling, Mary decided that she liked Tina. You knew where you were with people like her – they said exactly what they thought; no beating round the bush, no bullshit. It made a refreshing change after all the lies of the past few years.

Yes, she could easily see herself becoming good friends with Tina – and that was exactly what she needed right now.

PART THREE

22

Jane sang along with the radio as she got ready. Lining her eyes carefully, she waggled her hips as she slicked on a layer of glossy pink lipstick and pulled a brush through her shiny blonde bob. Stepping back when she'd finished, she looked herself over and smiled. Gorgeous – even if she did say so herself.

Pulling her jacket on, she checked that all the plugs were switched off and headed out to work with a spring in her step. She was only a barmaid at The Crown down the road, but she loved it. In fact, she loved most things about her life, these days.

A lot had changed in the years since she'd lost David. She'd sunk so low after that, she'd thought she would never get back on her feet. But she had. Time was like that. It moved on regardless – dragging you along in its wake, forcing you to eat, breathe, sleep . . . Recover.

Still, that was the past, and Jane didn't visit that place too often – not even in her head. Right now, the only thing she had to worry about was her weight.

Not that it really bothered her. She quite liked her size, as it happened. Pleasantly plump, she liked to call it. And at least she had boobs now – even if they did come with their own support-cushion of a stomach. The men at The Crown certainly seemed to like it, anyway. There wasn't a night went by that she didn't get a compliment – and that wasn't bad going for a chubby twenty-don't-ask-year-old.

Alf was waiting on the doorstep when she got to the pub.

'Thought you weren't coming,' he grumbled, shoving the keys into her hand.

'As if I'd let you down,' Jane said, helping him down the steps. 'You sure you're up to driving tonight?'

'There's nowt wrong with me,' he insisted, staggering towards his clapped-out old Rover. 'Nowt Sadie can't fix with a bit of hanky-panky, anyhow. See you tomorrow. And don't forget to lock up.'

Smiling, Jane waved as Alf crunched into gear and took off. Wincing when he almost took the wing off a parked car, she shook her head. His eyes were deteriorating, but he wouldn't admit it in a million years – not if it meant giving up driving, which would put an end to his Tuesday-night dates with his two-hundred-year-old ballroom-partner-cum-girlfriend. They were a pathetic sight – him in his white suits and dickie bows, with his spit-lick hair dyed boot-polish black; her in her frothy sequinned frocks, her thinning hair a garish orange. But you couldn't knock the walking corpses for trying to keep the romance alive.

The usual three-pints-a-night merchants were sitting around the bar when Jane went inside.

'Evening, luvvies,' she greeted them, making her way behind the pumps. 'How's the wife, Ken? . . . Had any luck at the bookie's, Phil? . . . That cream sort your 'roids, Harry?'

'Still a bitch, same as ever.'

'Must've handed a grand over that counter this year, and the bastards still haven't give none back.'

'Worked a treat, thanks, pet.'

Smiling, Jane hung her coat up and wiped away the spills that Alf had left behind. Now the chat was out of the way, all she had to do was refill whoever's glass was empty then she'd be free to watch *EastEnders* in peace. It was back-breaking work, but someone had to do it.

The night crawled by at its usual Tuesday snail's pace and Jane had been yawning for half an hour solid when the door opened at just gone ten. Taking her elbows off the bar when three men and two women she'd never seen before came in, she gave them a welcoming smile – amused by the muttered complaints of the regulars who hated strangers invading their space. Nice as it was lounging around all night, she loved a bit of new blood every now and then – it woke her up.

One of the men came to the bar while the others went to sit around a table beside the door.

'What can I get you?' Jane asked.

'Two rum and cokes, and three double Scotches,' he said, adding with a wink, 'and one for yourself, gorgeous.'

'Celebrating?'

'Too right!' Snatching up one of the Scotches when she'd poured it, he held it aloft. 'To Strangeways . . . May it burn to the ground – and everyone in it!' Downing the drink, he banged the glass down and ordered another.

'Got a thirst on, have you?' she teased.

'God, I can't tell you,' he groaned. 'It's been torture sniffing the hops from my cell night after night. They shouldn't be allowed to put a brewery so close to a prison, but that's what the cunts get off on, innit? I ain't *never* going back inside, me.'

'He says that now,' one of the women at the table shouted. 'But he'll be back inside in a week, you watch.'

'Fuck I will!'

'Aw, shut up yakking and fetch us our drinks,' one of the two other men yelled impatiently.

'Yeah, get a move on,' the woman agreed, picking up an ashtray and banging it down on the table. 'Drink . . . drink . . . drink . . .'

'Settle down,' Jane called to her. 'You'll have us closed

down if you're not careful, *then* where you gonna celebrate?'

'You tell her!' the impatient man cackled. ''Bout time someone put her in her place.'

Looking up from the pint she was pulling, Jane grinned at the woman, letting her know she was only teasing.

Slapping the man beside her, the woman grinned back. Then, squinting, she tilted her head to the side and peered hard at Jane. Getting up after a moment, she pushed her way out from behind the table and approached the bar with a strange smile on her face.

'It *is* you,' she said when she was right in front of Jane. 'Oh, my God, I can't believe it! Don't you recognise me?'

Peering back at her, Jane frowned. She did look familiar, but Jane couldn't quite place her.

'Mary!' the woman blurted out. 'Your bestest mate in the whole wide world!'

'No way!' Jane gasped, bringing a hand up to her mouth and staring at her in disbelief.

'Yeah!' Mary affirmed, grinning broadly. 'God, I haven't changed *that* much.'

'You bloody have,' Jane countered, laughing even as her eyes filled with tears. 'You had dark hair last time I saw you. When did you go all Marilyn?'

'About the same time I lost my virginity for the umpteenth time,' Mary quipped. 'Anyhow, never mind that – get your arse round here and give us a hug! Jeezus, I can't believe it's really you. How long has it been?'

'Too long.' Jane blinked rapidly as she rushed around the bar. 'I never thought I'd see you again.'

'Me neither.' Mary hugged her tightly. 'Christ, I missed you when you left. What happened? Did you have the baby?'

'Yeah.' Swiping at the tears, Jane nodded. 'A boy.'

'*Really*? Wow! What's his name?'

'Well, I called him David, but I've no idea what he's called now. He was taken off me after I got home. Haven't seen him since.'

'Oh, shit, I'm sorry.' Mary gave her a sympathetic smile.

'It's all right,' Jane told her, shrugging. 'It was years ago. Anyway, what about *you*?' Holding on to her friend's hands, she stepped back, shaking her head fondly. 'I was dying to see you after I'd had him. I took him round to yours, but your mum said she hadn't seen you. How is she, by the way?'

'Dead,' Mary told her quietly. Then, shaking off the flicker of sadness that always came over her when she thought about her mother, she said, 'But that's was years ago, an' all. So, what have you been up to?'

'How long have you got?' Jane grinned.

Before Mary could answer, one of the men yelled at her to quit gossiping and get her arse in gear before they missed all the free drinks. Flipping a V over her shoulder, Mary rolled her eyes.

'My fella, Dave,' she explained with a sheepish grin. 'I suppose I'd best get going. Him and his mate only came out of nick this morning and we're doing a celebration crawl. We only popped in here for a quick one on our way to a club. Here . . . you don't fancy coming, do you?'

'I can't,' Jane told her regretfully. 'I'm on till eleven, and there's no one here but me.'

'Close up early,' Mary pleaded, squeezing her hands. 'Come on, it'll be great.'

'I'd love to.' Jane sighed heavily. 'But I can't – honest. This lot would never forgive me, and my boss would have a fit.'

Just then, the other woman in the group came over. Standing beside Mary, she looked Jane up and down.

'Oi! Don't be giving her the evil eye.' Mary nudged her sharply with her elbow. 'This is Jane – my best mate from when we were kids. We haven't seen each other for years. Jane, this is Tina.'

'Her best mate *now*,' Tina said, giving Jane a grudging smile. 'Dave says hurry up or he's off,' she told Mary then.

'He'll go, as well,' Mary grumbled. 'Look, have you got a pen and paper, Jane? I'll give you my address. You can come round when you've got a night off and we'll have a proper get-together.'

'You in tomorrow?' Jane asked, reaching behind the bar for the order pad.

'Yeah, Dave's got his mates coming round to watch the United match.' Mary jotted the address down and gave it to her. 'Come round at about seven. We can have a proper natter without being disturbed.'

'Oi! Mary! Last warning . . .'

'Better go,' Mary said, backing towards the door. 'Don't forget to come.'

'As if!' Jane grinned, waving until Mary had gone.

Going back behind the bar then, she beamed at the curious men.

'That was my best mate.'

'Very nice, love.' Smiling, Harry shoved his empty glass towards her. 'I'll have a stout, seeing as we're celebrating.'

Phoning Alf the next evening, Jane did something she hadn't done in months and pulled a sickie, putting on a pathetic voice and telling him she'd come down with a bug. Thanking him when he told her to take a couple of days off and have a proper rest, she felt as guilty as hell when she hung up. But she soon shook it off. Some things were just too important to miss.

Taking a bus to town, and another to Moss Side, Jane's excitement began to turn to apprehension. Getting off at her stop, she gazed at the all too familiar scenery with a sickening sense of déjà vu. It had been almost ten years since she'd been there, but nothing had changed. It was like a time warp: same old dirty streets, same old shifty-looking people. Cheetham Hill, where she lived now, was a grotty dump, too, but here there was an added dimension of darkness – a shadow of danger that seemed to envelop everything.

Making her way to where Mary now lived, the depressing high-rise overlooking the indoor market, Jane's stomach churned when she glimpsed the hulking tops of the Crescents above the terraced houses opposite. Averting her gaze, she stared fixedly at the flats instead, trying to guess which was Mary's from the curtains hanging in the windows – anything to keep the memories in check: her mum, her dad, Aunt Margaret, Del . . . David.

Reaching Mary's door at last, she rang the bell with a shaking hand. She shouldn't have come. It was too late to pick up the pieces after all this time. They didn't know each other any more. What if they absolutely hated each other and had nothing to say? She should have made an excuse and stayed away, leaving the sweet memories intact . . .

Opening the door, Mary rushed out with a delighted smile on her face. Throwing her arms round Jane, she said, 'God, it's great to see you! I'm so glad you came. You look fantastic. Come in.' Holding on to her hand, she pulled her inside, still babbling excitedly: 'Let me get you a drink. I got some Jamaican rum in specially, but I've got brandy, whisky and lager as well, so you can take your pick. Shit, remember your mam and her gin . . . ?'

'Mmm.' A little overwhelmed by the enthusiastic welcome, Jane smiled tightly.

Following Mary into the living room, she was a little dismayed to find all the same people from the night before sitting there. Mary had said that Dave and his mates would be watching the football, but Jane had half hoped that they'd have changed their minds and gone out. It would have been nice to have a few hours alone, just the two of them.

'This is Dave,' Mary said, beaming proudly as she introduced him. 'I've already bored him stupid talking about you, so I'll give you all the gossip about him in a bit.'

'You bleedin' won't,' he grunted.

'Don't get your dick in a twist,' she teased. 'I wasn't talking about *that*.' Turning back to Jane, Mary gave her a conspiratorial grin, mouthing, *Men!* Then, aloud, she said, 'Take no notice of grumpy drawers. He's just miffed that he won't be able to watch the match in peace.'

'Yeah, I will,' Dave piped up again. 'You lot can piss off in the kitchen where you belong and leave us in peace. It's serious man-business, footie.'

Dismissing this with a tut, Mary said, 'These are Dave's mates – John and Jim. Bit confusing, I know, but you'll soon get used to them. And you already know Tina, don't you?'

'Yeah.' Smiling at the woman – and getting the barest of lip twitches in return – Jane pushed her hands deeper into her pockets. This was going to be horrible.

'Oi, shift your arse,' Dave grumbled. 'They'll be calling the match off in a minute thinking there's a fuckin' storm brewing – the shadow you're casting on the screen.'

Blushing furiously when the men burst out laughing, Jane moved as far away from the TV as possible.

'Stop being such a bastard!' Mary slapped at Dave's head. 'What did I say about being nice to her? Take no notice, Jane.'

'Yeah, take no notice,' Dave agreed, twisting his head to wink at Jane. 'I'm only messing. You're not *that* fat. Not like you, eh, Tina?'

'Fuck off, you skinny twat!'

'Ooh, go on . . . I love it when you talk dirty.'

Hissing, 'Stop showing me up,' Mary gave him a warning glare and pushed Jane towards the kitchen. Motioning with a jerk of her head for Tina to follow, she said, 'Come on, girls, we'll have more peace in here. *And* we'll have all the booze to ourselves.'

'Here, don't be letting Tina-tum-tum loose on my Scotch,' Dave yelled after her. 'I haven't had any yet.'

Sticking her fingers up, Mary backed into the kitchen and slammed the door in his face.

'Sorry about that, Jane. He's a right wind-up sometimes.'

'Never mind her,' Tina complained, parking herself on a kitchen chair with a scowl. 'It's me he insulted.'

'Yeah, but *you* know he's only messing.' Reaching up, Mary took three glasses from the cupboard. 'Jane might think he means it.'

Jane suspected that he did, but she kept her opinion to herself. He was Mary's boyfriend, and she was obviously fond of him. Anyway, he was right about Tina – she *was* gross, and not too nice, from the little that Jane had seen of her so far. She had a face like a vicious backyard dog – and a snarling gob to match.

When they were all seated, Mary poured the drinks and handed them out. Holding hers up, she said, 'To women – God help us!'

'And death to all men,' Tina added with a grunt.

'They've got a word for people like you,' Mary chuckled.

'Well, it ain't dyke, so don't even go there.'

'No, that other word . . .' Mary gave a thoughtful frown. 'I know its misogynist when men hate women, but what d'y' call it when it's the other way round?'

'*Piss*-ognynist,' Tina deadpanned. 'I sure as hell hate the pissy-arsed bastards.'

Jane smiled. Maybe Tina wasn't so bad, after all. At least she seemed to have a sense of humour.

Resting her elbow on the table, Mary propped her chin on her hand and gazed at Jane.

'God, you look amazing, girl. I love your hair short like that.'

'Yeah, I like it.' Jane self-consciously reached up and slotted it behind her ear. 'So much better than when we were kids and it just used to hang around my face.'

'So, what else has changed?' Mary asked. 'What have you been doing with yourself?'

'God, where do I start?'

'With the baby. That was the last time I saw you, wasn't it?'

'I can't believe it's been so long,' Jane murmured wistfully. 'You haven't changed a bit – well, apart from *your* hair, obviously. You're still as gorgeous as ever.' Pausing, she peered closely at Mary's face. She'd always been so beautiful, and time hadn't stripped her of it. Yes, she had a few lines around the eyes, but she still had that certain something about her that had made all the boys want to get her into bed. Jane had envied her so much back then – wanting to look like her, smell like her, *be* her.

'It seems like yesterday in some ways, doesn't it?' she said. 'But like a lifetime ago, too.'

'So, you had a baby?' Tina chipped in peevishly, forcing herself into their cosy little reconnection. Mary had been her best mate for almost six years, and she wasn't too happy about this Jane tart turning up out of the blue and monopolising her.

Snapping out of her nostalgic haze, Jane nodded. 'Yeah. But I was only fifteen, so I had to give him up.'

'Bet that was your mam's doing.' Mary sneered. 'She'd never have let you keep it. *Far* too shameful.'

'Actually, it wasn't her in the end,' Jane said. 'She tried telling me to get rid of him, but I told her to get stuffed. It was the Social Services, after I went to them for help. They put me in a home for under-age mothers and did a *proper* job on me – convinced me I was too young to look after him.'

'You were,' Tina interjected disapprovingly. 'Sorry,' she

said when she got a warning frown from Mary. 'But that's my opinion. It ain't fair, leaving babies with kids who can't even look after themselves.'

'That's what *they* said,' Jane murmured. 'And they were right, I know that now. I thought I was so grown-up at the time, but I wasn't.'

'Must have been tough?' Mary gave her a sympathetic smile.

'Yeah, but it would have been even tougher if I'd tried to keep him with no money and nowhere to live.' Sighing deeply, Jane shook her head. 'Anyway, never mind that. What about you? Have you got kids?'

'Not me,' Tina said bluntly. 'I'd rather die than go through all that. Give me a cat any day.'

'I had one, but he died just after he was born.' Downing her drink, Mary lit a cigarette and took a deep drag.

'Oh, God, I'm sorry,' Jane said quietly. 'And there's me moaning 'cos I gave mine up. You must have been to hell and back.'

'I survived.' Mary shrugged, hiding the pain in her eyes behind a wall of smoke. 'Anyway, his dad was such a cunt, it was probably for the best. He was a useless husband, and he'd have been a worse father.'

'You were married, then?'

'If you can call it that, yeah. He only did it to get a passport. He took off as soon as he had it – on the morning of me mam's funeral, would you believe.'

'Bastard,' Jane gasped.

'Too right,' Tina agreed. 'Should have seen the state of her after. You'd have thought she was *dead* if you couldn't hear her breathing, she was that skinny.'

'Oh, you were there, then?' Jane asked, noticing the glint of bitterness in the other woman's eyes. 'Did *you* know that's what he was up to?'

'If I'd laid eyes on the little shit, I'd have known,' Tina

replied scathingly. 'All them refugees are the same, and I'd have told her not to trust him from the start, but I only met her after he'd gone.' Turning to Mary, she smiled. 'Got you back on your feet, though, didn't I, Mare? Kept you on the straight and narrow.'

'Yeah, you were great,' Mary confirmed, giving Jane a despairing side glance. Tina *had* helped – a lot – but it was years ago now, and it pissed Mary off that the other woman still insisted on treating her like a recovering invalid. Tina was so protective sometimes, Mary wished she'd never told her in the first place. But she *had* been a good mate, and Mary wasn't about to start knocking her.

'Anyway, enough of this maudlin rubbish,' she said, snatching up the bottle and refilling their glasses. 'Let's get back to positives. How long have you been working at that pub, Jane?'

'About two years.' Jane smiled fondly. 'The pay's crap, but I like it. Alf – the landlord – pretty much lets me get on with running it, so it's cool.'

Peering at her, Mary shook her head. 'Never thought *you*'d end up a barmaid. I always thought you'd be a doctor, or a lawyer, or something.'

'*Did* you?' Jane was genuinely surprised.

'God, *yeah*,' Mary laughed. 'The way your mam ponced about like you were the royal family, or something. She used to look at me like I'd just crawled out of some dog's arse-hole. I thought she'd have you straight in the uni when she got you away from *my* bad influence.'

'Like they'd have *had* me,' Jane chuckled. 'I wasn't exactly bright, was I?'

'Not bright,' Mary scoffed, turning to Tina. 'This from the kid who walked straight into the top set at school.'

'Only 'cos my mum convinced them I'd been top of my class at my old school,' Jane admitted, blushing. 'They must have got a hell of a shock when they realised how thick I was.'

'You were never thick,' Mary told her fondly. 'You were just insecure. And who could blame you, with a mother like yours? I hated her for the way she treated you. But I got my own back. You should have seen the bitch's face when I offered her out.'

'You didn't!' Jane's eyes widened. 'How come?'

'It was the day they sent you away,' Mary explained, grinning wickedly. 'I didn't know, obviously, so when you didn't call for me, I went to yours. Christ, she was in one – telling me it was all my fault, and how dare I show my face there. Well, I didn't have a clue what she was on about, so I let her have it good-style. Told her she was a disgrace for getting pissed all the time and making your life a misery.'

'Oh, my God,' Jane laughed. 'I bet she went mad.'

'Oh, she *tried*,' Mary confirmed, smirking. 'Called me a cheeky bitch and went to slap me, so I called her bluff and told her to bring it on.'

'What did she do?'

'Nowt.' Mary shrugged. 'Your dad came out and dragged her in. That's when I found out about the baby. I don't think he believed that I didn't know anything about it, but he was cool. Anyway, I never saw them again after that. I got a job and ended up falling out with my mam and had to move out. Last I heard, they'd moved.'

'Yeah, I got told when I rang his office,' Jane murmured, her eyes glinting with sadness. 'It was two years after I lost David, and I know I should have done it sooner, but I was too messed up. Anyway, they wouldn't tell me where he'd gone. Said it was against company policy to give out employees' personal details.'

'Even to family?' Mary frowned. 'What a load of tossers. Your dad wouldn't have minded you knowing. He really loved you.'

'Yeah, I know.' Jane sighed. 'But it's too late to worry about it now.'

'Christ,' Tina moaned, frowning irritably. 'Change the subject, for fuck's sake! You'll have me cutting my wrists in a minute. Let's get pissed and talk about something happier.'

'All right.' Mary grinned. 'Men!'

'That's even worse.'

'You're just jealous 'cos you haven't got one. Bet you have, though, eh, Jane?'

'No way,' Jane snorted. 'I've had more than enough of men to last me a lifetime. If they're not married, they're screwing around behind your back.'

'Not my Dave.' Mary smiled smugly. 'He's totally committed.'

'He *should* be,' Tina sniped. 'To a bleedin' loony bin.'

Sensing that the banter between Dave and Tina hadn't been as friendly as she'd assumed, Jane raised an eyebrow. This could be interesting.

'How long have you been with him?' she asked.

'Too bloody long,' Tina muttered under her breath.

Ignoring her, Mary said, 'About three years, off and on, but this is the first time we've lived together. He used to have his own flat in Gorton but the landlord chucked all his stuff out when he was sent down, so I said he could move in here when he came out, 'cos he needed a fixed address for his probation.'

'Should have let him rot in jail,' Tina grunted.

'Will you put a sock in it,' Mary hissed, eyeing the door nervously. 'He's not that bad. You just got off on the wrong foot with him, that's all.'

'If you say so. But I think I've known him long enough to have my own opinion, and I reckon he's a grade-A piss-taker. And you're a mug for putting up with it.'

'Don't call me a mug.' Annoyed now, Mary downed her

drink and refilled her glass, slamming the bottle down on the table. 'It's *my* business if I give him a second chance.'

'Try second *hundred*.'

'Back off. He's making an effort.'

'He's bound to be *acting* nice now he's getting his leg over after a year without,' Tina argued. 'It's only been two days. How long before he's up to his old tricks – that's what I want to know.'

'What's all this?' Jane was unable to stay her curiosity any longer.

'Nothing.' Mary flapped a dismissive hand. 'It got a bit rough before he went down, that's all.'

'Bit rough,' Tina snorted incredulously. 'He battered the *crap* out of you.'

'Only 'cos he was off his head.'

'What kind of excuse is that?' Tina's eyes were blazing now.

'He hit you?' Jane was aghast. 'How come you took him back?'

'He's changed,' Mary insisted, jutting her chin out defensively. 'He was only like that because he was doing so much coke before he went in. He's sorted now.' Turning to Tina, she gave her an accusing glare. 'You know he was all right before he got into the powders.'

Shaking her head, Tina looked at Jane. 'You can't tell her nothing when it comes to him.'

'So, stop interfering,' Mary told her icily. 'I love him, and I *know* he's changed. But, even if he did hit me again, do you really think I'd be stupid enough to put up with it?'

'You put up with Ali for long enough,' Tina reminded her sarcastically. 'And he turned you into a junkie and a prostitute.'

'*Tina!*' Mary's face had turned scarlet.

'Christ, Mary,' Jane murmured disbelievingly. 'Is that true?'

Sighing heavily, Mary grasped her glass between her hands and nodded. 'Yeah. But I've been clean from the day I walked out, and I've never so much as *thought* about selling myself again – and never will,' she added, glaring pointedly at Tina. 'So, quit going on about it like I'm gonna slide back into it if you don't keep an eye on me. All *right*?'

'I'm only looking out for you.'

Shaking her head, Mary inhaled noisily. 'Aw, Jeezus . . . this is doing my head in. How did we get started on it in the first place?'

'Don't look at me,' Tina huffed, throwing an accusing glance in Jane's direction.

'Hey, it's not *my* fault,' Jane protested. 'I didn't know anything about it.'

'Enough!' Mary slammed her hand down on the table. 'From now on, we leave the past well and truly alone. We don't talk about it – we don't even *think* about it. Pact?'

'Pact,' Tina agreed, placing her hand over Mary's.

'Jane?' Mary raised an eyebrow.

'Fine with me,' Jane lied, placing her hand at the top of the pile. She had no intention of leaving the past behind till she knew everything about Mary's colourful life. 'I just want to get to know my best mate again.'

'Me, too.' Mary smiled. 'And no one's leaving you out, you moody old tart,' she said then, noticing Tina's affronted expression. 'So quit sulking, and get the drinks topped up.'

Working their way through the rest of the bottle, time flew as the women relaxed and chatted about happier things. Before Jane knew it, it was two a.m.

'God, look at the time,' she groaned. 'I'd best get moving before I fall asleep.' Standing unsteadily, she stumbled. Reaching out to steady herself, her hand landed flush on Tina's enormous breast. 'Oops! Sorry, love,' she giggled tipsily. 'Didn't see you there.'

'Help yourself, why don't you?' Tina replied dryly.

'See!' Mary chuckled, pointing a finger at Tina. 'I *told* you there was a name for birds like you.'

Snorting softly, Tina said, 'Not me, mate. I'd take a scabby cock over a fish split *any* day.'

Grimacing at the image this conjured up, Jane asked if she could ring a taxi.

'I'll do it,' Mary said, using both hands to push herself up from her seat. 'They'll do you a discount if they know you're a mate of mine.'

Hugging Mary when the car horn sounded down below a few minutes later, Jane promised to come back soon. Then, saying goodbye to the others, she left with a mile-wide grin on her face.

Climbing into bed that night, Jane was happier than she'd been in a long time. The reunion had been much better than she'd expected – and far more revealing. Who'd have guessed that smart, gorgeous Mary would end up hooked on smack and on the game? Still, she seemed to be back on her feet now – even if it was a bit worrying what Tina had said about Dave. She just hoped that Mary was right about him having changed. Now that she'd finally found her again, she'd hate to see her hurt.

23

It was a mammoth trek, having to take two buses there, and expensive, catching taxis back – even at a discount – but Jane thought it was worth it to be around Mary again. Only problem was, the more time she spent with her, the less time she spent at work.

It might not have been the best job in the world but Jane really enjoyed it, and the money came in very handy. But the more time she skived off, the more guilty she felt – and the less inclined to go in.

When she confided this to Mary a few weeks down the line, Mary made a suggestion that really got her thinking.

'You could always find bar work round here, you know. In fact, I don't see why you don't just move back, then we'd be able to see each other every day – just like we used to. It'd be great.'

Jane was seriously tempted, but she didn't see how she could pull it off without upsetting people and messing things up. Alf would never forgive her if she walked out on him. He was having a hard enough time managing on the odd days she took off in the week – how would he cope if she went for good?

And it would be hard finding somewhere to live, as well. The rent on the flat she had now was fixed at the same low rate that it had been when she moved in. She'd never find anywhere as cheap as that anywhere else.

Mary didn't think any of this was a problem.

'Alf will easily find himself another mug,' she reasoned. 'He's not exactly done you any favours with the crap wages he's been paying you. As for finding a cheap place to live . . . well, you could always put your name down with the council and move in here until they've found you something.'

Jane would have jumped at the chance if it had just been Mary she'd be staying with. They'd been getting on really well since meeting up again – like they'd never been apart, in some ways. But there was no way she could even *consider* living with Dave. She couldn't stand him, and the more she saw of him the more the feeling intensified. And it was obviously mutual.

He was such a snidey little shit, always taking pops at Jane and Tina – disguising them as jokes by slotting them in among the *hilarious* stories of crimes he'd committed and violence he'd inflicted. She didn't find him the slightest bit funny, but everyone else seemed to – Mary included. It was the one thing that Jane was beginning to find irritating about her.

After everything Mary had said about her ex-husband, Jane couldn't believe she had fallen for a bastard like Dave. But Mary thought he was just *wonderful*, and never tired of raving about his athletic physique, his tousled dark-blond hair, his mesmerising ice-blue eyes, his dangerous, sexy grin . . .

Hard as she tried, Jane couldn't see it. Dave just looked skinny and moody to her, his hair looked dirty, and his eyes were horrible – too pale, cold, and bulging. When he stared at her, as he frequently did when he was taking the piss, he gave her the heebie-jeebies. She'd only tolerated him so far for Mary's sake, but she knew that one of them would end up dead if they lived under the same roof – and it wouldn't be her.

Not wanting to say any of this to Mary and offend her, Jane refused her offer. But she did agree to put her name down with the council, saying that it would give her time to sort everything out with her landlord and give her a chance to help Alf find a suitable replacement.

Expecting a long wait after signing on to the council register, Jane almost died when a letter came just two weeks later offering her a tenancy in the Crescents.

Ringing them to turn it down, she was dismayed when they warned her that she'd be lucky to be offered anything else for another two to three years if she refused.

Too committed now to the idea of living near Mary to wait that long, Jane reluctantly agreed to take it, convincing herself that it wouldn't be too bad. She didn't have to spend any time there, but it would give her a base close to Mary from where she could apply for a transfer.

Packing proved to be a bigger job than Jane had expected. She'd had no idea of the amount of junk she'd acquired over the years – ornaments she hated, books she'd never read, clothes and shoes that didn't fit . . . And more of the same that she'd totally forgotten about still in their bags in cupboards and under the bed. Being brutal with herself, she threw away everything she didn't need, determined to leave the past behind and make a fresh, uncluttered new start.

Prepared as she was, when the moving day finally came Jane was overtaken by a feeling of panic as she stared around the flat. It was small, dingy, and in desperate need of modernising, but it had been her home for most of her adult life. Within those walls she had laughed, cried, loved, lost, sung, danced, partied . . . Everything she had once been and since become was contained there, and it was a massive risk to give it all up to start again in the very place where her troubles had all begun.

Yes, she'd have Mary to support her through the move. But she'd also have Daye to contend with. And if he succeeded in driving a wedge between Mary and herself as she knew he was trying to, she'd have nothing – no job, no friends, and no easy way out.

On the other hand . . . If she didn't give it a try, she might be missing out on something wonderful.

Weighing up the pros against the cons, the pros eventually won.

The new house was far bigger than the flat that Jane had left behind. Totally unfurnished and uncarpeted, it echoed with memories of the families who had inhabited it when the Crescents were first erected.

It hadn't been so bad back then, when working-class families like her own and Mary's had lived there. But now it just seemed to be full of students and druggies. No one had any familial links, and the atmosphere was all the colder for it – and more dangerous.

Jane did her best to make the place look like home, but she couldn't bear to spend time there and would go to Mary's as soon as she woke up, not returning until it was time to go to bed.

Jane's depression at living in the Crescents increased as the tension continued to build between her and Dave. She found that she was constantly on edge, waiting for something to snap, and it soon began to affect her relationship with Mary. But she struggled on in the hope that Mary would see that she wasn't the cause and would kick Dave into the gutter where he belonged. But the longer it went on, the more she knew that it was never going to happen.

Six months down the line, Jane was seriously contemplating

giving the whole thing up as a bad idea and crawling back to Cheetham Hill to recapture her old life. She despised Dave, couldn't stand Tina, and she didn't like John or Jim much either. In fact, if it hadn't been for Mary she'd have gone a long time back. But Mary was her best mate, and there was no way she was giving up without a fight.

But, as always happens when two people are pulling a third in opposite directions, things finally came to a head.

24

Lying on the bed in his boxers, Dave was frowning darkly as he watched Mary putting her make-up on at the dressing-table mirror. They were supposed to be going out, but he wasn't in the mood. In fact, the only thing that was stopping him from fucking the whole thing off was the thought of seeing Big Jock and Stan the Man again, two of his old mates from Strangeways.

They'd written to him last week, saying that they were up for release this morning and would be calling round tonight. Made up, he'd told Mary to get her glad rags ready because they were going on a mega booze-up. He should have known that the silly cow would immediately go and invite her fat-twat mates along, but it hadn't occurred to him to tell her not to until it was too late.

He *had* hoped that she'd have the sense to realise that this was *his* special night. But, oh no . . . the thick bitch was too selfish for that. And that was why he was so pissed off.

Dave saw enough of Mary's mates as it was without them spoiling his big reunion. He'd known Tina before he'd got banged up, but absence hadn't made his heart grow any fonder – he'd hated the ugly cow then, and he hated her just as much now. But nowhere near as much as he hated Jane.

She was one *miserable* cow, her. It had been bad enough having her round two or three times a week, but since she'd moved to the Crescents he couldn't fart without seeing her ugly, disapproving mush. And she was as thick-skinned as they came. No way could he get rid of her, no matter how hard he tried. His insults hit home, he knew that from her constant slapped-arse expression, but could he shake her out of Mary's nest . . . ? Could he bollocks! He was convinced she was a dyke, but Mary wouldn't have it. She just reckoned it was because they were mates from way back.

And that was the *main* reason Dave hated Jane.

It really pissed him off that she shared a history with Mary that didn't include him. He could just about stomach them yakking on about the good old days, but it infuriated him when Jane encouraged Mary to talk about her no-good ex. Mary was with Dave now – her mind should be on *him*, not on some foreign cunt she'd shagged back then.

Dave could have put his foot down and banned Jane from the flat, but it was too much of a gamble while Mary was still so hooked on the novelty of having her around. If he forced her to choose, she might just do the unexpected and turn on *him*. It was doubtful, but it wasn't worth the risk – not while he still needed her address. The magistrates would have him back inside to finish his three years in a flash if he didn't keep up this show of stability and good behaviour.

Still, much as Dave despised Jane, he had to admit that he got a perverse kick out of making her life a misery. He wanted rid of her, but he was determined to make *her* look like the baddie when it all blew up. It would give him a great deal of satisfaction to see Mary stuff her back into whatever hole she'd crawled out of.

He just didn't know if he had the patience to wait that long.

Mary gave Dave a nervous smile when she saw him looking at her in the mirror. He'd been in a funny mood since he'd told her about his mates coming round, and she was praying he wasn't building up to a full-scale wobbly. He could be really unreasonable when he flipped, and she had to pull every trick in the book to get him out of it.

He hadn't hit her since he'd been out. But she'd seen sparks of the old Dave in his eyes lately – Mad Dave, as they'd called him back then, when the drugs had made him think he was invincible and he'd pick fights with the weediest men in the pub just for the hell of it, then come home and batter Mary for dessert.

Still, that was then and this was now. He'd been good since he came home, and hadn't so much as mentioned speed, smack, or any of the other shit that had sent him loco. He *was* drinking a lot, but she supposed that he needed *some*thing to wipe out the stress of being on probation. And booze had to be better than getting hooked on skag again.

Getting the old familiar twinge in her gut at the mere *thought* of heroin, Mary snatched up her brush and yanked it roughly through her hair. She hadn't touched smack in years, but the whispering siren lived on in her brain – hiding among her everyday thoughts, waiting to ambush her and drag her back into its satin cage.

Not thinking about it . . . Not thinking about it . . .

Cutting the thoughts dead, she concentrated on her reflection. Frowning at the dark roots splitting her peroxide hair down the middle like an axe wound, she wished she'd never bleached it. But Dave had said it would suit her – and Dave *always* got what he wanted.

Oh, the things Mary did to keep that man happy. She just wished he'd try a bit harder to keep *her* happy. She didn't complain about *his* mates, but he was always moaning about the girls. Especially Jane.

She'd really wanted him and Jane to get on. Not *too* well, of course. Best friend or not, Mary would rip Jane's head off if she got up to any of that shit with Dave. But then, Jane wouldn't do that. She was way too loyal – unlike Mary herself, all those years ago.

It made her sick to think how close she'd come to being landed with that smooth-talking gyppo's baby. Christ, she'd been stupid back then. But time was a great one for forcing you to grow up. Now she'd sooner stick her head in a bubbling pan of chip fat than shag her best mate's fella – if she'd had one, which Jane didn't.

That was something Mary planed to rectify tonight. If Dave's mates were as great as he made out, she was hoping to get Jane off with one of them. If Jane got laid she might stop being so uptight, and Dave would see how nice she really was and lay off her.

And pigs might fly . . .

The sound of the doorbell brought her out of her thoughts. Getting up off the stool, she turned around and gave Dave a sexy smile. He'd soon cheer up when he saw his mates, but it wouldn't hurt to help things along.

Whipping her dressing gown open, giving him a flash of the nothing she was wearing beneath, Mary's hopes lifted when he gave her a dirty grin in return. Thanking God that his cock ruled his head, she sashayed across to him and gave the stiffening bulge in his boxers a squeeze.

'You just stay right there,' she told him seductively. 'I'll be back to sort you out in a minute.'

'Where's Mary?' Jane asked when Tina let her in twenty minutes later.

'Bedroom,' Tina grunted, rolling her eyes as she went back to the living room and plonked herself down on the couch with a suck-lemon scowl. 'Supposed to be getting dressed, but they're making enough noise about it. If you ask me, they're having a sly shag – dirty bleeders.'

Jane groaned, wishing she'd gone with her instincts and stayed at home. It was going to be a barrel of laughs if Mary and Dave were all loved-up and Tina was in one – *not*!

The doorbell rang again.

Going to answer it, Jane was confronted by two strange men – one small and skinny with shoulder-length, greasy brown hair; the other hugely fat and bald with a bushy red beard.

'All right, blondie,' the little one said, parting his curtain-like fringe to ogle her tits. 'You Dave's bird?'

'No, I'm her mate,' Jane snapped, folding her arms to obscure his view as she stepped back to let them in. 'Go through. They'll be out in a minute.'

Thanking her, Big Jock pushed Stan up the hall ahead of him. They'd only been out a few hours but Stan was already getting them into trouble. He was like a rabid dog on heat, leering at every woman they passed and making lewd comments about their *assets*. Jock would have to keep a close eye on him tonight, or they'd end up having to lamp some offended husband and land back in nick.

Walking into the living room, Jock immediately forgot his concerns when he saw Tina. It was rare to meet a bird who could match him pound for pound in this anorexic day and age, but it was the killer scowl on her face that really caught his eye. There was nothing sexier than a bad-ass mutha with a bit of meat on her bones.

Grinning, he plonked himself down beside her, his weight momentarily lifting her out of the dip she'd moulded into the cushion over the years.

'The name's Big Jock, but you can call me *any* time,' he quipped, extending a meaty tattooed hand.

Ignoring it, Tina turned to his mate. 'And who are you?'

'Stan the Man,' Jock answered for him, giving her a playful nudge in the ribs. 'Big in heart as he's small in size – if you get my drift.'

'Not as big as your gob, though, eh?' she sneered.

'Or his belly,' Jane muttered, wondering if the couch could take their combined weight.

'Much bigger than both,' Stan drawled, waggling his eyebrows lewdly as he rested a bony elbow on Jock's huge shoulder.

Looking at each other, Jane and Tina burst out laughing.

'Have we missed the joke?' Jock asked bemusedly.

'You look like a bleedin' ventriloquist with his dummy,' Jane explained. 'We're just wondering where you put your hand.'

'Up me arse!' Stan deadpanned. 'Any booze in this place, or what?'

'In there.' Tina pointed at the sideboard. 'But you'd best wait for His *Lord*ship to play the dutiful host or he'll sulk.'

'He don't scare me.' Smirking wickedly, Stan jumped up and yanked the sideboard door open. Grinning when he saw how many bottles were in there, he said, 'Wa-*hey*! Houston, we have lift-off!'

'What you got?' Jock asked, opening the pack of cigarettes he'd just discovered down the side of the cushion and offering them around.

'Aldi's finest Scotch,' Stan called back over his shoulder. 'Rum . . . *Gin* . . . ?' Pausing, he grimaced. 'And *your* favourite, you fat fuck – a six-pack of blow-your-tits-off Special Brew. What's your poison, ladies?'

'That ain't no lady, that's my wife,' Jock quipped.

'Fuck me, I thought it was your guide dog,' Stan said, turning to peer at Tina's face. 'Oh, sorry, love. I could have sworn you was a pit bull.'

'Up yours, you cheeky bastard!'

Taking even more of a shine to her for having such a mouth on her, Jock chuckled. He couldn't be doing with ladylike women who acted like you'd shat on their mothers' heads if you farted. He had the feeling they were going to hit it off.

Sauntering in just then, reeking of Kouros and looking like a Teddy-boy throwback with his slicked-back hair, long black jacket and drainpipe trousers, Dave grinned and spread his arms.

'G'wan then, you pair of cunts! Took you long enough to get here, didn't it? Get extra time for being ugly, did you?'

'How's it hangin', y' wanker?' Stan laughed, throwing a shadow-punch at Dave's stomach. 'Still putting the old Vaseline on your knob every night?'

'In your dreams,' Dave snorted, clipping him around the ear. 'That was you, that.'

'Great to see you, man,' Jock said, getting up to shake his hand. 'You're looking good.'

'Feeling it.' Dave grinned, clapping him on the shoulder. 'There's nowt like the love of a good woman to get you up and running.'

'So, where is this lovely lady of yours?' Jock asked, sitting back down. 'Can't wait to meet her.'

'She's just finishing her hair,' Dave told him, going to the sideboard. 'Who wants a quick one before we set off?'

'Beat you to it, mate.' Stan waved the Scotch in the air. 'Not opened it yet, though, so you can do the honours if you want. Heard you like to play *host*.'

'Keeps this lot in their places.' Dave flicked a thumb in Jane and Tina's direction. 'The amount of time they spend round here, you'd think it was *their* gaff, not mine. What's everyone having?'

Being deliberately awkward because she knew it was the one thing he didn't have, Tina said, 'Brandy for me. I can't stand lager – it gives me wind summat chronic. And whisky's for alkies, innit?'

'Give over, you prickly bint!' Stan snorted. 'It's good stuff, is that. I'll 'ave a big 'un, our kid.'

'Special Brew for me, mate.'

Catching the can when Dave tossed it to him, Jock tore the tab off and downed a noisy mouthful. Wiping his mouth on the back of his hand, he turned to Tina and burped loudly in her face.

'Stop flirting,' Stan sniggered. 'She ain't interested – not with that bleedin' hedge on your chin, anyhow.'

'I happen to like beards,' Tina informed him frostily. 'I think it suits him. It makes him look like a big cuddly caveman.'

Flicking her an incredulous glance, Jane was disgusted to see Tina giggling at something Jock had just whispered into her ear. This was all she needed – *both* of her mates hooked up with Dave and his lot. Well, if they had any ideas about setting her up with Stan the scrawny Man, they could forget it!

Just then, Mary came out from the bedroom, looking gorgeous in stilettos and a tight red dress with a plunging neckline and a thigh-high hemline. Her make-up was immaculate, and she'd managed to tie her hair up so that the roots weren't so obvious.

'Here she is.' Dave beamed proudly. 'Come and meet the lads, babe. Big Jock . . . Stan the Man.'

'Nice to meet you.' Mary smiled at them. 'Dave's told me all about you.'

'He'd best not have,' Jock chuckled. 'We'll have to do him in if he's given all our dirty secrets away.'

'Yeah, right!' Dave snorted. 'You and whose army?'

Nudging him without taking his eyes off Mary, Stan said, 'Here . . . how did an ugly twat like you land a belter like her?'

'Oi, he's gorgeous, if you don't mind,' Mary scolded

light-heartedly. Planting a quick kiss on Dave's cheek to stop him getting uppity about his mate complimenting her, she said, 'The others not here yet?'

'Nah, but it's still early.' Dave glanced at his watch. 'It's only half-eight. Anyhow, Jim can't make it, so we're only waiting on John and that mad bint from upstairs. Christ knows why you invited *her*.'

'Ah, I felt sorry for her.'

'Er, *John* . . . ?' Stan cut in, frowning. 'I hope you don't mean that cunt from D Wing?'

'That's the one,' Dave confirmed. 'But don't worry, he don't have owt to do with her no more.'

'Good job!' Stan grunted, knocking back his drink and holding his glass out for more. 'I wouldn't have come if you'd said he'd be here.'

'What's this?' Mary gave Dave a questioning look. 'Not trouble, I hope?'

'Nah, they just had a bit of grief in the Strange,' he explained. 'Nowt to worry about. John knows he was out of order.'

'Too right he was,' Stan agreed bitterly. Turning to Mary then, he said, 'He copped off with my bird when we was banged up.'

'He *didn't*?'

'He fuckin' did! Sneaked a look at a nuddy photo she'd sent me and nicked her address off one of me letters. Next thing I know, she's telling me she's met someone else and don't want to know me no more. He's lucky he got out when he did, or I'd have sliced his cock off in the showers.'

'What are you playing at?' Mary turned on Dave accusingly. 'How could you invite them both round at the same time after that? Are you trying to start a war, or something?'

'Take it easy.' Dave waved his hands in a calming motion. 'He didn't want nowt to do with it once he saw its mush.

He didn't even stop to say hello – just legged it and jumped in a taxi. Talk about speedy bollocks,' he added with a laugh. 'I've never seen anything move so fast.'

Frowning thoughtfully, Mary said, 'Here, you're not talking about that bird that was hanging about at the gates the day you and John came out, are you?'

'Yup.'

'*Ooeer!* She was a *right* dog.'

'Oi, that was my tart,' Stan protested. 'She was well fit.'

'Bollocks!' Jock snorted. 'Come on, man, you was gonna finish it when you got out, anyway. He did you a favour.'

'Not the point,' Stan muttered sullenly. 'Mates don't shit on each other like that.'

'Yeah, well, he probably won't even come, 'cos I told him you'd be here,' Dave said, pouring himself another drink and screwing the cap tightly back on the bottle. 'Who says we get moving before we've got no booze to come back to?'

'What about Hannah?' Mary reminded him. 'I told her nine.'

'Sack her,' he sneered, downing the drink and heading for the door. 'Just tell the daft bitch her clock was wrong.'

'Don't be horrible.'

'You don't get nowt for being nice in this world.'

Filing out of the flat, they almost collided with Hannah who'd been about to knock. Jumping as though she'd just been caught doing something naughty, she looked ready to burst into tears.

'You only just made it, love,' Dave said, sounding as friendly as could be now. 'We thought you'd blown us out.'

'Oh, no, I wouldn't do that,' she twittered. 'I just couldn't remember if Mary had said eight or nine. If it was eight, I wouldn't have had time to do me hair proper. But it was such a mess, I thought, no, Hannah, you take your time, an'—'

'Very nice, too,' Dave said, cutting her short before she

could list every breath she'd taken and every thought she'd had all day.

'D'y' think so?' Blushing, she reached up to pat the nest-like backcombed botch-up.

'You look perfectly extinguished, my dear,' Stan drawled, shouldering her out of the way. 'Now shut the fuck up about your hair, an' let's go. I've got some serious drinking to catch up on.'

Dave, Stan and Jock were first down the stairs. Spilling out onto the pavement, they set off down the road, chanting: 'Man United for the cup . . . Shitty City get t' fuck!'

Scowling when Mary and Tina started laughing and linked arms to follow the men, Jane folded her own arms and set off after them.

'Wait for me,' Hannah yelped, struggling to free her handbag strap from the heavy entrance door.

'Oh, for God's sake,' Jane hissed between her teeth. This was going from bad to worse. As if it wasn't enough that Mary seemed to have forgotten her, now she was going to be lumbered with the bint from hell. Much as she hated to agree with Dave about *any*thing, she was with him on this one . . . Mary had lost her marbles, letting dopey Hannah tag along.

Freeing her bag, Hannah ran to catch up. Giving Jane a sheepish grin, she said, 'Sorry about that. I always forget how fast that door shuts. I'll get my head stuck in it, one of these days.'

'I doubt God likes us that much,' Jane muttered scathingly.

'Oh, do you believe in God?' Hannah cheeped. 'I do, but people think you're a bit daft if you say it, don't they?'

'Do they *really*?'

'Oh, yeah. They can get really nasty about it. But Mary's all right. She never takes the mick, or nothing. She's really nice, isn't she?'

Really soft, more like, Jane thought.

'Dave's all right, too,' Hannah went on. 'I've not known him long, but I think he's really nice. And he makes Mary happy, you've got to give him that.'

'Oh, yeah, I'll give him that,' Jane snarled through gritted teeth. 'But we'll see how long it lasts before I trust him to look after her properly.'

'What do you mean?' Hannah gazed up at her uncertainly.

'Forget it,' Jane snapped, regretting ever opening her mouth. 'I just don't reckon he's as nice as he makes out, that's all.'

'Oh.' Frowning, Hannah mulled this over for a moment. Then, 'You don't fancy him, do you?'

Turning on her furiously, Jane said, 'What are you talking about, you stupid cow? Why the hell would I fancy *that*?' Eyes ablaze with indignation, she marched away with her nose in the air.

Breaking into a trot, Hannah quickly caught up with her.

'I'm sorry,' she spluttered. 'I didn't mean to upset you. You're not mad at me, are you?'

Exhaling loudly, Jane shook her head. Hannah was annoying the tits off her, but at least she was bothering to talk.

'No, I'm not mad at you. But I do *not* fancy him. *Okay?*'

'Okay. Sorry.'

Up ahead, Dave and the others were in full swing, singing rude songs now.

'I knew a girl called Mary, who came from Tipperary, who very very rarely washed her smalls . . . The vicar came a-calling, said Mary it's appalling, something BIG is crawling up your hole!'

Hannah giggled but quickly stopped when Jane gave her a dirty look.

Coming to an abrupt halt outside The Western pub, causing a near pile-up as everyone crashed into each other, Dave said, 'I know we're supposed to be going straight to The Nile, but who fancies a quick one in here?'

'Great!' Mary yelped, rushing for the door. 'Last one in's a wanker.'

Pushed aside as the others stampeded inside, Jane was astounded when the door slammed shut in her face. Staring at it, she wondered if this was an indication of how things were going to be with Jock and Stan on the scene. If it was, she didn't hold out much hope for the future. Mary was already sucking up to Tina like nobody's business – which Jane thought really hypocritical considering Mary didn't even *like* her. She was always slagging her off, telling Jane she was sick of Tina's mood swings and how she wished she'd stop winding Dave up all the time. But she didn't seem so bothered by her now.

Popping her head out just then, Mary saw Jane standing there and said, 'What are you doing? Are you coming in, or what?'

'Oh, so you've remembered I'm here, have you?' Jane sniped, folding her arms.

'What's up with you, narky arse?'

'Like you care.' Jane's mouth tightened into an angry knot.

'What you acting up for?' Mary demanded, frowning now. 'We're supposed to be having a good time.'

'Yeah, well, you and *Tina* obviously are,' Jane complained jealously. 'Oh, and thanks for landing me with that stupid bitch, by the way. You know I can't stand her.'

'Oh, grow up!' Mary snapped. 'We're all having a laugh, but if you're just gonna put a downer on it, you might as well piss off home.'

Jane's mouth flapped open with disbelief when Mary went back inside. Well, that did it! She knew where she wasn't wanted. Wrapping her coat tight around herself, she turned on her heel and marched away.

'Where's droopy drawers?' Dave asked when Mary came back to the table alone. 'Dropped down a crack in her own ugly mug, has she?'

'She's gone,' Mary said, thanking Jock when he handed her a drink off the tray he was carrying. 'Ta, love.'

'What's wrong with her?' Hannah asked, frowning concernedly. 'Isn't she well?'

'No, she ain't, but not in the way *you* mean,' Dave said, circling a finger at his temple. 'She's a bit – you know.'

'Is she?' Hannah's eyes widened. 'You can't tell, can you? I mean, I know she's a bit snappy, but you wouldn't think she was like *that*.'

'A bit snappy?' Tina snorted. 'She's a moody bitch, through and through. And I don't know why you think so much of her.' She looked at Mary now. 'If it was me, I'd kick her right out on her arse – pulling her face all the time.'

'Well, well!' Folding his arms, Dave gave a triumphant sneer. 'So it ain't just me, eh? There's me feeling guilty for slagging her off, and all the time no one else can stand her, either.'

'She seemed all right to me,' Jock remarked, dwarfing the stool beside Tina.

'You're probably a bit thick, then, aren't you?' Tina huffed.

'Eh, up . . . Methinks someone's got a bit of green-eye,' Stan teased, nudging Jock. 'You ain't supposed to let on that you fancy their mates if you want to get into their knickers, you know.'

'I never said I *fancied* her,' Jock protested. 'I just said she seemed all right.'

'Well, if you want my opinion,' Dave said smugly, 'I reckon she's a pussy-licker, and she don't like me 'cos I've got Mary.'

'Don't be so stupid,' Mary hissed, downing her drink and slamming her glass down on the table. 'She's my oldest mate. I think I'd know if she was like that.'

'Oh, I don't know,' Tina interjected snidely. 'She grabbed my tit that time, remember?'

'Oh, belt up,' Mary barked. 'You know that was an accident.'

'Don't believe us, then,' Dave said, including Tina with a conspiratorial smirk. 'But I bet you anything you like she blames this on me next time you see her. And you know why? 'Cos she's desperate to split us up and get you all to herself.'

'Bullshit,' Mary snapped.

'We'll see,' Dave countered with a sneer.

'Oh, I've had enough of this.' Pushing her stool back, Mary stood up and headed for the door.

'Where you going?' Dave called after her.

'To see if I can find my friend before she goes home,' Mary tossed back over her shoulder. 'Some of us know what loyalty means, you know!'

25

Thump! Thump! Thump!
THUMP! THUMP! THUMP!

'All *right*!' Jane yelled, cursing whoever was hammering on the door. 'I'm coming!'

Swiping at the grit in her eyes, she focused on the bedside clock and groaned. It was only nine a.m. What kind of idiot disturbed people at this time in the morning?

Official idiots.

Shit! She hoped it wasn't Norweb coming to cut the electric off. She'd been meaning to pay that bill for ages, but like everything else lately, she hadn't got around to it.

The knocking started up again.

Falling out of bed, she stumbled to the window just as a small stone hit it.

'What the hell are you playing at?' she squawked when she threw the window open and saw Mary standing down below. 'That could've smashed the bloody glass!'

'Oh, belt up, you moody old tart,' Mary yelled up to her. 'Hurry up and let me in, it's freezing out here.'

Snatching her keys off the dresser, Jane threw them down and slammed the window shut.

By the time she got dressed and went downstairs, Mary was lounging on the couch, dipping a chocolate digestive into the brew she'd made.

'Oi! Don't snatch!' Mary scolded when Jane flopped angrily down and grabbed the biscuit packet. 'I've only had two.'

'Yeah, and I'm Greta bleedin' Garbo!' Reaching for the cup Mary had left on the table for her, Jane dunked a biscuit into it with a splash.

Watching her, Mary shook her head. 'You know what, you're going funny in your old age, you.'

'Oh, so *I*'m going funny, am I?' Jane spluttered. 'Well, that's ripe, coming from the bitch who told me to piss off home last night. What have you come round for, anyhow? You didn't bother coming to find me then, did you?'

'I bloody did, as it happens,' Mary shot back at her – grimacing as she watched a piece of soggy biscuit trail slowly down Jane's chin. Didn't she know it was there? 'I came back out to say I was sorry for having a go at you, but you'd already gone off in a strop. What was up with you, anyway?'

'Never mind,' Jane snapped grumpily. 'Pass us me cigs. They're by your feet.'

Reaching down, Mary picked them up. Opening the pack, she saw that there was only one left. Lighting it, she tossed the empty pack to Jane.

'Cheeky bitch!' Jane protested, flinging it back at her.

Ducking, Mary took a massive pull on the cigarette and blew the smoke at Jane. Laughing when Jane exaggeratedly wafted it away, she said, 'Keep your knickers on, baggy eyes. I've got twenty in me pocket.'

'Well, hand them over and stop winding me up,' Jane grunted.

Throwing them to her, Mary shook her head again. In all the years she'd known her, she'd never seen Jane as moody as this. It was as if she'd had a sense-of-humour transplant. And much as Mary loved her, it was beginning to wear a bit thin.

'Gonna tell me what's up?' she asked, watching as Jane puffed agitatedly on the cigarette. Reaching out when Jane didn't answer, she poked her in the ribs. 'Oi! I'm talking to you.'

Turning to face her, Jane pursed her lips. 'You really want to know what's up with me, do you? Right, well, I'll tell you, then . . . It's *him*!' Spitting the word out, she launched into a vitriolic assassination of Dave's character, pouring out all the resentment and anger she'd been harbouring against him for pushing her out and trying to split her and Mary up.

Listening in stunned silence, Mary began to feel sick. Dave had been right all along – Jane *was* jealous, and she wasn't going to be happy until she'd ruined everything.

'Right, stop!' she said when she'd heard enough. 'This is just rubbish, Jane. None of this is Dave's fault – it's *yours*. Christ . . . I've been defending you for months, but I can see it for myself now.'

'Oh, thanks a bunch!' Jane spat, her eyes ablaze with indignation.

'It's *true*,' Mary insisted, her own eyes serious. 'You used to be a right laugh when we were kids. Bit possessive when lads were into me, but I didn't really mind, 'cos it amused me.'

'So, I was just a joke, was I?' Jane's lips tightened even further.

'No, you were like my little *sister*,' Mary corrected her quietly. 'I loved you to bits, and I missed you like *mad* after you got sent away. That's why I was so made up when we met up again and you moved back to Hulme. But I can't *believe* how much you've changed.'

'I haven't changed,' Jane protested sulkily. 'If anyone has, it's you.'

'Yeah, maybe I have,' Mary admitted. 'But only 'cos I've grown up. The me I am inside is still the same me as I was back then. But you're different – inside *and* out. You can't take a joke, and you're never satisfied unless you're stirring things up.'

'Bollocks! It isn't me who stirs, it's *them*.'

'Come off it.' Mary gave her an incredulous look. 'We were all getting on fine until you came along and started putting a downer on everything. Shit, even *Tina* says you're moody, and that's saying something.'

'Like I give a toss what *she* thinks.'

'Yeah, well, maybe you should, 'cos she's not the only one.'

'I suppose you're talking about *Dave*?'

'Not just him, no,' Mary replied coolly. '*Every*one. Even dozy Hannah was asking what was up with you last night.'

'Pfft!' Jane snorted, folding her arms. 'So, you're gonna side with that lot against me, are you?'

'I wasn't going to, no.' Mary gave a slight shrug. 'Actually, I *was* going to ignore the fact that you ruined last night for me. Me and Dave nearly had an argument over you, you know – 'cos he slagged you off and I had a go at him. But after all the shite you've just come out with, I shouldn't have bothered.'

'No, maybe you shouldn't,' Jane agreed, gritting her teeth. 'Like you shouldn't have bothered coming round, 'cos it's perfectly obvious God all-bloody-mighty *Dave* is the most important thing in *your* life.'

'Shouldn't he be?' Peering at her, Mary's eyebrows puckered together. 'He *is* my boyfriend.'

'Best get back to him then, if that's how you feel.'

'Best had, eh?' Standing up, Mary looked down at Jane, waiting for her to say something – *any*thing – to show that she felt as bad about this as Mary did.

'Bye,' Jane clipped, staring straight ahead.

Sighing, Mary flapped her hands in a gesture of defeat. Then, turning, she left.

★　　★　　★

Jane stayed where she was for a long time after Mary had gone, chewing on her nails as the tears trickled down her cheeks.

She was furious with Mary, but even more furious with herself – ashamed, in fact, for blurting out all that stuff about Dave. She'd just made herself look jealous and possessive, and Dave would laugh his head off when Mary told him. It was so humiliating.

Covering her face with her hands, she cursed herself for letting her guard down after months of biting her tongue. She'd really blown it now. And what if Mary was right and this really *was* her fault? She'd have thrown away the best friendship she'd ever had for *nothing*.

There had to be something wrong with her, Jane decided. Maybe she was going through the change, or something. There was no other explanation for wanting to smack Dave in the mouth every time she saw him when everyone else seemed to get along with him. But then, he wasn't as nasty to them as he was to her. And what was she supposed to do when he insulted her – *ignore* it? She'd have to be a bloody saint to do that.

It was so unfair. She'd sacrificed everything to come back here, and now, thanks to Dave, she had nothing – just as she'd feared. No job, no friends, no money . . . no Mary.

Needing to do something physical to ease the frustration that was twisting at her gut and squeezing at her heart, Jane marched into the kitchen and grabbed the polish and duster from under the sink. Polishing the living room like a woman possessed, she went over in her mind everything that had just happened.

Mary wouldn't come back, she was sure of that. There had been something about the way she'd said goodbye – something sad and *final*. It would be strange, not seeing her after doing everything together for the last few months, and

Jane didn't know how she was going to cope. Who would she go shopping with? Who would tell her funny stories that made her nearly wet herself? Who would comfort her when she was upset?

Swiping at the tears as her pride began to resurface, Jane threw the duster down and pulled herself together.

Maybe she *had* been wrong to say what she'd said, but Mary had said worse. And if she wanted to make it up she'd damn well have to come here and beg.

Until then, Jane was on her own. But so what? It wasn't the first time, and it certainly wouldn't be the last. If there was one thing she'd learned in this life, it was that you couldn't rely on anybody but yourself.

And that was exactly what she'd do from now on, Jane vowed. Starting tonight, with a visit to the local pub to see if there was any work going. It was time to get her life back on track.

She'd show Mary that she could manage without her . . . She'd show them all!

26

Dave was whistling as he strolled into The Grapes. It was weeks since Jane had shown her ugly face, and that made him very happy indeed. She'd been a major pain in the arse, that one – always dropping snide hints about his comings and goings, trying to make Mary as suspicious as she was herself. Without Jane's sour influence, Mary was back to her old laid-back self – waiting on him hand and foot while he pleased his lazy-arse self. Just how it should be.

Yep, life was looking pretty good.

And it was about to look even better – on the surface, at least.

'Usual?' Diane, the barmaid, asked when he reached the bar.

'Yeah, thanks.' Smiling, he slapped his money on the counter. 'And one for yourself while you're at it.'

'Feeling flush, are we?'

'Nope, just showing appreciation for the good service. Your man not around?'

'Over there.' Diane nodded towards the smoky pool-table area at the rear of the pub.

Turning, Dave spotted Diane's huge, evil-tempered land-lord boyfriend in deep conversation with several heavy-looking black guys. The glint from their assorted gold chains, rings, and diamond-encrusted watches was blinding, and Dave felt a twinge of envy. What he wouldn't give to be a Yardie and get his hands on some of that. But, even if he hadn't been as white as they came, he knew he wasn't cut out for it. You had to have the Devil in your heart to mete out the types of punishments those guys did – dousing men in petrol and setting them alight just for *looking* at their birds. No . . . he wasn't cut out for that.

Seeing Goldie eyeing him just then, he raised his hand in a polite wave, cursing himself for being caught staring.

Giving the slightest of nods in return, Goldie turned his attention back to his homies. Guys like Dave were nothing but legitimate money on the books to him – nothing to worry about unless they showed disrespect, which few were foolish enough to dare.

'Meeting anyone tonight?' Diane was asking now, putting his drink on the counter.

'Nah. Just fancied a quiet one before I head into town,' Dave told her. Gulping when she rested her elbows on the bar, making her porn-queen breasts almost spill out of her top, he said, 'I'll, er, just go and grab a seat before you get too full up. See you later.'

Snatching up his pint, Dave made his escape to a table in the corner. Sipping it, he cast a nervous glance at Goldie, relieved to see that he was still in deep discussion. Nice as it was to look, it was wise to avoid birds like Diane. They could be the death of you.

A group of noisy students came in a short while later. Pissed off when one of them bounded across to the jukebox and wasted good money on a Duran Duran track that he hated, Dave downed his pint and went back to the bar.

Churlishly shouldering the waster's mates aside, he slammed his glass down and ordered another, knowing that Diane would serve him ahead of the students. Moss Siders didn't take kindly to strangers invading their turf – especially not these spotty, oiky student types.

Glaring when one of the lads complained under his breath

that they'd been there first, Dave smirked when they all looked the other way.

'Pussy cunts,' he sneered, picking up his pint and making his way back to the table.

The students didn't stay long after that. Already unnerved by Dave's unwelcoming greeting, an evil stare from Goldie when they got a bit loud soon sent them fleeing – straight into the arms of the muggers who'd followed them there and were waiting in the shadows outside to march them off to the cash-point machines.

Dave saw it all through the window, and it gave him a buzz to know that he had no worries on that score. He was a local face, so he could walk the streets undisturbed and drink where he wanted to. It was good to belong.

An hour and three pints later, he was about to head into town when a blast from the not too distant past walked in: his one-time cell mate, Kenny Butler. Kenny had been transferred to Wakefield for kicking the fuck out of a screw when he'd had just a couple of weeks of a ten-stretch left to serve. He was so hard that he hadn't given a shit about the extra year they'd lumped on him. It had given him legendary status – and Dave felt honoured to be one of the privileged few that he considered a mate.

Getting up now, he followed Kenny to the bar and gave him a friendly slap on the back.

'Wotcha, mate! What *you* doing here? Done a runner, have you?'

Turning, Kenny frowned as he tried to recall where he'd seen the face before.

'It's Dave . . . from the Strange,' Dave said, grinning idiotically.

Remembering the no-hoper little smack-head who'd ingratiated himself by running errands for him, Kenny nodded.

'Ah . . . so it is. How's it going?'

'So-so.' Dave shrugged. 'You?'

'Better now I'm free.'

'Yeah, it's great, isn't it?' Dave agreed. 'How long have you been out?'

'Few weeks.' Kenny's gaze flicked every which way. 'Went to Nicksy's in Marbella straight after. Just got back the other day.'

'Lucky git,' Dave said enviously, getting his money out to pay for the drink that Kenny had ordered. 'What's he doing over there?'

'Running a bar,' Kenny told him. 'It's a regular old face paradise – more dosh floating about than they've got in all the fuckin' banks put together over here. I'm thinking of going back when I've sorted my shit out.'

'Got something lined up, then, have you?'

'Haven't I always?' Kenny gave a secretive grin. Dave Riley was a dickhead, but he might come in useful if he'd been back on the scene for a while. To get into business round here, you had to know who was doing what, and where. You couldn't just barrel in or you might end up stepping on the wrong toes and get your head blown off.

'You having another?' Diane asked Dave when she'd pulled Kenny's pint.

'Yeah, and keep the change to pour 'em again when we're finished,' he said, handing her his last twenty. He wouldn't be going clubbing now, but it was worth missing out to cultivate a mate like Kenny Butler.

'So, what you up to?' Dave asked, leading Kenny back to his table. 'Got anything in the pipeline? You know I'm available if you need a driver or a lookout, or owt like that.'

'I'll keep it in mind,' Kenny lied, having no intention of *ever* involving Dave in his business. Checking his watch, he frowned and glanced at the door.

'You waiting on someone?' Dave felt a thrill of excitement.

Since he'd been out, he hadn't been involved in anything worthwhile. Jock, Stan and the other guys were all right for hanging out with, but they were hardly in Kenny's league. He'd been heavy shit with a capital H in his day, with a real knack for making money. He reckoned he'd lost thousands last time he was busted. The pigs had seized all his assets, including a well-padded bank account, a couple of expensive motors, and a shitload of hard drugs. If Dave could get in with him, he'd be set for life. And he wanted that – badly.

'Just some of my boys,' Kenny told him evasively. 'So, tell me, what's been going on while I've been away? Who's running things nowadays?'

'Skag?' Dave sipped his pint.

'Coke, crack, speed . . .' Kenny shrugged. 'Is there a main man, or is it open season?'

'Well, Goldie's got a pretty tight hold on the Moss,' Dave told him, lowering his voice. 'But there's nothing much going on anywhere else. Just a few chancers doing small-time shit.'

'Goldie?'

'The landlord.' Dave gave a surreptitious nod in Goldie's direction. 'Took over the licence last year. *Not* to be fucked with.'

Glancing across, Kenny saw the heavies for what they were and decided to give them a wide berth – for now. The last thing he needed was to go up against Yardies before he'd got his feet back on the map.

'You say he's only running the Moss?'

'As far as I know,' Dave said, adding conspiratorially, 'I don't think he can be arsed with anything else. Word is, he's got overseas shit going on – importing, exporting, that kind of stuff.'

'Gear?'

'If it is, there's not much stays round here. It's been dry

for a while now. I've even had junkies asking *me* where to get hold of a bit, and I haven't touched it for ages.'

'Stayed clean, did you?' Kenny narrowed his eyes.

'Yep, and I intend to keep it that way.' Dave raised his glass. 'This is the only shit I need.'

'So you wouldn't be interested in a bit of coke, then?' Kenny patted his pocket.

Dave's pupils burst to greedy life. 'You got some?'

'No point coming home without a few gifts for your old mates, is there?' Kenny drawled. 'It's boss white, this – fresh out of the mule's arse.'

'No shit?'

'Better fuckin' not be!' Kenny chuckled. 'Want a taste?'

'Shit, *yeah*!'

'Thought you was staying off?'

'You know me.' Dave gave him a broad grin. 'Never turn down a freebie.'

'Know anyone else who'd fancy a bit?' Kenny asked, taking the wrap from his pocket and slipping it to Dave under the table. 'Good rates, seeing as you're a mate.'

'You're fuckin' kidding, aren't you?' Dave spluttered. 'I know about thirty cunts who'd suck your dick for it here and now. How much you got?'

'As much as I need for now, and there's plenty more I can get my hands on.' Pausing, Kenny nodded at three men who'd just walked in. Turning back to Dave, he said, 'Look, go sort us a couple more drinks while I have a word with the lads, eh?'

Getting up as the men approached the table, Dave went to the bar. He was a little put out that Kenny hadn't included him in the meet, but it was early days, he supposed. Ordering the drinks, he went to the toilets to check out the wrap.

He groaned with lust when he saw the small square of

glistening white powder. It had been a good while since he'd *seen* any, never mind had it in his hand – or up his nose. Like he'd told Kenny, it had been dry round here, and he'd never have dared ask Goldie to set him up. This was a real godsend – even if it did shatter his good intentions.

Licking the tip of his little finger, Dave dipped it into the powder and rubbed it along his gums. The hit was instant, and blissfully clean and bright – like opening the curtains on a brilliant summer morning and throwing the window wide to let the fresh air in. Laying out a thin line on the cistern, he leaned down and snorted it up.

Kenny was alone at the bar, sipping his drink, when Dave came back. Seeing the wide grin on his face, Kenny gave a knowing smirk.

'Sorted?'

'Aw, fuck, man!' Dave exclaimed ecstatically. 'It's *buzzin*'! I could shift that for you in two minutes flat, no danger. Want me to sort it out?'

'We'll talk about it,' Kenny said, motioning with a downward swipe of his hand for Dave to keep his voice down.

'Where have your boys gone?' Dave whispered, struggling to contain himself.

'They only came to update me on something,' Kenny told him. 'Anyhow, never mind that . . . How safe are these punters you've got in mind?'

'Safe as fuck,' Dave assured him. 'You know some of them from nick. Remember Big Jock and Stan the Man?'

'Oh, aye? They out now, are they?'

'Yeah, but they're still on probation so they're not up to much. Look, they'll be over at my place now. Why don't you come back and sort them out while I give a few others a ring?'

Checking his watch, Kenny shrugged. 'Yeah, why not?'

*   *   *

Mary frowned when Dave walked in with Kenny. She'd never seen Kenny before, and didn't like the look of him. He was too big for her small living room, and she felt instantly claustrophobic. Dave should have known better. He knew she got paranoid when she was smoking skunk. He should've phoned to say he was bringing someone round – given her time to get used to the idea.

'All right, Ken!' Jock exclaimed, standing up to greet the man. 'Long time no see.'

'How's it going, mate?' Kenny clapped him on the shoulder. 'And you, you little runt. Keeping out of trouble, are you?'

'Course!' Stan grinned, leaping to his feet and pumping his hand. 'Fuck me, mate, you're even bigger than last time I saw you. What they been feeding you at Wakefield? Elephant stew?'

'Same shite as the Strange,' Kenny told him, patting his stomach. 'This is paella, this.'

'He's been stopping with Nicksy in Marbella since he come out,' Dave explained as proudly as if he'd been there himself. 'He's over there running some bar for old faces.'

'So, what've you lot been up to?' Kenny asked, irritated with Dave already.

'Klish,' Jock grunted, sitting down. 'There's nowt going on worth putting yourself out for round here. Anyhow, me and Stan are behaving ourselves so we don't end up back inside.'

'Smart move.' Kenny nodded approvingly. Looking at Mary then, he raised an eyebrow.

'This is my bird, Mary,' Dave told him boastfully, pleased that she'd remembered to put her make-up on today. 'Mary, this is Kenny – my old cellie from the Strange.'

'Hi.' Mary gave him a tight smile.

'I don't bite,' Kenny teased, extending his hand. 'Nice to meet you.'

Relaxing when he gave her a warm smile, Mary shook his hand.

'Sorry about that. I'm a bit wasted and it makes me jumpy.'

'Skunk?' He sniffed the air. 'Yeah, it makes me paranoid, too. I stick to the Leb, myself. It's not such a head-fuck.' Pulling a lump of draw from his pocket he handed it to her. 'Here . . . have that on me.'

'You sure?' She gave him a questioning look. 'It must be an eighth, this.'

'Don't worry about it,' he assured her, smiling. 'I've got shitloads of the stuff.'

Pleased that Kenny and Mary seemed to have hit it off, Dave rubbed his hands together and went to the sideboard. If this went well, he'd soon be as flush as a virgin's pussy at a gang bang.

Taking out a bottle of Scotch, he went to get some glasses, calling back over his shoulder, 'By the way, Kenny's got some top gear if anyone's interested.'

'Gear?' Mary's smile slipped.

'Coke,' Dave corrected himself quickly, tipping Kenny a wink. 'And it's well clean. You couldn't get hooked on this shit if you tried.'

'Oh, *great*,' Tina muttered, glaring at Dave as he retreated into the kitchen. What kind of idiot brought a powder dealer around an ex-junkie?

Sensing her deteriorating mood, Jock threw an arm around her shoulder and gave her a hearty squeeze, telling Kenny, 'This is my bird, Tina.'

'Girlfriend, not bird,' she corrected him, shrugging him off and staring rudely at Kenny.

Kenny almost laughed in her ugly face. He didn't give a toss about her, or *any* of them, come to that – Dave included. All he wanted was a steady line of punters to get the ball rolling.

'So, you were in Strangeways with Dave, were you?' Mary asked, deliberately drawing his attention away from Tina – whom she could punch right now for being so rude after Kenny'd been so generous.

Looking at her, Kenny narrowed his eyes. Her hair was a mess, but she was a bit of a looker, all the same. Nice teeth, good figure. Sitting beside her, he put his arm along the back of the couch and peered deep into her stoned blue eyes.

'Yeah, we were cellies. But he never said he had a beautiful woman like you stuck away at home. Can't say I blame him, mind. You tend to keep your good stuff secret inside. Stops you losing it.'

'Tell me about it,' Stan grumbled. 'Remember that John cunt off D Wing? He nicked my bird's address off one of me letters and sweet-talked her knickers off.'

'Did he bollocks.' Jock gave a weary sigh. 'You know he didn't want to know her once he got out. Will you just get *over* it?'

'No, I bleedin' won't!'

'So, what do you do?' Kenny asked Mary, cutting Jock and Stan dead. 'Let me guess . . . I bet you're some sort of private secretary, or something?'

'Do me a favour,' she snorted, flattered by his assumption that she was intelligent enough for that. 'I'd rather die than do dictation for some fat slob. No, I'm more kind of . . .' Pausing, she pursed her lips.

'A lazy bitch?' Stan supplied, chuckling good-naturedly.

'Don't be so damn cheeky!' Mary retorted. 'I was *going* to say sociable.' Turning back to Kenny, she smiled. 'I like meeting people and having a laugh. I used to work in a pub before I met Dave, and I really liked that.'

'You never told *me*,' Dave said accusingly, coming back with the glasses.

'Yes, I *did*.' Mary rolled her eyes at Kenny, embarrassed that Dave was pulling her up in front of him. 'When Jane was talking about her job at The Crown.'

'Don't mention that fat bitch to me!' As he poured Kenny a glass of Scotch, Dave's scowl morphed into a smile. 'There you go, mate. Have a taste of that. It's well smooth.'

'Stop showing off,' Mary clipped, giving him a dirty look. 'It's only from Aldi.'

'Yeah, well, you didn't pay for it, so keep your nose out.'

'I bloody *did*! I get more money than you, remember?'

'What – 'cos you're a better sponger? I wouldn't be so proud of that, if I was you.'

'You've got room to talk about sponging!' Mary snapped, all set to give him a rundown of his inadequacies in the finance department.

Blushing when Kenny coughed beside her, she whipped her head around and forced herself to smile.

'Oh, God, sorry . . . We shouldn't be squabbling in front of guests. You must think we're awful.'

'Not at all.' Downing his drink, Kenny placed his glass on the floor and stood up. 'I'd best get going, as it happens.'

'Already?' Mary was disappointed. 'Oh, well . . . You'll have to come again, now you know where we are.'

'I will.' Smiling, he tipped her a wink. 'It was nice meeting you. Thanks for the drink.'

'What about the gear?' Dave asked, pushing himself out of his chair.

Taking a couple of large wraps from his pocket, Kenny tossed them to him. 'Have them for now. I'll give you a bell in a couple of days – see if you want any more.'

Beaming, Dave handed the wraps to Mary and followed Kenny out into the small hallway, asking, 'How much do we owe you?'

'Nowt, this time.'

'Really? Wow! Thanks, mate! Still want me to ring round for some punters?'

'Yeah, you can put the feelers out,' Kenny said, lighting a cigarette. 'Only don't tell no one where it's coming from.'

'You know me, mate.' Reaching for his hand, Dave pumped it. 'I won't tell a soul.'

'Make sure *they* keep it zipped, an' all.' Kenny motioned with a nod towards the living room.

'They won't say owt,' Dave assured him confidently. 'You know Jock and Stan are safe, and Mary's sweet as a nut. She never opens her mouth about nothing.'

'She's a nice-looking bird,' Kenny told him with a hint of admiration. 'You could be doing a lot worse for yourself.'

'She's all right.' Dave puffed himself up self-importantly – emboldened by the half-wrap he'd polished off in the pub and the top-up snort he'd had in the kitchen. 'But I don't tell *her* that. You can't let 'em think they've got you by the curlies, or you never get no respect.'

'Suppose not,' Kenny agreed, twisting the latch and opening the front door. Stepping out into the communal landing area, he adjusted his jacket and smoothed back his hair. Didn't do to look less than your best when you were out and about.

'Don't forget to keep me in mind for any jobs that come up,' Dave stage-whispered from the doorway. 'We'll show Goldie who's boss, eh? Now the Butler man's back in town, there's no room for no one else.'

'We'll see how it goes,' Kenny said, flicking his ash impatiently. The idiot had only had a tiny sniff, and he was already mouthing off. Checking his watch, he headed for the stairs, calling back over his shoulder, 'I was never here, yeah?'

'Got you.' Grinning, Dave gave his nose an exaggerated tap, then stuck his thumb up and held it there until Kenny was out of sight.

Going back inside, he was rubbing his hands together when he rejoined the others in the warmth of the living room.

'Top bloke, that Kenny. Can't go far wrong with a mate like him.'

'Sound as a pound,' Stan said, helping himself to another glass of Scotch.

'He seems really nice,' Mary agreed.

'Well, I don't trust him,' Tina stated bluntly. 'He looks at you like he's sussing out what he can get off you.'

'Behave!' Mary scoffed. 'He's not trying to get anything. Jeezus, woman, you'd pay near enough sixty quid for all this stuff he's given us, and he didn't want a penny.'

'Yeah, button it, you gobby cow,' Stan joined in, squeezing himself in between Tina and Mary to get nearer the drugs. 'You don't know when your bread's buttered, you.'

Pursing her lips disapprovingly, Tina folded her arms and kept her opinions to herself. Kenny might have given it to them this time, but they were fools if they thought he wouldn't want paying. Sooner or later, they'd be paying through the nose – literally.

'Christ, that *is* nice,' Mary gasped when she tested a bit of coke on the tip of her tongue.

'See!' Dave exclaimed proudly. 'Didn't I tell you you'd like it?'

'Let's have a taste.' Stan greedily eyed the sparkling powder that Mary was tipping onto a small mirror.

'I've got a better idea,' Dave said, putting the flat of his hand on Stan's face and shoving him back in his seat. 'Let's chop it up, then we'll *all* get some. We'll be fucked if *he* gets his big fuck-off fingers on it.' He thumbed towards Jock.

'He's not having any,' Tina informed him huffily. 'Tell him you don't touch that shit no more, Jock.'

'Only 'cos I've never got no money,' Jock said. 'But I'm not averse if it's going free.' Beaming, he hefted himself out of his seat and dropped to his knees in front of the table to get in line.

'Steady on, you fat cunt!' Dave laughed, hanging on to the table as if to stop it collapsing. 'You nearly took the fucking floor out with that earthquake!'

'Oh, har-de-fuckin'-har!' Jock retorted good-naturedly, patting his enormous belly. 'Maybe I'd best have it all, then? We all know it's good for slimming.'

Smirking, Dave cast a sly glance at Tina. 'Sure *you* don't want some?'

'Fuck off!' Pursing her lips even tighter, she flipped Dave the finger and glared at Jock, furious with him for laughing at her. There was no way she was getting into an argument with him in front of everyone, but if he thought he was getting a leg-over when he walked her home, he could think again. No coke-head was getting *her* knickers off!

27

It was a week before Kenny went back to Dave and Mary's – plenty of time for even the most frugal user to have finished the wraps he'd left and be climbing the walls.

As he'd expected, they treated him like a conquering hero returned from the war, and vied with each other to roll him a spliff, pour him a drink, smile most brightly . . . Anything to earn his approval and get a little more of Kenny's white magic – oblivious to the fact that it was cut with heroin. Not enough to notice, just enough to get them well and truly gagging for it.

Dave had quite a few punters lined up already, and they were soon knocking it out like nobody's business, but it still wasn't enough for Kenny. Getting back on top was proving more difficult than he'd anticipated after a decade inside. He'd made a fair bit of profit on his initial investment, but nowhere near enough to pull off the one big deal he needed to put him back on his feet. Trouble was, none of his old contacts was willing to help him out. He'd been away too long – too much had changed, and nobody trusted anybody any more.

In Terry Hardman's day everyone had scratched each other's backs, and there was a real sense of power in unity. Now, with the influx of gun-running Yardies and crazy Triads fronting protection rackets and brothels everywhere you looked, all the decent criminals had gone underground, leaving Kenny in no man's land – unknown to the new, unwanted by the old.

Unable to move forward without the necessary funds, Kenny began to toy with the idea of pulling a few jobs. Nothing big enough to draw too much official attention, but enough to net him what he needed. Reluctant to put himself on the line, he decided he needed a fall guy – and who better than knobhead Dave? Even *he* couldn't screw up a couple of armed raids on out-of-the-way post offices.

Giving him a ring from the pub one night, Kenny told him to bring the night's takings over as soon as, adding that he had something important to discuss with him.

Dave was buzzing when he got the call, and hoped that Kenny had decided to up his cut of the profits. He was doing well with the dealing, and thought he deserved at least a bonus, if not a raise.

He was a big man on the streets of Hulme these days. People who wouldn't have given him the snot out of their noses a year back were treating him like their best friend – and he didn't blame them. *He* couldn't get enough of this coke, never mind them. It was so much cleaner and lusher than the poisonous shite he'd used in the past. Trouble was, it was *so* more-ish, he was spending every penny he made on it, and Mary was busting his balls big time.

All she ever did was nag about bills, and housework – like Dave didn't have better things to worry about. The last straw had been telling him to pack in snorting if he couldn't afford to help out. That had really taken the biscuit, that had. He didn't see why the hell he should go without when she was sitting on her fat, lazy arse, snorting to her heart's content.

Mary had even tried to goad him into giving it up, telling him that he was getting hooked – which was a joke. They both knew this shit was too clean. Anyway, it wasn't that he *couldn't* quit – he just didn't *want* to. Not until he had to.

And, with any luck, he *wouldn't* have to, because Kenny

would show some long-overdue appreciation and up his money.

'I need you to do something,' Kenny said, when Dave had paid for the drinks and carried them to the table. 'But keep it to yourself, 'cos if word gets out I'm involved, I'll be straight back inside – and you'll be dead. We straight on that?'

Sitting down quickly, Dave nodded. Whatever this was about, it looked serious.

Glancing furtively around, Kenny lowered his voice and said, 'I've got some jobs lined up – of the armed variety.'

'For real?' Dave spluttered, excited enough to almost piss himself.

Narrowing his eyes, Kenny gave a half-smile. 'I take it you're up for it, then?'

'Fuck, *yeah*!' Dave squawked, immediately clapping a hand over his mouth to quieten himself. Leaning forward then, he grinned. 'I thought you were never gonna let me in on the big shit, man. Not that I'm not grateful for setting me up with the dealing, and that – 'cos I am. But I could really use some extra cash, what with Mary always moaning about bills, and shit.'

'Squeezing your bollocks, is she?' Kenny sat back in his seat and looked casually around to make sure that no one was listening. There was hardly anyone in tonight, but you could never be too sure.

'You can say that again,' Dave grumbled, glad of a chance to get his complaints aired. 'She's on at me over everything, these days – leccy this, gas that. Christ, she must be the only mug in the whole of fuckin' *Manchester* paying for the *water*! I mean, come on, man, get real. It comes from the fuckin' *sky*.' Pausing to take a swig of beer, he shook his head in despair. 'You think she'd be a bit fuckin' smarter with *her* background, wouldn't you? I mean, how many pros pay for owt that's going free? And it ain't like she's got the money, neither. She's only getting sixty-odd a week off—'

'Did you say *pro*?' Kenny interrupted, his brow creasing with disbelief. 'Mary was a pro?'

'Aw, shit.' Slumping back in his seat when he realised what he'd said, Dave ran a hand across his face. 'Christ! I shouldn't have told you that. She'll fucking kill me.'

'So, it's true?' Kenny was a little disappointed. He quite liked Mary – had entertained the idea of slipping her one when he had a bit of time to kill. But there was no way he was going there if she'd done that. All the pros he knew were skanky bacteria bins. He'd never be that desperate.

'Yeah, it's true,' Dave admitted glumly. 'But do us a favour, and don't say I told you. She's clean now, and she don't need reminding of the past.'

Never one to dwell on what-could-have-beens, Kenny picked up his glass and peered at Dave over the rim, his eyes glinting as a new moneymaking scheme sprang to mind. He didn't know why he hadn't thought of it before but it was so obvious it was laughable. He knew loads of tarts who'd *jump* at the chance of having him as their pimp. Only trouble was, he didn't have the time to chase around after them, and he wouldn't trust any of them to collect the money for him. But if he had *Mary* on board . . .

'Funny you should say that –' he gave Dave a sly grin '– but that's one of the businesses I'm thinking of starting up.'

'Oh, yeah?' Dave muttered, too pissed off with himself for revealing Mary's sordid past to catch the underlying meaning of Kenny's words. What would Kenny think of him now, knowing he'd shacked up with a whore?

'Aw, cheer up, for fuck's sake,' Kenny jeered, tossing him a cigarette. 'I ain't gonna say nothing to her. I'm on *your* side, man. It'd do my head in if I was out there flogging my guts out while my bird was getting up to all sorts back home.'

'What d'y' mean?' Dave's brow collapsed into a frown as he leaned forward to get a light. 'She don't get up to nothing.'

'You reckon?' Kenny said, sounding unconvinced, his shoulders rocking with a chuckle as he blew his smoke out.

'I reckon.' Dave was gritting his teeth now, his face growing darker by the second. 'She knows what she'd get if she fucked me about.'

Drawing his head back, Kenny squinted at Dave, his eyes suddenly serious.

'Never took you for the jealous type, Dave. And I've got to say, it ain't very reassuring.'

'How so?' Dave was confused. Every man he knew felt the same way about their birds. It was all right for the blokes to fuck anything that moved, but God help the women if they tried pulling the same stunt.

Shrugging, Kenny said, 'What use are you to me if you can't leave her alone for two minutes 'cos you're worried what she's getting up to? Think about it, man . . . How can I bring you in on these jobs if your head isn't on it? You'll be a fuckin' liability.'

'My head *will* be on it,' Dave insisted quickly, seeing his dreams going up in smoke. 'And I'm not jealous, man. It's just summat you say, isn't it? I don't give a flying fuck *what* she gets up to, so long as she ain't holding *me* back.'

'Yeah, right . . .' Kenny smirked at Dave as if he was stupid. 'She's already got you running round after her like a pussy.'

Squirming in his seat at the mocking tone, Dave said, 'No, she ain't. It's the other way round, mate. She does everything for me.'

'So how come you're working and she's sat on her arse giving you grief?' Kenny countered smoothly. 'Something ain't right with that. You should *both* be pulling your weight, but you're letting her get away with taking you for a twat. If it was me, I'd have her out doing what she does best. Think of all the money you're missing out on, man.'

Getting up on that note, he went to the bar, leaving Dave to chew over what he'd said. Seeing the conflicting emotions in Dave's eyes when he came back a few minutes later, he knew he had him. Blokes like him hated letting their birds crawl out from under the thumb, but they'd sell their own grannies if the price was right.

'About them jobs,' Dave said, right on cue. 'I wanna do it. And I won't balls it up – trust me.'

'Ah, but it's not just about trust,' Kenny told him coolly. 'It's about availability, and you're no use if you can't get about.'

'I can.'

'Sure about that?' Kenny raised a disbelieving eyebrow.

'I'm sure.' Dave was adamant. He wanted in on this – wanted it badly. 'And you're right about Mary,' he went on, his tone bitter now. 'She *is* taking the piss – doing nowt while I'm grafting my arse off.'

'So, what you gonna do about it?'

'Set her fuckin' straight.' Dave snatched up his pint and took a long drink. Slamming his glass back down, he looked Kenny in the eye. 'This business you're thinking of starting up . . . Where does Mary fit in?'

Chuckling, Kenny took a swig of his own drink. 'Fighting words, my man . . . What makes you think she'll go for it?'

'She won't have no bleedin' choice,' Dave growled. 'She did it for that cunt of an ex-husband of hers. I reckon it's about time she did something for me.'

Sitting back in his seat, Kenny joined his hands behind his head and grinned. Well, well, what a turn-up. Mary had nous *and* experience – the perfect combination. And with her own boyfriend *persuading* her to do it, she couldn't refuse. It was in both their interests, after all.

At least, they'd *think* it was.

Mary was asleep on the couch when Dave rang to say that he was bringing Kenny round to tell her something. Jumping up as soon as she'd put the receiver down, she reapplied her lipstick and gave her hair a quick brushing.

She liked Kenny and didn't want him to see her at her worst. But it wasn't a fancying kind of liking – although he wasn't half bad when you got used to how big he was, and how pale with his head newly shaved to the bone. It was more that she enjoyed talking to him. He always gave her the impression that he was listening even when he probably wasn't, and he treated her with respect – unlike Dave, who was all too often offhand and abrupt these days.

Giving the room a quick going-over when she was satisfied that she herself looked fine, she made herself a cup of tea and sat down on the couch to wait.

Mary hoped this was about money – God knew they needed it. Despite running all over the place like a blue-arsed fly doing his deals, Dave's always paltry contributions to the household expenses had completely dried up lately. He was spending every penny he made on himself and just expected her to keep him – like food grew out of the walls, or something.

She wasn't doing that well, as it happened, but Dave wouldn't listen when she tried telling him how far behind she'd fallen. The phone was due to be cut off any day, and she didn't even want to *think* about the stack of final reminders at the back of the kitchen drawer.

It was her own fault for liking the coke so much, but Mary didn't see why she should go without when Dave was living it up. Much smoother and more relaxing than the speed-driven buzz of old, this coke had a bright, happy edge to it – like being wide awake in a bath of hot velvet. It might not solve any of her problems, but it sure made it easier to ignore them.

Smiling expectantly when the men came in and sat on either side of her, Mary crossed her fingers and waited to hear the good news.

'Me and Kenny have been talking,' Dave said, jumping right in and pulling no punches. 'And we think you should go back on the game.'

Sure she'd misheard, Mary squinted up at him. '*What?*'

'Oh, you heard.' He flapped his hand impatiently. 'Look, just think about it. It ain't like you haven't done it before, and Kenny reckons you'd make a mint.'

Mary's eyes flashed with indignation. Of all the things she'd been expecting, this hadn't even crossed her mind.

'Since when have you had the right to discuss my private business?' she demanded, glaring at Dave with the sharp glint of betrayal in her eyes.

'Don't be offended,' Kenny interjected smoothly. 'I was asking about you and he let it slip. To be honest, I wasn't surprised.'

Nostrils flaring, Mary turned the glare on him, the glint one of injured pride now.

'Oh, so I look like a slag, do I?'

'Not at all,' Kenny assured her, softening his words with a smile. Creeping didn't faze him. He could be as persuasive as the best of them when he wanted something. 'There's just something about you. I mean, you've got to be pretty fuckin' amazing to survive what you've been through. I've got nothing but absolute respect.'

'That right, is it?' Mary gave a contemptuous sneer. If he laid it on any thicker, she'd need a chisel to chip it off. 'And I suppose you think the same, do you?' She swivelled her stare back to her treacherous so-called boyfriend.

'Yeah, I do,' Dave told her bluntly, pissed off, considering her past, that she was being such a self-righteous bitch. 'Just hear him out – you'll see it's the right thing to do. Go on, mate,' he said to Kenny. 'Tell her.'

'Yeah, go on, *mate*.' Mary was barely suppressing the rage now. 'Tell me this great idea of yours.'

Sitting forward, Kenny rested his elbows on his knees and gazed deep into Mary's blazing eyes. He had no doubt that, if she'd been a bloke, she'd be trying to punch his lights out by now.

'I know you're pissed off with us for landing it on you like this, but look on the positive side. No offence, girl, but you're living in a shit-hole, just about surviving on the dole. Don't you think you deserve better?'

'Oh, I *know* I'm worth more than this,' Mary retorted icily. 'But there's not a lot you can do when you've got no one helping out, is there? If he –' she jabbed an angry finger at Dave '– got off his lazy arse and got a proper job, we'd be fine. But he leaves everything to *me*.'

'Which is exactly why I reckon you should give this a go.' Kenny slipped his point in neatly. 'You shouldn't have to work your arse off and get nothing back.'

'No, according to you, I should just work my arse off, full stop,' she sniped.

'You'd have money in your pocket twenty-four-seven,' he persisted in an infuriatingly reasonable tone. 'You could pay all your bills without worrying, and buy whatever you wanted . . . new sofa, bigger bed, better clothes.'

'What's it to you what I've got?' Mary challenged, offended by Kenny's implication that she needed to make such vast improvements in her life. 'I *like* what I've got. And as long as we're paying for the coke, it's none of your fucking business how we live. Anyway, where do you get off, making out like you're better than us? You're only an ex-con *dealer*.'

Smiling slyly, Kenny said, 'Oh, I know what *I* am, sweetheart. But I know *you* better than you think, an' all. You know you want more than this, and *I* know you could get it – if you put your mind to it.'

'What, by lining your pockets? I don't think so!'

'Shut the fuck up,' Dave chipped in irritably. 'You do my bleedin' head in sometimes.'

'Shut it, you!' Whipping his head around, Kenny gave Dave a warning stare – scoring himself a couple of much-needed points with Mary.

Snapping his mouth shut, Dave pursed his lips. He wasn't worried – it was all part of the plan.

'That's one thing that's gonna change round here if you're going to work with me,' Kenny went on, his voice low and threatening as he held Dave's gaze. 'You'll show this lady of yours the respect she's due. And you can start right now, by making us a brew while me and her talk things over. Go on – shift it.'

Watching as Dave took himself off sulkily into the kitchen, Mary felt a small thrill of smug pleasure. She loved him to bits, but she could kill him right now. He'd had no right to tell Kenny about her past life – and even less right to suggest that she should take it up again.

'If it wasn't for you, I'd have lamped him one ages ago,' Kenny snarled when they were alone, his cheek muscles jumping as he feigned indignation on her behalf. 'I'm *sick* of him talking to you like that.'

Sighing, Mary rubbed a hand across her eyes. Much as Dave pissed her off, she didn't want him hurt.

'He's all right. He just doesn't know when to keep his mouth shut.'

Shaking his head, Kenny looked her in the eye. 'He don't deserve you, you know. But it's your life.'

'Yep.' Folding her arms defensively, Mary nodded.

'Fair enough,' he conceded. 'But this is between you and me, and you don't need his permission to *think* for yourself – do you?'

'Course not,' she told him huffily. 'I don't take orders from *any*one.'

Kenny gave a sly smile, thinking, *Oh, but you will.*

'That's exactly what I need,' he said. 'A woman with a mind of her own. Which is why I thought of you for this. You'd be perfect.'

'Oh yeah?' Mary held his gaze, curious to hear what he had to say even if she had no intention of going along with it.

Lighting two cigarettes, Kenny passed one to her – another point in his favour. She loved a bit of good old-fashioned chivalry, did Mary.

'This ain't something I've come up with off the top of my head. I've been planning it for ages. Dave just happened to let slip that you'd done it before, and it got me thinking. See, I've already got some girls lined up, but I don't trust none of them enough to run things. That's where you come in.'

'So, what you saying?' Leaning forward, Mary picked up the ashtray off the table and placed it between them. 'You're setting up a brothel?'

'Eventually.' Kenny nodded, sensing that she was interested in that idea. 'But not until I've got the money together, so you'd have to work the streets to start with.'

'Oh, no . . .' Snorting softly, she shook her head. 'Sorry, but there's *no* way I'm doing the streets.'

'How about here, then?' he suggested.

'Are you *mad*?' Mary gazed at him incredulously. 'Dave would have a fit! Anyway, I couldn't do that again. I only did it last time because I needed the money.'

'And you don't now?'

'I was a junkie then. I had no choice.'

'Yeah, but this time you *have* got a choice – and you'd be clear-headed enough to enjoy it. Think how it'd feel to be in charge of all the other girls. You'd be raking it in.'

'It don't work like that,' Mary told him, bringing her hand up to her mouth and chewing on her fingernail. 'It'd all end up in your and *his* pockets.' She jerked her head towards the kitchen. 'I'm not that stupid.'

'No, it wouldn't,' Kenny assured her, lowering his voice. 'You can give that loser the heave-ho for all I care. He ain't gonna see *none* of it. This is between you and me.'

'I'm not interested. I've been sweet-talked into it before, and it ended up really bad.'

'Your ex-husband?' Kenny nodded understandingly. 'Yeah, Dave mentioned him. Sounded a bit rough.'

'Understatement of the year. He was a *cunt*, through and through.' Mary shook her head adamantly. 'No. Ali fucked me up once. I can't let it happen again.'

Frowning, Kenny said, 'Did you say Ali?'

'Yeah, why?' Looking at him, her eyes widened when she saw the expression on his face. 'Oh, Christ, you *know* him, don't you?'

'I think so, yeah. Used to be a Paki guy called Ali who lived on Claremont Road. Must be ten, fifteen years back now. Him and his mate—'

'Raiz?'

'That's him. Jeezus . . . Small world.'

'Too bloody small,' Mary muttered, folding her arms as it suddenly occurred to her that Kenny's arrival in their lives might not have been quite as simple as him just *happening* to bump into Dave. 'All right, cut the crap, Kenny. What's going on?'

'Eh?'

'Don't come the innocent.' She was glaring at him with

open suspicion now. 'He sent you here to get back at me, didn't he?'

'I don't know what you're talking about.' Kenny gave a little shrug of genuine confusion. 'Get back at you for what?'

'You know full well what.' Jerking her chin up, Mary held his gaze, refusing to back down and say that she'd been wrong to do what she'd done. She'd been *right* – and she'd do it again if she had to.

'I think we've got our wires crossed,' Kenny said softly, looking at the sparking defensiveness in her eyes. 'I haven't got the foggiest what you're on about.'

'Grassing him over that bloke he knifed,' she spat, knowing full well that he knew *exactly* what she was talking about. 'He knows it was me, and he's sent you to punish me. Well, forget it. You can do what you want, but you're not making me go back on the game so *he* can—'

'*What* did you say?' The blood had all but drained from Kenny's face.

Drawing back from him as he balled his huge hands into fists, Mary's brow puckered. If he was trying to intimidate her, he was doing a damn good job of it.

'You heard me,' she muttered, standing her fearful ground. 'I'm not doing it.'

'This bloke he knifed,' Kenny snarled, his voice low and threatening. 'Who was it?'

Mary was genuinely scared now. Kenny looked like he wanted to kill her. His eyes were harder than she'd ever seen them before, and he was breathing heavily, his broad chest rising and falling beneath his shirt like that of a bull about to charge. She glanced at the kitchen door, hoping to see Dave, but it was closed.

'Who *was* it?' Kenny said again, his teeth bared now.

Jumping, Mary said, '*I* don't know. Some dealer – Terry something or other. I only read about it in the paper after

Ali buggered off. Christ, what's *wrong* with you? You're acting like *I* did it. Is that what he told you? 'Cos it's a lie, if he did. I never knew anything about it. I was just his alibi.'

'And you knew that at the time, did you?' Kenny was holding himself in check – just. 'Thought you were smart, covering up for him?'

'Course not!' she protested vehemently. 'D'y' really think I'd have *married* him if I'd known he was a murderer? Nobody told me a thing till he got his passport. Soon as I knew, I grassed him up.'

'To the police?'

'Course! Who else was gonna give him what he deserved?'

'*Me*,' Kenny growled murderously. 'I'd have ripped his fuckin' heart out.'

Hearing the pain and anger in his voice, Mary realised that he hadn't known, after all. A shiver of relief passed through her. Angry as he was, at least he wasn't here at Ali's behest. They'd *both* been screwed by him.

'That slimy little *cunt*!' Kenny slammed a fist down on his leg. 'I should have known he was lying! I should have fucking *known*!'

'Yeah, well, I wish *I'd* known before I let him get me hooked,' Mary muttered. 'Turning up in the middle of the night, making out like he was some kind of big shot with all his gear!'

Turning his head towards her, Kenny narrowed his eyes. 'He had gear that night?'

'Yeah, a big bag of it,' Mary affirmed, holding out her hands to demonstrate the size of the package. Then, seeing the look on Kenny's face, she said, 'Oh, Christ. Don't say it was yours?'

'Terry's.' Shaking his head, Kenny stared down at his hands, which were tightly clasped now. 'I told the stupid bastard not to carry it about, but he wouldn't be told.' Laughing mirthlessly when he suddenly remembered something else, he said, 'Shit . . . I bet you were the bird Ali reckoned he'd been shagging when Terry got knifed.'

'Yeah,' Mary admitted guiltily. 'He asked me to lie for him if anyone ever asked. Reckoned some blokes were after him over some girls who'd set him up. If I'd known what he'd done, I'd have kicked him right out on his arse.' Frowning now, she said, 'You *do* know it was nothing to do with me, right?'

Sighing heavily, he nodded. 'Yeah, I know.'

'Thank God for that.' She gave a nervous grin. 'I thought you were going to say I owed you for that gear. That bastard's cost me more than enough already.'

'So, you grassed him up?' Kenny cracked his knuckles sharply.

'Yeah, but I don't know if they got him. I moved out the next day and did a cold turkey. I didn't leave the flat for near enough three weeks, and I didn't hear anything after that. It was enough to know I'd done my bit to fuck him over.'

'Yeah, well, I want to make *sure* he's fucked.'

Something in his tone sent a shiver of apprehension down Mary's spine.

Looking up, Kenny noticed the fear in her eyes and smiled. 'I owe you one.'

'So why do I feel so guilty?' she murmured, dropping her gaze and drawing her knees up to her chest.

She'd got Kenny all wrong – accusing him of being in league with Ali when he was as much a victim as she was. Ali had stripped her of her pride, dignity, and self-respect. But he'd taken something far more precious from Kenny – and she'd unwittingly helped him.

Watching Mary struggling with her conscience, Kenny didn't feel sorry for her. He was more interested in how to use her guilt against her. Settling old scores – as important as that was – wasn't the most pressing matter on his agenda right now. Terry was long gone; it wouldn't hurt him to wait a few more years for vengeance. But Kenny was alive and kicking – and in desperate need of fast money.

Reaching out, he patted Mary's leg. 'Look, forget what we were talking about. You've been through enough without me raking up the past.'

'It's okay.' She smiled sadly. 'You weren't to know.'

'No, but I had no right to ask you to do something like that. I'll just have to find someone else I can trust.' Exhaling loudly, he let his shoulders slump. 'You know, it really fucks me off to see cunts like Ali abusing women. These girls came to me to get away from blokes like him.'

'They came to you?' Mary raised an eyebrow.

'Yeah.' Kenny nodded. 'You must remember what it's like out there. There's some real rough bastards taking everything they've got and beating the shit out of them. I can't be doing with that.' Turning his face, he peered at her solemnly. 'Was Ali ever violent?'

'Not really,' she admitted, wishing she could say that he had been – that he'd battered her senseless, and *forced* her to sell herself.

'What about Laughing Boy?' Kenny jerked his chin in the direction of the kitchen.

Blushing, Mary shook her head and looked down at her hands.

'Yeah, well, he'd better not,' Kenny growled protectively. 'He ever lays a finger on you, you just give me the word, yeah?'

Smiling shyly, she nodded.

Winking at her, Kenny reached into his pocket and pushed something into her hand. Folding his own hands around hers, he gazed sincerely into her eyes.

'That's for you – and I don't want to find out that you've shared it with him. He can pay, same as usual.'

Looking at the small clear-plastic bag when he finally released her hand, Mary frowned when she saw the two small white rocks.

'What's this?'

'That,' Kenny grinned, 'is a bit special. You are gonna *love* that, believe me. Anyway, I thought it was time you had a change from the powder. Strong as you are, you have been doing a bit much of it lately. This will clean your slate and give you a fresh start.'

Hard as she tried, Mary couldn't fight the thrill of anticipation that was surging through her. She loved drugs – always had, probably always would. There was something amazing and almost orgasmic about being lifted out of the humdrum day-to-day routine and let off the gravity leash. It was like being back in the warmth and safety of the womb after a year in a cold-water tank, but with wings to fly far above the rest of the world.

Glancing gratefully up at Kenny, she said, 'Thanks. And, about these girls of yours . . . You really going to look after them?'

'Yeah, course.'

'And you'd be looking to set up a proper house for them?'

'As soon as I've got the money together, yeah.'

Pursing her lips, Mary took a deep breath. 'All right, I'll do it.'

'You sure?' Kenny frowned concernedly. 'I don't want to pressure you into it.'

'You're not,' she assured him. 'But you're right about the money – I could use some more. Dave's useless, God love him. And I can't see me working at Netto, somehow.'

'Too right,' he agreed. 'You're way too good for that. I can see you in a year's time, lady of the manor, with your

bottle of bubbly and your little gold mirror and straw –
taking it easy while the other girls do all the work. If Ali
had any sense, he'd have seen your potential and you'd have
been rolling in it years back.'

'Yeah, well, he was too thick to see past his next fix,' Mary
said bitterly. 'But forget him . . . When are you planning to
get started?'

'I'll get the girls together in a week or two,' Kenny told
her, already mentally planning who he would approach. 'Let
you give them the once-over.'

Nodding, Mary frowned and flicked another glance at
the kitchen door.

'You sure Dave's all right about it? He might say he is
while you're here, but I don't want him going off on one
when you've gone.'

'Just leave him to me,' Kenny said, trying not to look too
victorious. 'And not a word to anyone. This is *our* business,
right?'

'Absolutely,' Mary agreed, shuddering at the prospect of
any of the others finding out what she was planning.

And God only knew what Jane would say if *she* knew . . .

But no . . . *Sod them!* It was her life, not theirs. And she
didn't see any of them rushing to pay her bills.

Like Kenny had said, she was a woman with a mind of
her own. She knew exactly what she was doing, and this
time she was doing it for herself. If Dave didn't like it –
tough! She was through with struggling. This time next year,
Mary would be queen of her own little empire.

28

Tina had stopped going round to Mary's weeks back, unable to stomach seeing them squabbling over the coke like a little pack of dogs. And, worse – fawning over Kenny like he had solid gold bollocks and a diamond dick.

She couldn't stand the man. She'd seen through him from the start and didn't understand why everyone else seemed to worship him. He was on the make as sure as night followed day, but the more she'd voiced her unpopular opinion, the more her so-called friends had turned against her.

Tina had never been into powders, but even she could see that there was something funny about this one. They all reckoned it was too clean to get hooked on, but they definitely were hooked. Why else would they spend so much time talking about it, doing it, trying to get money for more? But they wouldn't admit that – not even to themselves, it seemed.

Mary had laughed in Tina's face when she'd tried to warn her, telling her to chill out before she turned into Jane. And if that hadn't been insulting enough, Jock had agreed, saying it was just a bit of fun – and why didn't she want him to enjoy himself?

That had stung because she'd gone quite soft on Jock.

Soft enough to carry on seeing him after she stopped hanging out with Mary, but *not* soft enough to be fooled by his assurances that he could stop the coke any time he liked.

She wanted to believe him, she really did, but she was sure he would prove himself wrong.

And that happened much sooner than Tina had anticipated.

Jock came round to visit – with Stan in tow, as usual. Letting himself in with the key that Tina had given him, he barrelled into the living room, bringing a blast of chill air with him.

'Colder than a butcher's bollock out there,' he declared, leaning down to give her a kiss.

'Sit by the fire,' Tina told him, putting her crossword book down. 'I'll make a brew.'

Getting up, she waddled into the kitchen leaving them to take their coats off and make themselves comfortable. She tutted softly when she heard Stan switching the TV on. She'd been enjoying the quiet, but Stan couldn't bear it. He'd watch The Teletubbies rather than sit in peaceful silence. Still, much as he irritated her at times, she'd rather have him here if it meant Jock spending less time at Mary's.

After pouring the water into the teapot when the kettle had boiled, Tina opened the fridge and saw that she had no milk. Knowing it was pointless asking either of the men to go, she went into the hall and pulled her coat on, calling over her shoulder, 'Won't be long, I'm just nipping to the shop.'

The instant the door closed behind her, Jock leapt up from his seat and rushed to the window. Easing the curtain back, he smiled when he saw the woman from three doors down come out of her gate and walk down the road with Tina.

'She's yakking to that bint from number seventeen,' he said. 'She'll be ages.'

Rubbing his hands together, Stan got up, took a small paper bag from his pocket and waved it at Jock. 'Come on, then, fat man . . . Let's go test the merchandise!'

Giggling, they ran upstairs like a couple of naughty schoolboys, not giving a shit about the noise they were making as their thunderous footsteps shook the small house to its foundations.

In the bathroom, Jock slid the bolt across and sat down on the floor. There was no blind at the window and the last thing they needed was for the nosy next-door neighbour to see them and report back to Tina. She'd forbidden them to do anything stronger than weed in her house and would have a complete shit-fit if she knew they were doing this.

It wasn't that Jock was scared of her, or anything, he just didn't want her to ban him from the bedroom. She was the first bird he'd ever met who didn't mind him bouncing up and down on her. Not like thin birds, who made out like you were killing them if you took more than five seconds to come.

Sitting beside him, Stan opened the bag and took out the small glass pipe that they'd bought at one of the head shops in Affleck's Palace that afternoon. Holding it up, he gazed at it as if it were the most wondrous sight he'd ever seen.

'Oh, that is *mint*,' he said, slotting his greasy fringe behind his ears and sucking on the mouthpiece. 'Well smooth.'

'Yeah, well, get something in it and quit dry-humping,' Jock told him irritably. 'We haven't got all night.'

'All right baldy, keep your hair on.'

'Oh, har-de-fuckin'-har!'

Sniggering, Stan took from his pocket the rocks they'd scored from Dave on their way over and loaded one into the bowl of the pipe. Ordinarily, they'd have done it at Dave's place, but he'd been in a bit of a rush to get them out tonight, for some unknown reason. Sparking the lighter, Stan held the flame up and grinned.

'I hereby christen this pipe Rocket Man.'

'Stop arsing about and get on with it,' Jock complained.

'Cool down,' Stan drawled. 'You know you should never rush a virgin.' Taking his sweet time, he brought the pipe to his lips and lowered the flame into the bowl. 'Oh, Ker-*iist!*' he exclaimed, sucking up the smoke, his grin a mile wide now. 'That is fuckin' *hot*, man!'

'Hand it over.' Jock impatiently reached for the pipe. Sucking wetly on it, he didn't hear the front door clicking shut down below.

Anna from number seventeen had only gone as far as the corner, so Tina had got the milk and come straight back. Hanging up her coat now, she popped her head around the living-room door en route to the kitchen. Frowning when she saw that the TV was playing to an empty room, she wandered all the way in and stood with her hands on her hips, cursing Jock and Stan for letting her go to all that trouble if they hadn't intended to stay – the bastards!

Mid-curse, her eyes narrowed when she spotted their coats still slung over the back of the couch. Annoyance turning to suspicion, she put the milk down on the coffee table and crept silently back out into the hall and up the stairs.

Listening at the bathroom door, Tina's suspicions were confirmed when she heard them talking in hushed tones inside.

'Hurry up and give us another go, man,' Stan was saying. 'She'll be back in a minute.'

'She'll still be yakking,' Jock replied confidently. 'Anyhow, we'll hear the door. Pass us the lighter.'

Inflamed, Tina yanked the handle down and shoulder-barged the ineffectual bolt off.

Jock and Stan gaped up at her guiltily, the only light in the room coming from the moonlight bouncing off Jock's head – and the flame of the lighter that he was holding to the bowl of the pipe.

Glaring at them, Tina didn't know if she was more angry or upset. He'd promised never to do this in her house, but the minute her back was turned he was at it. And not just coke now, but *crack*.

'Right, that's it!' she yelled, her whole body quivering with rage. 'Get out of my fucking house and don't ever come back!'

'Aw, come on, babe,' Jock drawled, giving her his best cuddly-caveman grin. 'It's only a bit of—'

'Don't you dare say *fun*!' Rushing across the room, Tina snatched the pipe from his hand and hurled it at the wall. 'Since when have you been doing fuckin' *rock*, you dick-head?'

'Christ, Tina!' Stan protested, leaping to his feet. 'Chill out, will you! That was half mine, that pipe. I fuckin' paid for that!'

Balling her hands into fists, Tina spun around and threw a punch at him.

Ducking just in time, Stan scooted past her onto the landing, yelling, 'You fuckin' mad bitch! No wonder he needs to get off his head all the time. You're enough to turn a man queer, you!'

'Get *OUUUT*!' she roared, thundering after him as he fled down the stairs. 'I'll fuckin' kill you, you little puff!'

'Tina, don't!' Running after her, Jock caught up with her at the door and put his arms around her, trying to calm her down. 'Look, there's no need for this, babe. If you hadn't come back so fast you'd never have known, so where's the harm?'

Using all of her strength to shove him out to join Stan in the garden, Tina said, 'You've done this before, haven't you? In *my* house! After everything I said . . . After *promising* you wouldn't.'

'Aw, come on,' Jock wheedled, trying the special grin

again. 'We've only done it a couple of times. Anyway, you like it when I've had a bit of coke. You said it yourself – it keeps me up. What does it matter where I do it?'

'Coke *might* keep you up,' she countered angrily. 'But crack just sends you fuckin' loopy, and you know that as well as I do, so don't even bother arguing. And don't think I'll forgive you for going behind my back, 'cos I won't. You've blown it – *good* style!'

Slamming the door in his face, Tina leaned her back against it and covered her ears when Jock knocked and pleaded for a second chance. Painful as it was to end it like this, she couldn't let him make a fool of her. And that's what he was doing, she could see that now. All the time he'd been coming round here, agreeing with her that Kenny was a cunt, that Dave was a shit, that Mary was an idiot . . . All the time, he'd been laughing at her. Stupid Tina who objected to what he was doing but still let him get his end away. Well, no more! Enough was enough.

Exhaling wearily when Jock finally gave up and went, taking a grumbling Stan with him, she got their coats and tossed them onto the small patch of garden. Pulling her own coat back on then, she went out, double-locking the door behind her. She hadn't given Jock the key for the mortise, and she would get the Yale changed tomorrow to stop him paying any unscheduled visits.

Right now, she needed a friend to moan to and, since Jane was out of the picture, that only left Mary. She hadn't seen her in weeks, but she was sure Mary wouldn't turn her away.

Tina got a shock when Mary answered the door. The difference in her appearance was startling. She'd lost a lot of weight, for one thing, but it was what she was wearing that was most shocking. Her skirt was so short that it barely

covered her knickers, and her top was so low-cut that her
nipples seemed to be the only things holding it up. And her
make-up was far more *obvious* than usual – her eyes darkly
outlined, her lips a deep, glossy red. She looked like a whore.

Frowning when she saw who it was, Mary said, 'All right,
Tee. What's up?'

'I need a moan,' Tina said, frowning when she had to
squeeze past her friend to get through the door. 'What's up
with you? Aren't I welcome any more, or something?'

'Course,' Mary lied, going through to the living room.
'It's just that I'm about to go out.'

'Well, I'd put some proper clothes on if I was you, 'cos
it's bloody freezing out there,' Tina warned, following her.
'What are you all tarted up for, anyway?'

Before Mary had a chance to answer, Dave came through
from the kitchen with Kenny in tow.

'Mind your own business,' he told Tina sharply. 'What
d'y' want? We're busy.'

'I've come to see *her*, not you,' Tina retorted huffily. Then,
turning to Mary, she said, 'What you letting him do your
talking for? Since when have I had to go through him to
talk to my best mate?'

Shrugging her jacket on, Mary frowned. 'Look, you'll have
to leave this for another time, Tee. Like I said, we're on our
way out.'

Tina's trouble antenna was beginning to twitch like a newly
slaughtered lamb. Narrowing her eyes, she said, 'Where?'

'Didn't I just tell you to keep your fucking fat nose out?'
Dave snapped, stepping between them and glaring at her.

'All right, *Dave*,' Mary cut in peevishly. 'I have got a
tongue of me own, you know.'

'Oi!' Kenny barked at her. 'Less of the lip. Let's get moving.'

Turning on him, Mary scowled. 'What you sticking up
for *him* for? I thought you were on *my* side.'

'Get a grip,' Dave snorted. 'He don't care what *I* do. Ain't you figured that out yet?'

'Oh, fuck off, you wanker!'

'Wanna say that again, do you?' Sneering contemptuously, Dave thrust his face into hers. 'Come on, I *dare* you.'

'Shut it, the pair of you!' Kenny cast a warning glance in Tina's direction.

Staring at the three of them with open suspicion, Tina said, 'What the hell's going on here? Why are you talking to her like that? You don't *own* her.'

Whipping around, Dave brought both hands up and slammed them into her chest.

'Fuck off, you fat cunt. And don't come back.'

'Keep your bleedin' hands to yourself,' Tina warned, stumbling as he propelled her backwards from the room. Catching Mary's glance over his shoulder, she said, 'You gonna let him treat me like this?'

Turning her head, Mary folded her arms.

Mouth gaping in disbelief, Tina brought her arms up and whacked Dave's hands out of the way.

'Right, what's the game?' she demanded, her tone as fierce as the look in her eyes. 'And don't tell me it's nowt, 'cos I can see something funny's going on.'

Smiling nastily, Dave reached behind her and pulled the front door open, saying in a low, mean voice, 'She don't want you here, that's what. And *I* sure as hell don't, so why don't you just piss off back to your little shit-pit and leave us alone, eh?'

'I'm going nowhere till you tell me what's going on.' Tina stood her ground. 'If you're hurting her, I'll—'

'He's not.' Coming up behind Dave, Mary jerked her chin up proudly. 'I've moved on, Tee, that's all. I'm fine, so why don't you do yourself a favour and go, eh? You're only winding yourself up for nothing.'

'You don't *look* fine,' Tina contradicted her worriedly. 'What they doing to you, Mare?'

Stepping around Mary and Dave, Kenny shoved Tina out onto the communal landing.

'I think you've outstayed your welcome, don't you?' he snarled, towering over her menacingly. 'Now, have a bit of respect and fuck off, 'cos they don't want you here. Got it?'

'Yeah, I've got it,' Tina muttered, casting a betrayed glance at Mary who was too busy chewing her nails to notice.

'Bye-bye, then.' Smirking nastily, Kenny waved her towards the stairwell.

Giving him one last reproachful glare, Tina turned and made her way down the stairs.

Outside, she stepped into the shadows of the bin cupboard and lit a cigarette, surprised to see that her hands were shaking. It took a lot to rattle her but that had been weird, and she was more concerned for Mary than ever. Whatever was going on in that flat, Mary was in danger and Tina wouldn't rest until she knew the score.

Hearing the main entrance door opening a couple of minutes later, she ground the cigarette butt out with her heel and pressed herself back against the wall. Listening as Mary and Kenny came out and began to walk away, she waited a few moments, then followed them at a distance.

Hiding behind a wall when Mary and Kenny stopped at the park gates on Alexandra Road, she watched as three girls ran across to join them. As if a light had been switched on in her mind, Tina suddenly knew exactly what was happening.

The stupid bitch was back on the game!

Disgusted, disappointed – *saddened* – she gave up her surveillance and walked home. There was no point confronting Mary about it. She had obviously chosen to do this, and nothing Tina or anyone else said would make the slightest bit of difference.

Pausing at her gate, Tina saw that Jock and Stan's coats had gone. Wondering if they'd come back for them, or if they'd been nicked, she felt an extra layer of sadness settle upon her heart.

It was over . . . Her and Jock . . . Her and Mary. She was right back to where she'd started – nobody left to cling to but herself.

Sighing, she made her way inside the solitary little house, hung up her coat, sat down and picked up her crossword book.

PART FOUR

29

Dressing for the party, Jane looked herself over in the mirror and smiled. She'd never have dreamed of wearing a hippie dress in her previous life, but Mimi had persuaded her to buy this one – and she was glad now that she had. Long, black and slimming, it had a lovely embroidered bodice and floaty sleeves. It really suited her, and she felt good wearing it. In fact, she felt pretty good about herself altogether. Hanging about with genuinely nice people, who complimented her for her strengths but didn't take the piss about her weaknesses, had boosted her self-esteem no end. She was almost back to her old self – and that was fantastic after the misery of the previous year.

Pulling her jacket on when she'd done her make-up and brushed her hair, she headed out and made her way around the landing with a light heart. Mike's parties were great. Every offbeat, oddball weirdo in Hulme turned up, bringing booze, weed, and all manner of musical instruments for the night-long jam-and-hash session.

In some ways, it was just like any normal day at Mike's place, but there was an added excitement when the word 'party' was attached, and the flat – which normally had six or seven people in it at any given time – would be chock-full of old friends, new friends, friends of friends, friends of *friends* of friends . . .

Jane felt privileged to be one of Mike's everyday friends, along with Pete, Mimi, Jonas and Kim – *and* their glued-on mate, Genghis: a tiny, shrivelled-up, reformed alkie, who had a beaming toothless grin and the kindest eyes Jane had ever seen.

She loved them all as if they were family – even Donkey, the peculiar little dog that had attached itself to Mike at one of the peace camps he'd visited over the years. Convinced he was as human as the rest of them, Donkey smiled when he was happy and sulked when he was sad – and he even knocked on the door when he wanted to get back in after a toilet trip. He was a cool dog.

Trotting down the stairs to Mike's floor a few minutes later, Jane's smile dropped when she heard the distinctive swish and rumble of roller skates on concrete. Oh, great! Roy the skating speed-freak. Just what she needed – not!

Of everyone she'd met since falling out with Mary and getting to know Mike and the others, Roy was the only one that she truly disliked. He was mad as a hatter, and really creepy-looking with his jet-black hair and coal-black eyes. Forever prattling on about demons and aliens and assorted spiritual matters that – according to him – only he was privy to, he also had an annoying habit of bursting through the front door and roller skating around Mike's uncarpeted front room for hours on end – which pissed everyone off, not least Mike.

'Stop *doing* that,' he'd yell when the door flew open. 'I keep thinking it's the fuckin' drug squad!'

But Roy would just laugh and say, 'You should lock it, man. You don't know *what* could be lurking out there.'

Jane was praying for the day when Mike would ban him from the flat, but she knew it wouldn't happen. Mike was too soft-hearted to turn anyone away – however certifiably insane they were.

Hiding around the corner now until she'd heard Roy going

inside, she waited a couple of minutes, then followed him in.

Kim was the first person she saw, her long red hair brushed to a gleam, her unmade-up face glowing with youth. Shaking her head in mock despair, Jane tapped her on the shoulder. She was only a decade older, but these girls made her feel like a pensioner sometimes.

Turning around, Kim saw her and made herself even more beautiful by breaking into an enormous smile.

'Jane!' she exclaimed, throwing her arms around her. 'You look *amazing*. And I love what you've done with your eyes.'

Hugging her, Jane thanked her and said, '*You* look gorgeous, as usual – you *cow*.' Smiling, she let her go and asked, 'Who's here?'

'Everyone.' Kim beamed, shouting to make herself heard above the music. 'Want a drink? Jonas is flitting about somewhere with a pile of cans. Just let me find him. Won't be a minute.'

Gazing around when Kim had dashed off, Jane saw people sitting, lying and standing in every available space. In one corner, four men were playing bongos, penny whistles and guitars. In another, Mike and two men were immersed in a serious-looking game of cards. Some young girls Jane recognised from the pub where she now worked were hogging the centre of the floor, attempting to dance to the complicated rhythms that the stoned musicians were belting out. And everywhere, the fog of marijuana smoke drifted between heads and swirled around legs.

'Hey, Jane . . . You look great.'

Turning at the voice, Jane smiled at Kim's gorgeous boyfriend, Jonas. His Mohican was dyed a shocking pink tonight, and he was wearing matching eyeshadow and lipstick. He looked amazing – even if he did clash with his girlfriend.

'Don't just stand there gawping, give her a drink.' Smiling adoringly up at Jonas, Kim stood on tiptoe and planted a kiss on his lips. Taking one of the cans from the six-pack he was holding, she passed it to Jane, then glanced around. 'Where's Geng?'

'Waiting to lose his giro,' Jonas told her, nodding across the room.

Frowning when she saw their strange little friend sitting cross-legged on the floor beside Mike, Kim said, 'Oh, Christ. He'll be skint for the next two weeks if they let him play.'

'That's right, babe,' Jonas called after her as she headed off to rescue Genghis. 'You go sort him out . . . I'll just stop here and have a toke for you.' Giving Jane a conspiratorial wink, he rubbed his hands together and flopped down onto a beanbag next to a couple of lads who were busy loading a heap of Gold Seal black resin into an oil-blackened bong.

Shaking her head with amusement, Jane dropped her coat onto the pile covering the chair beside the door and followed Kim across the room. Avoiding Roy, who was squatting against the wall like a black-eyed nightmare, she tiptoed over an obstacle course of legs. Reaching Mike just as Kim hauled Genghis away from temptation, she squatted beside him and kissed his cheek.

'Winning?' she asked, stroking Donkey's head – until he rudely shoved her hand away with his snout.

Winking at her, Mike said, 'Don't distract him. He's spying.'

'He'd best not be!' one of the opponents protested, turning his hand so that Donkey couldn't see his cards.

'Stop faffing about,' the other one snorted. 'Donkey ain't a cheat. You're just making excuses 'cos you're losing.'

'You're *both* losing,' Mike cut in smugly. 'You'll never be good enough to beat me, and you know it.'

'Only 'cos Donkey's telling you what we've got!'

'Bollocks!' Mike chuckled. 'He only speaks *German*. I wouldn't understand him.'

'So *you* say!'

Laughing as they squabbled, Jane stood up and left them to it. Stopping every couple of steps to chat to people, she gradually made her way to the kitchen. Finding the door closed, she gave a tentative tap, then opened it a crack and peeped inside. The last thing she wanted was to walk in on some couple having it off on the ledge.

Pete and Mimi were standing by the sink, talking to two young girls Jane didn't know. They looked even younger than Mimi and Kim, but they had an added aura of naivety – as if they'd just landed on Planet Hulme and couldn't believe what they'd found there.

It was obvious at a glance that both girls had taken quite a fancy to Pete, who must have seemed like some sort of Bohemian god to them with his waist-length dreadlocks, his goatee beard and his easy, laid-back manner. Flanking him, they were thrusting their pert breasts at him and fluttering their mascara'd lashes like crazy.

Waving her in, Pete said, 'Hurry up, Jane. We're having a secret meeting.'

'Secret, eh?' Smiling, she went in and closed the door. 'What kind of secret?'

'Take no notice,' Mimi said, kissing her on the cheek and handing her a spliff. 'We're talking about dreams, that's all. This is Melanie and Della, by the way – old friends of mine from back home. They're staying with me for the weekend, so I thought I'd bring them to meet my friends. This is Jane,' she told the girls then. 'My big sister.'

'Really?' Della gazed from one to the other of them in disbelief. 'You don't look anything like each other.'

'I didn't even know you *had* a sister,' Melanie added.

'We're all sisters in spirit,' Mimi twinkled. 'Anyway, finish what you were saying, Del. You got a letter, and . . . ?' She gestured with her hand for the other girl to continue.

'Oh, yeah . . .' Della frowned thoughtfully. 'Well, I had this envelope in my hand and I'm wondering who it's from. So, I'm looking at it and smelling it, and what have you, but I can't figure it out. So, then I start feeling it, and it's all sort of bumpy, and I'm thinking, *Oh, God, what's that? I hope it's not rabbit eyes.*'

'You *what?*' Pete interrupted with an incredulous snort. 'Why on *Earth* would someone send rabbit eyes through the post?'

'*I* don't know.' Della shrugged, smiling shyly. 'It was only a dream. Anyway, it was upside down when I opened it, so everything fell on the floor.'

'What was it?' Melanie asked.

'Teeth,' Della told her, grimacing as she added, '*My* teeth.'

'No way!'

'Honest to God.' Della nodded grimly. 'They were in thousands of tiny pieces, and I'm looking at them all over the floor, but I can't scream 'cos there's more in my mouth and I know I'll lose *them* as well!'

'You know what that means, don't you?' Mimi told her knowledgeably. 'When you dream about teeth crumbling like that, it either means that *you*'re saying stuff you shouldn't be saying, or someone's gossiping behind *your* back.'

'Really?' Della frowned. 'That's weird that, 'cos there *was* a rumour going round about me a while back, but I never found out who was spreading it.'

'Look closer to home,' Mimi intoned, folding her arms. 'It's usually someone you thought was a friend.'

'Don't look at me,' Melanie protested.

'I wasn't,' Della said – but it was obvious from the way that she'd narrowed her eyes that she had been.

'If you ask me, it's a warning to stop eating sweet things,'

Pete interjected, chuckling. 'Sounds like your mouth's trying to tell you something.'

'Shut up!' Mimi scolded, giving him a playful shove. 'There's nothing wrong with her teeth.'

'Yeah, look.' Thrusting herself even closer, Della gave Pete a huge smile.

'Watch it!' he yelped, just managing to stop the spliff he was building from going into the sink as her breasts jolted his arm.

Casting a disapproving look at her friend, Melanie turned to Jane.

'What about you? You must have had some wild dreams in your time?'

Exchanging a bemused glance with Pete, Jane said, 'With me being such an *ancient* old thing, you mean?'

'Oh, God!' Melanie threw a hand up to her mouth. 'Sorry! I didn't mean it to come out like that.'

'Don't worry about it.' Jane laughed good-naturedly. 'We're way past vanity when you get to our age – eh, Pete?'

'Oi, don't make out like I'm a fossil like you.'

'You're *older* than me.'

'According to *you*.'

'Yeah, well, we both know the truth.' Giving Pete a smug grin, Jane turned back to Melanie. 'Anyway, no . . . I hardly ever dream, as it happens.'

'You probably do, but you don't remember,' Della said. Then, turning to Pete as if addressing the Guru of the West, she said, 'Was it Jung or Freud who said that every dream really means that you want to shag your own mother?'

'No idea,' he drawled. 'But, whoever it was, they were probably talking about Roy.'

Slapping his arm, Mimi said, 'Ssshhh! He'll hear you.'

'So what?' Jane sneered. 'He's right. If ever there was a fucked-up excuse of a motherfucker, it's *that* freak.'

'Yeah,' Mimi agreed, giggling quietly. 'But you don't want to go setting him off, do you? You know what a weirdo he is.'

Bored at being left out of this in-crowd stuff, Della clapped her hands together sharply until they were all looking at her – oblivious to the bemused smiles on Jane's and Pete's faces as they both wondered if she was a primary-school teacher, or something.

'Talking about weird,' she said, her voice too loud and pushy for the small kitchen. 'Tell them about that dream *you* had, Meems.'

'Which one?' Mimi frowned. 'The one about the boy in the goldfish bowl?'

'No, the one you rang me about last week – about the woman in the sea.'

'Oh, *that* one.' Remembering, Mimi's eyes widened. 'God, yeah, it was weird, that. It didn't half freak me out.'

Lighting his spliff, Pete leaned back against the sink, a teasing smile curling his lip.

'Was it your *mother*?'

'No, it was not! I've no idea who it was, actually. It was just this woman I've never seen before. She was really beautiful, and—'

'Go *on*, then!' Pete waggled his eyebrows lewdly. 'I love a bit of girl-on-girl.'

'Are you gonna let me finish telling you, or what?'

'Carry on.' Grinning, he waved a hand. 'Can't wait to hear all about your wet dream.'

'It was *not* wet, for your information.' Mimi pursed her lips primly. 'Not in the way *you* mean, anyway. It was just—'

Before she had a chance to say another word, the door opened and Roy rolled slowly in. Narrowing his eyes, he looked at everyone in turn, a sly smile lifting one side of his mouth.

'What's this, then? Private party, or can anyone join in?'

'Private,' Jane snapped, folding her arms.

Smirking nastily, Roy glided right up to her and circled a finger in front of her face.

'See you . . .' he murmured, his voice whispery and slow as if he were tranked out of his head. 'You're under my command.'

'Oh, piss off,' she snorted, swatting his finger away.

'Is that the weird one you were talking about?' Della asked Pete worriedly, pressing herself even closer into him.

Grinning, he nodded and waved her to be quiet. This ought to be fun.

Staring intently into Jane's eyes as if there was no one else in the room, Roy began to whisper-sing: 'The Devil's on his way, the Devil's on his way, E-I-Ad-E-O, the Devil's on his way.'

'You are one fucking nutter,' Jane barked, losing patience and jabbing him in the chest with a recently filed and polished nail. 'And if you keep bugging me I'm gonna knock you out. Now, why don't you do us all a favour and piss off, 'cos no one likes you.'

'*Schwizameezle*,' he hissed, wafting his hand rapidly in front of her face. '*Cabbajabeezah!*'

Laughing out loud, she said, 'Christ, you really are off it, aren't you? Where's the men in white coats? Shouldn't they be coming to take you back to the home by now?'

Roy's complexion darkened several shades.

'Don't believe me, then,' he growled venomously. 'But when he gets here, don't say I didn't warn you. You're going to fall on your knees and *beg* me to save your miserable soul!'

'Right, that's enough.' Suppressing the laughter that was making his guts ache, Pete disentangled himself from Melanie and Della who were gripping his arms now and stepped between Jane and Roy. Putting his hands on Roy's shoulders, he rolled him smoothly back towards the door. 'Come on, mate, time you got going.'

Holding up his hands in a placatory gesture, Roy said, 'It's all right, man. I'm the sentinel. I'm only doing my job.'

'Yeah, well, why don't you tell me all about it when there's no girls around to scare?' Still smiling, Pete shoved Roy out and closed the door in his face.

Shuddering, Mimi said, 'God, he's getting worse. Did you see his *eyes*? It's like there's – I don't know – some sort of red glow behind the black.'

'*Devil* eyes,' Pete hissed, bringing his hands up zombie-like. 'He's gonna *get* you.'

Slapping him on the shoulder when she noticed the fearful expressions on Mimi's friend's faces, Jane said, 'Pack it in, you idiot. You're scaring the crap out of them.'

'I'm all right,' Melanie protested shakily. 'There's loads of nutters round our way.'

'And where's that?' Pete asked, relighting his spliff and settling back against the sink.

'Bridlington,' both girls said at once.

'Where I grew up,' Mimi reminded him, rolling her eyes as she added, 'bog end of nowhere.'

'Subject of sea,' Della piped up. 'You never finished telling them about your dream.'

'God, you've got a good memory,' Melanie snorted. 'I forgot all about that.'

'Yeah, well, I didn't. But that's why I got five A levels and you only got three Os, isn't it?'

'Get lost!'

'Mee-*ow*.' Pete chuckled softly. 'Put the claws away, girls. We're all friends here.'

'I've forgotten it now, anyway,' Mimi said, checking her watch. 'It's gone a bit *dark* in here. I think I'll nip to the all-night Spar for some incense. Anyone coming?'

'No,' Melanie and Della both said, flicking adoring glances at Pete.

Jane smiled to herself. They obviously couldn't bear to tear themselves away from him, but they had more chance of marrying each other and having seven beautiful babies than they had of getting off with him. He was a brilliant bloke, but he hadn't had a girlfriend in the whole of the year she'd known him. He reckoned he was a born-again virgin, saving himself for the woman of his dreams.

'I'll come,' Jane said, pushing herself away from the ledge where she'd been lounging. 'I could do with a bit of fresh air after all that Devil shite.'

'Oh, well, if you're both going, I'll take you,' Pete said. 'I'm nearly out of rolling gear, and I fancy a bit of brandy. No one's brought any tonight. It's all beer and bloody cider.'

'We'll come, then,' Della immediately said.

'Sorry, love.' Pete gave her a regretful smile. 'My van's full of junk. There's only room for these two.'

'Never mind,' Mimi told them, opening the kitchen door. 'There's loads of people to talk to while we're gone. And we won't be long.'

Groaning with disappointment, Melanie and Della followed her out into the living room. Spotting Jonas, Della brightened up in a flash.

'Hey! There's that lad!'

'Oh, yeah!' Melanie yelped excitedly. 'He's well fit. Let's go chat him up.'

Shaking her head when the girls rushed to ambush Jonas, Mimi said, 'Sorry about them. I keep forgetting how silly they are.'

'How old are they?' Jane asked, opening the front door and stepping outside.

'Nineteen, same as me,' Mimi said, following Pete out and pulling the door shut. 'But they've never been away from home before. And back in Bridlington, no one grows up until they hit their thirties.'

'What happens then?' Pete asked, trotting down the stairs.

'Pension City,' Mimi groaned. 'Honest to God, I swear the duffel coats and bubble perms just grow on you overnight on your thirtieth birthday. Why do you think *I* got out when I did?'

'Smart move.' Wrenching the back door of his two-seater van open, Pete hopped in and climbed over the assorted tools, sleeping bags and rubbish to get to the driver's seat.

Clambering in after him, Jane sat in the passenger seat and squashed herself up against the door to give Mimi room to squeeze in after she'd pulled the back doors shut.

Starting it up on the fifth attempt, Pete crunched the rust bucket into gear and set off. Taking the back roads to avoid being pulled over by the police and gripped for having no road tax, MOT or insurance, he kept to a strict thirty all the way – which felt almost as slow as walking.

Flicking the radio on, Mimi began to sing along to the old soul records, her high, sweet tone clashing with Jane's tuneless huskiness when she joined in.

'We both know that it's wro-ong . . . ooh, but it's much too stro-ong . . . to let it go no-ow . . . We meet ev-ery da-ay, at the sa-ame café, six-thir—'

Stopping abruptly when she realised that she was suddenly going solo, Mimi turned her head to see why Jane had stopped singing. Seeing the shocked expression on her pale face, she said, 'What's wrong, babe? You look like you've seen a ghost.'

'I'm not sure,' Jane murmured, twisting her head to stare out through the grimy rear window. 'Did you see those girls standing on the corner back there?'

'The pros?' Pete chuckled. 'Yeah, I saw them.'

'You would!' Mimi admonished him. 'Who was it, Jane? Someone you know?'

'No.' Shaking her head, Jane turned back to face the front. All she'd seen was a fleeting glimpse of blonde hair. That didn't mean anything. 'I must have been seeing things.'

'You sure you're all right?' Mimi peered at her concernedly.

'Yeah, I'm fine,' Jane assured her, giving her a quick hug. Mimi was so sweet. She was probably dying to know what the story was, but she was far too polite to stick her nose in where it wasn't wanted. Anyway, there was probably nothing to tell.

After picking up Mimi's incense and Pete's tobacco, skins, and brandy, they went back to Mike's, but Jane had completely lost the party spirit. Despite telling herself that she'd been wrong, she couldn't shake the feeling that she'd just seen Mary up to her old tricks. She sincerely doubted it after everything Mary had said about staying on the straight and narrow, but now that the seed was planted . . .

Assuring Mimi for the umpteenth time that she was okay, that she was just tired and her head was starting to ache with all the noise, Jane made her way home.

Back home, Jane sat in the darkened living room, smoking a cigarette and mentally rerunning the moment when they had passed the women on the corner – trying to latch onto the fleeting glimpse and hold it in place so that she could scrutinise the faces in her mind. Hard as she tried she couldn't, but, somehow, she just *knew* that Mary had been among them.

It was almost a full year since they'd had their fight and gone their separate ways, and Jane had neither seen nor heard from Mary in all that time. She told herself that she didn't care, but it wasn't true. She *did* care – deeply. But she'd forced Mary out of her mind a long time ago, vowing to forget about her for turning her back on Jane in favour of that scumbag Dave. And she had succeeded – until now.

Stubbing out her fourth cigarette in an hour, Jane got up and snatched her jacket from the back of the chair where she'd flung it. There was no point sitting here mulling things over; just as there was no point going to bed, or even back to the party. Nothing was going to quieten the voices in her head until she'd seen with her own eyes that Mary hadn't fallen off the wagon and got herself into some sort of trouble. She'd just have to go round to Mary's flat. Then, when she'd seen that Mary was all right – and she sincerely hoped that she was – she'd say her goodbyes and come back to her new life with a clear conscience.

Bypassing Mike's flat where the party was still going strong, Jane pulled her collar up around her ears and hurried out of the Crescents, marching purposefully past the shops, the pub, her and Mary's old school, and on through the estate to Moss Side.

Looking up when she reached Mary's block, she counted along the windows on the fifth floor until she located Mary's place. Seeing that the light was on, she gulped down the lump that was forming in her throat. She wanted to turn and run, but she couldn't let herself. She *had* to see this through – even if it killed her.

Steeling herself, Jane made her way up the stairs and, taking a deep breath, knocked on the door.

30

Squinting out through the spyhole in the centre of the door, Dave couldn't see anybody. Bending down, he cautiously raised the letter-box flap.

'Who is it?'

'It's me,' Jane replied, her nose wrinkling at the mere sound of his voice.

'Who the fuck's *me*?' Relieved to hear a female voice, Dave opened the door an inch and peered out at her through the crack. 'Oh, it's you. Ain't no one ever told you y' knock like a bleedin' copper? Whaddya want?'

'I need to see Mary.' Jane kept her voice as level as possible. 'Is she in?'

'No, she ain't,' Dave grunted, looking her up and down. 'And even if she was she wouldn't wanna see you.'

'If she's just nipped out, I'll wait,' Jane persisted, putting a hand out to stop him closing the door.

'You're not waiting in here,' he snapped. 'Anyhow, she won't be back for hours yet, so piss off.'

'Look, I don't want an argument,' Jane said evenly, hoping that Dave wouldn't hear her pounding heart. She had *so* wanted Mary to be here to prove her wrong. 'I just want to see her. Tell me where she is and I won't bother you any more.'

'Oh, that's priceless, that is!' Giving a contemptuous snort Dave opened the door a little wider and mimicked what she'd just said: '"Tell me where she is and I won't bother you no more."' Then, in his own nasty voice, he said, 'Truth is, Jane, you *always* bother me. I mean, *look* at you.' Lip curling, he flicked a hand at her dress. 'What *do* you think you look like?'

Biting her lip to stop the smart remark that was on the tip of her tongue from escaping, Jane peered coolly back at him. Any fool could see that he was off his face. His pupils were too large, making his bulging eyes look positively manic, and he was skinnier than ever, his stained jeans hanging like a dirty nappy between his legs. It didn't bode well for Mary, but Jane *still* didn't want to believe what her heart knew to be true. She prayed that he was lying – that Mary was in bed asleep, or out clubbing it with a friend. Anything but *that*.

Using every ounce of will-power that she possessed, she forced herself to smile.

'Please, Dave. I really didn't come for a fight. I just want to tell Mary that I'm sorry for being such a bitch about . . . well, about *you*, I suppose.' Another forced smile to cover the nausea at having to grovel to the runt. 'I was wrong and I know that now. I just want the chance to make it up to you both. Please let me see her.'

Flinging the door back so hard that it slammed into the wall, leaving a doorknob impression in the plaster, Dave stepped out onto the landing and jutted his face forward until he and Jane were nose-to-nose.

'Don't fuckin' creep round me, you two-faced, ugly bitch,' he snarled through gritted teeth. 'I don't want your apology. You can stick it up your arse and fuck it doggy-style, for all I care. I just want you out of here, and I don't ever want to see you again. Got that?'

'Fine!' Jane hissed, returning his glare, refusing to be intimidated. 'Just tell Mary I'm here so I can tell *her* I'm sorry. You don't mean anything to me, but she does.'

'That right, is it?' Drawing his head back, Dave contorted his face into an ugly, scornful sneer. 'You wanna see your precious mate that bad, do you?'

'Yes, I do.'

'Right, well, she's with all the other dick-lickers down the park, earning my money!' Grinning evilly, Dave rubbed his fingers together. 'Ain't life beautiful.'

Stepping back to escape his stinking breath, Jane glared at him. 'You're lying,' she said, knowing full well that he wasn't. 'She hasn't done that for years.'

Laughing nastily, he patted himself on the heart. 'She does it all for love. Oh, but you wouldn't know about a woman's love for her man, would you – you being into pussy. Ain't quite the same, is it?' Eyes gleaming madly now, he stuck his tongue out and licked her cheek.

Jerking back, Jane grimaced with disgust and swiped at the wetness with the back of her hand.

Cackling loudly, Dave went back into the flat and slammed the door.

Jane was seething. She felt like kicking the door in and killing the bastard stone dead. And she could, because Dave was no match for her – not in the state he was in now. All she'd have to do would be to sit on him and he'd snap – like the feeble, dried-up little *twig* that he was.

Resisting the urge with some difficulty, Jane turned on her heel and marched back down the stairs.

Reaching Alexandra Road, Jane spotted the same group of women that she'd glimpsed from Pete's van. They were standing now at the gates of the GP's surgery opposite the park. She wasn't sure if Mary was among them at first because they all looked so skinny and small, but there was no mistaking the laugh that floated to her. It was the dirtiest laugh she'd ever heard. It was definitely Mary.

Narrowing her eyes as she approached, Jane located Mary holding court in the centre of the group. She knew it was her, but she still couldn't believe it. No way was this the Mary she knew and loved. *That* Mary had always seemed bigger than she actually was because she stood tall and her breasts were large and proud. But *this* Mary was small and stooped, as if age had not only caught up with her but had trampled her into the dirt on its way past.

Jane felt the anger surge into her throat on a rush of acid bile. This was *that* lousy bastard's doing! Mary hadn't worked the streets for years, and Jane had believed her when she'd said she never would again.

Just then, one of the women spotted her and nudged Mary. Jane's heart skipped a beat when her friend turned around. She looked even worse than Dave.

Putting her hands on her hips, Mary tilted her head to one side and grinned, revealing a dark gap where one of her lovely teeth had once been.

'My *God*!' she drawled. 'Am I seeing things, or what?'

'No, it's really me.' Forcing herself to return the smile, Jane walked right up to Mary and peered at her, taking in the lines on her face, the gaunt cheeks and sunken eyes. 'How are you?'

'Me? I'm just great, me!' Still grinning, Mary twirled around on the spot as if she were modelling the latest fashions. 'Got eyes, haven't you? How do *you* think I look?'

'You're certainly . . . *thinner*,' Jane murmured, struggling to find a kinder word for the scrawny mess standing before her. Then, unable to keep up the pretence, her brow collapsed into deep ridges of concern. 'Aw, Christ, Mary . . . What have you *done* to yourself?'

'What d'y' mean?' Frowning, Mary looked down at herself. 'Oh, I see . . . It's me diet, innit?'

'*Diet?*' Jane gave an incredulous snort. 'You look bloody anorexic. And what the hell's happened to your teeth?'

Shrugging casually, Mary said, 'Shit happens, and there's nowt you can do once it's done. Anyhow, never mind me. What's with *you*?' Looking Jane up and down now, she laughed. 'Since when have you been into all that flower-power shite?'

A couple of the girls standing behind Mary began to snigger, but they soon stopped when they got a murderous glare from Jane, and moved a few feet back. Staring at them until she was satisfied that they were far enough away, Jane brought her gaze back to Mary.

'Why are you doing this? Surely you're not that desperate?'

'Jane, Jane, *Jane*.' Shaking her head, Mary gave a disappointed sigh. 'I haven't seen you in weeks, and all you can do is insult me.'

Correcting her, Jane said, 'It's nearly a year, actually, but that's not the point. *This* is.' She flapped a dismissive hand towards the other girls. 'You said you were never gonna do it again.'

'Yeah, well, things change, don't they?' Mary retorted defensively. Then, snorting softly, she added, 'Not that *you*'ve changed much, mind. You're still the same old lard-arse.'

Jane gave a loud, dry sniff. It was a childhood habit that only reared up when she was upset – and she was *really* upset now. Not just because Mary looked such a state but because she was being so flippant about it – acting as if it was all a big joke. And as for her *diet* . . . Oh, yeah, Jane could see the effects of that, all right. Mary was at least two stone lighter than the last time she'd seen her – and it didn't suit her.

Rolling her eyes at Jane's pained expression, Mary said, 'Look, love, there's no point getting all uptight about it. I'm doing all right for myself.'

'All right for *Dave*, you mean,' Jane snapped, unable to contain the anger. 'And don't bother denying it 'cos I've *seen* him. He's got you into this, hasn't he?'

Mary's smile disappeared in a flash.

'Get this straight,' she snarled, vehemence spilling through her words. 'I'm not doin' this for no one. Yeah, I give him a bit of money, but that's my business. He can do what the fuck he wants, but I'm doing this for *me*.'

'For what?' Jane goaded her. 'Your *diet*?'

'If that's gonna make you happy. *Yeah!* I'm doing it for me diet. Satisfied?'

Looking at her livid face, Jane knew that Mary was strung-out. Her eyes had the same manic quality as Dave's and her movements were quick and jerky. Jane had assumed they were doing gear, but this wasn't the behaviour of any smack-head she had ever seen. When they were doped up they were too zonked for normal conversation, but even withdrawing junkies weren't this aggressive.

Unsure of exactly what she was dealing with, but sensing that there'd be no talking to Mary if she pushed her too far, Jane changed tack in an effort to calm things down.

'Look, why don't you come back to my place for a bit?' she said, smiling again. 'We haven't seen each other for ages and we've got loads of catching up to do.'

'Can't.' Mary folded her arms. 'I mean, I'd really like to chat, an' all that, but I'm working. Sorry.'

'Surely you can take one night off? Anyway, you don't sound overly desperate to get back to Dave. You could always stop with me till you're back on your feet.'

'Back to where it all began, eh?' Mary chuckled. 'Back to staying at me mate's till I've sorted my mess of a life out.'

Confused, Jane frowned. 'What you talking about?'

'Does the name *Lynne* ring any bells? I only went to stay with her for a bit, and look where *that* got me.'

'Yeah, but this is different. And, by the looks of you, you couldn't be doing much worse than you are right now. What have you got to lose?'

'Oh, for fuck's sake!' Throwing her head back, Mary stared up at the clouds, her cheek muscles jumping as she ground her teeth. 'Why can't anyone ever keep their nose out of my business? I'm sick to bleedin' death of people interfering and telling me what I can and can't do.'

'I'm not *people*,' Jane protested peevishly. 'I'm your best mate.'

'Some mate!' Snapping her head down, Mary glared at Jane, shoulders hunched, nostrils flared. 'Coming here with your airs and graces, making out like you're better than me. Well, you're not! Never have been – never will be!'

Jane could feel the girls gawping at them – wondering if they were going to fight, no doubt. She was beginning to wonder the same thing herself. Mary had always been quick-tempered – more than capable of lashing out at the slightest provocation. But, tough as she had been, she was too messed up to try and take Jane on in this state. She wouldn't stand a cat in hell's chance.

Just as suddenly as the fight had come into Mary, it left again. Shoulders slowly drooping, she said, 'Look, I don't need this crap. Why don't you just piss off and leave me alone, eh?'

Jane's mouth flapped open. For a moment, she didn't know what to say. Mary had told her to piss off, but she'd sounded so weary and defeated, it was weird. And the light had suddenly gone from her eyes, leaving them dull and sad.

Desperate to lighten things up again, Jane folded her arms and forced herself to grin.

'Don't tell me to piss off, you cheeky cow. I'll have you down to Mother Superior if you don't watch it, and you know what'll happen then, don't you?'

'Christ!' Mary yelped, grinning herself now. 'How did you remember *her*?'

'Just walked past the old school,' Jane told her, wrinkling

her nose. 'You can *still* smell that horrible bleedin' cabbage.'

'Holy Mary Mother of God!' Crossing herself, Mary shook her head reflectively. 'How long ago was that?'

'For ever. And talking about *long* . . .' Reaching out, Jane flipped Mary's jacket open and prodded one of her sausage-skin breasts. 'These are getting a bit friendly with your knees, aren't they? Where's your bra, woman?'

Quickly covering herself up, Mary said, 'I told you – I'm on a diet. Your tits are always the first thing to go.'

'Yeah, right,' Jane snorted. 'Well, if it's that easy, I think *I* should go on this diet of yours. So, what is it? Cabbage water? Dry toast?'

'Do me a favour!' Mary chuckled, turning to wink at a giggling girl in a raggy knitted dress who was sitting on the wall behind her. 'You wouldn't catch me sticking that crap in my mouth. A bit of the old white magic, more like. Does wonders for the old belly.'

'Yeah?' Jane felt like a crocodile as she determinedly maintained the grin. 'And how often would I have to take this amazing magic stuff to get rid of this?' She patted her stomach. 'Once a week? Once a month?'

'Get *real*!' Mary cackled. 'Try every morning, noon and night!'

Infuriated by the giggling girl, Jane pointed a warning finger at her. 'Shut the fuck up, you, before I kick your stupid face in!' Then, to Mary, she said, 'Are you off your head, or what? What you messing with that shit for?'

Mary's surprise at the sudden outburst quickly turned to anger.

'Because I *like* it! And because I can do *what* the hell I like, when*ever* the hell I like – all *right*?'

They glared at each other for what felt like an eternity, Jane's eyes alive with the rage of concern, Mary's ablaze with defiance. Jane knew they were just seconds away from scrapping on the floor like a couple of kids, but she couldn't allow it to get to that – she just couldn't.

Holding her hands up in a placatory gesture, she said, 'Look, don't let's fall out again. I only want to spend a bit of time with you. Even if you decide to carry on with all this crap in the end, at least just come and spend the night at mine and think about it. For *me*?'

The anger fell from Mary's face only to be replaced by a resigned weariness that made Jane want to cry for the strong, independent woman her friend had been.

'I can't, love,' Mary murmured. 'Honest, I just can't.'

'Yes, you can!' Jane insisted, seizing her hands and squeezing them. 'If you want to, you *can*.'

'I'm in too deep.' Mary gave her a sad little smile.

'Don't give me that. All you have to do is walk to my flat, and that's it – over. What d'y' say?'

'I say, give up, love, that's what I say. I've made my bed, now I've just got to lie on it.' Shrugging, Mary pulled her hands free and stuck them deep into her pockets.

It began to drizzle. Shivering violently when the first tiny drops hit her face, Mary pulled her chin down into her collar. Jane was still standing there with that stubborn look on her face that clearly said she wasn't going anywhere until she'd got what she came for. Mary wished she'd give it up before they both got soaked – or, worse, Kenny arrived. He'd be here soon, and there'd be trouble if Jane was still hanging about.

'Look, you were right about Dave,' Mary said, hoping that if Jane felt vindicated she'd be satisfied and go. 'He *is* a bastard and I should've listened to you. But I didn't, so what can you do? Anyway, I really appreciate you trying to help,' she went on, trying – and failing – to inject sincerity into her voice, 'and I'll think about what you said, but I need time to get my head around it. So, why don't you give me a day or two? I'll sort something out and come to see you. Okay?'

Refusing to be fobbed off so easily, Jane folded her arms. Mary was her oldest friend, and there was obviously more to this than she was letting on.

'What's really going on?' Jane demanded. 'Has he been hitting you again? 'Cos if he has, it's not a problem. Just come with me and I swear he'll never get to you again. And if you don't want to risk him finding you at *my* place, I've got a friend who'd let you stay at his.'

Jane held her breath and prayed that Mary would say yes when she stared at the ground and seemed to be considering the offer. Jane had nothing against prostitution in itself; she just didn't think that Mary should be doing it again – and certainly not because an abusive bastard like Dave was forcing her to.

Mary hummed and hahed for an age, then shook her head, saying, 'No, sorry, I can't. I don't even know this bloke you're talking about. How can I just turn up on his doorstep and expect him to let me stay? Even you've got to admit that's pushing it a bit.'

'Take my word, it'll be fine,' Jane assured her, smug in the knowledge that Mike would like nothing better than to be instrumental in rescuing a damsel in distress.

When Mary shook her head again, Jane opened her mouth to make one last plea, but she didn't get a chance.

'Heads up!' Knitted Dress hissed, jumping down from the wall and tugging on Mary's sleeve as she motioned with a nod to something behind them.

Glancing over Jane's shoulder, Mary's eyes widened. 'Shit!'

Frowning, Jane turned to see what was freaking them out. There was nobody in sight but a man crossing the road up ahead. Even from this distance, she could tell that he was huge. Some of his width was probably an illusion created by the padding in his bomber jacket, but his height was no illusion. He was well over six feet, with long legs that were so muscular his trousers seemed almost welded to them.

As he lurched across the road and strode purposefully towards them, Jane noticed that most of the girls had suddenly disappeared. Before she could ask what was going on, Mary had gripped her arm and was dragging her away.

Glancing back as she stumbled along beside her, Jane saw that the man had reached Knitted Dress. Cowering back as he towered over her, the petrified girl was shaking her head as he gestured angrily after Mary and Jane.

'Who's that?' Jane asked, shaking Mary's hand off. 'And why are you pulling me away? Don't you want me to meet your new friends?'

'Don't be so bloody sarcastic!' Mary snapped, stopping at the corner and glancing fearfully back. 'And stop being such a pain in the arse, 'cos I'm doing you a favour here. You do *not* want to know that bloke – believe me. You'll get yourself seriously hurt if you mess with him.'

'Ow!' Jane protested when Mary gripped her arm again. 'Stop *doing* that. Anyway, it's *you* I'm worried about, not me.'

'Look, just piss off,' Mary hissed. 'I can't be doing with any more hassle right now. Just go home and forget about me – *please.*'

Swiping her dripping hair from her eyes as the rain lashed down on her head, Jane stood firm.

'No. I'm not leaving you like this. I don't know what's going on, or why you're so spooked by that guy, but I know you're in a mess and I'm not going till you tell me what's wrong.'

Just then, the man whistled. Jumping as if she'd been shot in the back, Mary wrapped her jacket tighter around herself, and said, 'I've got to go.' Turning, she ran head down towards the man.

Jane felt the anger bubbling in her gut when he gripped Mary's arm and marched her out of sight around the corner. She felt like following and giving him a piece of her mind, but she instinctively knew that her interference would only make things worse.

Giving up, she headed back to the Crescents, deep in thought.

Hauling Mary into the shadows behind the church, Kenny slammed her up against the wall. He was furious – and paranoid as hell, having just been warned by his nark at the local police station that he was in line for a flash raid tomorrow. Just what he didn't need when he had a shit-load of powders on his hands that weren't due to be moved for another three days. What he *did* need was somewhere safe to stash it until the heat was off – and that was supposed to be Mary's job.

Much as he despised her cunt of a boyfriend, Kenny still liked Mary. Not as much as he had before she'd let herself go, but it was there all the same – a tiny worm of something indefinable that he felt in his gut whenever she was on form. Which wasn't often lately, he had to admit – and even less so since Dave had relieved her of one of her teeth. But he still trusted her – to a degree – and she was shit-hot at keeping the girls at it.

But, all that aside, he wouldn't hesitate to wring her neck if she'd set him up. He'd never have believed it of her, but given what he'd just witnessed he wasn't sure. The woman she'd been talking to could have been a plain-clothes for all he knew. She'd looked too straight by half.

'Who was she?' he demanded now, holding Mary in place with a hand on her chest. 'What have you been saying about me? If you've grassed me, I swear I'll kill you.'

'Have I hell grassed you!' Mary protested, struggling to keep from crying as the rough brickwork dug into her back. 'Jeezus, Kenny, what d'y' take me for?'

'So, who *was* she?'

'Just an old mate I bumped into. Christ! D'y' think I invited her to come and watch me work, or something?'

Drawing his head back, Kenny stared down at Mary with suspicion in his eyes. This didn't feel right. The woman hadn't looked like any of her mates that he'd ever seen. She looked too straight and clean – like an undercover.

'Look, you've never seen her 'cos we fell out before you came on the scene,' Mary told him when he voiced what he was thinking. 'Her name's Jane. You've heard me talking about her loads of times. She's the one I knew when we were kids – the one Dave can't stand.'

'Oh, yeah? So, what was she doing here?'

'I don't *know*. She was just walking past and stopped to say hello. Honest, Kenny, that's all it was. I was telling her to piss off when you turned up. I swear it on me mam's grave.'

'For real?' Kenny peered at her narrow-eyed, almost convinced that she was telling the truth . . . *Almost*.

'On the Bible,' she assured him, crossing her chest with a finger. 'You know I wouldn't lie to you. I don't tell *no* one your business – not even Dave.'

'Best not, neither,' Kenny grunted. 'Anyhow, I didn't come for a chat. I need you to stash something, and it's got to be *double* safe. If that wanker so much as *looks* at it, you're both dead.'

'How much?' Relieved to be off the hook, Mary stuck her hands deep into her pockets and hopped from foot to foot as the wind ate at her bare legs.

'A lot,' Kenny whispered, glancing around furtively. 'Thirty gee's worth.'

Mary's eyebrows rose sharply. 'Aw, shit, Ken. Where am

I supposed to hide *that*? You can't squeeze a flea in my place without squashing its cousin.'

'That's your problem,' he grunted. 'Anyhow, it's only till I'm in the clear with the dibble.'

'*Dibble*? Aw, you're not gonna land me in it, are you? I've already had three pulls this month. I'll go down if they get me on anything else. Can't you leave it with one of the lads?'

'Think I'd be leaving it with you if there was anywhere fuckin' else?' Kenny barked aggressively. 'And since when have you argued with me?'

'I'm not,' Mary bleated. 'I'm just worried, that's all. It's a load of pressure, this.'

'Pressure!' He snorted. 'What the fuck do *you* know about pressure, you stupid cunt? It's *me* who's gonna get my fuckin' arse split by some twat of a copper! All *you*'ve got to do is stash a bit of gear and keep that thieving scrote away from it. What's so hard about that?'

'Nothing,' Mary murmured, wincing when Kenny raised a hand and rubbed agitatedly at his brow – a sure sign that he was stressed enough to give her a slap if she wasn't careful.

'Yeah, that's right,' he said. 'Nothing. So quit moaning before I swing for you.'

'Okay.' Mary held up her hands in a gesture of compliance. 'I'll keep it safe. You can trust me. Where is it?'

'Col's got it in the car.' Sighing wearily now, Kenny indicated back down the road with a jerk of his head. 'Come on. We'll drop you off.'

'D'y' want the takings?' Falling into step beside him as he set off across the road, Mary reached into her inside pocket for the money she'd just collected from the girls when Jane turned up.

'Nah, keep hold of it till I come for the rest,' Kenny told

her, wrenching his collar up around his ears and striding ahead. 'I don't want them finding anything on me when they pull me. They'll only fuckin' confiscate it again.'

Quickening her step to keep up with him, Mary asked Kenny what was going on.

'Nowt for you to worry about,' he told her. 'Just do your bit and don't ask no questions. All being well, I'll be here at the usual time tomorrow and I'll take you to pick it up. If I don't come it's 'cos they've fitted me up, and you'll have to hang on to it till I'm out. No fuck-ups, right?'

'Right.'

Reaching the car, Kenny turned to give her a final warning. 'Oh, and by the way, Mary . . . Don't be slacking because you think I'm off the scene. It's business as usual as far as you're concerned, and if I hear different you'll be sorry.'

Frowning as she climbed into the back of the car, Mary folded her arms to still the shivering that Kenny's not-so-veiled threat had caused.

She'd stashed stuff for him before, but never an amount as large as this. And much as *he* didn't seem to think it was a problem, *she* did. What if he got banged up? How the hell was she supposed to keep the girls in line, herself in business, *and* stop Dave getting his hands on the gear? She'd just have to pray that Kenny didn't go down. The stress, if he did, would kill her.

31

Mimi greeted Jane with a delighted smile when she arrived back at Mike's.

'Hey, babe! How you feeling?'

'Fine,' Jane lied, not wanting to bring Mimi down because she was obviously buzzing along nicely, if the glazed look in her lovely blue eyes was anything to go by. 'Where's Mike?'

'In his room,' Mimi giggled. 'I think the penny whistles were doing his head in. Oh, and you'll never guess what?' she went on excitedly. 'He kicked Roy out!'

'Really?' Jane was amazed. 'Wow. I never thought I'd see the day. What for?'

'The usual head-fuck nonsense.' Mimi shrugged. 'But don't get too excited, he said he could come back tomorrow if he'd learned to behave. Between you and me, I think he was pissed off with him for upsetting you.'

'Oops!' Jane gave a guilty smile. 'Oh, well . . . If it did the trick and got rid of Roy for one night, I don't think anyone will be too annoyed with me.'

'Annoyed?' Mimi laughed. 'They think you're the dog's licky bits, girl! Anyway, Mike's still awake if you want to go and see him.'

'Yeah, I think I will.' Kissing her on the cheek, Jane made her way through the bodies lying all over the living-room floor and tapped on Mike's door. Popping her head around it after a moment, she said, 'Only me. Am I disturbing you?'

Sitting cross-legged on the mattress, Mike was rocking his head to the strange atmospheric music coming from the portable tape-player on the low table beside him. Flicking his long hair back from his face, he smiled and waved her in.

Jane joined him on the bed and took the spliff he offered her. She'd always liked this room, it was so peaceful with its deep terracotta walls and its colourful Indian throws. In daylight, you could see the holes in the material and the thick layer of dust that carpeted the floor. But like this, with candlelight dancing off the walls, it was stunning – like an Arabian harem.

'So, what's up?' Mike asked, lowering the volume of the music. 'You look like you've got the weight of the world on your shoulders.'

Giving him a sheepish smile, Jane said, 'If you'd asked me what's *right* I'd have known where to start 'cos the list would be smaller.'

'Like that, is it?' Chuckling softly, he reached across to the table and picked up a half-full cup. Passing it to her, he said, 'Get that down you. You'll feel better in no time.'

Presuming it to be alcohol, Jane raised it to her lips. Grimacing when the all too familiar smell of boiled magic mushrooms assailed her nostrils, she shook her head. '*Oooeer*. No, thanks.'

'It's fresh,' Mike assured her. 'I've had it in the freezer. Thawed a batch out when I got rid of Roy. I think we *all* needed it.' Nudging her, he nodded at the cup. 'Go on . . . You can tell me your problems while you're waiting for it to come on. You know how focused you get after a good trip. You'll wonder what you were ever worried about.'

'No, honestly, I'd better not.' Jane handed the cup back. 'I've got too much on my mind; I'd probably freak out.'

'Fair enough.' Handing her a glass of red wine instead,

he reached beneath Donkey's tail for his tobacco tin. 'I'll roll up while you tell me what's going on.'

'After listening to Jane's story in silence, Mike said, 'So, who was the bloke?'

Shrugging, she said, 'I've no idea, but he looked a proper nasty piece of work. I reckon he might have been her pimp.'

'Mmm,' he murmured thoughtfully. 'Doesn't sound too good, does it?'

'Not really.' Jane slumped further down on the bed and rested her chin on her hand. Looking up after a moment she saw Mike peering at her and the concern in his eyes made her smile. 'You must think I'm a right sad case getting all worked up over something and nothing. She's probably fine, like she said, and here's me moaning on to you about it.'

'Don't be daft.' Reaching out, Mike gave her hand a squeeze. 'That's what friends are for, isn't it? So, you've definitely never seen him before?' he said then.

'Nope.' She shook her head. 'And I don't *want* to see him again.'

Tapping a fingernail on his teeth, Mike said, 'Tricky. If we don't know anything about him we won't know what we're dealing with. What about her fella? D'y' think *he*'d know him?'

'I suppose he must if it is her pimp. He knows she's back on the game.'

'Right, then! Let's go talk to our friend Dave.'

Stopping Mike when he began to rise, Jane said, 'Er, I don't think that's a very good idea. He was acting weird enough before, but I reckon he'd get nasty if I turned up with you in tow.'

Dismissing this with a wave of his hand, Mike said, 'Don't worry about me, I can handle him.'

'No, really, I don't want to,' she insisted. 'Not just yet,

anyway. I need to think about it. Anyway, you've had the mushrooms. That could make for a very weird encounter.'

'Okay, it's your call,' he said, grinning because he thought it would make for a *fascinating* encounter. 'How's about you tell me a bit more about your friend. You say you've known her since you were kids?'

'Yeah.' Jane smiled sadly. 'She rescued me from some bullies at school, and we were best mates from then on.'

'And you lived round here?'

'Yeah. Charles Barry.'

'So, how come you left?'

'Long story,' Jane muttered. 'I don't want to bore you with all that old rubbish.'

'Bore away,' Mike insisted.

Sipping the wine, Jane frowned. She didn't want him to think badly of her, but she wasn't quick-minded enough to invent a less damning account of her past. So she told him the truth.

'I got pregnant when I was fifteen, so my mum and dad sent me to stay with my aunt in Wigan,' she said, her voice wistful. 'I was supposed to have the baby, then give it up and come home. But when it came to it I couldn't do it.'

'So you kept it?'

'Yeah ... well, sort of. My mum went mad when I brought him back home. She said *I* could stay, but *it* couldn't.'

'That's shit.'

'Yeah, I know.' Jane tightened her grip on the glass as her cheek muscles clenched. 'I reckon my dad would have been all right about it, but he was always weak when it came to standing up to *her*. Anyway, I told her to piss off and walked out. I might have only been a kid, but I felt different after having David. I really wanted him, you know?'

Glancing up, Mike nodded understandingly. Having lost the baby he'd fathered many years before when his wife ran away to live on a kibbutz in Israel, he knew well the force of love for one's own flesh and blood.

'Anyway,' she continued, determinedly shaking off the sorrow, 'Mary wasn't around 'cos her mum had kicked *her* out while I was away, so I went to the Social Services for help. And that's when I lost David. They put us in a home for under-age mothers and kept at me until I agreed to give him up.'

'Bastards. They can't deal with the problem, so they take the problem away.'

'That's about the strength of it, yeah.' Jane gave a tiny snort of disdain. 'Still, I suppose they were right. I was way too young. He'd have had a shit life with me as his mother.'

'I don't think so.' Mike gazed at her sincerely. 'I think you'd have been a brilliant mother.'

'Thanks.' She smiled sadly. 'Too late to worry about it now, though, eh?'

'I suppose it is,' he agreed, sensing that it was a regret she'd carried around for long enough without him adding what-ifs to the equation. 'So, what happened once you'd given him up?'

'They kicked me out,' Jane stated bluntly, the bitterness more than obvious in her scathing tone. 'I wasn't a single-mother-desperate-cow any more, so they didn't have any responsibility to help me. I was sixteen by then, so I was quite capable of looking after myself in their eyes. But I wasn't.' Pausing, she gritted her teeth. 'I started drinking – that's how grown-up I was.'

'You probably needed it.' Mike passed the spliff to her. 'Like me with this stuff. I'd have gone off my nut many a time if I'd had to stay straight.'

'It's not the same,' Jane said, taking a drag and blowing the smoke out. 'This relaxes you, but drinking just makes you crazy. The amounts *I* was knocking back, anyhow. I did exactly what I'd despised my mum for, only worse. She used to keep herself to herself, hiding behind a respectable façade. But me . . . I had to let everyone see what a mess I was. I can't tell you how many times I woke up on some piss-wet bog floor covered in bruises from scrapping with anyone who got in my way, with my knickers round my ankles 'cos I'd shagged some bloke I couldn't even remember.' Pausing, she gazed down at the glass in her hand, too embarrassed to meet Mike's eye. 'I'm lucky I haven't had a thousand fatherless kids by now – or, worse, Aids.'

Mike didn't say anything, he just exhaled loudly. He couldn't disagree . . . Jane *was* lucky, by the sound of it. *Very* lucky.

'Anyway,' she went on, rushing to a conclusion now, 'I finally came to my senses and straightened myself out. That's when I moved to Cheetham Hill and started working at The Crown. I'd been there a few years when I met up with Mary again and moved back to Hulme. We fell out and I got my job at The Eagle. That's when I met you – and the rest you already know.'

Releasing a long shuddering sigh, Jane let her head flop back. She'd never really talked about all of that stuff before – only to Mary, and she hadn't even told *her* that much. She was exhausted, and more than a little ashamed.

Reaching out when he saw the tears glistening in her eyes, Mike gave her hand a squeeze.

'You should be proud of yourself for surviving, not hating yourself for not being able to cope. You were a child in pain. You'd been rejected by your mother and you'd lost your baby. You'd have been a very strange girl if you'd shrugged that off without getting into a pit. But you climbed out, and look at you now: smart, beautiful, loads of fun, and a great mate.'

'Sorry,' Jane said, swiping at a tear that was trickling down her cheek. 'No one's ever said anything like that before.'

'Yeah, well, it's true. Anyway, what happened to David? Have you seen him since?'

'No.' Shaking her head, she sniffed loudly, struggling to stop her chin wobbling. 'You're not allowed to contact them when they're adopted. They say you've got to wait for the child to make the first move.'

'Why don't you write him a letter?' Mike suggested. 'They'll keep it on file and give it to him if he ever goes looking for you.'

'Maybe,' Jane murmured, knowing full well that she wouldn't. It would be too painful waiting for a reply that would probably never come.

Sensing that she was all talked out, Mike said, 'How you feeling?'

'Fine.' She gave him a sheepish smile. 'Thanks for listening. I think I needed that.'

'Any time,' he said, reaching out to tuck her hair behind her ear. 'Think you're up to going out there?' He nodded at the wall, indicating the hubbub coming from the other side.

'Are you?' she asked, quite enjoying the peace.

Pursing his lips, Mike peered at her for a moment, then nodded. 'Yeah, why not? That lot had theirs just after you went home. They'll all be peaking by now. We can have a laugh at them.'

'Mind if I stay here?' Jane asked, wrinkling her nose. 'I'm a bit too knackered to watch everyone trip, and I don't really fancy walking home again.'

'Not at all,' he assured her. 'Get your head down for a bit. I'll make sure they keep the noise down.'

It was pitch dark when Jane woke up, and very quiet except for the soft sound of breathing coming from the next room. She couldn't see anything, and her back was aching.

Groaning, she tried to sit up, but it was agony. She was

curled up like a foetus on Mike's mattress and her body screamed in protest when she forced it to unfold, it was so cold in the room. Shivering violently, she wrenched the blanket out from beneath her and wrapped it around her shoulders.

Struggling to her feet, she stumbled into the living room. Looking around, she made out the shapes of several sleeping bodies on the floor. Mike was huddled under a blanket on the couch. Donkey was on top of him, his snout resting on Mike's open, snoring mouth.

Sucking his breath out, Jane thought with a shudder.

Stepping over a body lying prone behind the door, she headed for the kitchen.

'Whoever that is,' Mike mumbled from the living room, '*please* put the kettle on.'

'It's me, and I am,' she called back.

Trotting in, Donkey sniffed his empty bowl hopefully. Jane looked around for food, but all she could see was an open packet of cornflakes. Taking a handful, she dropped them into the bowl, saying, 'Sorry, boy. It's all there is.'

Sniffing at them, Donkey gave her a dirty look and trotted back to his master.

Mike was sitting up when she carried the teas in.

'Want some?' He held his spliff out to her.

'God, no.' Jane shook her head. 'Way too early for me.'

'Feeling all right?'

'Yeah, fine,' she moaned. 'If my head wasn't caving in, and my tongue didn't taste like the dried crap at the bottom of a birdcage!'

'Can't say I've ever tried it myself.' Mike laughed. 'But each to his own, eh?'

Jane rolled her eyes, envying his ability to be happy whatever the time of day. It shouldn't be allowed. But, then, neither should red wine.

'I've been thinking about your friend,' Mike said quietly. 'And I think I've got a plan. What time will she be out tonight?'

'I saw her at about two last night,' Jane told him. 'And she told me once that they usually stick to the same times.'

Mike nodded thoughtfully. 'Right, well, if we set off at about half-one, that'll give us plenty of time to get things ready. We'll have to sort the bedroom out and get it properly secured, but that shouldn't be a problem. I'll just take the bolt off the bathroom door and put it on the outside of the bedroom door so we can lock it from this side.'

'Whoa.' Jane held up her hand. 'What are you talking about?'

'We're going to bring her here and nurse her through a cold turkey,' Mike explained, as casually as if they were discussing a dinner party. 'And the sooner the better, if she's as bad as you say. That's why I'm planning to get it ready for tonight.'

'Christ,' Jane murmured, gazing at him in disbelief. 'You're serious, aren't you?'

'Absolutely,' he affirmed. 'She'll thank you for it in the end, you'll see.'

Jane shook her head, amused by his confidence. He was so sure he could pull it off, but he had no clue how stubborn Mary was.

'All right,' she said. 'Supposing I go along with it. How are you planning to get her here?'

Grinning sheepishly, Mike said, 'I'm going to pose as a punter. But I'll need you to tell me how to go about it 'cos I've never done it before.' Snorting softly then, he said, 'I've done just about everything in my time, but I have *never* paid for a shag.'

'Yeah, I bet.'

'Watch it!'

Catching Mike's tobacco tin when he threw it at her, Jane

rolled herself a straight and tossed it back, thinking what a contrast he was to Tina. In all the time she'd known her, Tina had only ever taken cigs without ever giving any back.

'Hey!' she squawked as her mind seized the thought and made it relevant. 'Tina! I bet *she*'d know that bloke.'

'Tina?'

'Yeah, she's a mate of mine and Mary's. Well, more Mary's than mine, but she'll know more about what's going on. They're still mates, you see. It was only me they fell out with. Do you think I should go and see her?'

'Worth a try,' Mike said. 'It'll give us a better idea of what this pimp's capable of. Forewarned is forearmed, as they say. I'll come with you.'

Glancing at the clock, Jane tutted impatiently. She'd have to wait a good few hours yet. There was no way Tina would be up at a time like this.

'Anyway, Madame,' Mike grinned, affecting a French accent. 'Never mind zat . . . What I need to know ees, 'ow does one go about zee mucky business of luring zee common prostitute back to one's abode?'

'Who's pickin' up a prozzy, then?' a girl's groggy voice asked from the floor behind the couch.

'Mike,' Jane giggled.

'Oi!' he protested good-naturedly. 'I'm going to have to stop hanging about with you. You're doing my reputation no good.'

Waiting until the girl had eased herself up and staggered into the bathroom, Mike said, 'So what time do you want to set off for Tina's?'

'Whenever.' Jane shrugged. Then, remembering something, she said, 'Oh, God, I can't. I'm working.'

'You could always pull a sickie.'

'No, I can't.' She shook her head. 'That's how it started when I met up with Mary. I don't want to lose this job.'

'Well, I'd develop a bad cold or something before we get into this,' Mike told her seriously. 'We're going to need you here.'

Feeling a shudder of apprehension at his grim tone, Jane nodded.

'Okay, I'll take my holidays early. They shouldn't mind. I haven't had a day off since I started there. But I'll have to work today. I'm only doing lunch till six, so we'd best go to Tina's this morning before I start.'

32

Tina answered on the second knock and Jane only just stopped herself from gasping out loud at the sight of her. She'd changed so much – and not for the better. She was even fatter, for one thing, and her face looked shockingly moonlike, framed by a new, too-short, too-tight perm. Only one thing hadn't changed, and that was the suck-lemon expression.

'Oh, it's you, is it?' she grunted, folding her arms. 'What brings you round here?'

'Can we talk?' Jane smiled nervously.

'Whatever.' Turning, Tina waddled up the hall, leaving the door open.

Taking it as an invitation, Jane stepped inside and gestured for Mike to follow.

Plonking herself down in her wide, weight-battered armchair, Tina took a cigarette from a pack on the table and lit it.

'So, what d'y' want to talk about?'

'Mary,' Jane said, sitting beside Mike on the couch.

Tutting, Tina rolled her eyes. 'I take it you've made friends, then?'

'I never *wasn't* friends,' Jane reminded her. 'You know I only stopped going round there 'cos of that bastard Dave.'

Snorting with contempt at the mention of his name, Tina said, '*Him*? He's nowt but a piece of piss. It's that Kenny Butler who's the real bastard.'

'Kenny Butler?' Jane exchanged a quick glance with Mike. Surely it wasn't going to be this easy. 'Who's he?'

'A proper cunt, that's who. Big-shot pimp with a nice little sideline in powders. Huh!' Sneering, Tina took a deep pull on the cigarette.

'I don't think I know him, do I?' Jane prompted.

'Nah. He only started coming round after you stopped. That brainless shite Dave fetched him round. Knew him from the Strange, apparently, then bumped into him in the pub and brought him back to Mary's.' Pausing, Tina shook her head in disgust. 'Fancy bringing a dealer round after everything Mary went through to get off it. Messed everything up for her, that did.'

'She's not back on the smack, is she?' Jane asked, knowing full well what the answer would be.

'And the rest,' Tina snorted. 'You name it, she's doing it. And you know what else she's doing, don't you? She's only out on the street again – working for that Kenny, to pay him for the shit he's feeding her.'

'Why doesn't Dave put a stop to it?' Jane asked, amazed that they were getting so much from Tina. She'd thought it would take hours to coax anything from her, but it had taken all of two minutes. It was almost as if she'd been storing it up, just waiting for a chance to pour it all out.

'Dave?' Tina laughed mirthlessly. 'He's so far off his bleedin' head he couldn't do anything if he wanted to – which he obviously don't, 'cos he's getting money out of it, isn't he? That's all he's bothered about at the end of the day.'

'How come?' Jane persisted, needing to get the full picture. 'I mean, if Kenny's her pimp, why's Dave getting money?'

Raising an eyebrow, Tina said, 'Have you seen her lately?'

'Yesterday. Why?'

'Well, you've seen the state of her, then, haven't you? How's she supposed to defend herself if Dave kicks off?

She knows she can't fight him, so she gives him a bit of what she's got left after Kenny takes his cut.' Pausing, Tina gave a bitter laugh. 'And she thought Kenny would keep Dave off her back, the stupid cow. *He* only gives a shit about what she does for *him*. He don't give a toss what Dave does to *her*.'

'Why does she put up with it?' Jane was becoming angrier by the second, wishing she'd gone with her instincts and kicked the crap out of Dave last night.

''Cos she's thick! She only keeps enough back to pay for her drugs, and she hardly ever eats. If you've seen her you'll know how skinny she is.'

'Yeah. She told me she was on a diet, but I knew it was drugs. How bad is she? You see her more than me.'

'Not any more I don't,' Tina admitted, sighing heavily. 'I couldn't stand all the drugs they were doing. Then when I knew what she was getting up to, well, that just sealed it for me. I saw her a couple of times after and tried to warn her. I said, you'll end up dead one of these days. If the drugs don't do for you, one of them mad bastards will. But would she listen . . . ?'

'They're not *that* bad, are they?' Jane frowned, sure that Tina had to be exaggerating. 'I can't believe she'd take all that crap lying down.'

'Hey, lying down's what she does best at the moment,' Tina quipped.

'You know what I mean,' Jane said, not at all amused. 'It's not like her.'

'Yeah, well, it is now,' Tina stated flatly. 'I couldn't *stand* the way they pushed her around. That Dave running round after Kenny like a bleedin' lapdog, telling Mary what to do all the time. "Go make Kenny a brew, Mare . . ."' she mimicked scathingly. '"Go get Kenny some cigs, Mare . . . Kiss Kenny's scabby bleedin' arse, Mare!"'

'She doesn't do it, does she?'

'She bloody *does*. God, I wanted to beat the crap out of him last time I went round there. If it hadn't been for that cunt Kenny, I swear I'd have had him. But he's not right, that Kenny, so I did one before it got nasty.' Stubbing her cigarette out, Tina immediately lit another one.

Realising they weren't going to be offered one, Mike took his tin from his pocket and rolled two. Lighting them, he handed one to Jane.

'So who are you, then?' Tina asked, peering at him from beneath her unplucked eyebrows. 'I haven't seen you before, have I?'

'Mike.' He held out his hand. 'I'm a mate of Jane's.'

Shaking his hand – after making him wait a few seconds – Tina turned back to Jane. 'So, how are you, anyway?'

'I'm okay. I was worried about Mary, really. And it looks like I was right, 'cos if you're not going round there now she won't have anyone looking out for her.'

'I couldn't just sit there watching her going under,' Tina muttered guiltily. 'It was doing my head in.'

'I know what you mean,' Jane agreed. 'I'd have felt the same.'

'Well, at least you're not blaming me, 'cos I blamed myself for long enough. And that fat twat Jock didn't help. He put me on a right guilt trip, him.'

'I take it you're not seeing him any more, then?'

'I never *was*!' Tina retorted indignantly. Then, 'All right, yeah, I admit we had a *thing*. But I wasn't *seeing* him as such. Anyhow, I don't want to talk about him. I suppose you'll be wanting a brew?'

Grinning, Mike said, 'Thought you'd never ask. Coffee, please – black, three sugars.'

'You still take it white with two?' Tina asked Jane.

'Yeah, thanks.' Jane was surprised that she'd remembered.

Coming back with a laden tray a few minutes later, Tina put it on the table and, gesturing at the plate of biscuits, told Mike to help himself.

'Don't mind if I do,' he said, snatching two chocolate-chip cookies. 'Lovely house you've got here.' He cast an approving glance around the room. 'You must be proud of it.'

'Yeah, it's all right.' Tina sat down with the faintest hint of a pleased smile on her lips. 'So, where are you from, Mike?'

'Ah, now that's debatable,' he said, mid-dunk. 'I'm what you might call a drifter.'

'Eh?'

'He travels a lot,' Jane explained possessively. Tina was looking a little too interested in him for her liking, and she didn't want them to get too friendly. It reminded her too painfully of how pushed out she'd felt when Tina had monopolised Mary. 'He stays at peace camps all over the place,' she went on. 'Protesting about war, and nuclear arms, and that.'

'Not been to one in a while,' Mike interjected wistfully. 'You'll have to come with me next time I go, Jane. You'd love it.'

Beaming smugly, Jane took a sip of her coffee. She almost choked when Mike went on to say, 'I'll give my mate a ring when we've sorted Mary out – find out where the nearest one is.'

'Sorted Mary out?' Tina pounced, her eyes narrowed to slits. 'What's that supposed to mean?'

'I don't think we should talk about this right now.' Jane gave Mike a warning look. 'Tina might not—'

'Tina's no idiot,' Tina interrupted coldly. 'And she's not deaf, neither. I heard you whispering when I was making the brew. I know you're planning something, and if you don't trust me enough to tell me you shouldn't have come round.'

'It's not that I don't trust you,' Jane lied. 'It's just that, well . . .' Lost for a good excuse, she bit her lip. There was no point beating around the bush. Tina was as black and white as they came – and more than capable of warning Mary that they were up to something if they didn't tell her. 'All right, yeah,' she admitted. 'I *am* worried about you knowing. Because I *know* you, Tina. If you don't like it, you'll mess everything up.'

"Cos I'm such a bitch and I don't care about Mary as much as you?' Tina retorted, cocking an eyebrow, challenging Jane to deny she was thinking that. 'I mightn't show it as much as you,' she said when Jane didn't answer, 'but I *do* care. And I'm not averse to a bit of foul play if it gets the right result. So, why don't you tell me what you're planning? You never know, I might be able to help. I know more about what's going on with her than you do, don't forget.'

'Sounds logical to me,' Mike said calmly. 'But it's your call, Jane.'

Holding up her hands in a gesture of surrender, Jane said, 'Go on, then. You might as well tell her.'

Tina listened intently as Mike outlined his plan. When he'd finished, she pondered it in silence for a while, then nodded.

'I think we should do it. Mary's so messed up right now she doesn't even know how bad she is. And she won't be thinking about stopping, because she genuinely doesn't see anything wrong with it.'

'Good point,' Mike interjected respectfully. 'From what you told me, Jane, she thinks she looks great.'

'Yeah. She did the full twirling-round-to-show-off-her-figure bit.'

Tina shook her head. 'Looks like shit, but she still thinks she's some sort of supermodel. Sad, isn't it?'

'Yeah, it is,' Jane agreed. ''Cos she really was gorgeous before she started on that.'

'Which is why we've got to do this,' Mike cut in. 'Force her to open her eyes and see herself the way you two do. And I think you *should* help,' he went on, turning to Tina now. 'So, why don't you come round to mine later? Meet the others and get this rolling.'

'We're telling the others?' Jane had a hint of panic in her voice now.

'They'll be sensible,' Mike told her, patting her hand. 'Anyway, we'll need them if we're going to pull this off. It's going to be hard work, you know.'

33

Tina arrived at seven that evening.

Letting her in, Jane introduced her to Mimi, Pete, Jonas and Kim – who'd wisely left Genghis at home. Lovely as he was, he wasn't of sufficiently sound mind to get involved in something like this. And neither was Roy – who also hadn't been invited, much to Jane's relief.

Doing only the slightest of double takes when she saw Jonas's pink Mohican, Tina plonked herself down on the couch beside him without further ado, and Jane released the breath she'd been holding. She'd been worried that Tina would be her usual obnoxious self when she saw the way they all dressed, but Tina seemed perfectly happy to be there and was soon chatting away as if she'd known them all her life.

After a while, Mike brought the subject round to Mary, explaining the situation to the others and telling them about the plan.

'I know it sounds like heavy shit,' he said, looking at each of them in turn. 'And we'll understand if you don't want to get involved, but we asked you because we need a strong team to pull it off and you lot are as sound as they come. If you want in we'd be really grateful . . . But if you don't, that's fine, too. Just do us a favour and forget we said anything.'

'I'm in,' Pete declared without hesitation.

'So are we,' Kim agreed with a sparkling smile.

'Well, you know I am,' Mimi said, as if it had never been in question.

'Great.' Mike nodded his approval. 'I thought you would.'

'Er, just one thing,' Tina said, the darkness of her tone indicating that all would not be as well as the present atmosphere promised. 'I forgot to tell Jane and Mike earlier, but a word of warning about Kenny Butler . . . He's got a shooter.' Pausing briefly to let the weight of what she'd said hammer home, she added ominously, 'And don't think for one minute he wouldn't use it, 'cos I'm telling you now he would. Ever since he got his feet back on the map, he's been getting real heavy.'

Digesting this, Pete folded his arms and pursed his lips thoughtfully.

'Okay,' he said after a minute. 'So we'll just have to tread carefully. Everyone knows how nasty pimps and pushers can get when their territory's invaded, but they're not exactly the smartest animals on the farm. We should be able to outwit him if we put our minds to it.'

'Yeah,' Mike agreed. 'But we'll have to be really vigilant all the same. Make sure absolutely *no* one is hanging about when we approach Mary.'

'How's about we split up?' Jonas suggested. 'Keep watch from all sides to give warning if someone comes.'

'If we time it right we'll catch her between Kenny's checkups,' Tina interjected casually.

All eyes swivelled her way.

'Check-ups?'

'Yep. Twice a night without fail. First one to check they're all there and doing what they're supposed to be doing. Second, to take the money and give them their drugs. Mary collects whatever they make after that and Kenny picks it up in the morning. He's got it well covered.'

'How do you know so much?' Mimi asked politely. 'Only

you said you didn't go round there any more, and I really think we need to be sure of the facts before we do anything.'

'I'm *sure*,' Tina said with certainty. 'I mightn't go round, but I still see Hannah at the bingo from time to time, and she keeps me updated.'

'Hannah?' Jane sneered. 'What does *she* know? She's thick.'

'Hey, she's not as daft as she looks.' Tina drew her head back, doubling the size of the fat roll around her neck. Chuckling then, she said, 'All right, she *is* as daft. But she *does* know what's going on, 'cos Mary tells her.'

'Mary wouldn't tell Hannah anything.' Jane's frown deepened. 'She can't stand her.'

'Yeah, she can. It's Dave who hates her. Mary's always had a bit of a soft spot for her. And I can't say I blame her. It's any port in a storm when you've got no one else to talk to, isn't it?'

'Suppose so. But I still can't believe she'd confide in *her*.'

'Never mind all that,' Mike cut in impatiently. 'Let's just concentrate on the matter at hand for now. You were there when Kenny turned up last night, Jane. What time was that?'

'About two, half-two.'

'If she was as strung-out as you reckon,' Tina mused, 'that was probably his second visit. Hannah reckons he makes sure the girls are desperate before he does the drop-off 'cos he knows they'll work extra hard if they're gagging for it. If they haven't made enough he holds it back, and they're not allowed to score off anyone else because he'd kill them. Just like he would if he thought they were chatting his business – which is probably why he got pissed off when he saw Mary talking to you.'

'Oh, no,' Jane muttered guiltily. 'You don't think he'd have hurt her, do you?'

'He probably gave her a slap.' Tina shrugged. 'But don't

worry about that. She might be a mess but she's not totally stupid. And we might hate what she's doing, but you've got to remember that she's quite happy playing her little game.'

'How can she be?'

'Believe me, she is,' Tina stated sagely. 'Mary feels good 'cos Kenny put her in charge of the other girls. And I know for a fact he still goes round to hers for a brew, so he can't exactly *hate* her, can he?'

'You think there's something between them?' Mike asked, frowning. A romantic entanglement would complicate things in a way he hadn't anticipated.

Tina shrugged again. 'Doubt if it's personal in *that* sense, but they've definitely got an understanding.'

'It's fucked up,' Pete commented, shaking his head. 'Classic abuser manipulation. Make her totally dependent by putting the fear of God into her and getting her hooked on drugs only *he* can supply, but keep her sweet by giving her a bit of status with the underdogs, so she feels respected and he's got someone to run things if he can't be there.'

'Exactly,' Tina confirmed, looking at him as if at last she'd found someone as astute as herself.

Sighing, Mike said, 'Look, we're wasting time with all this talking. If we're going to do this, we've got to get things sorted. If anyone wants to back out, speak now or for ever hold your peace.'

There was a general shaking of heads.

'Right, then.' He rubbed his hands together. 'Let's get cracking.'

34

It was one-thirty when Jane, Mike, Pete and Tina set off. Jonas was disappointed not to be included in the *dangerous* bit, but Pete persuaded him that he should stay to look after Mimi and Kim in case something went wrong. Adding that a shocking pink foot-high Mohican would stand out like a sore thumb in a plaster cast, making it a little difficult to stay undercover.

They hadn't wanted to offend him by telling him the truth: that they didn't want him along because he'd be about as much use as a chocolate fireguard if anything kicked off – him being so young and *delicate*.

A very disgruntled Donkey was also left behind, with the strict instruction to 'Guard the house!' He immediately went to his cushion in the corner to sulk. He was always being left behind these days, and he wasn't impressed.

Driving into the car park at the back of a supermarket on a side street near Alexandra Park, they left the van there and walked the rest of the way. Sticking close to the shadows of the overgrown bushes draped over the old church wall at the junction, Jane peeped around the corner.

Spotting Mary leaning in through the window of a car at the park gates across the road, she whispered, 'She's here.'

'Right, everyone back,' Mike hissed, waving them to hide.

Climbing the low wall, they pushed their way through the bushes until they had a clear view of the gates and the road without being visible themselves. A few seconds later the car took off at speed, and Jane stifled a giggle when Mary stuck two fingers up after it and yelled obscenities at the driver.

'Bloody state of her,' Tina hissed disapprovingly.

Sobering, Jane nodded. Mary looked particularly trashy tonight. A miniskirt was one thing, but *that* was nothing more than a belt. And her top was little better – all but see-through, Jane could clearly see the saggy remnants of her friend's once-full breasts through it. Mary had obviously lost all sense of shame.

Staggering back onto the pavement when the car disappeared from view, Mary tottered over to the lone lamp-post and leaned heavily against it, her already pasty face made all the more sickly by the orange glow that the light cast.

'Do you think Kenny's already done the drop-off?' Pete asked.

'If he has, it'll have been a while back,' Tina told him, squinting to see Mary more clearly. 'She'd be nodding out if she'd only just had it. She looks more like she's getting ready for her next bit. He could turn up any time. We might have to give it a miss for tonight.'

'Well, at least I know what she looks like,' Mike whispered. 'So I'll recognise her if I have to come back. I still think it's worth a shot, though.' Nudging Jane, he pointed to a gap in the bushes. 'Have a look and see if he's hanging about anywhere.'

'All right, but it's your fault if I fall straight through,' she warned.

Shuffling forward a couple of inches, Jane stuck her face through the branches and scanned left and right. There had been one other girl walking about when they'd arrived, but she'd just gone off in a Mercedes. But for Mary, the road was deserted.

'Looks like she's getting ready to go,' Mike whispered, motioning with a nod towards Mary who was yawning and checking her watch now. 'I'd best make my move while it's quiet.'

'Are you sure about this?' Jane was having serious doubts now that the moment was upon them. What if Mary kicked off, or Kenny turned up and got nasty? 'Maybe we'd be better waiting a few nights. Watch her – see what her routine is.'

'We might never get a better chance,' Mike reasoned. 'We could come back tomorrow and find she's changed her times or her beat, or something.'

'He's right,' Tina agreed. 'There's no point waiting if it means missing a perfect opportunity like this. He's best off just getting it over with before she goes.'

Muttering, 'Suppose so,' Jane gazed at Mike and gave him a tiny, concerned smile. 'Just be careful, yeah?'

'Don't worry about me,' he told her reassuringly. 'I'll be fine.'

Scrambling back the way they'd come, Mike appeared on the pavement a minute later. Pausing just inches from where they were hiding, he whispered, 'Wish me luck,' then set off across the road.

Hands deep in his pockets, he headed straight for Mary . . . and carried on going.

'What's he doing?' Tina hissed.

'No idea,' Jane murmured, wondering much the same thing. When Mike turned around seconds later and headed back towards Mary, she breathed a sigh of relief. For one terrible moment, she'd thought he was bottling out.

Everyone pressed forward when Mike approached Mary and there was a collective intake of breath as they strained to hear what he was saying. Finding it impossible from that distance, they had to content themselves with watching as he pointed towards the Crescents – obviously telling her where he wanted to take her. Their hearts sank when she shook her head.

'She's not going for it,' Jane groaned.

'She will,' Tina wheezed, finding it difficult to breathe in the confined space. 'As soon as she sees the dosh, she'll be off like a shot.'

As if on cue, Mike pulled out his wallet and opened it for Mary to inspect. Obviously satisfied that he was good for her asking price, she nodded and, at last, they were off.

Mike whistled as he passed the church wall with Mary's arm linked through his, letting the others know that the first stage was complete.

Waiting a couple of minutes before climbing out of the bushes, they made a mad dash to the van.

Back at Mike's flat, Pete gave Mimi, Kim and Jonas a quick rundown of what had happened. Then everyone got into position.

The bedroom was ready – the bed made, all potentially harmful items removed, and the bolt from the bathroom screwed firmly onto the door. As an extra precaution, Jonas had nailed a piece of wood across the window, ensuring that once Mary was in there there was no way she was getting out without their say-so.

After the group had turned out the lights, their eyes quickly adjusted to the gloom – aided a fraction by the faintest of street-lamp glows bleeding in through the curtains.

'Everyone ready?' Jane hissed when she heard Mike's key in the lock some minutes later. There were a few muffled yeses, then silence as everyone held their breath.

35

'Take your bleedin' time, why don't you?' Mary complained as Mike made a meal of opening the door.

'Sorry,' he murmured, ushering her in. 'Dodgy lock. Make yourself at home.'

Wandering in, Mary gave a tiny shudder as the darkness enveloped her. She hated not being able to see her surroundings; it unnerved her.

Whirling around when she heard the sound of the mortise key turning in the lock behind her, there was a note of real panic in her voice when she said, 'Here . . . what's going on? Don't be locking me in, you bastard! What d'y' think you're doing?'

'Helping you,' Mike replied calmly, flicking the light on and pushing her firmly into the living room.

'What's that supposed to mean?' Mary squawked. 'I don't need any help! I just—' Stopping mid-sentence when she saw everyone emerging from their hiding places, she glanced wildly at the strange faces. Then, spotting Jane and Tina, the confusion crossed her face like a shadow. 'What are you two doing here?'

'Like Mike said,' Jane explained, coming towards her. 'We're trying to help you.'

Squaring up to her, Mary put her fists on her hips. 'And like *I* said, I don't *need* any fucking help!'

Stepping forward, Tina grabbed her arm and yanked her round.

'Yes, you do, you stupid cow. Why d'y' reckon we went to all this trouble to get you here?'

'You didn't get me here,' Mary retorted angrily, tearing herself free and jabbing Mike viciously in the chest. '*This* sad tosser did. And if you think I'm staying, you're off your bleedin' heads. I'm going . . . *Now*!' Pushing past them, she made for the door, only to find her way blocked as Jonas stepped neatly in front of her.

'Hi, there,' he drawled, attempting to disarm her with a wide, toothy grin. 'You must be Mary. I've heard so much about you.'

Stopping in her tracks, Mary drew her head back and weighed him up. Then, lashing out, she landed an almighty slap across his face.

'Get out of my way, you little shite!'

Slim as he was, Jonas easily held her back as she tried to force her way past him. Laughing as she struggled to get her bitten-down nails into his flesh, he said, 'Now, now . . . no scratching. It's not very ladylike.'

'*BASTAAARD!*' Mary screamed, growing wilder by the second, kicking and biting and tearing at his pride-and-joy Mohican.

Marching across, Jane and Tina took an arm each and hauled Mary off Jonas.

'Are you gonna stop fighting?' Tina yelled, struggling to keep her grip as Mary continued to thrash about. 'I don't wanna hurt you, but if I have to I *will*.'

Knowing she stood a cat in hell's chance of beating Tina, Mary stopped struggling and allowed them to lead her to the couch. Dropping sulkily down onto it, she rubbed her arms and glared at everyone reproachfully.

Sitting down beside her, Mike calmly explained what they were doing.

'You're all *mad*,' she snorted when he'd finished, looking

around as if she were in a room full of aliens. 'You don't really think you can *kidnap* me and keep me here for God knows how long and I'm just gonna *let* you, do you?'

'You've got no choice,' Tina told her evenly. 'We're doing this for your own good.'

'Who are *you* to decide what's good for *me?*' Mary snarled, glaring at her hatefully. 'What the hell do *any* of you know about me or my life? As for *you*,' she pointed an accusing finger at Jane, 'I haven't seen you in *yonks*, so how could *you* know what I need?'

'I care about you,' Jane murmured guiltily, but Mary had already turned to Tina.

'And *you* buggered off and left me in the lurch, an' all, so don't *you* start telling me what's good for me.'

'We're your mates,' Tina yelled back at her, losing patience now. 'We're not just gonna sit back and watch you kill yourself.'

Laughing hysterically, Mary said, '*Me* kill myself, that's a good 'un. It's *you* lot that'll bleedin' kill me if you keep me locked up in here! Kenny's expecting me. I've got to go.'

'Tough!' Tina pushed her back into her seat as she lunged forward. 'You're staying, and that's that.'

'Fuck *off*!' Mary screamed, bringing her fists down on the couch cushion. 'You've got no *right*!'

'So what?' Tina challenged coolly. 'You're here now – deal with it. And while we're at it . . .' Yanking Mary's arms aside, she reached into her pocket. 'I'll have whatever you're carrying.'

'No!' Mary squealed when Tina pulled the plastic bank-bag containing the night's takings and her purse with the small wrap of smack and her works in it from her inside pocket. 'I need that! Give it back!'

'No way!' Stuffing the money into her own pocket, Tina snapped the works in half. 'You can have the money back when you're sorted, but the gear's going down the loo. And don't bother arguing, 'cos I mean it.'

Faced with Tina's calm determination Mary started to cry, in the vain hope that someone would take pity on her and make Tina back off. When nobody moved, she quickly gave it up. Wiping her nose on her sleeve she narrowed her eyes, trying to think up a different approach.

'Look, we're mates, aren't we?' Mary said after a moment, appealing directly to Jane now. 'And I know you're worried about me, but I'm all right – really I am.'

'Yeah, right,' Tina snorted. 'And I'm eight stone two.'

Ignoring her, Mary continued to target Jane, who looked the most uncomfortable of them all. Forcing herself to smile – which only served to contort her face into a grotesque grimace, she said, 'I know you're pissed off about Dave hitting me, but he's not that bad any more. I've got it all under control – honest.' Another grimace. 'It was seeing you the other week that did it. I thought, Jane's come all this way to see me 'cos she cares about me, the least I can do is sort myself out. So, that's what I did – I went home and got it sorted.' Sitting back, she gave a satisfied sigh, pleased with her performance – sure that they would see sense and let her go now.

'It was only last night,' Jane reminded her quietly. 'How could you have sorted anything out in that time?'

'Was it?' Mary frowned confusedly. 'I could have sworn . . . Oh, but, so what?' She flapped her hand. 'It don't matter *when* it was, I sorted it and that's what counts. I told Dave straight. I said, listen Dave, I don't need you giving me all this shit, and he says, all right.'

'Just like that?' Tina scoffed.

'Yeah!' Mary gave a bright, insincere laugh. 'That was all it took. I know I should have stood up for myself before, but I've done it now, so there's no need for any of this, is there? Eh?'

Unconvinced by the bullshit speech, Jane folded her arms. 'Never mind Dave. What about *Kenny*? Did you sort him out too?'

Mary's face dropped. 'Kenny's all right,' she muttered defensively.

Tutting loudly, Tina rolled her eyes. 'Oh, yeah, he's just *great*, him!'

'Make your mind up,' Jane said, peering down at Mary. 'You told me he was bad news. Said I'd get hurt if I messed with him. How's that, if he's *all right*?'

Mary was being backed into a corner, and she knew it.

'He . . . well, he's only *not* all right if he thinks you're messing him about,' she spluttered. 'He's got a lot of money invested in me, so he looks out for me. That's how it works.'

'You *WHAT*?' Tina roared, bringing her fist down on the back of the couch. 'My *God*, I've heard everything now. He's got *nothing* invested in you, you stupid bitch. He's taking *your* money.'

'I *OWE* him!' Mary retaliated fiercely. 'How d'y' think I get my drugs? He gives me what I want, and I *pay* him for it.'

'So, what exactly does he give you for all this money?' Mike cut in quietly, trying to break the tension.

Sensing sympathy, Mary turned to him. 'I'm not a junkie, you know. I only have a bit of rock to keep me going, then a bit of gear to bring me down – help me get to sleep, an' that. And I don't do it all the time – just when I'm feeling a bit rough.'

'And you don't think that's a lot?' Mike raised an incredulous eyebrow. 'I'm not being funny, love, but if you give him all your money—'

'Not *all* of it,' Mary corrected him.

'All right,' he conceded, holding up his hands. 'Most of it, then. You give him *most* of the money you've earned, and all *you* get is a *bit* of rock and smack. If that's right, I think you're paying too much. I mean, come on . . . He's getting the lion's share, and you're working your backside off to give it to him. Doesn't that sound wrong to you?'

'Not really,' she muttered, sniffing loudly.

'Look, what's really going on?' Mike persisted, his voice surprisingly gentle. 'You can't be doing this because you *want* to. Look at *me*. Can you honestly tell me that you wanted to come here and do the business with a complete *stranger*?'

'It don't make no difference,' Mary retorted sulkily. 'You, Joe Bloggs, Quasimodo . . . It's all the same to me. In fact, it's better if you *are* a stranger, 'cos at least I won't ever have to see your ugly mush again.'

'And what about the knife I'm going to slice your stupid *throat* open with?' Mike growled, changing tack so suddenly that Mary literally shrank away from him as he thrust his face towards her. 'Is *that* all the same to you?' Leaning over her now, his knee on the cushion beside her, his teeth bared, he said, 'And how about the *rope* I'm gonna wrap around your stupid neck and *hang* you with? Or this cigarette,' he held his lit one near her face, 'that I'm gonna stick in your fucking *eyes*?'

'Get him off me!' Mary shrieked, scrabbling to escape the glowing tip.

Snatching the cigarette from him before he got too close, Jane said, 'What Mike's *trying* to say, is that he could have been any old nutter picking you up, so how come you agreed to go with him?'

'Yeah,' Tina interjected scornfully. 'How stupid was that when you *know* there's a psycho running round out there? Remember them three girls who got raped and tortured in Moss Side last month, do you? Yet you still agreed to go to a man's flat.' Shaking her head, she pursed her lips disapprovingly. 'If you don't need help, who the hell *does*?'

Mary began to sulk again. It was fast dawning on her that it made no difference what she said, they weren't going to let her go. She'd tried threats, tears, and bullshit, and none of it had worked. She was already starting to feel like crap, and it was going to get much worse if she didn't get a proper hit soon.

'So, what now?' she asked, sounding too weary to fight. 'It won't be long before I freak out, you know. I only had a bit of that gear before. What you gonna do when I need it?'

'We'll deal with that when it comes,' Mike told her, his voice normal again. 'All we want is to get you clean. You've got to agree it's for the best.'

'Best for *who*?' Mary cast him a filthy look. '*You*, you weirdo?'

'Behave!' Tina warned her. 'You *want* to get off it, don't you?'

'Well, seeing as you're asking,' Mary retorted sarcastically. 'No – I don't *want* to get off it, thanks! I'm totally in control of it, and I *like* it. And I don't care what you lot say.' She glared around at them all. 'I'm still gonna do it when you let me go. And you *will* have to let me go *some*time.'

'Maybe so.' Tina shrugged. 'But at least we'll know we've done our best by you.'

By five a.m., Mary had worked herself into a state of hysteria. The withdrawal had properly kicked in and she began to scream and kick and thrash around, making so much noise that they decided it was time to put her into the bedroom. Carrying her there when she refused to walk, they bolted the door and left her to bang and shout.

Concerned for her safety, Jane paced the living-room floor, chewing her nails to the quick and wincing at each thud.

'Come and sit down,' Mike told her after a while. 'We all knew this wasn't going to be easy, but now we've started, we've got to see it through, haven't we?'

'Suppose so,' she murmured unhappily, joining him on the couch. 'But it just feels so *wrong*.'

36

'What d'y' mean, she ain't back yet?' Kenny roared. 'Where the fuck is she?'

'I don't know, man,' Dave whined, cowering back when Kenny towered over him and slammed his hands down on the arms of the chair. 'I swear to God!'

'Don't fuck me about, you little ponce,' Kenny spat. 'If you two are fucking about with my gear, you're dead.'

'We're not,' Dave squeaked, almost wetting himself with fear. 'Honest, Ken, I don't even know where she's put it. She said you told her not to.'

'That's right, I did,' Kenny confirmed meanly. 'And you know why? 'Cos I don't fuckin' trust you. I gave you enough chances, but you fucked everything up as usual, didn't you? You're nowt but a snivelling little cunt, and the only reason I haven't done you in is 'cos I can't be arsed knifing your miserable fuckin' throat. But, believe me, I won't think twice if you're up to owt with my gear.'

'I'm not!' Dave was almost crying now. 'She's got it stashed somewhere. I haven't even seen it. She don't tell me nothing – you know that.'

Shaking his head in disgust, Kenny pushed himself upright. God, how he despised this useless excuse for a man.

Glancing at his watch, he felt the anger churn afresh in his stomach. It was five a.m. He had things to do. But where the fuck was Mary? He'd told the bitch he'd pick her up. He'd have understood if she'd had a last-minute punter, but that would have only taken ten minutes. She should have been back long before now. This was a pure piss-take.

Marching to the window, he yanked the curtain aside and peered down at the road below. The boys were waiting in the car, but that was the only sign of life in the area. The road was deserted; there weren't even any cars on the flyover up ahead.

Letting the curtain drop, Kenny paced the floor, punching his palm with a fist. He'd taken a big risk leaving that much gear with Mary but he'd thought he could trust her. He should have known better. She was only a whore, after all – and a junkie one, at that. Well, he'd kill her if she'd taken advantage of his good nature. Kill her stone dead!

Just like he was going to kill that twat of a copper, Gibson, for giving him that bum steer about the raid. The snidey little bastard had blagged him good style, giving him the time, the date, and even the method the drug squad had supposedly devised to catch him unawares. He'd been bloody convincing, too. Convincing enough for Kenny to pay him two grand for the warning – two grand that the cunt would pay back in blood.

The raid had never happened – had never even been on the cards, according to another bent cop Kenny had had a quiet word with after waiting all day and most of the night in his cleaned-out flat.

Gibson was dead for fucking him over like that. *Doubly* dead, if his greedy little scheme led to Kenny losing the powder he'd left with Mary. Thirty grand's worth of pure coke was not something he was prepared to walk away and forget about.

Gibson would get his first, then Mary and this gimp.

Turning to Dave now, Kenny glared at him evilly.

'Right, you, I'm off. But I'll be back at two tomorrow afternoon. If she's still not back, you're fucked.'

*   *   *

Getting up when Kenny had gone, Dave tiptoed to the window and peeped out. Exhaling shakily when the big man climbed into the car and took off, he rushed to the door to check that it was locked. Then, going into the bedroom, he dropped to his knees and rooted through the dust-covered rubbish beneath the bed for Mary's secret stash. His nerves were in bits; he needed a fix to calm him down.

Locating the little box that she kept hidden inside a sock, Dave pulled it out and checked how much was there. It was nowhere near enough to zonk him out, but it would have to do for now. At least it would take the edge off; calm him down enough to get his head straight and look for Mary.

And what a fucking beating she was going to get for dropping him in it with Kenny like that. God only knew where the sneaky bitch had stashed that gear. Dave had searched the flat from top to bottom, but he hadn't seen so much as a grain of it. If he *had* found it, he'd have given it to Kenny just now and dropped Mary right in it. He'd have said that she'd *told* him where she'd put it, letting Kenny know that his precious little whore wasn't quite as trustworthy as he'd thought. Kenny would have battered the bitch senseless for that.

But she hadn't told Dave, had she, the fucking slag! She'd kept her little secret all to herself, leaving the man she was supposed to love to take the flak for her. Well, fuck her if she thought she was getting away with it. When Dave got his hands on her, he was going to teach her a lesson she'd never forget.

And Dave knew just where to start looking.

37

At six, Mike persuaded Jane to walk with him to the all-night garage, hoping that the fresh air would clear her head and give her back some of the energy that she'd lost fretting over Mary.

It didn't. All the way there, Jane continued to moan.

'You don't think we're overdoing it, do you? She could do herself some real damage if she keeps throwing herself around. And what if she gets really sick?'

'We won't let it get that bad,' Mike assured her. 'We'll wait till she calms down, then we'll get some food and drink down her. She'll be fine – you'll see.'

'But what if someone hears her screaming?'

Giving Jane a sceptical look, Mike said, 'Since when has anyone ever taken any notice of screams in the Crescents? Anyway, I went outside earlier when she was really loud, and I couldn't hear a thing. You worry too much, that's your trouble.'

Stopping when they reached the garage door, he held out his hand. 'Where's that list?'

Handing him the crinkled scrap of paper she'd been clutching, Jane said, 'Don't forget Tina's cigs. I didn't write them down.'

'Aw, what have you been doing with this?' He held the paper up with a grimace of disgust. 'Have you been blowing your nose on it, or something?'

'Get stuffed!' she protested, slapping him so hard that he

almost fell through the door. She was laughing as she followed him in, but what she saw inside stopped her dead in her tracks.

Peering at her, Mike frowned. 'What's up?'

Nodding towards a man who was standing at the counter with his back to them, she whispered, 'That's Dave.'

Mike turned to look just as Dave finished his transaction and turned around. Looking into the glazed, staring eyes, he immediately guessed that Dave was high as a kite.

Dave looked straight through him for a moment. Then he spotted Jane, and the malicious light of recognition dawned in the colourless orbs. Lurching across the floor, he came to a stop just inches from her – close enough for her to smell his rancid breath.

'Eh up! What've we got here, then? Me old mate Jane with a *whatjamacallit*?' He flapped his hand as if looking for an appropriate description. '*Hippie* dude!' he managed, lunging at Mike and throwing an arm around his shoulders. 'Y' all right, there, mate?'

'Excuse me.' Politely shrugging him off, Mike walked up to the counter.

''Scuse *meee*,' Dave drawled, pulling a face at his retreating back. Turning back to Jane then, he said, 'Well, this is a co-inky-dink. I was just coming to yours.'

'Why?'

'Oh, I think you know what I'm lookin' for. Or should I say, *who*.'

'I don't know what you're talking about,' Jane lied.

Dave didn't believe her. Scowling now, he said, 'Look, I know my Mary's up at your place, so cut the crap.'

'She's not,' Jane replied coolly.

Jutting his face towards her, Dave dropped his voice to a menacing snarl. 'Don't fuck with me, you ugly bitch. I know she's at yours, and I'm coming back there with you to get her.'

'She's not there,' Jane repeated truthfully, refusing to be intimidated by his threatening tone. 'Anyway, I'm not going home just yet.'

Dave narrowed his eyes, thrown by her calmness.

'Well, if she's not with you, how come she disappears straight after you turn up looking for her, eh?'

'I don't know.' Jane folded her arms and drew her head back. 'But I'm telling the truth. She's *not* at my flat.'

'Where *is* she, then?' Dave yelled, losing patience. 'She can't have disappeared into thin fuckin' air! Them tarts told me you was there last night, an' now she's *gone*. So where is she?' He grabbed Jane roughly by the arm. 'Tell me!'

Mike had been listening from a discreet distance. Deciding it was time to get Jane out before it really kicked off, he pushed himself between them, accidentally-on-purpose stamping on Dave's foot.

Pushing Jane towards the door, he said, 'Oh, shit, sorry, mate. Nice meeting you . . . Must be off now . . . Bye!'

Hopping around in pain, Dave screamed, 'You stupid bastard! You've broke me bleedin' toe!' But they'd already gone, and he was in no fit state to chase after them with his toe throbbing blue murder.

Mike and Jane started running as soon as they got out of the door.

'See!' Mike yelled back to her over his shoulder. 'I told you I could deal with him.'

'Yeah, but he's gonna come after us now,' Jane countered. 'He's convinced I've got Mary stashed away in my flat. That's where he was going just now.'

'Well, we'd best hurry up and get back to *my* place, then.' Grabbing her hand, Mike pulled her on.

'You're gonna *kill* me,' Jane gasped. 'I've never been a good runner.'

'Aw, shaddap!' Laughing, he upped his pace.

By the time they reached the Crescents, Jane could barely
make it up the stairs. Hauling her along to his flat, Mike
shoved her through the door, slamming it firmly behind
them. Rushing to the window, he eased the edge of the
curtain back to keep watch.

Shocked awake by their noisy entrance, Kim sat up and
rubbed her eyes. 'What's up? Is someone chasing you?'

'Dave,' Jane wheezed, leaning back against the door to
catch her breath.

Tina, who'd been half-asleep on the couch, jerked upright.
'Dave? Where?'

'At the garage. He was asking where Mary was. Said he
was just about to go to mine to look for her.'

'Jeezus, that was quick!' Tina exclaimed. 'What did you
tell him? Who was he with? Was Kenny there?'

'No, he was alone. And I told him the truth.'

'You *what*?' Tina squawked, leaping to her feet. 'You told
him *what*?'

'The truth,' Jane repeated, wondering how Tina had got
up so fast when she usually complained and groaned about
every movement. 'She's not at my flat.'

Tutting irritably, Tina flopped back down. 'Did he believe
you?'

'What do *you* think?'

'He's going up there now,' Mike called, watching as Dave
staggered up the stairs to Jane's floor. 'He's nearly there.'

Rushing to look for herself, Jane was just in time to see
Dave flop forward over the balcony ledge.

'What's he doing?'

'Puking,' Mike told her, chuckling.

Dave hung limply over the ledge for several minutes after
the last drops had fallen from his mouth. Then, just as Jane
was beginning to think he was unconscious, he suddenly
jerked himself upright and continued on his way.

Falling heavily against Jane's door when he reached it, Dave steadied himself, then started knocking, his voice echoing around the Crescents as he shouted, 'MARY! I know you're in there! Open the door . . . Come on, you bitch! Open the bleedin' *door*!'

Getting no answer, he beat his fists against the wood, pausing after a minute to press his ear against it. Maddened by the answering silence, he took a couple of staggering steps back, then hurled himself at the door, yelling, 'Come out, you fuckin' bitch! I'm gonna *kill* ya!'

'He's going to break it!' Jane yelped, panicked by the sound of splintering wood.

Squeezing her arm reassuringly, Mike said, 'Don't worry. It's only a door.'

'Yeah, but what if he gets in and trashes everything?' Jane moaned, thinking it was all right for *Mike* to say that when it wasn't *his* home being attacked.

'He won't,' Mike insisted. And then he smiled as no sooner were the words out of his mouth than Dave stopped kicking. 'See? I told you.'

Dave was panting for breath and feeling decidedly unwell after his furious outburst. He had no doubt that Mary was in there, laughing at him. But he didn't have the strength to get in – not just yet. He needed to go home and have another look for that gear. If he could just find that, he'd be able to sort his head out.

Taking one last kick at the door, he yelled, 'I'll be back, you back-stabbing, pussy-lickin' *WHORE*! I'll be back – you can count on that!' Then, turning clumsily, he stumbled away.

Watching until Dave emerged at the foot of the stairwell and headed off through the open garages, Mike breathed a sigh of relief and closed the curtain. Going to the couch, he flopped wearily down.

'Christ, that was close. I need a spliff.'

'Never mind that,' Tina said, making a grab for the bag he was holding. 'Where's the chocolate? And I hope you remembered me cigs – I'm gagging.'

Everyone laughed when Donkey, having heard the word *chocolate*, belly-crawled out from his sulking corner and wriggled over to lie at Mike's feet, gazing longingly at the bag.

The good cheer lasted only as long as it took to eat the chocolate. The atmosphere was soon as tense and uncomfortable as it had been before. The air was blue with smoke, and Pete made so many brews that the toilet seemed to be continually flushing.

At last, daylight began to filter through the curtains.

Rubbing her eyes, Kim said, 'God, I'm shattered. I'm going home for a kip. Coming, babe?'

'Yeah.' Jonas yawned loudly. 'Best see what Genghis has been up to while we've been out. Knowing him, there'll be all sorts of dossers in the place.'

'I'll walk round with you.' Getting up, Mimi stretched languidly. 'I've got to feed the cats. The poor things have been locked in for ages.'

'I thought you'd sent them back to Bridlington?' Pete quipped.

'Not Mel and Del,' Mimi giggled. 'I did send *them* back; they were doing my head in squabbling like a pair of kids. No, I meant my *furry* cats.'

'I'm only teasing.' Pete tipped her an affectionate wink. 'Anyway, the cats will be fine. They can amuse themselves for days.'

'Yeah, but they can't use a can-opener.'

'Touché!' Pete grinned. 'Want me to walk you round?'

'No, you stay here and get some rest,' Mimi insisted, pulling her jacket on. 'It's light now. We'll be fine.'

*   *   *

After they'd gone, the others tried to get a bit of sleep before Mary woke up. She'd been quiet for a while but they expected her to start stirring soon and knew they'd need more energy than any of them had right now if they were going to deal with her.

Hard as they tried, they couldn't relax enough to drop off. So Mike kept the spliffs coming, and Pete kept the kettle hot, while Jane and Tina sat in silence – smoking, drinking tea, and listening out for sounds of Mary waking.

None of them was relishing that moment. What had seemed like a very good idea a few hours ago had turned decidedly weird. It was all very well *planning* to hold somebody against their will, but now they were actually doing it, it didn't feel quite as right as they'd expected it to.

38

A t ten, Mary started banging her fist on the bedroom
door, chanting, 'Let me *out* . . . Let me *out* . . .'

Moving closer to Jane, Tina whispered, 'What happens
now?'

'I don't know,' Jane whispered back.

'We can't keep her locked up. What if something happens
to her?'

'It won't.'

Jane wished she felt half as confident as she sounded. In
truth, she was seriously worried. She hadn't actually considered how Dave would react to Mary not coming home, but
she hadn't expected him to turn up here. And he wouldn't
give up – not now he thought he was on the right track.
He'd be back, she was sure.

'One of us will have to go in,' Tina said. 'She must be
hungry, and she probably needs the loo.'

'I'll open up.' Getting up wearily, Mike went towards the
bedroom. 'Just be ready if she comes flying out. I don't
think I've got the strength to catch her.'

They stood at the door for a moment, listening to Mary
whimpering.

'We're coming in now,' Mike called through. 'Are you
gonna be good?' Hearing a mumble that he took to mean
yes, he slid the bolt back and slowly opened the door –
instantly recoiling when the stench hit him in the face with
the force of a cosh.

Sitting on the edge of the mattress, Mary was shivering violently, an odious mixture of snot, sweat and puke smeared across her face.

Grimacing with disgust, Jane and Tina helped her to her feet and walked her to the bathroom. Sitting her on the toilet seat, Jane supported her while Tina ran hot water into the sink and rooted around for something to clean her up with.

Spotting a sponge stuffed behind the sink, Tina gingerly reached for it, pulling a face when she saw the brown stained edges.

'Have you been cleaning the bog with this sponge?' she yelled, holding it aloft.

'The yellow one?' Mike called back. 'Nah, it'll be all right if you run it under the tap.'

'Dirty bastard!' Dropping it back where she'd found it, Tina glanced around for something else. Grabbing the cleanest towel from a heap of dirty laundry in the corner, she dunked it in the sink and rubbed soap onto it, then set about cleaning Mary's face.

'She could do with a bath,' Jane murmured, wincing at the roughness of the scrubbing. 'She's got it in her hair, as well. You won't get it all out with that.'

'I don't want a bath,' Mary protested, swiping feebly at Tina's hand. 'It's bad enough you've got me locked up without you stripping me as well.'

'Behave,' Tina snapped, slapping the protesting hand away. 'You've got nothing we haven't seen a thousand times before. Anyway, we're trying to help you, so shut up.'

'Some help,' Mary wailed. 'You're trying to kill *meee*!'

'Oh, Mary, we don't want to hurt you.' Distressed by her friend's unhappiness, Jane put an arm around her, only to be knocked back by the stench. Mary *really* needed a good soak. 'Look, if I run the bath, will you get in it if we leave you alone?' she asked.

Nodding, Mary sniffed back her tears.

Smiling, Jane turned the taps on, telling Tina to hold Mary up.

'No way,' Tina snarled, flinging the towel onto the floor and stomping out. 'If I wanted to be a fuckin' nurse, I'd be working at the bleedin' hospital!'

As soon as they were alone, Mary grabbed Jane's hand.

'Let me go, Jane . . . You're my best mate, an' I know you don't want to hurt me, but they don't even *know* me. They're gonna *kill* me, Jane. Tell them they've got to let me go. They'll listen to you . . . *Please!*'

Wrestling her hand free, Jane tried to calm Mary down, reassuring her that she wouldn't let anybody hurt her. Mary cried and pleaded, but Jane just gritted her teeth and shook her head. Bursting into tears, Mary fell to her knees and wrapped her arms around Jane's legs.

'*Pleeease*, I'm begging you!'

Popping his head around the door, Mike saw the distress on Jane's face and realised that she was having a really hard time. Going in, he peeled Mary off her.

'Come on, sweetheart. Let's get you sorted out, eh? We'll help you get undressed, then you can have a nice, long soak. You'd like that, wouldn't you?'

Speaking to Mary as if she were a child seemed to work. Calming down, she offered no resistance when they helped her out of her stained clothes and into the bath.

Looking up when Jane came out of the bathroom, Tina gave a small, tight smile.

'Sorry about that, but I don't think I'm cut out for the caring, compassionate bit. I can't be doing with all that mess.'

'You did your best,' Jane excused her. 'And the messy bit

won't last long. Mike said it only takes a few days to get past that, then she'll be much easier to cope with. And it's for her own good, remember?'

'I suppose so,' Tina agreed glumly.

Twenty minutes passed before Mary stumbled out of the bathroom. She was dressed in an odd assortment of Mike's clothes, with a towel wrapped around her shoulders. Teeth chattering wildly, she said, 'I'm freezing. Can I have a cup of tea?'

'Course you can.' Getting up, Mike pointed her towards the couch. 'Go and sit with your mates and get warm. Do you take sugar?'

'Four,' Mary said, casting a dirty look in Pete's direction as she squeezed in between Jane and Tina. Unresponsive to his smile, she continued to eye him with sullen suspicion until Mike came back with the tea.

Jane's eyebrows crept up when Mary smiled and said a polite 'Thank you'. Mike must have reached her in some way. Maybe he'd made her feel safer by being so gentle with her. Whatever it was, Jane was glad of the lull in hostilities.

Lapsing into silence, Mary drank the tea in little gulps. Immediately she'd finished it, she asked for another. Tossing Jane an *I-told-you-she'd-be-fine* smile, Mike went and made it. Mary drank the second cup quickly. Then, so suddenly that it took everybody by surprise, she turned towards Tina and puked.

'Oh, for fuck's sake!' Tina bellowed, leaping to her feet just in time to avoid being completely covered. 'I have *had* it with this shit!' Glaring at the few drops that *had* landed on her skirt, her fisted hands turned white around the knuckles as she fought the urge to lash out.

'*Ooops!*' Mary drawled, her eyes sparking with malice. '*So* sorry.'

Sitting forward to intervene if it kicked off, Jane held her breath. But after a few tense seconds, Tina turned on her heel and made for the bathroom. Before she'd taken two steps, she slipped on the puke and went down with a thud that shook the room.

Everyone moved at once, running to help her as she writhed on the floor, screaming, 'Me back! Oh, God help me! It's broke!'

Pushing Jane and Pete aside, Mike swung his foot back and kicked her.

Roaring with indignation, Tina sat bolt upright and clutched at her ankle. 'What the fuck did you do *that* for?'

Smiling apologetically, Mike said, 'At least we know you're back's all right. Sorry if I hurt you but, to be honest, I couldn't be bothered waiting for you to discover it for yourself.'

'Piss off!' Scowling furiously, Tina hauled herself up and limped to the bathroom, slamming the door behind her.

'Sorry.' Mike turned to Jane with a shrug. 'But she's doing my head in, moaning about everything.'

'It's okay.' Jane smiled. 'I forgot to tell you how much of a hypochondriac she can be.'

'I wouldn't mind,' Pete interjected quietly. 'But it isn't like we've known her for years, and she's *already* acting up. What'll she be like when we *really* know her?'

'Worse,' Jane chuckled. Then, turning to include Mary now, she said, 'Remember that time—'

Mary wasn't there.

Hearing a noise at the front door, Jane whipped her head around and saw Mary frantically fiddling with the keys – the keys Mike had left in the lock when he'd let Mimi, Kim and Jonas out that morning.

'MIKE! She's getting away!'

'Oh, shit!'

Running to the door. Mike wrestled the keys from Mary's hand. Wrapping his arms around her, he carried her kicking and screaming through the living room to the bedroom and dropped her unceremoniously onto the mattress. He quickly backed out as she struggled to her feet, sliding the bolt across just a split second before she reached the door.

'*BASTAAARDS!*' she screamed, hurling herself at it with futile rage.

Flopping down on the couch with a weary sigh, Mike ran a hand across his sweating face.

'With any luck she won't have heaved all that first brew back up. If any of it got into her, she'll soon settle down. I put a couple of sleepers in it so she won't feel the pain so much. She might even get some proper rest.'

Coming out of the bathroom just then, Tina apologised again for kicking off.

'Oh, just shut up and sit down,' Mike told her good-naturedly. 'None of us is perfect. If we fell out every time someone said something we didn't like, we'd be a sad old lot, wouldn't we?'

Grinning sheepishly, Tina moved towards the couch. Before she got there, there was a knock at the front door and she froze on the spot.

Staring at each other, everyone was thinking the same thing: Mary was making such a racket, someone must have heard her and called the police.

More knocking, and still no one moved. Then Mimi's voice came through the letter box.

'It's us! Hurry up and open the door!'

A collective exhalation of relief sounded around the room as Mike got up and rushed to the door.

'Listen to this,' he blurted out as he led the others in.

'Mimi's just seen four blokes on her block. They were asking around for Mary, and they stopped her—'

'I was on my way back here,' Mimi interrupted excitedly. 'I bumped into one of them at the bottom of the stairs and they surrounded me. I was *terrified*. I thought they were coppers at first 'cos they all had black leathers, and jeans and trainers – like the DS, you know? Anyhow, they said they were looking for a mate of theirs called Mary, and did I know her? So I said no, and if they didn't mind I was late for an appointment. Then they said how about a woman called Jane? They knew she lived round here – did I know *her*? I said I've never heard of either of them 'cos I've only just moved here, so they let me go. But they said to say that Kenny's looking for Mary if I *should* happen to meet her.' Pausing, she exhaled shakily. 'I'm telling you, they were *serious*, man.'

'Did *you* see them?' Pete asked Kim and Jonas.

They both shook their heads.

'We just bumped into Meems on our way here,' Kim said. 'She was in a right state.'

'This doesn't sound right,' Tina mused quietly. 'I've never heard of a pimp going to this much trouble for a runaway pro.'

'Me neither,' Jane agreed, her face drained of colour.

'Well, I don't know that much about it,' Mike said. 'But I've got to admit it sounds a bit heavy.'

Jane began to chew her nails again. There was nothing left of them, but it helped nonetheless. She was seriously scared now. The men had mentioned her, but she hadn't been around when Mary met up with them. And how the hell did they know that she lived round here? But, then, that was obvious, wasn't it? That bastard Dave must have told them.

*　　*　　*

They spent the rest of the afternoon trying to decide what to do. Mimi was shaken by her encounter and didn't really want to go home alone. Neither did Jane – worried what she might find there.

'I'll go and check it out,' Mike offered.

'Bad idea,' Pete cautioned. 'What if someone saw you with Mary last night and recognises you? *I*'ll go. I'll just walk past Jane's and check for damage.'

'I need to get changed,' Tina said, wrinkling her nose at the smell of puke she imagined was still on her clothes.

'How's about I walk with Mimi,' Kim suggested, 'and Jonas can go with Tina.'

'I don't need *him*,' Tina snorted. 'Just let Butler start any of his funny business with me and he'll get what for!'

'You'd best be careful,' Mike warned her. 'Don't forget what you said about him having a gun. And he knows you're one of Mary's mates, don't forget.'

Taking control, Pete held his hands up. 'Look, whoever's going where, we'll do it when it's dark. And we'll go one by one, not all together. Right?' Nodding when they agreed, he said, 'Good. I'll go first. I'll check Jane's flat, then take a stroll around the Crescents to see if those blokes are still around. If it's all clear I'll come back, then Tina can go, then Jonas, Mimi and Kim.'

'I still think I should go with Tina,' Mike said, frowning deeply as he turned to her, adding, 'No offence, Tina, but you have got a bit of a big mouth. You'll drop us all in it if Butler confronts you and you start giving him attitude.'

'No,' Pete told him firmly. 'I know what you mean, but there's no way you can risk it. She'll probably be able to blag her way out of it if Kenny sees her on her own, but you and her together – that'll be hard to explain if anyone *did* see you with Mary.'

'All right,' Mike conceded reluctantly. 'I'll stay here with

Jane – but only if Jonas follows Tina till she's safely home.' Turning to Jonas now, he said, 'You don't have to get too close, mate. Just keep your eye open in case anything happens.'

39

Pete went out as soon as it got dark. Minutes later he was back, and his expression told them there was bad news.

'Jane's door's been booted in,' he said. 'I don't know if anyone's still there because I walked straight past without stopping. But I glanced in and it looked like they've trashed the place.'

Jane sat down heavily. She was beginning to feel completely out of her depth. Who the hell *was* this Kenny Butler, and why was he so desperate to find Mary? It couldn't be concern for her safety, and it certainly couldn't be love. If he had any feelings for her he'd have kept her *off* the game, not put her *on* it. Mary had said that she owed him, so money could be his motivation. But why would a man like Butler let someone like Mary get so far into debt that she was worth tracking down? And it couldn't be loss of earnings either, because – in her state – there was no way Mary was making *that* much.

Hard as she tried, the only explanation that seemed even halfway feasible to Jane was pride. Kenny Butler was supposed to be some sort of big shot, so it would piss him off if one of his girls stepped out of line – especially if she took off when she was supposed to be working. That had to be it. In which case, he probably wouldn't keep this up for long.

Jane hoped.

* * *

Soon after Pete's return, Tina left, followed a couple of minutes later by Jonas. Spying him from the corner of her eye as he strolled casually along some way behind, she felt the irritation bubbling in her gut. She'd never needed a man to protect her – especially not some weird-looking slip of a kid like him. What use would he be if anything happened? *She*'d probably end up having to protect *him*.

Reaching the old school, Tina decided to do a detour and walk past Mary's block – see who was about, and maybe ask a couple of casual questions. But first she had to lose the shadow,

Hiding at the end of the narrow alley running down past the school wall, she jumped out when Jonas drew level – smugly gratified when he leapt a foot off the ground with shock. Just as she'd thought . . . Useless.

'Listen, love, you might as well go home,' Tina said. 'I'm just gonna take a walk round Mary's – see if I can find anything out.'

'But I'm supposed to see you home.'

'No need,' she assured him. 'Honest, love, I'm better off on me own. Anyhow, everyone knows me round here and you're likely to get your head kicked in if anyone sees you following me.'

Reluctantly agreeing, Jonas went back the way they'd come.

Watching until he was out of sight, Tina crossed the road and headed for Mary's block. Turning the corner, she got the shock of her life to find the road swarming with police, the flashing lights from their vehicles illuminating the faces of the crowd that was gathered behind the blue and white tapes.

'Yo, *Tina!*'

Whipping her head around at the hissed summons, she saw Jock and Stan loitering at the back of the crowd. Forgetting that she hadn't spoken to them since kicking them out of her house that time, she rushed towards them and asked what was going on.

Pulling her aside, Jock said, 'Haven't you heard? Dave's been shot.'

'Fuck off!' Tina gasped, her hand flying up to her mouth.

'Straight up.' He nodded grimly.

'When?'

'This afternoon.' Lowering his voice, Jock glanced fearfully around. 'Me and Stan found him.'

'You *didn't*!'

'I swear to God!' He put a hand to his chest. 'We only went round to get some money he owed us, but he didn't answer the door so we booted it in. We were gonna have his stereo away as payback, but he was lying right there in the hall with half his fuckin' head missing. There was blood and brains and all sorts of shit everywhere. It was *disgusting*.'

'Jeezus,' Tina murmured sickly. 'What did you do?'

'Got the fuck out – what d'y' think? There was nowt else we *could* do.'

'Who called the police?'

'Me and Stan – from the phone box round the corner.'

'You didn't give your names, did you?' She peered up at him worriedly.

'Did we fuck. We ain't that stupid. They'd fit us up good style with our records. Where have *you* been, anyway? We thought everyone in Manchester had heard by now.'

'I've been in town,' Tina lied. Then, 'So, who did it? Do they know yet?'

'Do they bollocks. And they never will, neither. Butler's well too crafty to get nicked, and no one in their right mind is gonna grass him.'

'Kenny?' Tina feigned shock at the revelation. 'No way! That's terrible. What about Mary? Was she there?'

Peering down at her, Jock gave a conspiratorial roll of his eyes. 'Word is, she's behind it.'

'*Mary?*' Drawing her head back, Tina looked at him as if he'd gone mad. 'Don't be stupid. If she wanted rid, she'd walk out.'

'I don't mean she's behind Dave getting done in,' Jock told her. 'Butler reckons she's gone on the run with a load of gear her and Dave nicked off him.'

'Bollocks!'

'Only saying what I've heard.' Jock shrugged. 'I wouldn't have thought she'd be that much of a cunt to leave Dave in it like that, but there's got to be something to it, 'cos she's supposed to have gone AWOL last night. Either way, Butler's after her – and that I *do* know, 'cos Stan got gripped by his boys earlier.'

'Oh, my God,' Tina gasped, shaking her head in disbelief as the blood pounded through her brain. 'This is awful.'

'You all right?' Jock peered at her with a frown of concern. 'Here . . . you haven't seen her, have you?'

'Have I hell,' she snapped. 'You know we fell out after she started using again. You should – it was the same time me and *you* fell out.' Casting a hateful glance in Stan's direction now, she said, 'I suppose you're still sharing pipes with your little *mate?*'

'Nah, we sussed it for a mug's game a while back,' Jock said, shoving his hands into his pockets and kicking at a stone. 'Wasn't worth losing everything for, was it?'

'No, it wasn't,' Tina agreed, folding her arms. 'Still, your loss, not mine.'

Smiling sadly, he nodded and looked her in the eye. 'I have missed you, you know. I, er, don't suppose you'd fancy meeting up for a pint, sometime?'

'I don't think so. Not if you're still up *his* arse.'

Tutting, Jock folded his own arms, adding to the wall she'd already put up between them. 'Oh, don't start that crap again. You know it ain't like that. We're mates, that's all. We did a long stretch together.'

'Yeah, and we all know what goes on in nick, don't we?'

'Maybe for some, but definitely not for me and him,' Jock growled. Then, glancing back at the police activity, his shoulders slumped. Turning back to Tina, he gave her a small smile. 'Look, I meant what I said about seeing you again – even if it's just to chat. This kind of puts things in perspective, doesn't it? If you can't care about your mates at a time like this, you're a sad bastard.'

'Suppose so.' She exhaled shakily. 'Look, I've got to go. Give us a ring sometime, if you want. See you.' Turning, Tina waddled away as fast as her shaking legs would carry her.

40

Mary had been quiet for a while. Putting his ear to the door and hearing nothing, Mike eased the bolt back and peeped inside. It took a moment to locate her in the dark but, seeing her curled up like a baby on the mattress, he backed out again.

'She's out like a light,' he said, going back to the living room where Pete and Jane were slumped side by miserable side on the couch. Stretching, he added, 'I wish I was, as well. I don't know about you, but I've never felt so bloody old and knackered in my life.'

'Speak for yourself,' Pete chuckled, determinedly shaking himself out of the mood of despondency. Nodding towards Donkey then, he said, 'What's up with the fur monster? He's been acting really weird all day.'

Lying in the same spot he'd occupied for most of the day between the couch and the window, Donkey wasn't sleeping – he was *listening*; cocking his ears up and down, and keeping his beady eyes on anything that moved. His hackles rose stiffly every now and then, but the growl was continuous – and so low that it almost sounded as if he was purring.

'Dunno.' Mike clicked his fingers. 'But he's not happy, are you, mate?'

Still grumbling, Donkey slunk over to him and lay at his feet.

'They sense the unseen,' Pete remarked, nodding sagely.

'They're a lot closer to nature than us. We clog our psyches up with material shit, but they live on their instincts.'

'This one certainly does.' Mike tickled Donkey's ear affectionately.

'Yep, he's got it sussed, all right,' Pete agreed. 'He knows where it's at, don't you, Donkey dick?'

'It'd freak me out if I *sensed* everything.' Jane gave a tiny shudder. 'Imagine your hair going up and down all the time. It'd be really weird.'

'You probably sense more than you think,' Mike told her.

'Yeah,' Pete agreed, stretching his legs and putting his arms behind his head. 'There's no point fighting it. You've just got to go with the flow, then it flows right back to you. Know what I mean?'

'Er, yeah,' Jane murmured, not wanting to appear stupid.

'Spiritual law,' Mike said, reaching for his rolling tin. 'What goes up must come down. What goes around comes around. Karma.'

'Yep.' Pete nodded. 'You get what you give in this life, but it's the rewards we get in the *next* we should be working towards.'

'But not as a means to an end.'

Confused, Jane shook her head. She'd tried to keep up, but they'd just lost her at the roundabout.

'I haven't got a clue what you're on about,' she admitted.

Laughing for the first time in hours, Pete said, 'It's like this . . . You can go to church every Sunday and say all the right words, but you can't fool the Man.' He pointed at the ceiling. '*He* knows the truth, and if you say one thing but do another, the words don't mean shit.'

Jane understood that, having spent four years being tortured by the frustrated nuns at school, those evil bitches who called themselves Holy, then beat the shit out of the kids if they so much as farted – surely an act of God,

Him having designed the gas outlet in the first place.

'You've probably got gifts,' Mike went on. 'Voices in your head, or something.'

'You calling me a schizo?'

'No, he's not,' Pete said, chuckling at Jane's indignant expression. 'But he's right – you probably have got some sort of psychic gift, but you just haven't realised it yet. You're a woman, aren't you.'

'What difference does that make?'

'A big one,' Mike said. 'Men really miss out on that score. We can't *empathise*.'

'Eh?'

'We're not sensitive enough,' Pete explained. 'You lot just cut through all the crap and get straight to the heart of it. You *feel* the truth.'

'Sorry to say it,' Mike added. 'But us men are only good for three things – shagging, boozing, and crapping!'

'Yes, my brother!' Pete laughed.

'A-*men*!' Mike raised his hand for Pete to slap palms.

They stopped abruptly when someone started hammering on the front door.

Rising slowly, Donkey cocked his head to the side and rumbled deep in his chest.

As the good humour of a moment ago evaporated, Jane felt as if the room was closing in on her. Forcing herself to breathe, she tried to shake off the feeling of impending doom – the claustrophobic waiting for the worst to happen.

Tiptoeing to the window beside the door, Pete peeped out. 'It's Tina,' he said, rushing to let her in.

Jane exchanged an alarmed glance with Mike. 'Christ, that was fast.'

Shrugging, he gave a nervous laugh. 'Maybe she was missing us.'

Falling through the door, Tina stumbled into the living

room, her face beetroot from the strain of having run all the way back from Moss Side.

'It's Dave,' she said when she caught her breath. 'He's dead.'

'*What?*' Jane squeaked. 'What d'y' mean, *dead*?'

'What the fuck does "dead" usually mean?'

'But . . . *how*? What happened?'

'I went over there on my way home to see if I could suss anything out,' Tina explained, swiping at the sweat pouring down her face. 'But the place was crawling with filth. I didn't know what the hell was going on.'

'Calm down,' Mike said, lighting a cigarette and passing it to her. 'Tell us everything – from the beginning.'

Taking a minute to regain her composure, Tina relayed what Jock had told her.

'Shit!' Mike muttered when she'd finished. 'This is going from bad to worse.'

Jane was stunned. 'I can't believe this. It can't be a coincidence, can it?'

Mike shook his head slowly. 'No. This is *way* too close. It's *got* to be something to do with that Kenny. One minute he's walking round asking for Mary, then her boyfriend gets blown away. And Tina's already told us he's got a gun. It's no coincidence.'

'And Jock *told* me Kenny did it,' Tina added grimly. 'And he definitely wasn't lying.'

'Did anyone see you come here?' Pete was concerned that she might have been followed.

'I don't think so,' she told him guiltily. 'I didn't see anyone, anyhow.'

'I'd best take another look around,' Pete said. 'Just in case.'

'Be careful,' Mike warned him. 'This is getting nasty, so don't be taking any chances. Wouldn't want to lose you.'

Pete nodded reassuringly. 'It's cool, man. Don't worry.'

Getting up, he went to the window to check that no one was outside before letting himself out.

'How was your place?' Jane asked when he'd gone. 'Had anyone been there?'

'How the hell would *I* know?' Tina snapped irritably. 'You don't seriously think I went round there after that, do you? I came straight back here.'

'Smart move,' Mike told her, frowning deeply. 'If they're going round everyone Mary knows, it's likely they've been to yours already. And I'll tell you what . . .' He turned to Jane. 'It's a bloody good job you were here when they went to *your* place.'

Losing what was left of her colour, she nodded. 'I know.'

'What we going to do now?' Tina groaned. 'We can't hide in here for ever.'

'I'd rather you did that than go back out there,' Mike told her grimly. 'If we hadn't brought you round here in the first place, you'd have been sitting at home when Butler's lot went looking for Mary.'

Just then, there was a quiet, urgent knocking at the door.

'Shit, what now?' Pushing himself to his feet, Mike went to the window and peeped out. Turning around with a strange look on his face, he said, 'It's Mimi and Jonas . . . They're on their hands and knees.'

'Let them in, then,' Tina ordered, sitting up straighter. 'Hurry up. They might be in trouble.'

Crawling in when Mike opened the door, Mimi said, 'We've just seen those blokes again. They're up at your flat, Jane.'

'Not again,' Jane moaned. 'What do they *want*?'

'They didn't see you, did they?' Mike closed the door quickly.

'No,' Jonas assured him, standing up and brushing the dust off his knees. 'We crouched down and watched them through the railings. They're not looking this way; they're just standing around the door, talking. *Definitely* up to no good, though.'

'You can say that again,' Mike muttered. 'Wait till you hear what's happened.'

When Tina repeated her story, Mimi and Jonas were as shocked as Jane and Mike had been, and they wholeheartedly agreed that it was a good job that Jane and Tina had been here today – and that they shouldn't even *think* about going out while all this was going on.

'I've *got* to,' Tina complained. 'I need to get changed.'

'I'll get you something from mine,' Mimi offered.

Looking at her as if she was a complete idiot, Tina said, 'What *size* are you?'

'Ten.'

'Do I *look* like a size bleedin' ten?' Tina tutted.

'That's not a problem,' Mimi said, stretching the elasticated waist of her long skirt. 'All my stuff's loose like this.'

Chuckling wearily, Tina shook her head. 'Thanks all the same, love, but that wouldn't fit round me *arm*.'

Another burst of knocking jarred the atmosphere. Jane struggled to quash her rising hysteria. It was them! They'd seen Mimi and Jonas coming in and they were going to shoot everyone.

It was Pete.

He'd been watching the men, too, from an empty squat on the opposite block.

'They were inside for a while,' he said. 'Then they stood on the balcony looking around. But they've gone now. Headed off Chorlton Road way.'

'Probably going to ask the pros if Mary's been working today,' Tina remarked glumly.

Nodding, Mike said, 'You could be right there. That's what I'd do if I was them.'

'Want us to walk to the garage to see if they're hanging about?' Jonas offered.

'Okay, yeah,' Pete said. 'But don't take any chances. If they see you, leg it.'

'Don't worry, we will,' Mimi snorted, heading for the door.

Moments after they'd gone, a noise came from the bedroom. Slinking into his corner, Donkey lay down and rested his head on his paws, whimpering softly.

'Oh, God, Mary!' Jane's hand flew up to her mouth. 'What are we going to tell her?'

'Let's just deal with *her* for now,' Mike said, making his way to the bedroom. 'We'll worry about the rest later.'

41

Mary was rocking herself to and fro on the mattress. Looking up at Jane with tears streaming down her face, she said, 'Let me go. I'm in agony . . . You've got to do something. I can't stand it . . . I'm *dying*.'

Pushing past Mike into the doorway, Tina glared down at her. 'All the trouble you've caused, and all you can do is feel sorry for yourself!'

'Shut up!' Jane snapped, sitting beside Mary on the bed. '*She* doesn't know what's going on. Do *you* want to tell her?'

Pursing her lips, Tina shook her head. There was no way she was doing the dirty work. Let Jane deal with it if she was so fond of the silly bitch. Turning on her heel, she stomped away.

Moaning, Mary rolled closer to Jane – her only salvation. Every inch of her skin felt like it was crawling with invisible insects, and her muscles were twitching and jerking as her tortured joints screamed for mercy. She was red hot, then freezing cold, then hot again – so hot, she could barely breathe.

'*Pleeeease!*' she moaned.

Jane's heart was breaking. Reaching out to comfort Mary, the stench of evacuated bowels assailed her nostrils and she jerked back involuntarily. Putting a hand down to steady herself, her stomach heaved as something cold, wet and slimy squeezed up through her fingers. It was everywhere – on the sheets, the blanket, the floor . . . on Mary.

This was turning into a nightmare. Jane had thought that Mary would be all right after a good sleep. That she'd wake up smiling and happy, asking for food, cigs – *whatever*. But not *this* . . . this foul-smelling, pathetic wreck pleading for her life. And how long was it going to last?

It already felt like for ever.

Gazing down at her friend, Jane wanted to cry. They were in this mess because of Mary, but it wasn't her fault – not entirely. They should have left her alone instead of playing God and trying to rescue her.

But it was too late for should-haves. They'd meddled in things they knew nothing about, and now it was blowing up in their interfering faces. Dave was dead, and there was more to come – Jane knew that with an absolute certainty.

If it was anybody's fault it was *hers*. Her fault that her oldest, dearest friend was suffering. Her fault that Dave was taking his last walk down the fiery steps. Her fault that none of them could rest for fear of what might happen next.

But this was no time for self-recrimination. She had to find out about Kenny – and quick.

Forcing herself to reach down, she stroked the hair away from Mary's eyes.

'Mary, love . . . Tell me about Kenny?'

Groaning, Mary rolled herself into an even tighter ball.

Pulling her around, Jane said, 'It's important, babe. We need to know why he's so desperate to find you?'

'Oh, God,' Mary wailed. 'I told you not to get involved. Why didn't you just keep out of it? He's gonna kill me – an' if he knows you've got me, he'll kill you too.'

'Why?' Jane persisted. 'What's going on?'

Slumping onto her back, Mary stared up at the ceiling. 'The coke,' she said flatly. 'He probably thinks I've done a runner with it. Thirty fucking grand's worth. He told me to stash it somewhere safe 'cos he was gonna get busted. He was supposed to pick it up last night. He'll think I've nicked it.' Crying again, she rolled her head from side to side. 'Why didn't you just leave me alone? Why, why, why . . .'

Tina had wandered back into the doorway a few minutes earlier and had heard everything. 'So it's true,' she snapped.

'Oh, fuck off,' Mary sobbed. 'Just fuck off and leave me alone.'

'Quit whining and tell us where you've stashed the gear so we can get it back to him.'

'I *can't*! You've got to let *me* go. If you turn up with it, he'll kill you. He hates you.'

'Yeah, well, it's fuckin' mutual,' Tina spat. 'I told you he was scum, but would you listen . . . ? Would you bollocks! Well, you were wrong, weren't you, you brainless bitch. And now look at the mess we're in!'

'The mess *you*'re in?' Mary screamed. 'How d'y' figure *that*? *I*'m the one who's in a mess. It's *me* who's gonna get fucking murdered.'

'Is that right?' Tina thundered, gesturing wildly out of the door. 'Well, how come he's out there right now, crawling all over the place, lookin' for *US*? And how come he's kicked Jane's door in, if it's just *you* he's after? An' he's probably been to mine, an' all! And if it's only *you* in a mess,' she went on, her face purple now, 'tell me why he's blown your boyfriend's fucking *HEAD OFF*?'

'*What?*' Mary gasped, staring up at her. 'What did you say?'

Glaring at her, hating her more right then than she'd ever hated anyone in her life before, Tina hissed, 'You heard. He's shot Dave. So, stop messing about and tell us where the gear is!'

Mary threw up, launching a hot stream of bile across Jane's legs. Then she began to jerk as a fierce spasm racked her body, her eyes bulging, her teeth clamping down on her swollen tongue, spraying a fine mist of blood into the air.

Panicking, Jane said, 'She's having a fit! What should I do, Mike? What should I do?'

'Hold her down!' he yelled, running to the end of the mattress. 'I'll get her head, you get her feet.'

They struggled to pin Mary down as she thrashed wildly. Then, suddenly, she went rigid – back arched, legs jerking. Then she was still, her eyes staring straight up – wide, glassy, lifeless.

'Oh, shit,' Mike muttered, pressing his fingers to her neck. 'There's no pulse.'

'Do something!' Jane screamed, pulling at his jumper until he jolted into action.

Kneeling astride Mary's now-limp body, Mike put his hands on her chest and started rhythmically pumping it. Turning to Jane, he said, 'Give her mouth-to-mouth. When I get to five, hold her nose and blow.'

Jane was petrified. 'I can't . . . I don't know how.'

'Just bloody *do* it!' he snapped.

She tried. When Mike reached five, she put her mouth down to Mary's greying lips and blew. The stench hit her like a cosh, and the bitter taste of bile sent her stomach into revolt.

As Jane threw up beside him, Mike carried on pumping Mary's chest and shouted for Tina to take over.

'You must be bleedin' *joking*!' she yelped. 'I've never done that in me life.'

'Well, now's your chance to learn,' he said, 'Three . . . four . . . *Blow*!' When Tina didn't move, he glanced up at her. 'For fuck's *sake*, you useless bitch, she's your *friend* – *help* her!'

'I *can't*,' she yelled back at him. 'You've seen what I'm like with puke and shit. I'll be sick! Anyway, you don't know what she's got. She's a whore. She could have Aids or anything by now.'

Pete pushed Tina out of the way with a sneer of contempt. God, she was a selfish bitch. Leaping onto the mattress, he put his mouth over Mary's and blew, sending a strong blast of his own life-force into her lungs.

'Come on, girl,' he urged as her chest rose and fell. 'Come *on.*'

Jane was beside herself with guilt as she watched them try in vain to revive her friend. And what had *she* done? Nothing. Just thrown up, like the gutless, stupid bitch that she was. She'd never forgive herself if Mary died – never!

Mike shouted for someone to fetch cold water and, at last, Tina moved. Running to the kitchen, she came back seconds later with the overflowing washing-up bowl.

'When I say "Now",' Mike directed, 'throw it all over her.'

'What for?'

Gritting his teeth, he glared up at her. 'To *shock* her – like in hospital, when they put pads on your chest.'

'Why don't you just do that, then?' Tina suggested stupidly. 'Rip the plug off something and zap her with the wire.'

'Oh, yeah, *right*!' Mike yelled, with such ferocity that Tina actually jumped. 'Let's just *burn* her, eh, so then we get done for torturing her as well as fuckin' kidnapping her. Just throw the damn water!'

With a sullen scowl, Tina sluiced the water over Mary – drenching both Mike and Pete at the same time. Nothing happened.

Slumping heavily, Mike shook his head, sending drips of water from his beard into Mary's staring eyes. 'It's no use.'

'You can't just give up,' Jane cried.

'Yeah,' Tina agreed. 'Keep pumping her chest. We'll go and phone an ambulance.'

'NO!' Mike bellowed as she turned to leave the room. 'Don't be stupid. It won't do any good. We've got to *think* about this.'

'We can't just do *nothing*,' Jane sobbed. 'Please, Mike, you've got to keep trying.'

'It's no *use*,' he insisted. 'It's been too long.'

'He's right,' Pete agreed quietly, wiping his mouth on his sleeve. 'We've been doing it for ages and she's still not breathing. She's gone, Jane.'

Peering down at Mary, Jane knew that they were right. Her friend's lips were dark blue now, and her eyes were empty – not a trace of the sharp, suspicious, sparkle that had been the essence of Mary.

'What we gonna do?' Pete murmured.

Mike shook his head. For once, he didn't have the answer. Pulling himself slowly to his feet, he walked from the room.

One by one they followed. Flopping down onto the couch, they stared at each other in disbelief. The pall of death was smothering them – polluting their lungs, their hearts, their minds, with its awful unreality. And the silence seemed to be hemming them ever deeper into the nightmare.

After a while Pete cleared his throat. 'Look . . .' he said, sounding so grim that Jane shuddered, 'I think our only option is the old OD trick.'

Mike sighed heavily. 'Yeah, I know.'

'What's that?' Jane asked.

'We take her down to the phone box later on when no one's around,' Pete explained. 'Phone the nines and say we've found an unconscious woman and they'll send an ambulance to pick her up. We'll have to stay out of the way, though, 'cos they'll bring the police in when they find her dead, and there's no point us getting ourselves dragged into it.'

'*Jeezus!*' Jane gasped in disgust. 'She's not a *dog*. We can't just *abandon* her. What if someone gets to her before the ambulance?'

'She's *dead*,' Pete reminded her bluntly. 'What they gonna do to her if they *do* find her?'

'There's some weird people out there,' Tina chipped in morbidly. 'They could do *all* sorts.'

'Oh, like what?' Pete snapped. Then, holding up a hand, he said, 'Second thoughts, I don't want to hear whatever twisted shit you've got going on in *your* head. Just tell me what you think we should do instead, hmm? Maybe you'd like to sit and hold her hand till the ambulance gets there and get us all arrested?'

'Why d'y' have to be so fucking sarcastic?'

'Better than being a bitch.'

'Stop it,' Mike cut in quietly, rubbing at his aching temples. 'We've got to stay together on this or we've had it. This is the best we can do to make sure she gets a proper funeral. We won't just be *dumping* her,' he went on, standing and motioning Jane to the window. Drawing the edge of the curtain back, he pointed out the phone box at the foot of the slope to their right. 'See? We'll be able to keep an eye on her until the ambulance comes.' Putting an arm around her shoulder he gave her a gentle squeeze. 'All right?'

Jane nodded. She still wasn't happy about it, but she had to admit that it was probably the only way of doing it without getting any deeper into trouble. Sloping miserably back to the couch, she sat beside Tina with a heavy sigh.

Looking at their miserable faces, Pete felt guilty for shouting at them. Mary was their friend; they were bound to be upset. Making a silent vow to cool his temper, he went and made another brew.

Tina rewarded him with a sheepish smile when he handed her a cup. 'I'm sorry,' she said. Then, to Jane and Mike, 'Really sorry.'

'Me too,' Jane murmured, her chin wobbling as the tears slid down her cheeks.

'We all are.' Reaching out, Mike gave both of their hands a squeeze. 'But we've got to get a grip. We can't afford to fall out – not now. Okay?' When they all nodded, he said, 'Right, now I know no one wants to talk about it, but we've got to plan how we're going to get her down to the phone box without being seen.'

'What are we going to tell the others?' Jane asked, reminding them that there were yet more loose ends to tie up.

'Nothing,' Pete said firmly. 'The less they know from now on, the better. We're in enough shit as it is without dragging them down with us.'

42

At ten, Mimi and Jonas called round to say they'd been on a walkabout.

'We've asked everyone we know if they've seen anything strange today,' Mimi said.

'But no one's seen Butler's crew since Mimi had that run-in with them.' Jonas picked the story up. 'All anyone's talking about is the shooting in the Moss, but that's common knowledge. It's been on the news, and everything.'

'We took a walk round there,' Mimi went on. 'It's totally cordoned off, and there's a few uniforms strolling about. But, apart from that, it's pretty quiet.'

Thanking them, Mike said, 'Good work, but I think it's best if you stay out of the way from now on. You can keep an eye out in case anything else happens, but don't come back here until me or Pete gives you the all-clear.'

'Why?' Jonas asked worriedly. 'You're okay, aren't you?'

'Yeah, we're just a bit shattered,' Mike lied. 'You know how it is.'

Hesitating at the door when Mike showed them out, Mimi peered deep into his eyes. 'I've got a bad feeling about this,' she whispered. 'You'll keep an eye on Mary, won't you?'

Swallowing hard, Mike dropped his gaze. 'Course I will.'

Mimi searched his face for a long moment before gently squeezing his hand. 'You just take care, yeah?' Turning abruptly, she walked away.

Closing the door, Mike leaned his brow against the cool

wood and sighed heavily. That girl was the closest thing he had to a daughter, and he'd dragged her into a living nightmare. Even now, when he was only trying to protect her from further involvement, he knew she'd go home and worry about him, and that cut him to the heart.

Walking back to his seat, he felt the heavy burden of guilt descending upon him like a ton weight. For lying to Mimi; for letting Mary's life slip through his fingers; for coming up with the crazy idea in the first place. What had he been *thinking*?

Mike wasn't alone. As they settled down to wait, it ate away at them all.

43

The only sounds in the room, apart from their own shallow breathing, was the rumble of distant traffic on Chorlton Road, and the occasional scream of rubber as a stolen car was screwed around the rat-run of the Crescents.

And the clock.

That was driving Jane crazy. She'd never noticed it before, but now it was all she could hear.

Tick . . . tick . . . tick . . .

Getting up, she winced as a knife-slash of pain sliced across her eyes. She had a terrible headache, and the unbearable tension wasn't helping.

'Anyone want a brew?' she muttered.

No one answered; they just carried on staring at the floor.

Hobbling into the kitchen, Jane sensed a movement outside the window. There was definitely somebody out there; she could see the shadow shifting slowly along.

When the knock came, Mike crept up to the doorway and pressed a finger to his lips before moving on to the front door.

'Who is it?' he called.

'It's me,' the shadow whispered . . .

44

Roy's weird visit sparked a row which proved to be the straw that broke Pete's back. Ordering them all to the bedroom, he marched ahead, his jaw set with an utter determination to get things moving as calmly and as dispassionately as possible.

The stench when he opened the door hit him in the gut, knocking the wind from his sails.

Close on his heels, Jane actually staggered back when it hit her.

'It's death,' Mike explained, reaching out to steady her. 'Try not to breathe through your nose.'

Gagging, Jane covered her mouth with her hand. It was an overpoweringly foul smell, with such a unique *flavour* that she knew she'd never forget it. It was the kind of odour that seeped into your brain and settled in the cells, festering unnoticed until you smelled it again, when it would burst up into your consciousness like a tidal wave and suffocate you from within.

Recovered, Pete knelt beside Mary's body and pressed his fingers to her throat with an intense look of concentration, as if expecting to feel a pulse. Watching him, Jane shuddered. Mary was staring right at him, and she didn't look at all peaceful like Jane had heard dead people were supposed to. She looked tormented – racked with a pain she couldn't possibly be feeling.

Standing in the doorway, Tina shook her head slowly from

side to side as she watched Pete and Mike roll Mary onto her back and straighten her legs out.

'How the hell did it get to this?' she whispered.

Beside her, with her knuckles clamped firmly between her teeth, Jane's shoulders twitched in a tiny, involuntary shrug. Just two short days ago, this had seemed like *such* a good idea. Now Mary, her best friend in the whole world, was dead – and about to be dumped in a phone box like a pile of old rubbish.

'Jane?' Pete broke into her thoughts as he pulled Mary's arm around his shoulder. Holding her semi-upright as Mike manoeuvred himself under the other arm, he nodded towards a heap of clothes and bedding in the corner. 'Be a love and see if you can find a blanket in that lot.'

Forcing herself to enter the room, Jane sidled past them and pulled a big brown blanket from the pile. It reeked of dog and she realised that it must be Donkey's. Saddened beyond belief that this filthy old article would be Mary's death shroud, she handed it to Mike.

Just then, Donkey began to bark in the living room.

'What now?' Pete hissed, freezing mid-grapple. 'Tina . . . go and see what's up with him.'

Doing as she was told, Tina went, but seconds later she came running back, her eyes wide with panic, her voice little more than a squeak as she gestured towards the front door. 'Someone's breaking in! The dog's staring at the door with his hair on end!'

'How do you know they're trying to break in?' Mike asked, desperately trying to maintain a modicum of calmness.

'They're fiddling with the *lock*,' Tina squealed, growing more frantic by the second. 'Don't just stand there! What if it's the police? We'll get life for this! Do something!'

Dropping the body, Pete and Mike raced from the room. Mary's head rolled grotesquely before coming to rest –

staring straight at Jane now. Throwing a hand up to her mouth, Jane stumbled backwards out of the room. This was too much. She'd never felt so guilty in her entire life.

Tina was right. Someone *was* fiddling with the door – and more than one someone, judging by the whispered voices.

Huddled together in the kitchen doorway, the friends listened with rising dread. It couldn't be the police because there were no crackling radios – a dead give-away every time. Just those low, sinister voices. It had to be Kenny Butler and his crew.

Suddenly, the letter box flapped open, and a voice called through in a gentle sing-song: 'Oh, Ma-*re-ee*! We know you're *in* there . . . Come out, come out, wher*ever* you are.'

No one dared move. Then there was an almighty thud as someone kicked the door.

'*SHIT!*' Mike yelped, running to barricade it. 'Pete . . . Grab a chair! Help me jam it, for God's sake!'

Pete looked wildly around, but there were no chairs *to* grab – only beanbags and the couch. Swiping cups and rolling gear off the coffee table, he snatched it up . . . Just as the door flew open.

45

Kenny Butler loomed into the doorway. He was breathing hard, and the gun in his hand was aimed straight at Mike.

Stepping inside, followed by his three-strong crew, he motioned the friends back into the living room. Gesturing one of his boys to close the front door, he followed them through.

'Tut . . . tut . . . tut.' Kenny shook his head slowly from side to side. 'Fancy not answering the door when visitors come calling. Very antisocial, that.'

'Very,' the man standing beside him agreed, bouncing a scarred baseball bat on the palm of his hand.

Behind them, the larger of the other two was also holding a bat, while the smaller, slightly deranged-looking one was lovingly stroking his fingertip down the edge of the blade of a knife, drawing little drops of blood and licking them off as he waited for action.

'Well, well.' Kenny was circling Mike now. 'And what do we have here, then? You wouldn't happen to be that sad old hippie one of my girls saw escorting Mary along Chorlton Road the other night, now *would* you?'

Without waiting for an answer, he turned and looked at each of his captives in turn. Reaching Tina, he gave a nasty laugh.

'Looky here, boys. If it ain't my old mate Tina!'

Moving towards her now, Kenny pressed the gun into her

stomach, so deep that the barrel almost disappeared in the fat. 'Long time no see, *bitch*,' he snarled. 'Now, you gonna tell me where she is before I splatter your blubber all over the fuckin' walls?'

'All over the *flat*, more like,' one of his boys quipped.

Laughing, Kenny turned abruptly from Tina and focused on Jane instead.

'Oh, look . . . Jane's here, too. It *is* you, isn't it?' he teased, cocking his head to one side, challenging her to deny what he already knew. Bringing the gun up under her nose, he trailed it slowly along her upper lip and smiled. 'Very elusive, you are, Jane. Been hiding from me, haven't you? Thought I wouldn't find you in here with your little friends, didn't you?'

'I'm not hiding from anyone,' Jane retorted stiffly, forcing herself to hold his gaze. 'I don't even know you.'

'No, but you've *seen* me, haven't you? When you was down my patch the other night, trying to steal my girls away from me. Think I wouldn't remember, did you?'

'Leave her alone.' Pete's voice was low, and deceptively calm.

Turning towards him, Kenny narrowed his eyes to slits. His malicious grin at odds with his soft tone, he said, 'And who's this knight in shining *tramp* gear?' Chuckling at his own joke, he looked Pete up and down as though he were nothing more than shit with a mouth. 'Say something, did you, Dread?'

'She's done nothing to you,' Pete replied steadily – surprisingly so, given that the gun was aimed at his balls now. 'So why don't you just put that away and leave while you've got a chance?'

Laughing out loud, Kenny turned to his boys. 'Regular fuckin' hero we've got ourselves here, lads. What say we teach him a lesson?'

'I'll do it,' the knifeman offered, sniggering. 'I'll cut him up and feed him to his mates bit by *bit*. She can have his dick.' He pointed the knife at Tina who was openly glaring at him. 'Looks like she could do with a bit, don't she?'

'Yeah,' Kenny snorted. 'And a *bit* is all she's likely to get from this wanker.'

Shoving Pete aside, he strolled to the couch and sat down. Crossing his legs nonchalantly, he rested the gun lightly in his lap and looked at each of them in turn.

'Cup of tea'd be nice. Who's gonna do the honours?' When no one moved, Kenny shook his head. 'Tell you what, you're a fuckin' unfriendly bunch, you lot.'

'You weren't invited,' Tina muttered, folding her arms.

'Shut it, you fat bitch,' Kenny warned her, bringing the gun up and aiming it at her face.

Lowering it after a moment, he turned to Mike. 'This your gaff, Hippie?' When Mike nodded, Kenny gave a smug sneer. 'Know how I knew? 'Cos it bleedin' *stinks*.' Pointing the gun at Donkey now, who was cowering behind Mike and growling with false bravado, he said, 'Is it the dog's fault it stinks? Want me to get rid of it for you?'

Mike felt a white-hot rage spark to life in his gut.

'Leave . . . the . . . dog . . . *alone*,' he snarled, savagely punctuating each word. 'And get the fuck out of my *flat*!'

Looking at each other, the intruders burst out laughing.

'*Oooh*,' Kenny jeered. 'We're *so* fuckin' scared! Show him how scared we are, Col.'

The man standing closest to Mike swung his bat, catching Mike flush across the back of the thighs with a loud *thwok*!

Crumpling to the floor, Mike writhed in agony.

Launching himself at his master's attacker, Donkey sank his teeth into the bat-wielding hand. Dropping his weapon as the blood began to spurt, the man shook his arm, trying to free himself from the razor-sharp teeth. But Donkey held on, his teeth sinking ever deeper until the flesh gave way.

Falling to the floor with the chunk of man in his mouth, Donkey hawked it up and was back on his feet in a flash, blood dripping from his snout, teeth bared. But just as he sprang, a thunderous roar filled the room and everyone gaped in horror as the dog's shattered body slammed into the wall and slid bloodily down.

The shock wave engulfed them all. In that frozen, isolated moment, no one quite realised what had happened. It was the kind of moment they'd all heard about but never experienced – the moment when something so traumatic occurs that the brain seems to grind to a halt and everything goes into slow motion.

Then Kenny's callous, boastful laugher shattered the silence, and the full realisation of what had just happened exploded like a bomb.

Mike screamed and, suddenly, everyone was moving at once.

Lunging at the second thug, taking him totally by surprise, Pete wrestled him to the ground and took his bat from him. Leaping to his feet, he raised it above his head and brought it down with such force that the hollow *pop* of shattered skull reverberated around the room. Without pause, he turned and took aim at the knifeman – just as Mike grabbed the same man's legs and toppled him, leaving the bat to whizz through empty air.

Taking advantage of Kenny's distraction, Tina hurled herself at him, sixteen stone of solid fat knocking the breath clean out of his lungs and pinning him firmly to the couch before he could even think about raising the gun again. Gasping for air, he was helpless to defend himself as she punched him and gouged at his face with her nails.

Jane glanced wildly around. She'd already failed Mary, but there was no way she was going to stand idle now. Focusing on the man that Donkey had attacked, who was trying to drag Mike off the knifeman with his uninjured hand now, she put her head down and charged him, knocking him flat on his face.

Catching his breath, he flipped onto his back and kicked out at her. Going for him with a ferocity that surprised even herself, she fell on top of him and, seizing his hair with both hands, pulled her head back and butted him as hard as she could.

Reflexively lashing out as his nose exploded, his fist connected with her jaw, stunning her. Bucking beneath her, he tossed her off him and scrambled up to straddle her.

Opening her eyes, Jane saw the rage in his eyes as he raised his fist and just *knew* he was going to finish her.

Then, suddenly, he was gone – lifted bodily away from her.

46

The police were rough, lashing out indiscriminately and kicking anything that moved in the tangle of thrashing bodies. Jane only just managed to avoid being coshed when a strong pair of arms grabbed her and deposited her on the floor beside the kitchen door. From there, she counted at least ten uniforms. Wincing as baton blows rained down on the bodies, she prayed that they'd realise who were the attackers and who the victims.

Watching open-mouthed when a policewoman planted her foot between Kenny's legs as he lay unconscious on the floor beside the couch, an hysterical bubble of laughter rose into her throat when she heard the woman say, 'Resisting arrest, sarge,' to the man standing beside her. Jane was too numb, though, to do more than raise the corners of her mouth.

When everything was under control, the devastation became clear. The blood was everywhere – on the furniture, the walls, the uncarpeted floor. The uniforms were sliding on it as they moved around the room, their muttered curses adding to Jane's sense of unreality.

She watched in a daze as Kenny Butler was dragged, cuffed and unconscious, to the van that was waiting outside.

Then she watched as the man who'd been about to punch her had his arms hoisted roughly up his back, his face contorting in agony as the cuffs were slapped on – the arresting officer seeming to deliberately scrape the metal over the man's torn flesh.

Then Jane saw Tina, spreadeagled on the couch with three uniforms sitting on top of her. They were yelling at her to lie still and stop fighting, but she wouldn't so they cuffed her.

Better gag her, too, Jane thought when Tina let loose a foul stream of abuse.

Her gaze drifted to Mike then. Propped up against the wall with Donkey in his arms, his shoulders were jerking as the tears streamed down his face. Sobbing, he rocked the bloody body to and fro as if soothing a baby and whispered quietly into the un-hearing ears.

Swiping at her own tears, Jane quickly looked away. That was when she saw Pete in deep discussion with a plain-clothed man in the corner. Her heart catapulted into her throat.

This was it . . . They were dead meat.

'I think you should take a look in there.' Pete nodded towards the bedroom door. 'There's a friend of ours in there, and I . . . I think she might be dead. Her name's Mary. She's been staying here – trying to avoid Kenny Butler and get off smack. It's her he was looking for when he came here this evening.'

'Dead?' DS Ray Green frowned. 'Shot?'

'I don't think so.' Shaking his head, Pete sighed. 'We didn't hear any shots – just screaming. There was nothing we could do. They were holding a gun on us.'

'All right, so she was screaming.' Frown deepening, Green folded his arms. 'What makes you think she's dead? Have you checked?'

Exhaling shakily, Pete looked ceilingward as if finding this hard to talk about. 'No, but he *told* us he'd killed her when he came out. Said he'd done her boyfriend in the afternoon, and now he'd done her. And he reckoned we were next – starting with the dog, because it attacked one of his men.'

'This boyfriend. You wouldn't happen to know his name?'

'Yeah, it's Dave, but I don't know his surname. He lives with Mary on Gretney Walk.'

'And Butler told you he'd done him before coming here?'

'Yeah.'

'Right, tell me everything – from the beginning. Be as accurate as you can about times and sequence. This is really important.'

Taking a deep breath, Pete told his story – making some of it up along the way using the information about times that he'd gleaned from Tina, but sticking to the truth as much as possible to simplify things.

'Stay there,' Green said when he'd finished. Moving a few feet away, he radioed the station. 'Yeah, it's DS Green . . . Re the incident in Moss Side this afternoon, I need a name and address a.s.a.p.'

'That was a Dave Riley. Flat 360, Gretney Walk.'

'Right, thanks.'

'One more thing, sir . . . We've just had word from the lab. Seems the bullets used on Riley came from the same gun as that used on PC Gibson this morning.'

'You're fucking kidding me!' Green's heart stepped up a beat.

'No, sir. They're absolutely positive.'

Thanking the voice, Green flicked his radio off. Shit! This was fantastic.

Turning, he scanned the room. Spotting who he wanted, he yelled, 'Jameson! Get your arse over here!'

Pete gazed off into the distance when another plainclothes hurried across the room. But his ears were as sharp as they had ever been as he listened to Green telling his colleague to clear the uniforms out and make *triply* sure that the gun was secure.

'Fingers crossed,' he crowed, 'but I reckon we've just solved the Gibson *and* Riley cases.'

'For real?' Jameson's mouth gaped.

'For real!' Green had a note of vicious jubilation in his voice. 'The lab's just confirmed that the same gun was used on *both* of them, and I've got info linking Riley to a stiff at this scene. Butler's arse is mine!'

'Right, clear 'em out,' he said then, snapping back to business. 'And get the white-suits in . . . The stiff's in the bedroom, according to our witness. I'm just going to check it out. Make sure Butler don't give them the slip.'

'I don't think he's going to be giving anyone the slip for a while,' Jameson chuckled. 'Don't know what's been going on here, but he's had a right good going-over.'

'Couldn't happen to a nicer bastard,' Green jeered, making for the bedroom. Pausing halfway, he whirled around and pointed a finger at Pete. '*You* don't even *think* about disappearing. As soon as you've been checked out at the infirmary, I want a full statement. This bastard is going down if I have to *drag* you to court by your dreadlocks – got me?'

'I'm not going anywhere,' Pete told him wearily. 'I just want it over with.'

'Yeah, well, it shouldn't take long. Not now we've got him.'

'Could you . . .' Gulping exaggeratedly, Pete wrapped his arms around himself and nodded towards the bedroom. 'Could you let us know if . . . you know?'

'Go sit down with your mates, son,' Green told him kindly. 'The ambulances will be here in a minute. I'll catch up with you when I'm finished here and get that statement.'

47

The friends were taken by ambulance to the hospital where, some time later, the corpses of Mary and the man whose head Pete had pulped – 'fatally injured during an armed siege' as it was described on the news that night – were transported to the morgue in an unmarked van.

Still unconscious, Kenny Butler was taken to a secure hospital unit. The remaining two of his men were taken to the police station and thrown into separate cells to await questioning.

Two police officers were stationed outside the emergency-room doors, but there were none in the treatment room itself, so Pete was finally able to brief his friends about what he'd said.

Speaking quickly and quietly, he said, 'I blamed everything on Butler. Said Mary turned up at Jane's asking for help because he was hunting her down, so Jane took her to Mike's, but she started withdrawing so we put her to bed and took it in turns to look after her. Then I said we got word that Butler was in the Crescents this morning asking if anyone had seen her, so we made plans to move her to a safe place when it got dark. But someone must have tipped him off, and he turned up this evening before we had a chance to move her.'

'Don't you think it's a bit suss saying they came this evening?' Tina interrupted. 'That'd mean they were there for hours.'

'Precisely.'

'I don't get that.'

'Just let him finish,' Jane told her irritably.

'Well, I said they booted the door in,' Pete continued. 'And that's obvious, so they won't doubt that. Then I said they held a gun on us and made us sit on the floor while Butler went into the bedroom with Mary. I said he was in there for ages, and when he came out he was bragging that he'd killed her, and how he'd done her boyfriend earlier – and now he was going to do the same to us for hiding her. I told them about Donkey going for the one that hit Mike – said Butler shot him first and that's when it went ape.'

'And they believed that crock of shit?' Tina sneered. 'How do you explain her being dead for hours, then? They can tell that sort of thing, you know. Anyway, she wasn't shot, and Butler never went anywhere near the bedroom. All they're gonna find is *our* prints. You've landed us right in it.'

'I don't think so,' Pete said. 'See, I heard that detective talking to his mate and it seems one of their own lot was shot in the morning. Seems the bullets used on him and Dave came from the same gun, so now they're checking Butler's to see if it's the one.'

Frowning thoughtfully, Tina said, 'You could have something there, you know. I remember one time at Mary's, Butler was talking to someone on the phone about a uniformed nark he had at Greenheys.'

'There you go, then,' Pete murmured. 'Anyhow, it doesn't matter that Mary wasn't shot. If it turns out to be the same gun, they won't give a shit what *we* did. They're after Butler's blood. All we have to do is stick to the same script and we're laughing.'

'We didn't actually kill her,' Mike reminded them quietly, speaking for the first time since it had all kicked off. 'She died of shock, or something, but *we* didn't do it. Butler's responsible, all the way down the line.' Looking up now, his eyes were dark and haunted as he added, 'First chance I get, I'm going to kill him.'

Reaching out to squeeze his shoulder, Pete said, 'With any luck the pigs will do it for you, mate. They don't take kindly to losing one of their own like that – no matter how bent they were.'

Just then, a nurse walked in.

'Jane Bates?'

'That's me,' Jane said, wincing as she eased herself up from the chair.

Smiling sympathetically, the nurse reached out to help her. 'Doctor's ready to have a look at you, love. We'll see if we can't get you a painkiller when he's done, eh?'

'You can get *me* one *now*, if you want,' Tina piped up. 'My back's bloody killing me.'

48

It was five-thirty when they finally got the all-clear from the hospital and finished giving their word-perfect statements. No one had any major injuries, just severe bruising and muscle strains. Jane's jaw was badly swollen from the punch, but an X-ray showed that it wasn't broken and she was released with the rest of them.

Climbing out of the taxi back at the Crescents, Pete paid the driver as the others traipsed wearily out onto the pavement. Without a word, Mike set off across the road, heading for the stairs leading up to his flat.

'Where you going?' Pete called after him.

'To get Donkey.'

Rushing after him, they stopped him at the foot of the stairs.

'You can't go up there, mate,' Pete reminded him gently. 'It's an official crime scene.'

'I don't care,' Mike muttered, gritting his teeth determinedly. 'They can do what they want, but I need to get him out of there.'

'He won't be there,' Tina said in a matter-of-fact tone. 'There's no way they'd want a bloody corpse under their feet while they're working.'

Turning on her, Pete yelled, 'Why don't you keep your fuckin' stupid mouth *shut*? If I hear one more nasty word coming out of it, I swear I'm gonna stick my fist so far down it you'll think you've given birth to it!'

Expecting her to retaliate, Jane was shocked when Tina burst into tears.

'I'm sorry,' she sobbed. 'I didn't mean it like that. Honest, Mike . . . I didn't.'

Reaching out, Mike drew her to him and held her close. 'It's all right. You're upset – we all are. It's been a terrible night, but it's over now. Just go with them and chill out. I'll be there in a bit. I've just got to do this. Okay?'

Nodding, Tina sniffled back her tears and wiped her nose on the back of her hand.

'Want me to come with you?' Pete asked, knowing there was no point trying to stop him.

'No.' Mike shook his head. 'Take these to Mimi's and get yourself a brew.'

'A spliff, more like.' Smiling wearily, Pete patted Mike on the back. 'See you in a bit, yeah?'

Watching until Mike had disappeared up the stairs, they made their way to Mimi's flat. They were surprised to find Kim and Jonas there.

'What happened?' Mimi demanded, pulling them in and lavishing hugs and kisses on them. 'Did they hurt you? Oh, God, look at your poor faces!'

'We're fine,' Pete assured her, forcing her to stop fussing so they could sit down and catch their breath. 'Anyone got a smoke on the go?'

As Jonas set about making spliffs, Kim went to the kitchen to brew up. When everyone had a cup of tea in hand, Pete relayed what had happened.

'I knew something was wrong,' Mimi declared when he'd finished. 'After we left Mike's earlier, I went to bed but I couldn't settle 'cos I had this really bad feeling.'

'So she came and knocked us up,' Jonas cut in, 'and made me go back to Mike's with her. I told her he'd said to stay away, but she wouldn't have it.'

'No, and it's a good job I didn't,' Mimi interrupted primly. 'They might all be dead, by now.'

'I doubt that.' Kim chuckled softly. 'Sounds like they gave much worse than they got.'

'Well, I'm still glad I did it,' Mimi insisted. 'If we hadn't noticed that the door had been kicked in and phoned the police it would have been too late, and I'd never have forgiven myself.'

'It was already too late for Mary,' Jane interjected sadly.

'I know, love.' Mimi hugged her gently. 'But she's all right now. I mean, she wasn't happy, was she? And I don't really think she'd have survived for too long the rate she was going, do you?'

'I suppose not.'

'So, *you* called the police?' Pete gave Mimi a sardonic grin. 'You, who never stops going on about them being the tools of the oppressors?'

'They come in handy sometimes,' Mimi admitted sheepishly. 'When they're working *for* us, not against us. Anyway, never mind that – what about that copper that got shot? Do you really think Butler did it?'

'We'll soon find out.' Pete handed her the spliff. 'It'll be all over the papers tomorrow.'

'It's already been on the news,' Jonas told him. 'They showed a picture, and everything. No real details, though. Just that he'd been shot sometime early in the morning and the pigs are following a lead.'

'His name was Brian Gibson,' Mimi added sadly. 'Poor thing was only twenty-seven. He had a girlfriend and two kids, as well.'

'Gibson?' Tina narrowed her eyes. 'Oh, well, it was definitely Kenny, then.' Turning to Pete now, she said, 'When I told you about him talking on the phone that time at Mary's, he kept saying the name Gibbo. I wasn't really listening, but I remember that dead clear.'

Raising his eyebrows, Pete gave a weary sigh. 'Fingers crossed he used the same gun he brought round to Mike's, then, eh?'

Just then, Mike arrived with Donkey wrapped in his jacket.

'How did you manage to get him out?' Pete asked, resisting the urge to say *Speak of the devil.* 'Didn't they need his body as evidence, or anything?'

'Don't care if they did,' Mike muttered, holding the bundle close to his chest. 'Anyway, he can't be that important to them if they didn't even notice me sneaking him out. He was in a bag by the door.'

'You what?' Jane was indignant. 'Like they were just going to dump him in the bin?'

'It doesn't matter,' Mike murmured wearily. 'He's already free. We're, er, going for a walk if anyone wants to come,' he said then.

'Absolutely.' Knowing instinctively where they were going, and why, Pete stood up and motioned with a slight jerk of his head for the others to join him. 'Want me to carry him for you, mate?' he offered, more gently than any of them had ever heard him speak before.

'No.' Shaking his head, Mike stood up. 'Thanks, but I need to do this myself.'

'Course you do.' Pete squeezed his shoulder. 'You go ahead. I just need to get something from my place. I'll catch you up in a minute.'

49

Southern Cemetery was beautiful in the moonlight, the atmosphere seeming to resonate with the sensation of souls old and new co-existing in undisturbed peace.

Leading the way along mist-smoked pathways guarded by rows of ethereal marble angels and ornately carved headstones, Mike took them to a heavily wooded area at the rear of the graveyard. Coming to a halt beneath an ancient, gnarled tree, whose branches extended downwards in spiky, finger-like tendrils, he laid Donkey gently down on the moss between its cradling roots.

'This is where he wants to be,' he said.

Bringing down from his shoulder the spade he'd gone back to his flat for, Pete handed it to him, then stepped back to join the others. Heads bowed, they watched in silence as Mike pushed the blade down into the soft earth and began to dig.

Soon there was a small mound of soil beside the tree. Laying the spade down, Mike picked Donkey up and placed him gently into the hole. Brushing the earth gently over him with his hands, he patted it firmly down. Then, closing his eyes, he said, 'I love you, you mad, sulky, *crazy* little shit. And don't you be worrying about me, 'cos I've got this lot to look out for me – and you *know* they're cool. So I'll say goodnight for now, but I'll see you soon, yeah?'

Standing around the grave that night, bathed in the amber light of the eerie blood moon, none of them had any idea that they were so close to the plot that would eventually be allocated to Mary. But they weren't surprised when it happened. Mike said he'd just *known* that it was the right place, and now Donkey could watch over her and make sure she didn't get into any bad company.

EPILOGUE

Kenny Butler never made it to court.

Two days after his arrest he died without regaining consciousness, suffering a brain haemorrhage caused by a severe blow to the head.

This could have been Tina's work, or the excessive use of force by the young, overzealous uniforms. Either way, it didn't matter. He was dead, and the police were satisfied.

Colin Spencer got seventeen years for his part in the murders. He received numerous stitches to the wound in his hand, and had to endure several subsequent skin grafts to try and replace the chunk that Donkey had bitten off. And, thanks to Jane's head-butt, which had shattered his nose, he suffered permanent breathing problems – which earned him a good many beatings from his cell mates who objected to having their sleep broken by his grunting and snoring.

The knifeman, Sean Delaney, admitted his involvement in everything except Mary's death. This he vehemently denied, insisting that he'd never even laid eyes on her that night and had only been in the flat for ten minutes. Nobody believed a word of it.

Delaney served just two months of his twenty-five-year sentence at Strangeways before a panel of psychologists ordered his transfer to a maximum-security psychiatric hospital. He never made it.

On the morning of the transfer, he was dropped head first off the upper landing of his wing – an act of retribution by a fellow prisoner whose wife Delaney had raped and mutilated some years earlier. Delaney had escaped justice at the time because his victim had killed herself before it got to court, too traumatised to face him and relive the ordeal that had left her permanently scarred.

With no witnesses among the hundred or so men who'd been making their way along the landing to slop-out that morning, the vengeful husband was never charged.

Soon after the trial, Mike packed up his bits and pieces and headed off to join a group of squatters down south.

His frequent letters back were filled with colourful tales of life around the backyard campfire, where he was surrounded by hairy-legged women in rainbow-striped jumpers, masses of communal children, and a multitude of assorted shapes, sizes and breeds of dogs. His version of heaven.

Settling their differences, Tina and Jock followed Mike's lead.

Packing everything they owned into a hired van – obligingly driven by Stan, who was determined not to be left behind – they relocated to Jock's home town in Glasgow.

Everyone was pleased for her when she wrote to say that she'd become *Mrs* Big Jock – not least Jane.

They'd had their problems in the past, but she'd seen Tina in a different light after *that* night. It had taken real guts to jump Kenny, knowing that he could have shot her, and there had been a definite change in Tina's attitude afterwards – as if she'd settled a demon or two in her own mind.

No one thought to ask where Tina and Jock had suddenly acquired the funds to move lock, stock and barrel to another part of the country. But, as the coke that Mary had supposedly stashed for Kenny Butler had never been found, Jane thought she could make a pretty fair guess.

Pete and Jane got together – which was as much of a shock to *her* as it was to her friends, who had thought she would end up with Mike, if anyone.

Jane wouldn't admit to her feelings for ages, convinced that the attraction between Pete and herself was nothing more than a codependence thing – survivor clinging to survivor. But Pete was far more clear-headed about it. He'd recognised a long time earlier that they had a lot in common and had finally persuaded her to give it a go, convincing her that they had nothing but the past to lose – and a great deal of potential future joy to gain.

Jane didn't know if they would last, just as she didn't know where she would be in another year's time, but she was happy to go with the flow for now.

As Mike was so fond of saying in his letters: *She'd know where she was at when she got there.*

MANDASUE HELLER

The Club

Are you in?

Jenna Lorde knows she's taking on a challenge when she inherits her dad's nightclub. But Zenith comes with a top class reputation and a location other clubs would kill for, so she reckons she's more than up for it.

Until she starts to realise that the dangers aren't just from other clubs. Beneath the glamour of the VIP lounge and the pumping music, sleaze and corruption are starting to creep in, and it'll take everything Jenna has to stop the rot.

The club's survival – and her own – depend on it.

HODDER

MANDASUE HELLER

Forget Me Not

Remember me?

Manchester's Westy Lane is the hunting ground for a killer who leaves a tiny blue flower in the torn body of each victim after he kills her.

Lisa Noone, twelve years old and wise beyond her years, lives too near the lane and her mother is a member of the oldest profession in the book. Their lives are far from perfect, but they will always have each other. Or will they?

Trust me

One night Benny arrives in Lisa's life. Tall dark, the most gorgeous man she's ever seen, Benny is not all he seems. While Lisa savours true love, Benny wants more from her than she will ever know.

HODDER

MANDASUE HELLER

Tainted Lives

Three abandoned children

Sarah has been in care since she was seven, put there by her drug-addicted mother. Trying to live with the rejection is bad enough, but there is more pain to come.

Harry's mother locked him in a cupboard so she wouldn't have to look at his ugly face. When he and Sarah meet for the first time, they forge an instant friendship.

Then Vinnie comes into their lives. A good-looking, calculating thirteen-year-old, this is his last chance to change his ways.

Three tainted lives

As the years pass and they become adults, their lives take very different directions. But when their paths cross again, one of them will commit the worst crime of all . . .

HODDER